Praise for C.

'I was utterly gripped and can't wait
for the next instalment. This is a hit
movie just waiting to be made!'
Ruth Hogan, author of
The Keeper of Lost Things

'A brilliant eccentric concept which hits
you like a fever dream. I'm very keen
to see where he goes next!'
Giles Kristian, author of *Camelot*

'*The Wolf Mile* is a thrilling ride and a heck of a debut.
C.F. Barrington knocks it out of the park.'
Matthew Harffy, author of
the Bernicia Chronicles

'*The Wolf Mile* blurs the boundary between fantasy and
real life with authoritative panache. The moment you ask
yourself if it could just be true, the story has you.'
Anthony Riches, author of *Nemesis*

'*The Wolf Mile* had me hooked from the first page.
Gripping and original – a terrific read!'
Joe Heap, author of
When the Music Stops

Also by C. F. Barrington

The Wolf Mile

THE BLOOD ISLES

Book Two of
The Pantheon

C. F. Barrington

An Ad Astra Book

First published in the UK in 2021 by Head of Zeus Ltd
This paperback edition first published in the UK in 2022 by Head of Zeus Ltd,
part of Bloomsbury Publishing Plc

A CIP catalogue record for this book is available
from the British Library.

9 7 5 3 1 2 4 6 8

ISBN (PB): 9781800246423
ISBN (E): 9781800244375

Cover design © Dan Mogford

Printed and bound in Great Britain by
CPI Group (UK) Ltd, Croydon CR0 4YY

Head of Zeus
5–8 Hardwick Street
London EC1R 4RG

WWW.HEADOFZEUS.COM

THE PANTHEON ORBAT (Order of Battle)

THE CAELESTIA (THE SEVEN)

Lord High Jupiter
Zeus
Odin
Kyzaghan
Xian
Tengri
Ördög

THE CURIATE

Europe Chapter
Russia Chapter
China Chapter
Far East Chapter
US Chapter

THE PALATINATES

The Legion ~ Caesar Imperator ~ HQ: Rome
The Sultanate ~ Mehmed The Conqueror ~ HQ: Istanbul
The Warring States ~ Zheng, Lord of Qin ~ HQ: Beijing
The Kheshig ~ Genghis, Great Khan ~ HQ: Khan Khenti
The Titans ~ Alexander of Macedon ~ HQ: Edinburgh
The Horde ~ Sveinn The Red ~ HQ: Edinburgh
The Huns ~ Attila, Scourge of God ~ HQ: Pannonian Plain

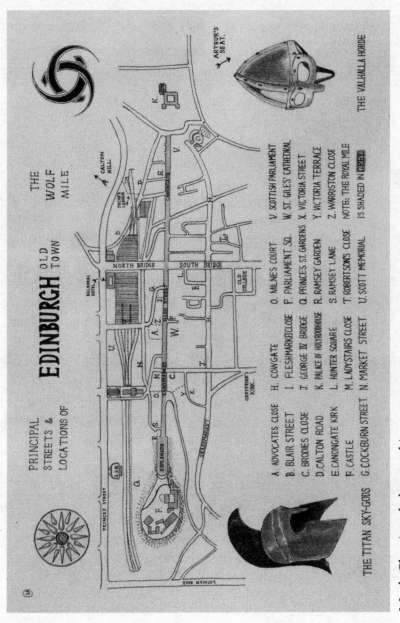

Mark Clay (markclay.co.uk)

*For my parents, who nurtured in me a passion
for books and who introduced me to the stunning
sands of my first Blood Isle.*

THE HORDE OF VALHALLA IN THE NINETEENTH YEAR

THE BLOOD SEASON

Strength: 189 shields
(214 at start of Year: 19 losses in Raiding Season and 6
to miss Blood through injury)

Odin ~ Caelestis of the Horde of Valhalla

Sveinn the Red ~ High King of the Horde

Radspakr ~ Thane of the Palatinate, Adjutant,
Paymaster, Custodian of the Day Books

Bjarke ~ Jarl (Colonel) of Hammer Regiment – Heavy
Infantry
13 x Litters. Total: 106

Asmund ~ Jarl (Colonel) of Storm Regiment – Light
Troops
Arrow Company – 3 x Litters = 24
Spear Company – 2 x Litters = 16
Total: 40

Halvar ~ Housecarl (Captain) of Wolf Company House
Troop
4 x elite Kill Squads = 28

Freyja ~ Housecarl (Captain) of Raven Company
House Troop
2 x elite Squadron of Scouts = 15

Litter Two, Wolf Company
Leiv ~ Hersir
Thegn Punnr (Tyler)
Stigr ~ Ake ~ Unn ~ Knut ~ Olsen ~ Hagen

Thegn Brante ~ Litter Three, Wolf Company
Thegn Calder (Lana) ~ Litter One, Raven Company
Jorunn ~ Litter One, Raven Company
Thegn Ulf – Litter Five, Hammer Regiment
Skarde ~ the Prisoner

THE TITAN SKY-GODS IN THE NINETEENTH YEAR

THE BLOOD SEASON

Strength: 147 troops
(176 at start of Year: 22 losses in Raiding Season and 7
to miss Blood through injury)

Zeus ~ Caelestis of the Titan Palatinate

Alexander, Lion of Macedon ~ High King of the Titans

Simmius ~ Adjutant of the Palatinate, Paymaster,
Custodian of the Day Books

Nicanor ~ Colonel, Brigade of Hoplite Heavy Infantry
Phalanx: 10 rows of 8. Total: 80

Cleitus (successor to Timanthes) ~ Colonel, Brigade of
Light Infantry
Total: 67. Broken down as follows:

Menes (successor to Olena) ~ Captain of Companion
Bodyguard
Total: 24

Agape ~ Captain of Sacred Band
Total: 16

Parmenion ~ Captain of Peltasts, Archers & Scouts
Total: 27

What Has Come Before

1. It is the Eighteenth Year of the Pantheon, a secret game bankrolled by the world's wealthy elite.

2. Two of the Pantheon's seven teams are located in Edinburgh: Alexander's Titan Palatinate are the masters of the rooftops of the Old Town, while Sveinn's Valhalla Horde dwell beneath the Royal Mile.

3. In the bleak darkness of a March night, Timanthes – Colonel of Light Infantry in the Titan Palatinate, and Olena – Captain of Companion Bodyguard, lead their troops into the subterranean tunnels of their foe, the Horde. But they are betrayed. Timanthes is killed, Olena disappears and the cream of the Titan Palatinate is wiped out. It will change everything.

4. And so begins the Nineteenth Year.

5. Tyler Maitland and Lana Cameron are confronted by Venarii recruiting parties and offered an opportunity to join the Pantheon. Along with a dozen other initiates, they become Thralls – trainees in the Valhalla Horde. They are whisked away on blindfolded car journeys to hidden vaults, where they are schooled in the arts of conflict by Housecarls Halvar and Freyja. Soon only six remain.

6. Tyler is convinced his sister – Morgan – is also part of

the Pantheon, but she has disappeared. He is determined to make it through the Armatura training to find her in the Horde.

7. The six Thralls are honoured with new Pantheon names. Lana becomes Calder (*cold waters*); Tyler becomes Punnr (*the weakling*); and they are joined by Brante (*sword*).

8. They are taken by train to a castle in the Scottish Highlands where they face their rivals – eight Perpetuals, *lost children* from the Pantheon's secret Scholae.

9. Released in pairs into the forest, the fourteen Thralls and Perpetuals must reduce their number to seven. It is kill or be killed.

10. The final seven swear loyalty to the Pantheon on the shores of a forgotten loch and are initiated into the Horde of Valhalla.

11. Now that he is part of the Horde, Tyler believes he will find Morgan, but she is nowhere to be seen and unwisely he makes his search known to Radspakr, Thane of the Palatinate.

12. The Horde returns to Edinburgh for the Raiding Season.

13. The new Thralls confront the rival Titan Palatinate for the first time at the *Agonium Martiale* – a starlit ceremony on Arthur's Seat.

14. The Pantheon masters have hidden four Military Assets around the city and the rival Palatinates have four nights to solve the clues. The Assets must be discovered by a White Warrior from each Palatinate and Punnr is selected to be Valhalla's – a role that instantly makes him the prime target of every Titan.

15. With the help of eleven-year-old Oliver Muir, the son of

his neighbours and an avid Pantheon fan, Tyler searches for solutions to the clues.

16. As the Raids begin, he realises his enemies are not only in the Titan lines. There is treachery on all sides.

17. He learns that his mentor, Halvar, was once Morgan's illicit lover and he also discovers why he cannot find his sister. He has joined the wrong Palatinate. Morgan was Olena, Captain of Companions in the Titan Palatinate. Because she abhorred being separated from Halvar across warring Palatinates, she betrayed her Titans during the original attack on the Horde's Tunnels in the hope that she could be united with him. But she has never been seen since.

18. Now enemies are circling Tyler too. Enemies who have much to lose if Olena is not found and silenced forever. His only chance is to fake his own death during the Third Raid.

19. Lana is distraught at his apparent demise and takes on his mission to find his sister, but this places her directly in harm's way.

20. At the final Raid in Edinburgh Castle, she is cornered and speared, but Punnr emerges from a secret tunnel to save her.

21. Now they must face their fates in the Blood Season.

Prologue

Conflict Season – Blood

He would never forget her face.

Sheet white. Ferocious. Streaked with rainwater and blood, a wisp of black hair plastered across one cheek and lips curled back in a snarl.

The clock on his dashboard said 2.27*am* as he cruised down the Royal Mile hoping for a final customer on this miserable night. He had just bitten into a ham and coleslaw sandwich when there was a whump on his rear bumper.

'What the...!' He dropped the sandwich onto his lap, hit the brakes and peered into his mirror. A shadow flitted across his line of sight. Little more than a darker piece of the night, followed by a shout.

'Bloody drunks.' They'd get a piece of his mind. He applied the handbrake and was about to heave himself out, when he caught movement again in his side mirror and froze, door ajar, cold air oozing into the stale interior. Only a glimpse. A flicker of bronze glistening rust-red in his rear lights. The whisper of a cloak and then gone.

He dropped back into his seat and closed the door. Not drunks. *Titans*. He stared again into his mirror and could now see them more clearly. Figures cutting across the Mile at a sprint, swords drawn, shields hauled onto shoulders. Others angled in front of the car and ran hard, uncaring if they were caught in his headlights.

'Okay, just keep it together. Nothing to worry about. Let them do their thing.'

There was something about the disarray of the figures. The abandon with which they hurled themselves across the street and disappeared into the shadows surrounding the High Kirk of St Giles. These troops weren't attacking. They were fleeing. In moments they had vanished and he peered to his left, towards the tight opening of Advocates Close from whence they had come. Rain arrived again, rattling on his roof, and it brought with it more figures from the close. But these were different. Their helmets bore no plumes, their mail was iron, their blades much longer and they howled with glee, like hyenas with the scent of blood in their nostrils.

And that was the moment she appeared.

A thud on the bonnet spun his attention back to the front and her arms were spread-eagled on the hood as though she had run blindly into his vehicle. Her shoulders heaved, ebony hair hung from her helmet and she gripped a shortsword, but if she had carried a shield that night, she had already dropped it in her haste. She glared at him through the windscreen, then pushed back and became emblazoned in his lights. He gawked at her, his jaw slack.

He had never seen someone so magnificently desolate. So feral and untamed. She might wear the bronze of a Titan officer, but there was horror in her eyes. Tears mixed with blood. Rage broke from her lips.

For a moment, her eyes pierced into him, then her attention was torn to her pursuers. She hurled a challenge back at them, turned and fled. The Vikings gave chase, but they were slower and he watched her charge across the court in front of St Giles and disappear under an arch beside the Signet Library. Some of the Vikings followed, but minutes later they returned and it was obvious from their frustration that she had given them the slip.

Good, he thought, though he knew not why.

The Horde loitered around the street. They yelled and hooted, swore at each other and swung their blades, but their noise was that of victors and they soon began to laugh and slap hands. He waited unmoving, numbed by the sheer incongruity of it all. The warm, air-conditioned interior. The mash of mayonnaise and bread between his legs. And the wild warriors of the night celebrating their battle honours.

When the last of them had gone, he eased the handbrake and slipped off the Mile onto South Bridge, but his mind was on the girl. Who was she? The last of the Titans to flee and a look in her eyes that would stay with him forever. He glanced at the seat next to him and swore when he saw his phone.

What a picture she would have made. What the papers would have paid for such a shot. A single image that summed up everything about the Pantheon. Its blood and its beauty.

*

Olena, Captain of Companion Bodyguard, ran. Her final look back had told her everything she needed to know. Timanthes, her colonel and one of the Pantheon's most illustrious servants, would not be setting foot again on the pavements of Edinburgh and nor would so many of the Titan Palatinate's best troops. That hot, stinking cellar was their burial chamber.

She wept for them as she sprinted through the archway beside the Courts and on towards the parking areas at the rear of the buildings. A rope was hanging in a corner – one of many readied as an escape route for the Titan Sky-Gods – but she ignored it. Her Companions would already be on the rooftops and watching for the final escapees, but she did not intend to join them. As she passed, she glimpsed the rope being hauled up to prevent any Valhalla lout – high on victory – thinking they too could take to the skies.

She could hear her pursuers on her tail and she kept running. Across a yard, through a gate and then threading between vans parked at the back of the Court complex. A building blocked her way and she knew if the final rope had already gone, then she was lost. The Horde would trap her there, edge her into a corner and cut her down. One more of the Titan elite taken out of the game that night.

She charged to the wall and peered each way. There it hung beyond the last window, straight and still. She sheathed her bloodied sword and lunged across, grabbing the length and hoisting her legs up the wall in practised movements just as the first Viking pursuers came hurtling around the vehicles. They howled at the sight of her, but she was already out of reach. A young face appeared over the parapet, unmasked.

'Go!' Olena commanded as she dragged herself onto the roof. 'I can do this.'

The Rope-Runt nodded in awe and dashed away into the night while Olena began hauling in the length. The lead Viking arrived below and made a grab for the end, but he was too late. Then a slender female warrior danced across the parking area, allowed her momentum to take her up the man's back and leapt for the rope as it disappeared. Olena felt the impact of the woman's hand on the other end, but the twine was wet and her grip failed. With a cry of exasperation, she fell back to earth and Olena yanked up the last few metres. Only when it was all safely coiled on the roof beside her did she peer over. Her adversary returned the look, pointed her blade, then stalked back between the vans and vanished.

A hush descended and Olena raised her eyes to the sodden rooftops around her. Nothing stirred. A diffused glow from the streetlights created an eerie orange dome over the buildings, as though shielding them from the impenetrable blackness above. A breeze jostled across the roofs and searched for her exposed skin. Her arms were shaking – although whether from the climb, the cold or sheer exhaustion, she could not tell. Her troops would already be well on their way to Ephesus and Thebes, and when they reached the safety of the Titan strongholds, the Armouries would fill with cries of treason, for any fool could see the Companions had been led into a trap.

Carefully, she raised herself and found her legs trembling too. She searched the shadows for the slightest movement, then began to navigate along the roof. But not towards the Titan strongholds. Instead she went north, back across the Court of Session and the Signet Library, the steeple of St Giles dead ahead. Then she cut west to the terrace over Lawnmarket where Timanthes had gathered his troops less than an hour before. She dropped to her knees and crawled to the edge. The Mile below was empty and resentful of her prying eyes. The Horde had gone and the entrance to Advocates Close squatted sullen and black. *Timanthes, forgive me.*

She pulled her gaze away and slithered across to a chimney, where the southern side provided shelter from the breeze. She seated herself on the wet tiles and leaned back against the bricks. She was shaking badly now as she attempted to wrap her cloak around her, but the cloth was already sodden and her fingers were stiff and clumsy. She unbuckled her sword belt and gazed at the leather and ivory scabbard. The blade would already be sticky with drying blood. It needed to be drawn, cleaned and oiled, but instead she simply dropped it and removed her helmet. She shook her lank hair and rubbed her face, then propped her head back against the chimney, took a deep ragged breath and gazed up at the starless heavens.

A cynic might say her plan had worked. Sow a belief amongst her Titan commanders that they had an asset in the Viking Horde. Lead the cream of the Titan companies to a door that this traitor said led to the heart of the Horde's Valhalla stronghold. Walk them into an ambush. Watch them butchered. Then in the forthcoming Grand Battle the weakened Titan lines would not be capable of holding the Viking onslaught and Alexander himself might fall. A chance to combine the Palatinates. To be, at last, together with her lover Halvar.

She dropped her gaze. A stupid plan. A plan only love could make sense of.

It is the nature of things that you reap what you sow. The Vikings were supposed to feign surprise, but they had marched into that cellar in full battle regalia. It was obvious they had been expecting the foe and now every Titan still breathing knew they had been betrayed. At that very moment messengers would be flying between Thebes, Pella, Ephesus and Persepolis, tallying up the living, accounting for the dead and soon all inquiries would lead back to Olena. Then the hunt would begin. She knew she should run. Discard her armour and flee into the arms of the city. Find a haven and disappear.

But her limbs refused to move. Halvar himself had not been present in the cellar and she wondered if he already hung in Valhalla's vaults, helpless against Radspakr's instruments. Everything had failed. Their clandestine love had led inexorably to a bloodbath that had felled even the great Timanthes. And there would be no mercy.

She squeezed the cloak tight and hunched lower, but the rain would not ease and the cold was groping for her, burrowing into her core and dissolving her thoughts.

Part One

The Cull

I

Pantheon Year – Nineteen

Conflict Season – Raiding

There was nothing. No time. No sense. No thought.

And then there was a dull light probing towards her in the darkness and a sound, something regular. She knew she needed to rise and suddenly – like cracking through an ice crust and emerging from frigid waters – her lids broke open and hard, blinding light surged into her.

A ceiling and flowing green fields. A beat too. And a smell, floral but sharp. Then her lids surrendered once more and took her away.

She could feel her daughter clinging to her. They were pressed against a wall that was hot to touch and before them was a passage. Something was coming. Something relentless and insatiable. It was growing, sending out tendrils, seeking them. *Mummy, help!* She was clinging to Amelia with every atom of strength, crushing her little daughter into her bosom, but something else had hold too. Amelia's tiny body was being drawn inexorably into the darkness. *No. Please... please don't take her!*

A dazzling white figure appeared at her shoulder and charged into the passage. The blackness pulsed in shock, surged once, then began to slither backwards. The figure was struggling in its core and dimming from view, but Amelia was being dragged too because a tendril of the dark was still wrapped around her little legs. *Mummy!* Her tiny hands were scrabbling desperately at her mother's clothing.

NO, my darling! Hold on! Come back!

But her daughter was gone.

This time her eyes flicked wide.

'It's okay,' said a voice above her. 'That was a bit sudden. Hello, Calder.'

She was on a bed and a woman was standing at the foot of it, pushing a clipboard back into a holder. The rolling fields were on the wall beyond, some sort of watercolour with buttercups and distant cows. A tube was hanging in her field of vision and there was a sensation down her right side, not so much a pain, more a weight. The woman came around the bed and took hold of Calder's hand with fingers that were warm and precise.

'Welcome back. I'm Nurse Monique. You'll be feeling groggy, but don't worry, everything's looking fine.' She nodded towards a machine in the corner, from which the beep was emitting. 'Pulse is good. Sixty-two. Fifty-eight. You're a fit lady. We're piping a little oxygen and there's a cannula in the back of your hand, which might feel uncomfortable, but it's providing important saline, salt and dextrose.'

There was a bitter taste in her throat and her mouth

was bone-dry. She tried to look down her body. She was wearing some sort of blue smock and beneath she sensed alien objects attached to her.

'Where am I?'

'In the best place you can be – with the best medical treatment money can buy.' Monique's voice was cheerful, with the baritone timbre of the Caribbean. 'Now let's have a quick look at your chest drain.' She inspected a bottle hanging below Calder's bed, tapped it and made an approving noise at the back of her throat. 'That's fine. Just a bit of fluid run-off – all normal.' She placed her hand on Calder's forehead. 'So, you're now five hours out from surgery and everything went well. You had a blade incision that entered beneath your right armpit and cut down the side of your chest. Some of your undershirt was forced into the wound, but you're cleaned and stitched now.'

Memories tiptoed back to Calder. The lights of the city far below. A cold night air seeking out the sweat beneath her chain mail. Her cumbersome and unresponsive limbs. A puddle caressing her cheek as she lay on the paving and another liquid, hot and viscous, pooling under her arm. She remembered the frenzy above her. Hard movements, cursing, frantic as life was taken. And him. The one in white. His helmet, his cloak. His arms turning her to him.

Monique lifted Calder's smock. 'Hmm... I think we'll do a dressing change.'

As Monique pulled on rubber gloves and busied herself, Calder tried to peer around. She thought she could make out light from a small window high on the wall behind. 'What time is it?'

'Three fifteen pm. You were admitted this morning at

five and went into surgery a little after nine. Goodness, but it's been a busy day. So many trauma incidents last night. We've been working flat out. It's the same every season. Long periods of nothing and then you all come at once!'

Calder's mind pieced together more fragments of memory. The view of the battle from the highest walls in the castle and Erland's tongue on her face, greasy and squirming. The white-hot pain of Ulf's spear punching across her ribs. Then a new caress amidst the carnage and a voice back from the dead. 'You're safe. We have you.' His arms had been steel as he carried her down Long Stairs from the batteries, her cheek pressed against his white enamelled mail. His grip had never loosened as he followed Halvar, searching, shouting, demanding help, until finally she felt herself released into the custody of Raven scouts.

She imagined the aftermath of the battle as the Vigiles picked amongst the prostrate and wounded, performing their task of *libitinarii*, removers of the slain, and she wondered how many more of the Horde were in beds just like this one.

'Where am I?'

'Like I said, the best place you can be.'

'I mean which hospital?'

'Don't you worry yourself about that. You're in good hands.'

Calder winced as the nurse cleaned her side. 'How long must I be here?'

Nurse Monique was taking the old dressing back towards the door. 'You're all the same. No sooner have you been chopped up than you're wanting to get out for a second round. We'll have you mended soon enough and back in the ranks in time at least for *some* of the Blood Season. Now rest a while and I'll bring you a little food.'

The door closed behind her and Calder heard the click of a lock.

A victory it might have been, but beneath the chest-thumping celebrations and ale-laced chants, there was bad blood in Valhalla.

The fourth and final Raid of the Nineteenth Season was complete and King Sveinn's Viking Palatinate had claimed all four strategic Assets from where they had been concealed at points across a radius of one mile from Tron Kirk on Edinburgh's Royal Mile. On the final Raid in the castle the Fates had conspired to bring the full force of both Palatinates together in the same place on the same night and hell was unleashed. As the Titan Heavy Infantry had surged towards them, the Vikings planted their feet on the ancient stones of the castle's roadway and swore no retreat. The lines had crashed into each other, bronze Hoplite shields meeting the Horde's limewood, and each attacked the other with murderous abandon. Blades, hilts, shield-butts, boots, elbows, even teeth, anything that would hurt the foe. They stabbed low. *Strike under the shields; get them in the legs; bleed them in the genitals; take them down.*

But, gradually, Titan discipline had begun to tell. A wedge had developed, its point driving closer and closer to the bulk of the One O'clock Gun. Somewhere in their midst was Lenore, the Titan White Warrior, awaiting her chance. If they got her to the gun, she would use her ultra-violet torch to find the hidden words of the clue and claim the Time Asset.

And then everything had changed. Punnr appeared, racing across Argyle Battery, followed by a wild and bellowing Halvar. Amongst the Viking defenders, astonishment turned to comprehension and new orders were yelled. *Envelop the White Warrior. Protect him.* The mighty bodies of Hammer Regiment parted, swallowed up the new arrivals, then wove once more.

From behind their shields, the Titans had also seen Punnr's arrival and knew the game had changed, for now the Horde could claim the Asset too. So the foe's White Warrior – presumed dead – must be felled all over again. Even as the wedge of Titan Heavy Infantry continued to drive inch by bloody inch towards the gun, a brutal rain of arrows fell from the sky and thundered around Punnr. Iron tips clattered onto helmets, thudded into shields and burrowed into flesh. Men cursed and dropped. Beneath his helm, Punnr remembered the pain of Freyja's arrows – shorn of their own killer iron tips – thudding into his mail at Old College on the third Raid Night and the thought made him crouch in fear and pray for the storm to pass.

'Keep moving!' Halvar yelled. 'And get your bloody shield up!'

Punnr had complied, just as three shafts plunged from the heavens and smacked into its wood. He stumbled to the gun and fumbled for the UV torch tied around his belt. He shone it up and down the barrel, back and forth, but he could see nothing. *Goddamn it! Where the hell's the clue?*

'Get on with it!' Halvar barked. 'They're almost through!'

Punnr had crawled around the undercarriage, between the wheels, along the length of the barrel.

'It's not here!'

'Hel's teeth, laddie, stand up! I've got you covered.' Halvar's giant figure loomed above Punnr and his shield obliterated the sky. A rough hand yanked Punnr to his feet. 'Find it!'

He stretched over the top of the gun, waved the torch and at last glimpsed words on the upper rim. He already knew what was written, but it was imperative to be able to see the words and prove precisely where they had been hidden.

'I have it,' Punnr shouted.

'So we go. Move!'

Then it had become a race. For the Horde to claim the Asset, Punnr must return to the Valhalla Tunnels alive and the Titans knew it. Further up the slope, behind the main Hoplite lines, only the keenest eyes would have spied the group that was released at a signal from the Titan command, the darkness hiding the colour of their cloaks. Blue.

The Sacred Band came for Punnr.

Only the gods knew how Punnr survived that flight back to Valhalla. He was flanked by Wolves and the line of retreat was protected by Asmund's Storm Regiment archers, but every step of the way they were harried by the Band. At one moment, Punnr was halfway down a ladder hanging below the ticket shop, when a cloaked figure swept across the wall towards him. It came in a graceful arc, blade extended, one hand clinging to a rope. Flying death. At the final moment, Punnr did the only thing he could and let go just as the Titan's shortsword hissed past his jaw. He plummeted groundward and began to roll helplessly down the hill, but hands grabbed at him and pulled him upright.

'That way,' said a Storm archer.

Punnr stumbled back to the track and hurtled towards the beckoning arms of Ramsay houses and the Tunnels of Valhalla beyond.

And so the Horde celebrated beneath the Royal Mile. Weapons and armour were removed for the Schola youngsters to clean. Warriors hugged, smacked shoulders and yelled exultantly. King Sveinn praised them for their courage and the audacity of the plan to fake their White Warrior's demise at Old College, then surprise the Titans with his arrival at the castle. He ordered them to drink and Punnr was pushed from one group to the next. No one allowed him to remove his white armour, for it was now the emblem of success, and he tried to grin and joke with them, although his body beneath was broken.

'Is Calder okay?' he demanded when he spotted Freyja.

'Aye, she's in the best hands. She'll pull through.'

Punnr clutched her arm. 'Are you sure? Tell me truthfully.'

Freyja prised his fingers open and met his gaze. 'She took a blade beneath her sword arm. Maybe splintered the ribs, but otherwise just a flesh wound. She'll be back with us soon enough.'

Punnr stepped back and nodded gratefully. 'Thank the gods.'

Sometime later, Halvar appeared. His wrinkled face shone with sweat and his hair was matted flat. 'It worked.'

He was right. It *had* worked. The whole crazy plan. A

fortnight earlier, when it seemed Punnr was destined to be killed either by the foe or by the treachery of his own Bodyguard, Halvar had come up with a simple concept. 'If you want to live, laddie, you're going to have to die.' They had taken the idea to Sveinn, and the King had seen its sweet beauty. It wasn't playing by the rules, of course, but neither was it strictly in breach of them. Punnr would die at Old College, taken down by Titan arrows in full view of both warring Palatinates and the cameras of the Curiate. But, in truth, the arrows would come from Freyja's bow and the Vigiles tasked with clearing his body away in the aftermath might question the circumstances when they found the White Warrior still alive and kicking, but they would register no formal objection.

So when the fourth and final Raid had begun three hours earlier, Halvar and Punnr slipped quietly from their hiding place at South Gate and ran to Old College undisturbed. The full forces of both Palatinates were focused on the castle and no one gave a thought about Old College. The quadrangle seemed so silent after the carnage it had witnessed the week before and Punnr had loped over to the fountain and claimed the third Asset. Then they retraced their steps to the Tunnels and Halvar ushered Punnr down hidden stairways, deep into the bowels of Edinburgh, until they came to a grated drain, which Halvar yanked open.

'You're now the only person outside the Council of War who knows about this, laddie. You'll guard its secret or answer with your life. Do you understand?'

Punnr had whispered *yes*.

'Then follow me.'

*

Halvar didn't stay for the celebrations. He took himself from the Hall and was one of the first to leave when the Raid Night was declared officially over at four in the morning. Punnr saw him go and wondered if the man was thinking about Morgan. Or perhaps he too sensed the same black omens that flitted across the faces of so many.

For destinies had unravelled that night and too many warriors were absent. The Horde drank and cheered, but beneath the noise, they glanced at each other and a new fear rippled through their bellies. What was happening this year? Were they still part of an enterprise with rules and parity, with a beginning and an end? Or was it different now? Like war.

II

The man's eyes met his, held them for a second and flickered away.

They were seated in the second carriage of a tram rolling westward between Haymarket and Murrayfield. It was mid-afternoon in late February and already the little daylight that had broken through the showers was fast receding. Radspakr was tired. He had spent the night pacing the Valhalla Halls with Sveinn as they awaited news from the battle. Then he had watched the chaotic celebrations from the sidelines, listened to Sveinn's speech, observed the Horde's adulation of Punnr and finally closed himself off in his offices. Valhalla quietened. Dawn matured into morning, and morning slipped into afternoon. At last, he had emerged, changed into his street clothes and taken his usual tram route to the Gyle Centre.

He studied the man opposite. Radspakr knew him – one of the Drengrs in Asmund's Storm Regiment – but he couldn't put a name to the face. The man was wearing smart jeans, a grey pullover and a raincoat. He had stepped on at the West End, thrown himself down into a seat and only then realised the Thane of his Palatinate was just across from him. Mortified, he sat staring into his lap. These sorts of meetings happened sometimes. It was part and parcel of life outside the Pantheon and was of little consequence so long as the individuals gave no more than a glance and passed on.

Today, however, Radspakr was in no mood to have his reverie disturbed and he waited irritably for the man to remove himself at the next stop. The tram lurched into Murrayfield and people clambered off, but the fellow remained seated. As the tram began to move again, Radspakr settled a hardened, unwavering gaze on the Drengr because this fool was outstaying his welcome. The man fidgeted uncomfortably and at last stole a glance across to his senior. When he saw the light in Radspakr's eyes, he gave a perceptible jolt, mouthed an apology and stumbled down to the doors to await the next stop at Balgreen.

Radspakr watched him go, then turned back to the darkening city. *Idiot*. It was not for some junior trooper to know that he took this tram route and it was absolutely out of the question that the man should observe where his Thane alighted. He forced himself to forget about the incident. It had been a bad day – a terrible outcome to the final Raid – and he needed some peace to think.

At the Gyle Centre he walked through the car park to his silver Range Rover *SVAutobiography*. With a five-litre, V8 engine and a price tag of two hundred grand, it was hardly the usual type of vehicle to leave in a shopping centre car park at night, but he preferred the anonymity of making the rest of his way to and from the city by tram. He slipped inside and accelerated smoothly towards the bridges, letting a Requiem by Berlioz wash over him. He liked driving across the Forth. There was something timelessly impressive about the three great bridges, each a product of a different age and together creating a magnificent industrial spectacle.

Once on the far side, he took the shore road through Dalgety Bay, Aberdour, Burntisland and finally arrived at the little fishing town he had called home these last twenty years. He eased the vehicle through his gates, waited as they closed softly behind him, then walked across the gravel to his front door. Beyond the garden was a yawning darkness, which he couldn't see or hear, but which he sensed in the air. It was the empty expanse of the sea. He paused and breathed it in. Not scented, not salty, but nevertheless the fresh essence of the coast and he loved it. He could afford the greatest of the townhouses in the city, but it was this quiet space that he preferred whenever he could break free from the tentacles of the Pantheon. The place suited him. It was sleepy and uneventful, with neighbours who respected his privacy. Here he could peel off the layers of Valhalla.

But not tonight. He made his way to the kitchen and found stew in the slow cooker from two days previous. He ate silently at the worktop, with a glass of cold Chablis as accompaniment, then wandered through to the drawing room and stood beside the chairs in an enormous bay window. The blackness of the Forth was punctured by shipping lights and the beam of the lighthouse on Inchkeith island. Beneath his garden wall, he could just make out swathes of sand disappearing into the night. *Good, the tide's out. That means it will be out again early tomorrow morning and I'll run a few circuits of the beach before the dog walkers emerge. It will do me good.*

He switched on a lamp and seated himself in one of the chairs, placing his Chablis to hand and reaching for a slim tablet. Working his way through the various security levels, he logged into the Valhalla accounts and ran his eyes down the figures sent through by the Vigiles. Thirteen Viking dead. Nineteen once the toll from the third Raid Night was taken into account as well. A further twenty-nine hospitalised. A total that was nigh on a quarter of the Palatinate. Numerically, it cancelled out the twenty-six Drengr that Sveinn had just recruited and the only silver lining was that the Titans had suffered as badly and could tolerate such loss of numbers even less than the Horde.

Radspakr needed to be very careful because questions would be firing around the Pantheon. Such a death toll undermined the financing structure of the whole operation. It rocked the planning of the Palatinates. It played merry hell with the wagers placed by the Curiate. Worse, it affected the morale of the troops. Each and every one of them readily faced the risks inherent in the Pantheon, but they didn't offer themselves up to its demands with the expectation of a one in four chance of injury or death.

And this exceptional count led firmly back to Radspakr's door, for it had been he who waded into the War Council's deliberations and had persuaded Sveinn to face the Titans head on at Old College during the third Raid. The other Housecarls had been aghast. Go for the castle first, they had argued. Let the Titans take the Old College Asset uncontested and Valhalla take the castle clue. Then each Palatinate could also avert full battle on the final Raid Night by aiming for separate objectives. But Radspakr had panicked. Without the confusion of conflict, his plan for Ulf and the Bodyguard to kill Punnr could never have succeeded undetected. He needed mayhem and so he had forced his way into the deliberations and persuaded Sveinn to take the gamble.

And now the Pantheon morgues were filled, the hospital overflowing, and the Caelestia demanding answers.

He tapped the screen and brought up an individual record. Tyler Maitland. Punnr. The Valhalla White Warrior. Still very much alive. *What the hell are you doing in my Palatinate?*

Radspakr reached for his wine and drank slowly as he studied the photograph of the young Thegn. Pantheon rules dictated that no siblings could be recruited and Atilius' Selection Committees were ruthlessly efficient. So, if the missing Titan traitor – Morgan Maitland – really was Tyler's sister, then how had the lad slipped into the Pantheon ranks? The question had been eating away at Radspakr's gut for weeks, always there, oozing through his bowels.

He chewed his lips and listened to the elements. It was no night to be on the water. He could hear wind in the chimney and the rain was returning, rattling against the glass. It wasn't Sveinn and the others who worried him, it was Odin, the Valhalla Caelestis. For six weeks now, Radspakr had sat on the information about the Maitlands. And it was a huge gamble.

Morgan Maitland – the hapless lover of Halvar – had been an asset too valuable to lose during the previous Pantheon year and Radspakr had recognised her worth. Radspakr himself had never been touched by love. He had never felt its force pulsing through his veins. His had been a life of service to the Palatinate. Nineteen years of marshalling and organising Valhalla. Nigh on two decades of nurturing it, managing its finances and shaping its growth. While the old fool Sveinn wore the king's mail and received the allegiances of his troops, it was Odin's money and Radspakr's ceaseless toil that kept the Horde fit and fighting.

Valhalla was, in truth, Radspakr's one true love and he would do anything to ensure its prosperity. So when Halvar had come to him and professed his love for an enemy officer, then proposed a crazy plan to unite the Palatinates – a plan only a lovesick, blind fool could believe – Radspakr had recognised it as an opportunity to learn of Titan intentions, prune their numbers and give Valhalla the glittering victory it craved in the Eighteenth.

But stupidly – so damn stupidly – he had told Odin of this traitor and the Caelestis had grasped the opportunity with vengeful alacrity. Trap her, he had ordered. Force her to feed them a constant flow of information about the Hoplite foe. But Odin didn't just want Titan bodies, he used the information to play the odds in the highest political circles of the Pantheon, amongst the Curiate and even the Caelestia itself. Forearmed with the traitor's whisperings, Odin shifted vast funds, placed them on long-shot bets and cheated the system. Radspakr had no idea of the true sums that must have been gambled using this illicit knowledge, but he knew the Titan ranks had been sorely decimated during the course of the Eighteenth Year and he could guess it had taken Zeus, the rival Titan Caelestis, close to fiscal breaking point. He also knew that if these illicit activities ever came to light, even a figure as mighty as Odin would fall – and Radspakr's life of love and service to Valhalla would come to an end on the edge of a blade or deep in the dungeons of Erebus.

Then the bloody woman had vanished before the Grand

Battle. Just up and gone. And nothing Radspakr had attempted could provide him with information about her fate. Neither he nor Odin needed telling of the gravity of the situation. Pantheon troopers did not simply vanish. Every individual was carefully monitored and exhaustively researched by Atilius' central Pantheon authorities. They knew their home lives, their histories, their bank details, their blood types, hell – even their shoe sizes. No one simply disappeared.

For a while last year, it had been touch and go. Odin was in no mood for security risks and Radspakr had actually feared for his own neck. But the crisis had passed and everything grew quiet. That was until Tyler appeared as a new recruit in the Valhalla Palatinate and sent Radspakr's heart into palpitations. Just get the boy killed. A Titan arrow, a Viking blade, he hadn't cared, as long as the boy was gone before Odin learned of this new threat.

But he wasn't. Not only was Tyler very much alive, he was being damn well feted as the hero of the Horde. Christ, what a mess!

Radspakr launched himself out of the chair, sending the tablet tumbling onto the carpet. He stepped to the window, placed his hands on the glass and peered through the raindrops at the shipping lights. *So what's the next move?*

He knew what he *should* do. He should crawl to Odin and tell him everything about Tyler. The boy wouldn't last long after that. But what if the Caelestis responded by eradicating the Thane as well?

No, he must find a safer plan.

*

Flat grey light stole around the curtains and slunk across Tyler's bedroom. There were voices in the gardens and comings and goings on the stairwell, but he lay unmoving beneath his duvet. Every fibre of his body ached and his head pounded from the endless beakers of thick ale that had been thrust at him by a Horde determined to drink away the shock of a fight like that. For a few hours they had needed a hero to toast and, dressed still in his white armour, the finder of all four Assets, he had been that hero.

Now his mind kept returning to the moment Halvar had shouldered open the chapel door and he had seen Calder's form slumped on the puddled cobbles. In those seconds, nothing else had mattered. Odin, Sveinn, the Titans, the Assets, the whole damn Pantheon could have gone to hell. All he could do was sweep her up into his arms and hold her and tell her it would be okay, while Halvar hacked Erland's head from his shoulders. Blindly, he followed the Housecarl down Long Stairs, no longer hearing the roar of the Palatinates, nor caring if arrow or javelin arced his way. Nothing mattered except the life of the woman in his arms.

At first he refused to pass her to the Ravens. He would have carried her from the whole damn castle and run with her through the streets of the city. But Halvar grabbed his shoulder and spun him.

'Give her up, you fool. They will get her to the care she needs and you have an Asset to claim.'

Reluctantly, he had relinquished his hold and other hands had taken her and she had slipped from him into the night. Then Halvar was yelling and they were running back up the thoroughfare, to Argyle Batteries, Mill's Mount and mayhem.

In the mundanity of a new day, the wild action of that struggle was beginning to lose shape. The hoarse yelling and cursing, the clash of steel on bronze and wood, the stench of death and terror, all were swirling and thinning and losing form, like blood in water. But the memory of Calder's weightless body in his arms was as sharp as a honed blade and the thought of her lying somewhere in the clutches of the *libitinarii* weighed down on him and locked him to his mattress.

It was a knock on his front door that jarred him back into the present. He guessed who it would be and he rolled out of bed with a groan, pulled on jeans and a shirt, and padded barefoot up the hall.

'Morning,' he said groggily as he opened the door.

Oliver looked at him with eyebrows raised. 'Afternoon, more like.'

Tyler mumbled and wandered back, leaving the door open. He pulled the curtains and peered out at a steel-grey city, shrouded in such low-lying cloud that the taller rooftops melted into nothingness. He reached for a cigarette and filled the kettle.

Oliver hovered just inside the room. 'I was sure I heard you return last night, but Mum wouldn't let me come over. How was your trip?'

'My trip?'

'Your friend Lana said you were on a trip when she came to pick up your things.'

Tyler frowned. 'Lana came here?'

'She said you needed a few clothes and also all my research about the Assets. I gave them to her on a USB. I hope you got it?'

'Oh... yes. Yes. Thanks lad. Very useful. You want a cuppa?'

'Okay, tea.'

'Make yourself at home.'

Oliver sat himself on the sagging sofa and looked around at the untidy room. Apart from the cigarette packet, it looked untouched since he had last been there a week ago with a harried Lana. 'I watched you on YouTube,' he said over the rumble of the boiling water.

'You what?'

'The battle near Old College – someone caught it on camera from an upper window and it's been shared everywhere. It's dark and confusing, but – wow, Tyler – there's no disguising the ranks of the Horde and the Titans. It's amazing! What a fight!'

Tyler brought the teas over and sat next to him on the sofa. 'And you saw me?'

'Just for a moment. The camera lurches up and you see a figure in white armour running past the main battle – that was you, wasn't it?'

Tyler sipped his drink wordlessly.

'Thought so.' Oliver grinned. 'So you weren't really on a trip.' He was interrupted by raised voices from across the hall. 'Oh god,' he said and hunched into himself. 'I'm sorry you have to hear that. Saturday afternoon and they're already sick of the sight of each other.'

'It can't be easy.' Tyler thought how often he had heard similar disagreements seeping through the walls.

'School nights aren't so bad, when they're too tired to care.' The boy gulped his tea. 'But I hate the weekends.'

'Is there anything I can do?'

'Just let me escape here sometimes… and tell me about your adventures. Let me imagine.'

Tyler looked at the boy's serious face and guessed that the true extent of his loneliness was kept closely hidden. 'Okay, that's a deal.'

Oliver made a conscious effort to brighten. 'You promised you'd draw the Valhalla Tunnels for me and you *must* tell me everything about that battle. I promise I'll keep it secret.' There was a crescendo of shouting and he closed his eyes and waited until it receded. 'You know, Tyler, sometimes I wish I could escape to the Pantheon like you. I lie awake at night and pray to Odin and Zeus that they'll find a need for a young boy like me in their Palatinates and will come and take me away.'

'You can't think like that. Your parents would be heartbroken.'

Oliver didn't respond and Tyler felt incapable of any better words, so they sat and drank.

'Where's your whisky?' Oliver asked eventually. 'I don't see it.'

'Heck, you're observant. I poured it down the sink last night.'

'Really?'

'An impulsive moment. I decided it wasn't doing me any good and I didn't need it.'

Oliver cradled his mug and looked around the room. 'I *am* observant – it's one of my skills. I don't miss much.'

'I called you a little watcher when we first met, you remember?'

'When you've got parents like mine, you spend a lot of time just watching. I notice things. Like the absence of that photo of yours, the one you always glance at, with the amulet over it.'

Tyler followed Oliver's eyes to the sideboard and jolted up in his seat. 'Where the hell's that gone?'

'Lana took it and the amulet.'

Tyler swivelled his gaze back to the boy. 'Why would she do that?'

'I don't know. She didn't want me to notice, but I saw her put them into the bag she was taking for you last week.' Oliver returned his look. 'She never gave you that bag, did she?' They were interrupted by a loud rap on the door. 'Oh god,' Oliver sighed. 'I'm really sorry.'

Tyler walked up the hall and opened the door. Mr Muir stood outside, arms folded across his chest. 'You got my boy in there?'

'I'm here, dad,' Oliver replied. He came down the hall and handed his mug to Tyler. 'Thanks for the tea.'

'Your mother's going to the shops on George Street and you're going with her, so you'd better get ready.' Muir stepped aside to let his son walk disconsolately back into the flat opposite, then returned to his position on the doorstep. Tyler had seen the man on several occasions, but spoken only in passing. Probably in his late thirties and turning fleshy around the edges, he was a buyer in the building trade and he looked smart enough suited and booted during the working week, but now his pose carried with it all the belligerence of the construction yard. 'You got a reason to have my son in your apartment?'

The back of Tyler's neck prickled. 'He came over to say hi. I made him a tea.'

'You like young teenagers?'

Tyler held his tongue. Muir took a step forward and pointed a finger in Tyler's face. 'My wife seems to think it's fine that Oliver hangs out with a twenty-something man across the hall, but let me be crystal – I don't. Keep away from him, you understand? I'm watching you.'

Tyler sighed and forced himself to be civil. 'My apologies. I was just being hospitable.' Without further ado, he closed the door and stalked back to his living room, shaking his head. 'Twat,' he said softly to himself and then stood looking at the empty space on the sideboard where the graduation photo had taken pride of place. He felt his stomach craving a dram of whisky, but he ignored it and instead stepped to the window and looked out across Learmonth Gardens. He guessed why Lana had taken the photo and amulet. She had thought him dead and she needed an image of Morgan so she could continue his search. Realisation sparked in him. *Oh, Lana. That's exactly what you tried to do, even though it put you squarely in harm's way*. Her actions must have attracted the suspicions of Radspakr and that was why Ulf and Erland had been sent for her blood at the castle.

My god, Lana, you did that for me. Something took flight in his gut and fluttered cautiously around his ribcage, seeking a chance to break free.

III

Calder was woken by the click of the locked door and Nurse Monique bustled in.

'Lunchtime,' said the big lady, placing a tray on the bedside table, which she wheeled in front of Calder. 'Chicken tagine with couscous, followed by cheesecake.'

Calder had lost track of time, but she thought this must be her fourth lunch taken in the bed. She was still roped in place by the chest drain and saline drip, and spent much of the time drifting in and out of sleep, but she felt stronger and in her waking moments she was starting to loathe the confinement. Early on day two she had questioned the need for the locked door and received short shrift from Monique, but later she had probed more delicately and the nurse had relaxed. Nugget by nugget, Calder had learned she was in a hospital reserved only for the Pantheon and this east wing housed the wounded warriors of Valhalla, while their Titan foe recovered in the west wing. She had asked about Brante and after much pressing, Monique had eventually said he was present and almost mended from his shoulder injury, and Calder could probably see him once she was well enough to leave her own bed.

At lunch on the third day, the nurse had brought Calder's

tray of food and then returned several minutes later with a mug of tea and a banana, which she proceeded to consume in the chair by Calder's bedside. Both women were of similar age, smiled at the same things and instinctively recognised that under different circumstances they could have been friends. During Monique's ten-minute break, Calder elicited that she was single and lived alone, hailed from Trinidad and Tobago, missed it like hell, had arrived in Scotland three years earlier and had a large family back home to whom she made monthly money transfers. She waxed lyrical about the wonderful Trinidadian meals she could produce for Calder if they would only let her loose in the hospital kitchens and they had both laughed about the effect the spices might have on Calder's delicate constitution.

Today's tagine looked good and Calder pushed herself up on her pillows. She might not think much of the room, but there was no question the Pantheon fed its patients luxuriantly.

'Is that all you have for lunch?' she asked, glancing at Monique's tea and banana.

The nurse grinned. 'The only New Year resolution I've managed to stick with so far! It would be okay if there weren't so many biscuits in the staffroom!'

'How many staff are there?'

'Oh it varies, girl. We're all on flexible contracts, so usually there's only a skeleton team and I don't see the inside of this place for weeks on end. Then suddenly you lot start hacking at each other and – boom – we're all called in!' She laughed deeply.

'So where do you work when you're not here?'

'I don't.' Monique went serious and shrugged. 'It's not permitted.'

'Oh.' Calder pondered this. 'So... you just come here when you're called. Is that... is that enough?'

'You mean how do I get by on a nurse's wage when I'm only called up occasionally?' Monique popped the last chunk of banana in her mouth. 'How d'you think, girl? Because this job pays incredibly well. You think we'd spend our time endlessly patching you lot up if it didn't?'

'I suppose not.' Calder scooped some couscous and Monique watched her for several moments.

'You know, Calder, I've talked with enough patients here to know that us nurses are in the same position as you. Okay, I don't dress up in the armour and run around at night slashing people – but I've sworn an oath on my life to the Pantheon. I'm as much a part of this whole nonsense as you are – whether I regret it or not – and in return they make sure my stay in this fine country is never questioned and grant me a wage that nurses in normal hospitals could only dream of.'

'And you send most of that back to Trinidad.'

Monique inclined her head. 'Most of us working here have family overseas. I think the Pantheon authorities prefer that.'

'How did you join?'

'I came to Scotland as soon as I'd graduated from the University of the West Indies School of Nursing. For eighteen months I worked the wards of the Royal here in Edinburgh and lived in a horrible shared room in Wester Hailes. But then my – let's say, *precarious* – status in Britain looked like coming to a quick end. That's when they came to find me.

They knew everything about me – showed me photos of my parents in Trinidad, my siblings and my San Juan family home, copies of my qualifications, my driving licence, even a copy of the letter I'd received from Immigration. And then when they'd got me sufficiently snared, they told me how they could help...' She forced a chuckle. 'So here I am! Almost twenty months now and I have a lovely flat on Livingstone Place in Marchmont, I work easy hours, I get paid five times what I could ever have earned at the Royal and everyone calls me Monique even though that's not my name!'

'Really? Oh no... I think Monique's a lovely name!'

The nurse laughed robustly. 'I'm afraid I can't say the same for *Calder* – but it's all I'll ever know you by.'

'No real identities in the Pantheon.'

'You got it, girl.'

They were quiet for a few moments and Calder was amazed how tired she felt from the effort of talking. Somewhere beyond the little window high on the wall behind her, children's voices called to each other.

'So do you care for the Titans as well?'

'We share some of the facilities – such as the operating theatres – and I can use the fingerprint scanners to access all the different parts of the hospital, but I don't attend to the Titans personally. No fraternising with the enemy!'

Calder smiled, but she was feeling really weary now. She had made little headway with the tagine.

'I've talked too much,' said Monique, rising and putting her banana skin in her empty mug. 'Tired you out. Why not try having some of the cheesecake. I need to go check on the others, so I'll give you some peace. The doctor will be around in another hour and then later, when you've rested, I'm going to get you upright and maybe we'll have a little walk out into the common area. It's important with chest injuries that you get mobile as soon as possible.'

She removed Calder's plate and pushed the dessert towards her, then headed for the door. 'I'll bring you coffee.'

When she returned ten minutes later, her patient was asleep. She wheeled the table back from the bed and studied the other woman's face. *Such delicate features. What road brought you to the Horde of Valhalla?* She reached out and brushed a curling strand of blonde hair from her face. 'Sleep now, girl. Get well.'

She picked up the lunch tray and left the room, locking the door behind her.

IV

The interior of the car smelt of leather, polish, pungent tobacco and a hint of something more citrus which – to Punnr's surprise – was emanating from Freyja in the front passenger seat. He peered at her and noticed how she had tied her braids back, exposing the curve of her neck and the swirls of her silver earrings, which shone dully against the dashboard lights. Asmund was next to him, his legs angled inwards so that his knee occasionally knocked Punnr's when the car rounded a corner. They had gathered by the lights on Market Street, just above the galleries, and his companions had been serious and reserved. Freyja was dressed in a smart trouser suit, accessorised with a shawl and heeled boots, while Asmund wore a white shirt under a tailored tweed jacket. As they stepped into the Mercedes, they could have been any well-to-do group taking an upmarket taxi for an expensive night out.

But they weren't. The wordless driver bore them west to the ring road and then south. Punnr tried to follow the route as they swept around the Pentlands and on to Penicuik, but as the streetlights dwindled and the night closed in, he lost his bearings and could guess only that they journeyed somewhere into the Border country. He wore jeans and a thick woollen jumper beneath his usual raincoat and on his lap he held a helmet, yet one so thin and light that it would probably dent if he dropped it, let alone take the impact of a Titan blade. It was large enough to cover only the top of his head, but silver eyepieces would still mask his identity. Freyja had handed it to him once they were in the car and given another to Asmund. Despite its frailty, Punnr could see it was beautiful, decorated with golden vines.

After an hour their car pulled onto a lane bordered by rhododendron. A stone arch loomed ahead and Punnr sat forward to stare over the driver's shoulder. Gates stood open, but figures waited either side and one stepped into the road and indicated for the car to halt. They were Vigiles, marked by their baggy trousers and red shoulder sashes. The driver opened his window and the lead Vigilis stooped to peer inside.

'Sit forward,' he said to the two in the rear, then clicked on a torch and shone it into the face of each passenger. Beyond him, fixed high on the arch, was a camera. 'Identify yourselves.'

'Housecarl Freyja of Raven Company House Troop, Horde of Valhalla,' responded Freyja, letting the torch beam glare on her. The Vigilis placed a finger on the microbud in his ear and listened, then nodded confirmation and swung the beam onto the rear seat.

'Jarl Asmund of Storm Regiment, Light Infantry, Horde of Valhalla.'

'Thegn Punnr of Wolf Company House Troop, Horde of Valhalla.'

The Vigilis listened to the voice in his earpiece and waved

them through. They swung up a long, looping drive, past ornamental gardens and a vast pond.

'Helmets on,' said Asmund as the car eased into a wide courtyard and they alighted. Ahead of them was a main building and to their right a second smaller one with lamps over an archway. Another Vigilis signalled for them to follow him under the arch. He opened a door onto a corridor lined with doors. The Vigilis led them to the fourth door and pointed to Freyja without breaking stride. 'You. In there.' She peeled off and slipped through the door. At the fifth, he did the same to Asmund and at the sixth it was Punnr's turn. 'Gather again at the front in five minutes.'

Punnr entered a small sparsely furnished room with a wooden exit on the far side, split into lower and upper sections. There was an old metal grate fixed in one corner and he realised it must once have been used to hold hay for a horse. *The stable block*, he thought. On a low bench was a set of clothes and a pair of boots. He gave a wry smile. *Of course*.

This time there was no armour, no chain mail and no weaponry. Instead, as Punnr walked back to the entrance, he was dressed in a velvet tunic of rich red with gold trimmings, dark leggings and smart knee-high boots. Over his shoulders was a cloak of spotless white and he guessed this marked him out as the Valhalla White Warrior. The others were waiting for him, attired similarly in velvet tunics and boots, but both with a cloak of deeper russet hues. The lantern lights played on their dress helmets and gold braid, and as Punnr saw Freyja appraising him with appreciative eyes, he felt a surge of exhilaration. *Perhaps I really am a*

*true Thegn of Valhalla – a million miles from the damaged
ex-addict who limped into Comely Bank last summer.*

They followed the Vigilis around the corner of the main
building and up to a colonnaded entrance that opened onto
the sparkle of chandeliers. The Vigilis stepped aside and
waved them into a grand hallway.

'Have you been here before?' whispered Punnr.

'No,' said Freyja. 'It's always somewhere different.'

'But always the same theatrics,' added Asmund with a
half-smile.

The hall flowed into a pillared saloon with an oak
stairway. If the newcomers had looked above, they would
have seen arched galleries and a decorative plaster ceiling,
but their eyes were fixed instead on a group of three figures
standing in front of a fireplace. Two of these were dressed
in formal evening suits and bow ties, while the third wore a
floor-length black gown that covered all except her hands.
Emblazoned in gold on each sleeve was an eagle with wings
unfurled and a sword grasped in its talons. They had been
talking quietly when the Valhalla warriors entered, but
now they offered no sign of welcome. Each held a flute of
champagne and all three were masked.

Freyja gave a small bow, then crossed the saloon to
another doorway. Beyond was a huge room, oak-floored,
lit with chandeliers, tapestries clinging to the walls. It might
have been a ballroom or an opulent dining hall, but now it
was bare of all furniture save for two high-backed gilt seats
on a platform at the far end. Another gallery ran above
and the ceiling had been transformed into a panorama
depicting the Roman gods in their celestial heavens.

To Punnr's astonishment, the best part of two hundred

people were gathered in the space. They were grouped informally in knots, and more figures crowded the gallery above. Each held a glass, yet the only movement came from a few waiters serving drinks and every masked head was turned to look at the three new arrivals. A floorboard creaked under Punnr and, to his nervous ears, it seemed to echo around the space.

Freyja and Asmund approached two figures on the far side. As Punnr followed, he realised they were Sveinn and Radspakr. They wore cloaks, short tunics and boots like him, but emblazoned in gold on the chest of each was the Triple Horn of Odin. Although both were helmeted, Punnr could feel Radspakr's brooding presence waiting for him. Sveinn, on the contrary, looked more regal than Punnr had seen him since the Oath-Taking and the King smiled briefly in his direction.

'Good. Valhalla is present and correct.'

There was the gentlest of hums as the throng finally let Punnr escape from its scrutiny and began to converse once more. A waiter appeared, dressed in white shirt and black waistcoat, as though he could have been serving at any city function, except that even he had a simple black mask tied across his eyes. The three newcomers each took flutes of champagne.

Punnr scanned the room and counted about twenty people in the robes with the eagles. The rest wore modern evening attire. The women looked resplendent in dresses and their masks were elaborate, accessorised with feathers and jewels. His attention was caught by another group across the floor. As one of them turned, he spied the Star of Macedon embroidered in gold thread across the man's chest and recognised the tall figure of Alexander. The King dipped his head towards him, but before he could respond, he glimpsed a flash of white from the back of the group and noticed Lenore, dressed too in a pure white cloak. Taking Alexander's cue, Punnr bowed before her. She looked surprised, but nodded once in his direction before turning her attention to the figure next to her. Punnr's focus shifted and he realised he was looking at the regal frame of Agape, sheathed in glittering silver, her long hair now dyed pale blue.

'A Thegn of Valhalla bowing to the foe?' said Radspakr behind him.

'Come now,' answered Sveinn. 'I believe we can be gracious in our victory.'

Punnr drained his champagne. Already the liquid was giving him a warm glow and he scanned around to see if he could catch a waiter for a refill. His eyes fell on more figures at the perimeter of the room. They were mostly women, masked and drinking champagne, but they held themselves separate from the groups and, unlike the female warriors in their tunics or the ladies in their formal evening attire, these women seemed distinct. Flowing hair, bare necks, naked shoulders, tight dresses. They watched the assembly and waited.

The hum of voices faltered as two Vigiles appeared at the doorway with scimitars resting on their shoulders. A waiter scuttled in front of the Valhalla group. 'Glasses, quick.' They handed him their flutes and he slipped on to the next group.

'And so the game begins,' murmured Asmund.

The Vigiles advanced and were followed into the hall by a further dozen. They marched in two ranks and fanned out into a line in front of the platform. They swung the swords down to touch the floor and then froze. Again there was movement from the door and into the room entered the Valhalla and Titan Caelestes, both dressed in the robes they had worn at the *Agonium Martiale*, with the same great helms encasing their heads. Behind them came Atilius, Praetor of the Pantheon, carrying a leather-bound book and wearing a plumed and gold-leafed helm in the style of a senior Roman officer, which also hid his features behind golden eye-pieces. It was the first occasion Punnr had seen him masked.

The Caelestes seated themselves and Atilius took up a position on the platform between them. He peered around the hall and allowed the silence to extend.

'Members of the Curiate, friends, associates. Welcome to the Blood Gathering of Scotland. It is good to see so many of you once more. Every year I ask myself where the months go, for it seems but a blink of an eye since we were gathered thus. If time really does go faster with age, then I must truly be an ancient man.'

In other circumstances this would have been greeted with a ripple of laughter, but the stony quiet was unbroken and Atilius seemed to expect nothing different. 'I know you have been awaiting this annual fixture with fervent anticipation, so I will not keep you long from the plentiful diversions on offer tonight. First, however, we have a few matters of business with which to attend.'

He smiled theatrically. 'The Nineteenth Raiding Season between the Titan and Valhalla Palatinates is complete. And *what* a Season it has been! Never have two Palatinates fought with such courage and determination outside of a Blood Season. Never has each dedicated so much in the struggle for victory. I trust you all enjoyed the footage and – even though I know there are losers as well as winners amongst you – I hope we can all agree on the sheer entertainment value of what we witnessed during these last weeks and can show our appreciation accordingly. Members of the Curiate, ladies and gentlemen – I give you Alexander of Macedon, Sveinn the Red, their Thanes and retinues, and the two Warriors of the White.'

This time it happened. Applause began in the gallery and swept down across the floor. Sveinn and Alexander took a step forward, bowed to the Caelestes and turned in a circle acknowledging the appreciation.

Atilius waited until the hall was quiet again and then opened the great book. 'The *Liber Sanguinis* – the Blood Book. Here resides the formal roll call of every Pantheon warrior, from every Palatinate, who has fallen in the nineteen Seasons to date. It is a roll of honour. A roll of heroes. Each has dedicated – and ultimately sacrificed – their life for the greater purpose of the Pantheon. Tonight the Blood Book will stand in state, so that you may ponder the names and remember all those who have fallen. Before that, however, I will confirm the results of the Nineteenth Raiding Season here in Scotland.'

He looked down at the pages before him and began to read.

'The Titan Palatinate.

Assets recovered – Two: Distance and Field.

Of the foe killed:
High King = none

Jarl = none
Housecarl = none
Hersir or Thegn x 2 = 8 credits
Wolf or Raven (elite) x 3 = 6 credits
Drengr x 14 = 14 credits

Total Blood Credits awarded to the Titan Palatinate: 28

The Horde of Valhalla.

Assets recovered – Four: Water, Distance, Field and Time.

Of the foe killed:
Lion of Macedon = none
Colonel = none
Captain = none
Platoon Commander = none
Companions or Band (elite) x 5 = 10 credits
Hoplite, Peltast or Archer x 17 = 17 credits

Total Blood Credits awarded to the Valhalla Palatinate: 27

May the fallen of both sides rest in peace and be remembered with honour.'

Atilius closed the book with a grim flourish. 'And so we enter the Blood Season. The finale of the Pantheon's year and one to send a shiver of excitement down all our spines. To each Palatinate I say, we honour you. Fight bravely and glory will be yours.' He bowed towards Sveinn and Alexander, and they returned the gesture.

'Now we come to the final piece of formal business this evening. The Initiatio. On rare occasions, when numbers and circumstances dictate, we provide opportunity for trusted friends of the Pantheon to submit their candidature to join the eminent ranks of the Curiate. Tonight is one such occasion and I am pleased to confirm that after the traditional thirty days of consideration by the Curiate, we have two Initiates present in this hall. Captain... if you please.'

The lead Vigilis stepped out of line and pointed to two of his men. Together they unwrapped a huge black banner and, pushing members of the audience aside, spread it out on the wooden floor before the platform. Punnr craned his neck and saw that emblazoned in gold on the banner was the eagle and its sword. The Vigilis captain walked through the audience and came to a short man in evening suit and mask. He motioned for the man to follow and kneel in the centre of the banner, then took up station next to him.

'Thank you, Captain,' said the Praetor, peering down at the figure. 'Do you know the words?' he asked the man.

'Yes, lord.'

'Then begin.'

The man paused to gather his thoughts, then started to recite. 'I promise to the Caelestia, the Curiate and all the Masters of the Pantheon, that I will, from henceforth, aid, keep and conceal the duties of this esteemed Body, from wife and child, from father and mother, from sister and brother, from fire and wind, from all that the sun shines on and the rain covers, from all that is between sky and ground. I will honour its priorities and its confidences, and I will not cease to do so for love or for fear, for gold or for silver, or for precious stones, and I will strengthen its jurisdiction with all my five senses and my power. What I thus promise will I steadfastly and firmly keep, as witnessed by those here present. If I should do anything contrary to this oath, I impose a curse upon myself encompassing the destruction and total extinction of my body, soul and life. May neither earth nor sea receive my body, nor bear fruit from it.'

'Rise.'

The man clambered to his feet and a second Vigilis came forward carrying one of the black and gold robes and helped him pull it on. With a bow to each Caelestis, the man stepped rigidly from the banner and melted back into the audience. Atilius motioned again and the Vigilis captain strode once more into the crowd until he came to a slim, elegant woman with silvering hair flowing beneath her mask. He touched her on the shoulder and she followed him gracefully back to the platform with heels tapping on the floor. This time the captain held out his hand so she could kneel in the centre of the banner.

'Thank you, Captain,' said Atilius once again and then studied the woman in front of him. 'Do you know the words?'

'Yes, lord.'

There was a long silence and some sixth sense tickled across the back of Punnr's neck. Atilius bent forward, so that he was closer to the woman's kneeling form. 'So perhaps you should have been more careful with your tongue.'

The woman's head jerked up and she started to speak,

but before a word could break free, the captain struck the back of her head and sent her sprawling. There was a gasp from the onlookers, but nothing more. In a whirl, two Vigiles broke from the line, grabbed the edges of the banner and rolled it around the prostrate form of the lady until she was completely wrapped and unable to move. They tugged her onto her back and then held her tight on the floor. She was panting and trying to speak through the material. Atilius jumped down from the platform and hunched beside her, holding her enmeshed head close to his. He seemed animated by the gravity of the situation.

'There, there, my dear,' he said soothingly. 'I'm sure you understand. Such laxity in protocol could compromise us all, so it cannot be overlooked. The Curiate have judged you guilty and now those gathered here tonight will determine your fate.' The wrapped figure groaned and tried to sit up, but the Vigiles had her locked in place. 'There, there,' said Atilius again, enjoying himself. 'If our friends here tonight are lenient, you will be transported to the dungeons of Erebus, there to live out your days in darkness. If they are not – well then, my dear, tonight you will have all the riches your actions deserve.'

Punnr tore his eyes from the spectacle and looked around. No one had moved. Freyja and Asmund were rigid. Radspakr was staring at the events in mortal fascination. Sveinn held himself still, eyes averted. All around, there was a sense of calm fatalism. Punnr wanted to speak, but his legs were rooted to the spot and he could only gawk like everyone else.

A third Vigilis appeared carrying a large bronze bowl with a flat base. He carried it ceremonially over to the little group and placed it with care onto the chest of the supine figure, then knelt next to his colleagues and held it in place. As if already aware of the punishment, she tried to rear up and throw it from her, but her captors forced her back and kept the bowl pressed against her.

Atilius rose and waved an arm and the waiters returned, this time carrying trays holding little bags. 'One hundred silver *denarii* per bag,' he said. 'An appropriate sum. You must each here tonight look into your hearts and decide if our dear lady deserves your generosity.'

He clicked his fingers at a waiter, who approached the two Caelestes and bowed, offering his tray. Odin rose to his feet, took a bag and stepped off the platform to look at the wrapped figure. Then he upturned the bag over the bowl and coins clattered onto the bronze. He flung the bag away and stalked wordlessly to the doors. Zeus took longer, refusing to accept the proffered bag for several seconds, then taking it slowly towards the group. He seemed ready to depart with the contents still full, but then reconsidered and tipped the coins from a much lower height so they slipped more quietly into the bowl. As he too departed, the waiters began circling the room offering out bags.

'Not us, you fool,' hissed Freyja as a waiter approached and Punnr had been turning to him. 'This is not our affair.'

Atilius broke the silence. 'I believe that brings us to the conclusion of the formalities and the evening is now yours to savour.' He raised his arms towards the gallery. 'Music. Play!'

From somewhere above, a string quartet stirred into action. It was Schubert or something – a waltz – but slow and sombre, the sound mournfully beautiful as it soared around the room, perhaps a memory of the once lavish balls that had been hosted in the exquisite space. Phalanxes of new waiters appeared bearing drinks and canapés, and the crowd began to shift and murmur. And all the time at the front, the Vigiles hunched quietly with their recumbent victim.

'What had she done?' Punnr whispered.

'That's not a question you ask,' Asmund said darkly. 'Keep your mouth shut and don't involve yourself in Curiate business.' He reached for a glass of champagne.

There was movement over Punnr's shoulder and he turned and froze, dumbfounded. Slowly, gracefully, a masked couple were dancing. Their eyes betrayed nothing and their jaws were fixed rigid, but their movements were lithe, almost sensuous, funereally becoming one with the music. Another couple joined them and Punnr couldn't drag his eyes from the scene. Around him, people talked, drank and even began to laugh. Men eased themselves to the edges and whispered with the bare-shouldered women. Groups were leaving the room and heading to diversions in other parts of the building. Three masked men, champagne flutes in hand, approached the platform and emptied their money bags into the bowl.

'Come with me.'

The voice was curt in his ear. Punnr swung round and found the Captain of the Vigiles next to him, black eyes watching him through their masking.

'Me?' he said with fear swelling through his stomach. 'Where?'

The Vigilis didn't reply, just strode away towards the doors. Punnr looked to the others and realised Sveinn and

Radspakr had already disappeared. Freyja stared back at him and behind her helm, he could sense her alarm.

'Just do as he says; it'll be fine.'

Mutely, Punnr followed the receding figure, eyeing the red sash hanging tight across his broad back and the scimitar resting nonchalantly on one shoulder. The pair walked through the saloon, past the staircase and along another corridor strewn with portraits and tapestries. Everywhere knots of people talked and smoked and drank and turned to look at him. He followed the Vigilis to a door and waited while the man knocked and moved aside to let him through.

He entered a small room that smelt of cigars and was painted deep blue, with bookcases and a huge desk. Sveinn and Radspakr were perched on chairs beside the desk and behind it sat Odin. He had removed his silver-horned helmet and now wore a smaller glittering mask that revealed a jutting chin and grey neatly-trimmed moustache. Punnr judged it was the face of a man in his sixties.

'Come over here, boy,' the Caelestis said in a North American accent.

Punnr walked forward, glancing at Sveinn and Radspakr. The latter was wide-eyed behind his helmet and sweating profusely.

'I wanted to meet my White Warrior. Punnr, isn't it?'

'Yes, sir.'

'Yes... *lord*. Punnr the Weakling, I believe. An interesting choice of name by our Thane Radspakr here.' Suddenly the man laughed. Not warmly, but not without mirth either. 'Looks like you damn well proved him wrong, boy, eh? Punnr the bloody Weakling, my ass.' He reached for a cigar that had been smouldering on an ashtray and sucked at it, blowing smoke across the room. Radspakr coughed lightly.

'So here's the thing, Punnr the Weakling, your little ruse almost fucked everything up for me. I had a *lot* of money riding on you and then you go and get yourself killed at Old College, don't you? Put me under quite a bit of heat. We weren't expecting our White Warrior to go charging out into the middle of the bloody carnage and get himself riddled with Titan arrows. That wasn't in the script, lad.'

He drew on his cigar again.

Sveinn sat forward and cleared his throat. 'My lord...'

'It's all right, Sveinn,' interrupted Odin, cutting him off with a wave of his hand. 'I'm just busting your balls. And from where I'm sitting, it looks like the boy here is sweating less than his King. So, tell me Punnr, whose idea was it to have you play dead?'

'Mine, lord.'

'Hmm. My eminent colleague, the Titan Caelestis was furious with your actions and launched a formal complaint.'

'That's his problem, lord.'

The man rumbled darkly and rolled the cigar around his mouth, chewing the end of it. 'Well, your plan worked. The Titan's complaint was overruled; Valhalla collected all four Assets; and I made a killing.' He laughed again and took the cigar from his lips. 'You played fast and loose with the rules, boy, but I like a rule-breaker. Rules are made to be broken.' He jabbed a finger at Punnr. 'As long as when you do so, you do it with style, you come out a winner, and you never *ever* think of doing it again without my say-so. You understand?'

'Yes, lord.'

'You damn well better.' He studied Punnr for a few seconds. 'Anyway, the Thane here says I should give you this trinket.' He tossed a silver arm-ring onto the desk. 'Wear the damn thing. It's supposed to show my pleasure. I suspect the extra ten grand in your account shows it clearer.'

Punnr took the ring. It was heavy.

Odin waved him away with a finger. 'You're dismissed. I have plans to discuss with the King and Thane. Enjoy your first Blood Season, Punnr the Weakling. It'll be a good one for Valhalla.'

Punnr stepped backwards and glanced at Radspakr, who was rigid, wide-eyed and still slick with sweat. The Thane made no movement, just stared at Punnr and opened his mouth once like a fish, so Punnr turned and got himself out of the room before any of them could change their minds.

In the corridor he fingered the arm-ring and wondered how the hell he was supposed to get something so heavy to stay on his skinny bicep. There was distant laughter and the air was redolent with tobacco and alcohol. He was drawn by music. Not the string quartet this time, but a single lilting violin coming from the far end. Light was escaping from a door and there were people leaning on the walls near it, one or two slumped on the floor. The music felt nearer as he approached and there was warmth coming from beyond the door; a closeness, an almost suffocating fug. He eased it open.

What he saw beyond would stay with him forever.

It was a richly furnished drawing room with lavish wallpaper depicting birds of paradise. There was a marble hearth and a vast white carpet. There were sofas and coffee tables and sheepskin rugs. The violinist stood in one corner, dressed head to toe in black, face hidden. He used no music and looked only out towards the dark gardens beyond the windows as he played the most beautiful, haunting melody. Around the edges of the room, men drank quietly and slumped against the walls, but they didn't interact. They had eyes only for the centre of the room. There – on the sofas, the rugs, the carpet, even over the tables – naked bodies indulged in each other. The movements were slow, silent, serious, as though following the music, yet there was no mistaking the raw intensity as limbs contorted. The participants all retained their masks and their featureless faces were a startling counterpoint to the whiteness of the flesh.

Punnr was rooted to the spot with his hand still on the door. Dimly his brain observed that the male bodies were mostly slack and shapeless with age, but his eyes were locked on the females and he knew they were the women who had stood apart in the hall. He could sense the incredible beauty of their physiques and the riches needed to enjoy them. Arousal flickered somewhere in his loins. One of them was looking at him and he remembered he still wore his white cloak. She was moving slowly and sinuously above a recumbent man and her eyes bored into Punnr. He wanted to step into the room and go to her.

'Sex and death,' said a voice just behind him and he turned to see Freyja watching the scene over his shoulder.

'What?' he whispered hoarsely.

'At the end of the day, no matter what riches you possess, no matter what wonders you own, everything boils down to man's twin obsessions. Sex and death. Nothing else matters.'

Punnr stared into her cinnamon eyes behind the helmet. His loins were still alight and he took in her ochre skin and the curve of her collarbone. 'And what of women?' he asked huskily. 'What are women's obsessions?'

She flicked her eyes from the scene and held his for several long seconds, then blinked, cast him an enigmatic final look, and walked away down the corridor.

Punnr peered again into the room. The woman had dropped her eyes and suddenly the whole scene felt raw and grotesque. He smelt anew the sweat and heavy aromas and his stomach roiled. Grimacing, he pushed the door closed and walked back past the lounging bodies. He thought of Calder lying in a Pantheon hospital and cursed himself for getting lost in the night's extravagance. He made it to the saloon, where the fire raged and the quartet was playing earnestly from the main hall. People were warming themselves by the flames. Two were crouched by a table and he could see from the state of their noses what they had just been snorting.

He was about to move through to the main hall, when he caught sight of another white cloak and realised Lenore was watching him from the bottom of the stairs. The Titans had that evening also discarded their heavy helmets and were wearing smaller dress helms. Theirs, however, failed even to cover the crowns of their heads and were little more than glittering silver masks, so Punnr could see Lenore more clearly than ever before, the pale skin, the red hair that fell in tresses over her shoulders.

'You arsehole.'

Punnr checked his approach. 'What?'

'You cheating arsehole.' Her tones were soft Scotch.

'I bust a gut in those Raids. I gave everything I possibly could to succeed. And then you cheated your way to victory.'

He could see her eyes were blue behind the helm and her alabaster cheeks were red with anger. 'I don't think...'

'I'll see you in the Blood Season.'

She pushed past him, banging her shoulder against his, and marched away. He watched her go, then followed the music back to the hall. The room was filled with dancing couples swirling around the floor. The quartet was playing with passion and the movements of the dancers were, at once, delightful and sorrowful.

Through the eddies of their bodies, Punnr could see the group by the platform. The woman was still lying in her black and gold wrappings, and her Vigiles guards still balanced the huge brass bowl on her. They watched him approach, but did not stir. He could see the *denarii* in the bowl were almost filling it now. Somewhere his mind worked unbidden on calculations. If there had been two hundred guests and they had each been given a hundred silver *denarii*, then there could be anything up to twenty thousand silver coins in that bowl. He had no idea what twenty thousand *denarii* might weigh, but he knew instinctively that there was no life in the body beneath.

'It's probably a better fate than Erebus,' said Asmund, who had followed him across the room.

'What's Erebus?'

'In classical times it was the place of darkness between earth and Hades where tortured souls were abandoned. And perhaps that's still an appropriate description for the Prison of the Pantheon.'

'Erebus is a prison?'

'Indeed. It's said that those who have contravened Pantheon Rules – but are deemed too valuable to die – are incarcerated in its dungeons. Many never see the light of day again, but some – those for whom circumstances provide a new worth – are occasionally resurrected.'

'Contravened?'

Asmund looked at him darkly. 'There are warriors for whom even the bloody opportunities of the Pantheon aren't enough, whose lust for violence can't be satiated. They are souls you don't wish to meet.'

As he was speaking, Punnr could see Freyja approaching. He glanced back at the body and at the black eyes of the Vigiles. With a ragged breath, he turned to Freyja. 'When can we leave?'

'Now.'

They walked between the dancers, past the statues, around the Blood Book standing in state at the doors and out into the startlingly clear night air.

V

You'll hate me when you read this. You'll curse and call me a bitch and punch something until your knuckles scream.

I've argued with myself every day about contacting you – wanting to write, then finding reasons not to. Christ knows why this evening's different. Maybe it's the three gins I've sunk. Maybe it's because it's June and it was always the summers – during the Interregnums – when we could most be ourselves and not our alter egos in the Pantheon. We could get away from Edinburgh and find places to be just another couple in love.

So I've started to write, for better or worse. And now it's happening, perhaps it feels okay.

I'll come in the small hours when you're with your Wolves. And being back in that house will be hard. The tick of the old grandfather on the stairs, the feel of your shirts in the wardrobe, the man-scent on your pillow. I'll probably sit on our bed in the dark and remember everything. Maybe I'll even flirt with staying until morning, until you walk up the path...

Sorry... that's the gins talking.

But I can imagine you walking back from the Halls of Valhalla in the dawn, away from the stranglehold of the city and into the birdsong and greenery of Morningside, as the sun bursts across The Braids. There'll be papers on the doorstep, blue tits on the feeder and flowers in the borders, because you may be the mightiest of the Horde's warriors, but you're also house-proud and punctilious (is that the right word?). The man I loved.

And I know that's all poetic bullshit, but it's how I feel as I write this.

And what about you? How will you feel when you see this letter? You'll know it's from me and I'm sorry for the brief hope that will surge through your veins. You'll scan the first few lines and then perhaps charge back out onto St Fillan's. But I won't be there.

Halvar must have read her words a hundred times. He sat in his study, feet on a stool, coffee to hand and a cigarette smouldering in the corner of his mouth. February rain clattered on the window as a sharp shower passed overhead, and the garden of his Morningside townhouse looked forlorn, denuded and clinging to the stone walls for protection. Something had drawn him to retrieve her letter. It was eight months since she had used her old key to enter his house and placed it by the kettle. And not a single bloody syllable since.

Fuck her. That was increasingly the sentiment that came to mind in his lowest, most solitary moments. He didn't mean it, but he was conscious enough of his emotions to sense how they had changed during the course of those hundred readings. Cooler now. Laced with steel. Gone was the hot-headed madness that had propelled them both through last year's Blood Season. Now, if the bedrock of his love still lay somewhere, it was dormant and buried.

Why had she done it? Why had she vanished without a word, without a goodbye, without the bloody courage to explain? Then to sneak back into his world and leave only the letter – well, that was just salt on his wounds. He stubbed the cigarette into a saucer, blew a wreath of smoke towards the bay window and took several long gulps of coffee. Then, with a concerted effort, he read on.

> *I can't describe the shock of that raid or the hell afterwards. Those weren't just my troops I took into that cellar, they were my comrades in the line and my friends. I – Olena, Captain of Companion Bodyguard – should have found them a better place to meet the axes of Valhalla than that stinking hole. I watched them fall, Halvar, and even as I led the retreat, I saw Timanthes taken on the knife of the one you call Freyja.*
>
> *Both of us planned that treachery, but it was me alone who had to carry it out. You've no idea what it felt like as I made my escape back onto the rooftops. An emptiness, a numbness, a loss of all direction in my life. I hunched against a chimney stack and listened to the Horde calling below. The cream of the Titan Palatinate lay scattered and it was all because of our selfish love.*

He paused in his reading. This next bit always got to him. The part when she finally put into words what he'd always suspected. That she blamed him for the mess they'd created, blamed him for telling Radspakr. Perhaps even blamed him for their relationship in the first place. He scowled out at the garden. He was unimpressed that he could read this passage countless times over many months and still feel it tear at him.

I knew then we'd been fools. Nothing we'd planned would ever come true. Damn you, Halvar, why did you ever tell that bastard? From that moment, he controlled us. We never had a chance. Whatever happened in the Grand Battle, we could never be together.

There. She had said it. A year ago, they had followed Radspakr's instructions and believed that pruning the Titan elite in the cellar would give Halvar's Wolves the opportunity in the Grand Battle to break through to Alexander and strike him down. The fall of the Titan Palatinate. It was what they'd dreamed about. The assimilation of the hoplites into the ranks of the Valhalla Horde and the joining of Olena and Halvar, together at last in the Pantheon. But she hadn't even waited for the hope of that outcome. Instead she'd fled from the cellar that fateful night, failed to show on the Field of the Grand Battle and disappeared from his life. It seemed it hadn't mattered to her if Alexander had fallen that day, because she'd already given up on their future.

It was Agape who found me in the first light. I was still locked against the chimney, chilled and sodden. I don't recall her words, but I do remember her look and it was terrible. I thought she was going to kill me and throw my body to the morning pedestrians. But the blow never came and in a small voice she told me she would cover for me.

I'm sorry, Halvar, but I told her about your plans to take Alexander in the Battle and I've heard since that she came for Leiv and his Wolf Litters just as they were about to strike the King. Perhaps it was for the best.

I hid in my flat, thankful that you didn't come looking for me at that critical time when all eyes were convinced of treachery. I had no plan. I thought Agape might arrive with answers, but she never did, and I began to realise the full measure of my actions. The Titans would be in uproar. Even in the moments of his death, Timanthes had yelled to me: 'We are betrayed.' It was obvious it had been a trap and now I was the only Titan unaccounted for. They'll come for me, I thought, but even that knowledge couldn't propel me into action. I wasted the time making Tyler a lasagne – like feeding him was going to make a difference.

And then come for me they did. But not the Titans. Nor Radspakr and his cronies. Not even the Vigiles. The one who appeared was so crushingly unexpected that you'd never believe me even if I could tell you and live.

So I suppose the purpose of this letter is to say I'm okay and, for what it's worth, to tell you I'm sorry. I think about you lots. I wonder how you are and if you're coping. When I come in the night, will I find your home messy, or will it still be the ordered sanctuary I remember? Weirdly, I don't know which I'd prefer.

I can't write to Tyler. Words would fail me and I don't think he'd ever understand. I've ensured he has enough funds in his account each month, but I worry about him on that horrible estate. Will you keep an eye on him sometimes – for me, for old times' sake? Just the occasional watch on his block? It would mean so much to me to believe you'll do that.

Stay strong, Halvar. Stay safe. Lead your Wolves in the Nineteenth Season and forget about me.

M

He refolded the paper and slipped it back into its envelope, then stood staring out at the rain. By god, girl, if you cared enough to make contact again – if not with me, then with your brother – you'd be surprised to learn that your good-for-nothing little Tyler is now Punnr, Thegn of Valhalla, trooper of Wolf Company, chosen White Warrior, finder of the Assets, victor of the Season of the White, hero of the Horde – and he's here in the Pantheon, Morgan, because of you.

'Brante!' The cry broke from her lips and she winced as her ribs throbbed in response.

He came striding towards her. 'Hello, my little one.'

It was the seventh day and Monique had brought Calder out to the communal area. Over the last forty-eight hours, such expeditions had become a regular part of Calder's recuperation. She was still rigged to the drain and saline, but these were attached now to a rolling IV stand, which she could lean on as she shuffled about like a geriatric resident in a care home.

Brante took her in a soft embrace and she was amazed at the relief that flooded through her.

'How are you?' he said, holding her away and inspecting her.

'Don't.' She laughed, embarrassed. 'I must be a real sight.' She thought he looked strained.

'It's wonderful to see you. I heard you were here, but the bastards have only been letting us out at separate times. It's like a bloody prison. Do you want to sit?'

She took his hand and they walked to the chairs. There were five other warriors reading or conversing, as well as two more over at a drinks counter making themselves coffees. She nodded to them and Brante shook the hands of a couple. They were all Drengrs and she recognised most of them, even though now they wore soft white dressing gowns. Brante himself was in jeans and a grey woollen polo neck jumper and he noticed her look.

'I'm leaving today. I think that's why they finally relented and let me see you.'

'Why wouldn't they before?'

'Because it's bad for morale to let us see injured comrades – or some bollocks like that.'

'Are you properly mended?'

'I'm fine. Shoulder's stiff, but it's well enough.' Brante frowned and lowered his head. 'Which is more than can be said for Punnr. I can't believe we lost him.'

'They haven't told you?'

'Told me what?'

She leaned forward and gripped his head with both hands. 'Punnr's alive.'

'What?' He searched her eyes for the truth. 'I saw him peppered with Titan arrows.'

'It was a ploy to fool the Titans. He appeared in the castle on the final Raid Night. But I don't know what happened after that. You've heard none of this?'

'Not a word. I could make out lots of activity last week and I guessed more injured souls must be arriving, but they kept me locked up and wouldn't explain. I've spent all this time blaming myself for not being near him when he fell at Old College, thinking I could have done something.' Brante stared at her, uncertainty flickering behind his eyes. 'You're sure you saw him?'

She thought again of the struggle beside the castle battlements, the strength of Punnr's embrace as he carried her down Long Stairs and his breath on her as he whispered again and again that she was safe. 'Oh, I'm sure.'

Brante beamed and then glanced at where the bandaging was bulbous beneath her gown. 'Is it bad?'

'Muscular mostly – a cut and bruised ribs.' She pondered whether to tell him about Ulf and Erland, but decided against it. 'A sword blow in the early stages of the battle.'

He could see the blue shadow on her cheek. 'And a punch as well.'

She tried to laugh it off. 'Yes, it's a real bed of roses – this thing we've joined.'

He smiled. 'It's so good to see you. This place has been driving me crazy. There's not even a proper window, so I've lost track of time.'

Her attention was wrenched from him by the sight of a Vigilis, helmeted and armed. One side of the common room comprised a half-glassed partition that looked onto a corridor. The Vigilis was walking along this and Brante followed her gaze.

'The bastards are always patrolling. Keeping tabs on us.' The man approached an unmarked lift, placed a finger on a scanner, the doors slid open and he was gone.

'Where do you think that leads? To the Titans?'

'I don't think so. My room's further up the end where there's a sealed door, which I'm pretty confident leads to the opposite wing.' He shrugged and made light of it. 'Who knows, maybe they're all slipping out for a fag break.'

Monique appeared. 'Now then, Brante – let's give our girl some breathing space. She needs to rest.'

'I know. Do you want a drink, Calder? The hot chocolate's good.'

'That would be nice.'

She watched him stride over to the counter and thought of him returning to the Valhalla Halls.

Monique noticed her wistful expression. 'Don't worry, girl, you'll be back with them soon enough.'

Bjarke scowled suspiciously at the plate in front of him. 'I presume that limp prick Ulf hasn't joined us?'

Radspakr pondered the warrior. They were seated in his Valhalla quarters. 'If, by that, you're asking whether I've become a serial boiler of young Thegns, then you can rest assured. I believe he's in the Practice Rooms.'

Bjarke muttered blackly and tucked into the chops, juices quickly greasing his beard. A serving girl entered with a pitcher of wine, which Radspakr took and then waved her away. 'So what do we do about him?' asked the big man as he thrust out his goblet for a refill.

'Nothing that will draw attention.'

'But he knows too much. Better a stiff corpse than a loose tongue.'

'He won't babble.'

'How can you be so sure?'

'Because, Jarl, his bowels will be leaking from the terror of knowing he failed us.'

Bjarke acknowledged the truth in this with a low harrumph.

'I think, however, you might wish to pay him a visit in the Practice Rooms to settle any doubts he may have.'

'Consider it done.'

'*Carefully*, Jarl. Our new Thegns seem to be dropping left, right and centre, so another one irreparably damaged will attract unwanted eyes.'

Bjarke snorted, but understood. Radspakr watched him maul the chops and wondered yet again at the wisdom of having this Neanderthal as an ally.

'And what of the White Warrior?' the man asked through a mouthful of meat.

Radspakr sighed and sat back in his chair, holding a goblet of wine. '*That* is more of a dilemma.'

'Give me his address and I'll gut him in his home. End of problem.'

'If only it were that simple, but the circumstances have changed. Consider this, Jarl – Punnr the Weakling is now the Horde's victorious White Warrior and, as such, no longer a non-entity who can simply disappear. Consider too the woman Calder, mending in the Pantheon hospital and – I suspect – fully aware of our less than charitable intentions. And then there's Housecarl Halvar, the man behind the White Warrior's timely disappearance during the Raids and most probably also the man who separated Erland's head from his shoulders. Our foe is growing in number and we must act with care.'

'So we just sit around with our hands up our arses?'

'We bide our time.'

Bjarke mopped his plate with a hunk of bread and sucked the grease from his fingers. 'And what of Sveinn?'

Radspakr looked at him sharply, gimlet-eyed. 'What of him?'

'The Gathering of the Palatinates will be upon us after the Battle. Perhaps the time is right for a Challenge?'

'Fool's talk!' Radspakr replied roughly, but bit back his words when he saw the warrior stiffen. Collecting a breath, he leaned forward and continued more gently. 'Jarl Bjarke – we have a bargain. You are my trusted sword arm and in return – when the time is right – I will support your Challenge. But you must understand that Sveinn's star is in the ascendance. He led Valhalla to a significant victory at the Grand Battle last year; he recruited well in the Armatura; and he's overseen the claiming of all four Raid Assets. The troops are behind him and – more critically – so is Odin, for now. So this is no time for a Challenge. You will lose.'

Bjarke glared, grabbed his goblet and drained it.

Radspakr held a finger out to draw his attention back. 'Have faith, Jarl. I've given you my word. There will come a time when Sveinn's luck will fail him and his troops will desert like so many grains of sand in an east wind. Then, I vouch, together we'll make your Challenge.' He could see he still needed to play Bjarke carefully, so, holding the Jarl's eye, he raised his own goblet with a flourish. 'To my future King. The next Sveinn.'

VI

Bjarke arrived in the Practice Rooms, glowered at the drilling troopers and told them to piss off. Ulf had been practising backhands against one of the pells stuffed with old clothes rather than sand or grain to provide a faster swinging target.

The Jarl was never one for subtlety. Once the room was empty, he approached the Thegn, spat dismissively on the flagged floor and smashed a huge balled fist into the side of his skull. The blow sent Ulf crashing against the wall and dropped him in a heap. Bjarke loomed above him and his fist came again, this time yanking Ulf's chin up so that he could see the fear in his eyes.

'One little girl. You're sent to kill one little girl. That's all you had to do. Two of you against her. Should have been a piece of piss. But what do I learn? That she lives. That she heals and prepares for her return.' He leaned in hard, pressing his full weight down on Ulf. 'If I had my way, I'd rip your prick off right here and bugger you with it. You think about that – you think about what that would feel like, boy.' He jabbed a finger in front of Ulf's face. 'Say one word and your death will be slow and terrible.'

He cuffed Ulf a final time, then pushed himself upright

and smoothed down his tunic. As he studied the scrawny Thegn, he found himself mildly impressed by the belligerent silence of the other man and decided he had made his point. Punching the nearest pell so it swung crazily, he stalked out of the room.

Ulf pulled himself gingerly onto a bench and touched the side of his head where the Jarl's fist had hammered the bone. How had it come to this? He had believed Punnr and the other Thralls would be pathetic competition to be destroyed in the forests during the Armatura. Instead, it was his Perpetual allies who had fallen like flies and now he found himself alone, despised, caught in an intrigue far greater than he understood and rapidly becoming Bjarke's butt-boy. He had fled for his life when a roaring Halvar burst from the chapel and decapitated Erland. He had run as fast as his legs would carry him, screaming incoherently like a child and convinced that the great Wolf was thundering after him. And behind it all he had glimpsed the White Warrior, alive and well.

Punnr. The bastard had proved more resilient than he had expected. He remembered him on the hill with the helicopters approaching and the shaft of sunlight playing on his cloak. Perhaps he should have realised then that Punnr was made of stern stuff. Now the bastard was revelling in his new-found fame as the victor of Valhalla, strutting the Tunnels, milking the attention of Hersirs and Housecarls.

Two troopers from Storm Regiment entered and retrieved wooden swords from the shelves. He rubbed his face, hawked loudly and walked stiffly to the Throne Room, then turned into North Tunnel towards one of the larger rooms where the door stood open and voices spilled out. The space was used as an instruction area and rows of benches were arranged in a semicircle. The year's new intake occupied them, dressed casually in tunics and soft leggings, murmuring together like students awaiting a tutorial.

Ulf slipped inside and placed himself on a bench near the door. Punnr was sitting at the front and talking with those around him. The bastard was loving the attention. He caught Ulf's eye and held it with a promise of retribution. Another figure came through the door and stopped to survey the room. Ulf glanced up and found himself staring into the face of Brante. The tall man regarded him coldly, then swung away towards the front benches. Someone cheered and then others began clapping and banging the benches. Punnr stood, a smile cracking over his face.

'Welcome back,' he said, holding out a hand.

'Hello, my friend.' Brante grasped the extended hand and threw his other arm over Punnr's shoulder in a bear hug.

Punnr noticed the stiffness of the movement. 'Still painful?'

'Not enough to keep me away from here any longer.'

'The first bit of proper action and you're stretchered off to the nurses.'

'If memory serves me correctly, it was one hell of a learning curve. One minute I'm practising my sword strokes with you buffoons and the next I'm in a blade fight with the Sacred Band.'

'We thought you'd buggered off for good.'

'I could say the same about you, Lazarus.'

Brante shook hands with a few of those close by, then the two men sat companionably together and Punnr leaned into his friend.

'Tell me about Calder. I've been worrying so much.'

'She's doing fine. She's up and about and almost her old self. She'll be back here causing havoc soon enough. She sends her regards.'

'Her regards? Was that all she said?'

Brante eyed him. 'Something along those lines.'

Punnr heaved a sigh. 'Well, it's good to have you back, *Thrall XII*. The place was lonely without you.'

'It's good to be out of that damn hospital. I've not seen daylight for two weeks.'

'Do you know where you were?'

'Not a clue. Windowless van rides. From the length of the journey, I'd say somewhere on the outskirts of the city, probably south.'

'Well do us all a favour and never go back there.'

'Agreed.'

The hubbub was interrupted by a loud oath from the doorway and heads swivelled to see Halvar glaring, hands on hips. 'Hel's teeth, wipe those grins from your faces!' He strode to the front of the room, followed by Freyja. 'What impudence is this, that two Housecarls can enter a Hall of Valhalla and be greeted by chattering children? How dare you cock and crow like victors in a playground brawl. Is that what you think you are? Victors? The gatherers of the Four Assets? Thor's balls, we're only days from the Blood Season and you'll not be so cocksure then!'

He pulled a table into the centre and began again in a more measured tone. 'All right, you maggots, we've gathered you here because you're what's left of this year's new intake. Thegn and Drengr. For each of you, this will be your first

Blood Season – and if you want to see another, you'd better shut up, wipe the grins and listen.'

He shifted his focus to Freyja, who had seated herself behind the table. When she spoke, her voice was stone-grim.

'Twenty-six Drengr were sworn into Valhalla at the end of the Armatura and seven Thegns. Thirty-three new warriors purchased with the Blood Credits won in the Eighteenth Year. Now there are nineteen of you.' She let the figure linger in the air. 'In just six weeks, fourteen have fallen; hospitalised or dead. I'll save you the arithmetic – that's forty-two per cent of the new intake.

'The figure is much lower amongst the senior troops in Valhalla because they've learned the cunning and the guile to survive, and over the years the weak have been eradicated and only the strong remain. It takes time to master your craft – and the Titans know that.

'The good news is that you've just lived through the most bloody and violent Raiding Season that's ever been witnessed between these two Palatinates and you've come out of it with your bodies in one piece and your minds intact. That is – at least – a start. But let me be crystal clear, the numbers of fallen amongst this new intake cannot be sustained. No Palatinate, however large, can absorb that rate of attrition for long.'

Halvar spoke again. 'So that's why we're here. King Sveinn wants you worms better drilled and better prepared for the Blood Season than any new intake before, otherwise this is going to be a hell of a ride. You'll train in the Practice Rooms until your weapons are part of you. Every given hour you'll work with your units and your Hersirs. You'll watch them and follow their instruction and do whatever they tell you until you know every detail of your role and your duties. But first – tonight – you'll start by listening to Housecarl Freyja. Her words are wise.'

All eyes focused on Freyja. 'Let me tell you what *should* have happened in the Raiding Season. It *should* have been about the mind and not the body. Each year our Pantheon masters set new Rules for the Raiding Season. They dream up challenges and prizes and timescales, all for the pleasures of their gambling friends. These challenges are important because there are points to be awarded and advantages to be won. Advantages like the four Assets that we now hold. Yes, there are always skirmishes and the trading of blows with the foe – these can hardly be avoided in a city of this modest size – but the rules are imposed to ensure they never descend into wholesale warfare.

'But it went wrong this year. The Rules were not enough to stop both Palatinates' core regiments going shield to shield. So that's why my colleague here is so angry when he sees you grinning. We may hold the four Assets, but don't imagine yourselves victors. We have never ended a Raiding Season with such a high body count.'

'And nor have we,' rumbled Halvar, 'entered a Blood Season with a foe so angry.' The audience fidgeted uncomfortably at this thought and there were a few mumbled oaths. 'Shut it,' growled Halvar. 'You need to listen to the lady.'

Freyja flicked him an irritated glance, uncertain she liked being called a lady in these circumstances. 'Let me tell you about the Blood Season. Each year it culminates with the Grand Battle and before that come a series of Blood Nights. The format of these Blood Nights may vary, but the principles remain much the same. Whereas the Raiding Season is designed to keep us apart, the Blood Nights find methods to throw us into the arms of our foe. This year is no exception. The Pantheon authorities have created a challenge, which they have named the Cull. Consider that term, find it in a dictionary. To cull – to select, to pluck. The key to this challenge will be to choose the best targets.

'The Cull will take place over six Blood Nights. Three nights together, then a break, then another three. Its mandates are few: Blood can only be spilled during the Pantheon hours of one in the morning until four; no bows, no spears; this time it's all about swordcraft. All activity must take place within a radius of one *half* mile of the Tron Kirk. That's half the radius you had to play with in the Raids. So it could get cramped. The total numbers to be culled will be announced before the first night. If the Blood Count hasn't reached that total by the end of the sixth night, the Pantheon will select the numbers still needed to reach the total and despatch them. That's it. All else is fluid.'

She scanned their faces. 'Tell me, whom do you think are the best targets?'

It was Brante who replied. 'Us,' he said, subdued.

'Your reasoning?'

'That's what a cull is – the removal of the weakest.'

Freyja nodded. 'The Rules of the Cull make no specific reference about who should be removed, only the total required. But make no mistake – in a tight spot, when the foe are present in force, no seasoned member of the Horde will risk themselves for you. If we must lose fighters before the Grand Battle, we'll lose our weakest. Some are even saying this challenge will represent the cleaning of the ranks. The surgical removal of the weakest. Just like wild animal populations, the Pantheon survives by maintaining only the strongest and fittest.'

She contemplated the faces before her. 'During these six Blood Nights, the usual order of rank and value is going to be ignored. It doesn't matter if you're the most senior Valhalla Jarl or the lowest Drengr, your death will be worth only one Blood Credit to the foe. However, there are two vital exceptions: the death of a warrior with just *one* kill to his or her name results in a reward of two credits to the opposition. And four credits are awarded to the Palatinate that can kill a Vestal.'

Halvar grinned humourlessly. 'Vestals. *Vestales* – the priestesses who tended the sacred fire in the shrine of the goddess Vesta in the Roman Forum. Virgins, all of them – and I wager we have a veritable gathering of those here tonight.'

He untied a small bag from his belt. Carefully he poured the contents into his palm and sifted through them with one finger, then walked towards the audience. At the first Drengr, he handed a small item to the man. At the second, he looked in the young face but gave her nothing. At the third he picked out two of the items, then he went by the next three onlookers without any action. So it continued around the room. To Ulf he handed two items, but he passed Punnr without a look and gave one final item to Brante. The process complete, he stepped back near Freyja and used his bulk to shield what they were doing. Finally, he turned and the troopers could see that both had fixed small circles of material to the left breast of their tunics. Halvar bore a gold circle and two red ones, Freyja a silver and one red.

Brante examined his own little circle of red material, poking at it in his palm. 'So what is this?'

'That,' said Halvar, 'is Eluf.'

Brante's eyes jerked up and widened, trying to see if Halvar jested, then he swore and tossed the material to the floor.

'What do you mean?' demanded Punnr. 'Why does he have a circle and I don't? Who's Eluf?'

It was Brante who answered. 'Eluf was the one I partnered in the forest in the *Sine Missione*.'

'Pick it up,' Halvar growled darkly.

Punnr was still struggling to understand. 'The Perpetual?'

'Pick it up,' Halvar said with more threat.

Brante heaved a sigh and bent to retrieve it. 'Yes,' he said to Punnr, suddenly angry, holding the circle towards him. 'Don't you get it? He's my Blood Kill.'

Realisation flooded around the room. Each trooper looked at the others and made note of who did and did not hold the circles. In that instant the unspoken pecking order changed.

From behind came Ulf's voice, his smugness revived. 'Two for me... Vidar... Gulbrand.'

Freyja spoke. 'These will be fitted to your *brynjar* mail and all warriors will wear them during the Season. When you make a kill – captured and confirmed on camera – you will be awarded a Bloodmark. Reach five and these become a single Bronze. Ten and it will be silver. Gold is fifteen.' All eyes looked at the circles on her breast and Halvar's, and calculated the kills. Eleven and seventeen respectively.

Brante stared at the material in his hand, twisting

it between his fingers and hardly hearing. He was lost somewhere with the man who had hunted him through the trees.

'Will the foe wear them as well?' asked a Drengr.

'Aye,' said Halvar. 'Exactly the same. So we can pick off their lambs too.' He stepped forward and placed himself directly in front of Punnr. 'Burn into your minds the values for a killing. One credit for the death of any warrior with two or more Bloodmarks. Two for a trooper with only a single Bloodmark. And four for the death of a Vestal – a Blood Virgin – a warrior with no kills. It is these who are now the real prizes.'

Punnr stared at the floor and his face burned. Gone was his aura as Valhalla White Warrior, replaced by the emptiness burning a hole in his palm.

'So,' said Freyja, 'What are our tactics?' She pointed to a Drengr in the back row. 'What do you think?'

The man looked shocked. He opened and closed his mouth, but no sound emitted.

Freyja pointed to a female Drengr further along the row. 'What do you say?'

The woman deliberated for a few seconds. 'We... go hunting for the Titan Vestals, find those without a Bloodmark, kill them, take the credits.'

'Who does the hunting?'

'Our finest. The Wolves.'

'And our own Vestals?'

'Conserve them and on the nights their units go out, we protect them, so we don't lose the four Blood Credits. The Palatinate did a good enough job protecting the White Warrior during the Raids, so we can do that again.'

Another Drengr spoke. 'Staying alive sounds like a commendable plan to me.'

There was strained laughter at this, but she scowled them into silence. 'After the toll of this Raiding Season, staying alive is an important ambition.' She trailed her eyes along the back of the room until she found Ulf. 'What say you?'

Ulf felt eyes on him and he wondered if they could see where Bjarke's knuckles had smashed into his skull. 'Sacrifice the Virgins,' he spat.

'You would actively let the Titans win all those Blood Credits?'

Anger rippled through Ulf's gut. She was toying with him. 'Why not? The Vestals have shown themselves to be useless to us.'

Freyja looked at Halvar. 'I think we can be glad our tactics are devised at the King's table.'

'Aye.'

She glanced towards the front row. 'What about you?'

Punnr was still staring at the floor with his fists gripped tightly. He met her eyes. 'I thought,' he said with belligerence, 'the purpose of the Blood Season was to kill the King.'

There was silence. Freyja inspected him and Halvar's face hardened. 'Kill the King?' she mused softly.

'Why are we wasting our time talking about pruning the weakest, when the real prize is Alexander? Isn't that our higher purpose?'

'Aye, laddie,' Halvar intervened. 'But not one that's ever been achieved.' The two men stared at each other and both were thinking of Morgan and her dreams to join Halvar in Valhalla by pruning the Titans in a trap and then allowing the Wolves to assault Alexander himself at the Grand Battle.

Freyja broke the tension. 'It may be our higher purpose, Thegn Punnr, but it's hardly the most realistic objective for our new Oathsworn to take into their first Blood Season.'

Punnr bit his tongue, glanced at Brante and wrinkled his nose angrily. Freyja ignored him and addressed the room. 'I know what you're thinking – especially those of you Vestals with no Bloodmarks. You're thinking you'll do anything to get out and earn your first. It's natural. But that's exactly what the foe hope you'll do.

'And there, in a nutshell, is the beauty of this task. The fine balance of tactics. The double-headed axe. If we conserve you and keep you safe, you'll march into the Grand Battle with your breasts still unadorned and the Titan army will come for you. But if we send you out during the Cull to earn your kills, you'll be easy credits for Titan ambushers. That's why, each day, King Sveinn and the Council of War will review tactics. We'll choose which units to release and which to keep in the Valhalla Tunnels. Nightly, we'll decide your fates based on the most opportune strategy.'

'So you lot,' Halvar summed up, 'be thankful those decisions are above your pay grade. Focus only on your own readiness. Your blades need to be clean, sharp and decisive if you hope to be standing at the end of this Blood Season. Use the Practice Rooms at every available hour. Listen to your Hersirs. Learn from your comrades. Master the sword. Know how to hold your shield so that a foe cannot see the Bloodmarks on your *brynjar*. And, when you're called upon by your officers, fight like Hel herself.'

There was silence as the room took this in.

'Questions?' Freyja asked.

A man in the second row raised his hand. 'What of prisoners?'

'Prisoners!' Halvar roared. 'Are you planning to surrender, laddie?'

'No, sir,' came the weak reply.

'They'll be no damn prisoners!'

Freyja waited again for Halvar to calm. 'It's against the Rules in the Raiding and Blood Seasons,' she explained. 'But – technically – it remains permitted during the Grand Battle. Although the reality is that it now never happens.

'In the early Seasons, it was advantageous to capture prisoners because they would then join the new Palatinate and their old comrades could not replace them. As a Rule, this was viable for the occasional prisoner cornered during the Battle. But it became a problem if larger numbers were involved. One year, the Legion surrounded and captured fourteen of their adversaries and they were duly assimilated into the Legion's ranks the following Season. The rival Palatinate was not permitted to replace these losses. That meant a swing in troop numbers of twenty-eight. It was too much and played merry havoc with the Curiate's gambles.

'There were calls to ban the taking of prisoners altogether, but in the end the Pantheon simply tweaked the Rules. Now a warrior unlucky or stupid enough to be taken prisoner is thrown out of the Pantheon altogether and their old Palatinate is allowed to replace them the next Season. There is, therefore, no advantage in capturing troops, so in the press of battle it has become only kill or be killed.

'The only exception to this Rule is that a Palatinate can decide to *keep* a prisoner it's captured. The prisoner will be assimilated into their ranks, but the Palatinate must then select one of its own troops to leave the Pantheon. There remains no numerical advantage and so it's more or less a redundant Rule.' She glanced mischievously at her colleague. 'Perhaps if the Titans capture Housecarl Halvar in the next Battle, they might decide he's worthwhile keeping and throw out one of their Vestales instead.'

'My arse, they'll capture me!' Halvar waved his arm grumpily. 'That's enough talk of yellow-bellied surrender monkeys. You lot have got training to do, so clear off.'

'You okay?' asked Brante as everyone began to rise and he saw Punnr's expression was still angry.

'Just forget about it.' But then he stopped. 'Actually, you go ahead. I want to ask Freyja something.'

'Let it go.'

'I'm fine. I'll see you shortly in the Hall.'

He stepped back to the table where Freyja was perched.

'The purpose of the Blood Season is to kill the King,' he said quietly. 'You know that. Kill the King. Combine the Palatinates. That has to be the primary focus of everything, the overriding strategic objective. I was expecting you to agree with me because we're the same – we come from the same backgrounds.'

'Excuse me?'

'I mean we were both recruited as Thralls. Plucked from the real world as adults and chosen because we can bring new ideas, new leadership. So why not use that leadership and explain to those Drengr about the importance of a strategy to kill Alexander?'

Freyja's face was expressionless. 'Tell me, Thegn Punnr – before you get ideas too far above your station – do you know where Alexander is on any given night? Have you been into his rooftop strongholds? Do you have any plan for getting through his Sky-God defences?'

His belligerence was caught by the questions. 'No. But if it's too complicated in the city then we wait for the Battle and deploy our ranks with the one aim of striking at him.'

Halvar had overheard and stalked towards them. 'Do your ideas about troop deployment extend to even one second's worth of genuine in-the-field experience?'

Punnr quietened. He wanted to blurt back that for all Halvar's seasons of genuine in-the-field experience, the Housecarl had still been foolish enough to believe a mad-cap plan with Punnr's sister might fell Alexander and while the Housecarl was still able to strut around Valhalla crowing about in-field experience, Punnr's sister was nowhere to be found. But he bit his tongue and just said, 'No.'

'In that case, I suggest you keep your ideas to yourself. You're not the White bloody Warrior any longer. You're an untested and unbloodied Vestal Oathsworn in one of my Wolf Litters and, as such, you'll keep your mouth shut and follow orders instead of filling your head with grand ideas. Have I made myself clear?'

Punnr reddened, but knew better than to argue. 'Yes, Housecarl.'

'Time to go, laddie.' Halvar brushed past him towards the door.

VII

The early morning sky was a cloudless indigo as Tyler turned into Learmonth Place. He'd shared a beer with Brante in the Hall, but pleaded forgiveness for his lack of conversation and the tall man had been mindful enough to drink up and join another group playing the board game *Hnefatafl*. It was seven thirty now and shockingly cold. The air burned his lungs and plumed from his mouth. Hands thrust in his pockets and face deep under his hat, he was lost in thought. A couple of blackbirds called from the Gardens and he found himself drawn away from the promised warmth of his building and, instead, fumbled for the residents' key that opened the gate to the Gardens. He trod across the crackling grass, seated himself on one of the benches with his coat wrapped around his legs and lit a cigarette. A squirrel bounded in front of him, froze when it saw him, then scurried away.

He brooded about the night just gone. Halvar's anger. Freyja's stubbornness. And the Bloodmarks that he didn't possess. Underneath it all, he found himself thinking about Morgan. If truth be told, in recent weeks his sister had been less on his mind. The final Raids themselves had taken up all his emotional energy and, somewhere beneath all the surface tensions, he had actually started enjoying the excitements of playing the White Warrior. In fact, he had been starting to view his place in the Pantheon not simply as a step on the path to finding his sister, but as a journey in its own right.

He heard the clang of the garden gate and looked up to see Oliver wandering towards him, wrapped in a winter coat that seemed several sizes too large. 'Hi, Tyler. I saw you from my window.'

'Hey, lad, it's early. Are you supposed to be getting ready for school?'

'Half-term.' Oliver seated himself on the other end of the bench.

'Already? It seems like Christmas was only a couple of weeks ago.'

'What are you doing out here?'

'Enjoying the quiet. And thinking.'

The boy peered at him. 'Another night in Valhalla?'

'You're not supposed to ask questions like that.'

'Sometimes I can hear you go out in the evenings, especially when the Connaughts' schnauzer yaps at you. And some nights I wake up and wonder what you're doing up there in the Old Town.'

'I hope you keep those thoughts to yourself?' Tyler glanced over to the boy's bedroom window. 'Your dad about?'

'No. Gone to a construction conference in Birmingham overnight. His job takes him away a lot. I'm sorry about last week.'

'Not your fault. But your dad doesn't want us hanging out together.'

'Like I said, he's away. What he doesn't know won't hurt him.'

Tyler dropped his cigarette and stubbed it out with his boot. 'What about your mum?'

'She's fine. Anything that gets me off her hands for a few minutes. Actually, now she knows my dad doesn't want me seeing you, her interest in you has doubled. She asks about you, whether you're in, whether you're busy, how you spend your time.'

'Why?'

Oliver shrugged. 'Isn't it obvious? You can be a new weapon in her armoury.'

Tyler didn't know how to respond and they sat silently listening to the blackbirds. Eventually Oliver spoke again, his tone perfunctory and off-hand. 'Anyway, he's lying. He's not at a conference. He's been waving the brochure around for days, so I hacked into their database and he's not on the delegate list. No one from his company is.'

'So where is he?'

'In a hotel room somewhere probably. Shacked up with the girlfriend he thinks is such a secret.'

Tyler puffed out his cheeks. 'Sorry, lad. That's not what you want to know about your father.' He studied Oliver. 'Anyway, how *do* you know all this stuff? How do you just hack into these databases?'

'Easy enough.'

'When I was your age, I was spending my life kicking a ball against a wall.'

'The whole world's a virtual one these days. Everything that's important is online. We're all just data really. Lines of code. Change any one of those lines and you can change lives. A new identity. A new nationality. A criminal record erased. A university degree here or a medical condition there. Even a completely different bank balance if you know what you're doing.'

'Can you do all that?'

The boy laughed. 'Not yet. But one day I'm going to get *really* good.'

They were interrupted by a woman's voice calling from the road. 'Oliver?' It was his mother, standing in a coat with one hand on the open front door. 'I'm out until lunchtime. Have you got your key?'

'Yes, Mum.'

She banged the door closed and walked down the steps to her car. 'Is that Tyler with you?'

Tyler rose and gave her a little wave. 'Hello, Mrs Muir.'

'Don't get cold out here you two. See you later, Oliver.'

They waited while she spent an age warming the car and backing slowly out of the parking spot. When she had departed, Tyler could see that Oliver was indeed getting cold and he realised it had seeped into his bones as well. 'You ought to be heading in. So what are you doing for the morning if everyone's out?'

Oliver shrugged as he rose. 'Not a lot. Welcome to my life.' Then he pointed more enthusiastically at Tyler. 'Hey – you still haven't talked me through Valhalla like you promised. This morning would be ideal.'

'You're right – I do owe you. First of all I need a shower, some food and a sleep – I've been up all night. But how about you come round at ten thirty – as long as your dad is definitely not making any sort of appearance today.'

'It's a deal.' The boy gave him a thumbs up and began to walk back to the gate.

Tyler watched him go. There was something nagging at the back of his brain. 'Hey.' Oliver turned. 'What you said about lines of data, how everyone's just code... are there ways of finding someone online?'

'Of course.'

Tyler thought through his next words. 'Could you find someone for me?'

'I might be able to. Who is it?'

'Her name's Morgan. Morgan Maitland.'

'Maitland? A relative.'

'She's my sister.'

The boy's face was shining now as he strode back to the bench. 'You've lost your sister?'

'Kind of.'

'When did you last see her?'

Tyler stared at the shrubs, at the sunshine beginning to creep across the grass. 'I lost her to the Pantheon. She was a Titan. They called her Olena – and now I don't know where she is.'

Oliver's legs gave way under him and he sank back onto the bench. 'Oh my god, Tyler. You lost your sister to the Pantheon? That is so *cool*.'

'That's not the word I'd use.'

'So do you have any idea where to start?'

Tyler shook his head forlornly. 'No – I really don't.' He looked at the boy. 'Will you help me?'

Oliver grinned from ear to ear. 'What do you think?'

★

'It's twenty-five,' said Sveinn, cutting straight to the point.

'Thor's bollocks!' spat Halvar. 'We'll barely have enough troops left at the Battle for a bloody football match.'

They were gathered around the great map in the Council Room. It was midnight on the third Tuesday of February and below them, Valhalla was quiet. Some of the new contingent still trained in the Practice Rooms and a few warriors shared ale and talked softly in the Halls, but most of the Palatinate chose to be warm in their own homes, saving themselves for the rigours to come.

Unlike the pomp surrounding the giving of the first clue at the *Agonium Martiale* at the start of the Raiding Season, this was a much more low-key affair. Everyone had become well versed in the rules for the new Cull challenge and all they awaited was the formal toll. It had arrived that evening in an email from Atilius to Radspakr, comprising nothing more than the figure "XXV". A similar message would have been sent to Simmius, waiting in one of the Titan strongholds, and they knew that the Titan officers would also be gathered tonight, digesting the news and forming strategies.

'It seems a reasonable figure,' said Radspakr flatly. He was dressed in his usual woollen robe and black sash, but his hair had been freshly cropped so that it was little more than a darker shade around his bald crown.

'It might in other years,' interjected Freyja. 'But in other years, we'd not already suffered the casualty figures of these Raids.'

'That's what we're here for,' said Bjarke from the end of the table where he was silhouetted against a fire, battling the cold seeping down through the city's foundations. 'To drive steel into bellies.'

'Who decided this figure anyway?' asked Asmund, ignoring Bjarke's comment.

'It came from Atilius,' replied Radspakr.

'I know. But who *really* decided?'

'Money, that's who,' said Halvar quietly, looking at the map. 'Odds, trends, risks, debts. The bloody Curiate will be addicted after the Raiding Season. Winners wanting more, losers needing a change of fortune. They'll be wagering on everything – first kill, first dead Vestal, toll on each night, toll in each Palatinate, which units fare best.'

'And they're doing it in penthouse suites from Tokyo to New York,' agreed Asmund.

'Aye. Greedy bastards. It's our blood they're addicted to.'

A derisive rumble came from the back of Bjarke's throat. 'So you pansies expect the Pantheon to go soft on us?'

Freyja looked at him coldly. 'The point, as I'm sure you understand, Jarl, is that if a wolf pack devours all its prey, it starves.'

The big warrior folded his arms belligerently, but bit back a retort, not entirely sure he did understand her point.

'It is what it is,' said Sveinn, ending the debate in a quiet tone. 'The purpose of this evening is to ensure those twenty-five don't come from our ranks.' He took himself over to the fire, where the light danced on his long silver hair and the whale's teeth hanging from his ears. 'Talk us through the figures, Thane, if you would be so kind.'

'Yes, lord.' Radspakr hooked spectacles over his nose and reached for an iPad. 'We cannot, of course, be certain of the precise return rate of the seventeen wounded; however, my hospital sources inform me that all but six should make it back in time to play some part in the Blood Nights. That being the case, then our number would stand at one hundred and eighty-nine shields, excluding the six of us present – down from two hundred and fourteen at the start of this Nineteenth year.'

'And the spread?'

'Even, my lord. The losses we suffered have not been concentrated in any specific unit. We can still field sixteen Litters in Hammer, five in Storm, four in Wolf and two in Raven.

'Good. What of the Vestals?'

Radspakr peered hawk-like at his screen. 'Many of the new intake were killed during the Raids. Of those remaining, seven are unbloodied in Hammer, five in Storm and one in Wolf.'

Freyja glanced at Halvar. Both knew who the one in Wolf was and it was a blight on his Kill Squads to have a member who was still a Virgin with the blade.

Sveinn turned from the fire and regarded his Council of War. 'That's thirteen multiplied by four credits. Radspakr?'

The Thane fussed with his screen. 'Er… fifty-two, lord.'

'Fifty-two.' The High King stalked back to his place around the table. 'Gut all our Vestals and the Titans could purchase fifty-two new troopers.' He stared hard at his council. 'So we're not going to allow them to do that.'

There was silence. The fire spat loudly and someone laughed from the Throne Room below.

'And what do we know of Alexander's strength?' Sveinn continued.

'More difficult to be precise, of course, lord. We know the Titans ended the Eighteenth Season with one hundred and fifty-nine and they used their funds to recruit seventeen. So they began the Raiding Season with one hundred and seventy-six, as we saw them at the *Agonium Martiale*. According to the Blood Book read at the recent Blood Gathering, they lost twenty-two during the Raids. I don't know the figures for their wounded, but we won't be facing more than a hundred and fifty over these next nights.'

Sveinn stroked his beard. 'Thirty – give or take – fewer than us. They're weakened, but not by much.'

Freyja interjected. 'But they *are* weakened where it hurts.'

'Aye,' Halvar agreed. 'The Band and the Companions.'

Sveinn nodded. 'The legacy of last year. Timanthes' suicidal raid into our Tunnels.'

Radspakr consulted his screen. 'We have no specific figures, lord, but I don't think the Band lost any more of their number during the Raids and the Companions not many. Nevertheless, I would still estimate that Alexander's Guard numbers only twenty-five and his Sacred Band a mere sixteen.'

'And his Vestals?'

'Almost certainly all in Nicanor's Heavy Brigade. Titan policy to place most of the new bloods there.'

'So there we have it,' said Sveinn, still stroking his beard. 'The question is what should we do? And, more importantly, what will Alexander do? Let me have your counsel.'

'If I were Alexander,' said Asmund, 'I'd be terrified of risking any more of my Sacred Band. Prune them further and they become almost redundant in the Grand Battle. So, too, his Companions. We got so close to him at last year's Battle. In those moments he knew how near he was to a Valhalla blade, so he can't risk losing more of his Companion Guard. That means it'll be Parmenion's Lights and Nicanor's Heavies that we face over these next nights. If we're bold, we'll have the advantage.'

'I agree,' said Halvar. 'Alexander *has* to be cautious. He'll send out his Heavies. He still has eighty of those. That said, if we can take twenty-five of those, he'll barely have a Phalanx worthy of the name in the Battle.'

'Let me at those bastards,' swore Bjarke. 'My Hammers have unfinished business with them after the castle. Fuck twenty-five, we'll cull the lot of them!'

'Send the Wolves out,' interjected Radspakr unexpectedly.

The King turned to him. 'That's a surprisingly forthright statement, Thane. Coming from one who doesn't usually lead our lines.'

'I was simply agreeing with Asmund. Alexander's caution means we can be bold. Release Halvar's Kill Squads over the six Nights and they will feast on the peltasts and Heavies.'

'Hm,' Sveinn harrumphed. 'I seem to recall your advice during the Raids hardly stopped us getting into considerably deep water.' Radspakr glanced around at the hard faces and dropped his eyes. Sveinn returned his attentions to the others. 'And what of the Vestals in Alexander's Heavy Regiment?'

Halvar scrunched up his face. 'That's where he'll be cautious. They might be useless turds, but a dead one's still worth four credits and he won't want to give us those resources. He'll only sacrifice them if he's taking too much of a beating to his more experienced troops.'

'Pussies,' spat Bjarke.

Sveinn switched his gaze to Freyja, who was studying the streets of Old Edinburgh on the map in front of them. 'You're quiet, Housecarl. What are you thinking?'

'I'm thinking of Agape, lord. After the slaughter of the Raid Nights, she'll not take kindly to being *preserved* in the Titan strongholds now.'

'It is for her King to decide what she does and does not do,' said Radspakr.

'But he'll listen to his best warrior and her blood will be up. She'll know the numbers are against them, so she'll want to rectify that before the Battle.'

'You think the Band will be abroad these Nights?'

'I do.'

Sveinn brooded, picking at his beard and staring at the map. At long last he shook his head. 'No. Alexander has no choice but to be cautious. He won't risk his best.' His words trailed away, but his officers knew better than to speak. Bjarke turned to the fire and warmed himself. Asmund glanced at Halvar. Freyja watched her King.

'But we'll begin cautiously as well,' he said eventually in his gravelly voice. 'Freyja, your Ravens, and, Asmund, two Litters from Storm, will start.' There was a hiss as Bjarke spat into the flames. 'Reconnaissance. Hit and run, if you get the chance. If you find Titan Heavies or Lights in number, I will send the Wolves for the slaughter. And, Jarl...' He addressed himself to Bjarke, who returned grumpily to the table, 'I'll hold Hammer until the time is right.'

The council members looked at each other. They had given their views and their King had spoken. There was no point in further debate.

'I have one additional ingredient to throw into the pot,'

continued Sveinn. 'Thanks to the endeavours of Thegn Punnr last Season, you will remember we have four Assets. One of these is Time. Perhaps the most precious of the lot – and one that Alexander doesn't hold. Time. To be precise, two weeks. None of us yet know the date of the Grand Battle. The Titans will be informed of this only twenty-four hours beforehand and they'll arrive at the Field only just transported from the capital and, presumably, disorientated and disorganised. We, on the other hand, will be informed of the date fourteen days prior. Assuming I learn of this during the Blood Nights, it will, therefore, be my prerogative to decide whether to transport Valhalla troops for the Battle early.'

All eyes were on him.

'So I may begin withdrawing units. The Titans, of course, must suspect nothing, so this withdrawal must be carried out with the utmost care. We thin our lines in the city and prepare ourselves at the Field, while appearing to be as strong as ever during the remaining Blood Nights. An interesting balancing act, and one, no doubt, this council will discuss in depth when the time comes.' He opened his palms to his officers. 'Thank you all. Brief your Hersirs. I look forward to six successful Blood Nights.'

VIII

Radspakr walked through the John Hope Building in the Botanic Gardens. The place smelled of coffee, burgers and floral room spray, and there were more people milling about than he expected on a damp weekday. Knowing there would be cameras, he steered away from the tills and marched straight through the main causeway into the fresh air beyond.

The Gardens themselves were nigh on deserted. On a grey winter's afternoon with the promise of rain, the plants were drab and forgotten. He bore left, following the main path through the trees. A squirrel bounded across in front of him and a child yelled from some distant point, but otherwise he was alone. He was dressed in a black overcoat and walking boots, with a tweed cap on his head.

The track took him through a giant beech hedge with limp brown leaves and on to a demonstration garden. In the high season, the rows of borders here would be filled with vegetables and cottage garden flowers, all labelled for the visitors to dream of reproducing in their own little patches. Now, however, the earth was bare. Even the staff were keeping indoors. A wheelbarrow filled with freshly dug weeds sat discarded and a robin perched on it, picking at morsels and watching him with a beady eye.

Radspakr despised himself for being there. He had always been a proud Viking and in the early Seasons he had even believed the Pantheon valued honour. But Odin's greed had changed all that. For the Caelestis, winning was everything and that meant trading secrets with the enemy and playing the off-stage power games. Fat Cleitus, the new Colonel of Light Infantry in the Titan Palatinate following the demise of Timanthes, had become Odin's whisperer. A man for whom money meant even more than winning. If Odin required information, Radspakr was required to make the illicit arrangements and Cleitus would meet the Caelestis and trade information for a flow of funds into his private accounts.

Now, much to his chagrin, Radspakr himself needed to make use of this channel. Not to furnish Odin with secrets. Quite the opposite. To smother one before it ever found its way to Odin's attentions.

He slowed and checked inside the scattering of greenhouses to ensure no one loitered. It began to spit and he pulled his cap down and swore under his breath, although if truth be told, it was better if it rained. Less chance of interruption.

A man approached from the opposite direction and Radspakr tightened. The figure was trim, athletic. No fat Cleitus.

The man came next to him and they stood, hands thrust in pockets, looking at an interpretation panel telling them about the abundance of wildlife to be found in herbaceous borders.

'Why hasn't he come?' demanded Radspakr without glancing at the other man.

'Because he didn't wish to. If you've something worth saying, Thane, then spit it out.'

Was this a trap? Could Zeus and Alexander have exposed Odin's channel? Radspakr turned on the other man and studied him. He had a hard face, clean-shaven like all Titans, but Radspakr recognised him as one of Cleitus' lapdogs. Across his mouth, embedded through both lips, ran a deep scar and Radspakr wondered how anyone could take a blade strike there and still have teeth.

Trusting his instincts, he said cautiously, 'We have a Vestal in Wolf Company this year.'

'A Blood Virgin in your Kill Squads? Dropping your standards a bit, aren't you, Thane?'

Radspakr ignored the barb. 'Tell Cleitus the man can be recognised not only by the lack of a Bloodmark, but also by a silver arm-ring.'

'Not easy to spot in the dark.'

'Stop giving me excuses and just make sure the man doesn't get through the Blood Nights.'

The Titan kicked a stone on the path and peered shrewdly at Radspakr. 'You have your own means for getting rid of undesirables, so I wonder what makes this Vestal important enough to bring the Thane of Valhalla out of his lair?' He grinned knowingly. 'You're flying under the radar. Odin doesn't know about this meeting, does he? This Vestal got something on you?'

Radspakr rounded on the man. 'If I were you, trooper, I'd think very, very carefully before bandying such questions around. Always remember you're expendable. Just tell

Cleitus we would consider this Vestal's demise a significant favour.'

'A nice clean kill in front of the cameras, which raises no suspicions. Nothing that could come back and bite you, Thane. I think we understand. So what's in it for us?'

'What's in it for you!' Radspakr exploded, then steadied himself. 'A Vestal's in it for you. Four credits.'

'That's all? You demanded a meeting just to give us that?'

Radspakr calmed himself with an effort. 'Tell Cleitus, kill the Vestal and I will be in his debt.'

The man thought about this, then nodded once and turned on his heel. Radspakr checked around. Only the robin, pecking away and still eyeing him, had witnessed the brief exchange.

The woman cycled across The Meadows and into the lights of the university quarter. It was cold, but she was dressed in only a tracksuit and white trainers. Her hair was tied back in a bun and she wore no cycle helmet, which amused her. How dangerously she lived! Max Richter played softly on her headphones, because on these nights she wanted ethereal music instead of the dance beats of her workouts. The incline steepened up Middle Meadow Walk, but she didn't need to rise in the saddle. She was early, always early, and she used these rides to warm her muscles and relax her mind. The rhythm of the tyres on the tarmac took her away from the person she was in daylight and focused her on the hours ahead.

She bore east away from the university, past the theatres, and then angled through back roads until she turned onto

Holyrood Road and dropped down towards Dynamic Earth and the Parliament. She let the bike take her, picking up speed, freewheeling, feeling the cold nip at her nose, then drawing to a halt near an alley that led north to intersect with the Royal Mile. She walked into the shadows and switched off her lights. It was a little after ten and she waited for a group to pass on their way to the cocktail bars further down, then ran her eyes casually up the road and along the skyline above.

Satisfied, she turned into the alley and wheeled her bike towards Canongate and the Mile. Halfway along, she stooped and flipped her back wheel inward. It was a Brompton and in moments she had folded it down. She removed her earphones and the hum of the city came to her. She let herself adjust to it, then alighted steps to a smart door with half a dozen business names beside it and pressed the buzzer for A&K Finance. She raised her eyes to a camera trained on her, there was an answering buzz and she pushed her way inside.

The entrance hall was well lit with opaque glass doors leading off to different office premises. She climbed the stairs, passed the environmental consultancy and solicitors on the first floor. On the second, the auditing firm had wide windows looking onto the stairs and she could see a few heads still hunched over desks. She padded to the final floor and approached the A&K Finance door. There was a click as she approached and a man in shirtsleeves swung it open.

'Evening, ma'am.'

'Evening, Terence. Everything quiet?'

'You're the first, as always, ma'am.'

She handed him the Brompton. 'Thanks. See you later.'

She strode through an open-plan office with about forty desks and terminals, all empty, turned through a door and came to a ladder that had been pulled down from a hatch above. As she climbed, the hatch opened and another man stood back to let her up. 'Hello, ma'am.'

'Hi Rich.'

'It's all yours.'

She was in a vaulted loft space, painted white. In front of her was a dividing wall, which hid the true size of the loft. In fact it extended not only across the breadth of the property, but on into neighbouring ones. There were two unmarked doorways in the wall and she walked through the right-hand one. It led her to a changing room and she took herself to her usual corner.

Eyes closed, she stretched her neck muscles and rolled her shoulders, then began a series of gentle meditative movements. The room was warm, moist and smelt of essential oils. When she was through with her routine, she stripped, placed her clothes and headphones in an open locker, untied her hair so that the tresses dropped down her back and then she walked naked through to the next area.

Before her, still as glass and lit only by six soft spotlights, was a pool. It was enclosed in black marble and the walls above were cast bronze and burnished so perfectly that she could see an almost untarnished reflection of herself. The water beckoned her. She sat and dipped her legs, letting the warmth caress her. An essence of aloe hung on the air and she breathed it in, then eased herself forward and sank beneath the surface. She allowed herself to drop to the bottom, crouched there foetus-like for long seconds, then extended her arms and pulled back up. She broke the surface and began an effortless breaststroke to the far end, slipped onto her back and returned. There were skylights above and she could see the stars. *It is a good night to begin.*

They called the place Persepolis, after the ancient Persian capital founded by Darius, captured and burned by Alexander in 330BC, and on Blood Nights it was her custom to come here early to be alone. She could spend an hour or more in this pool, swimming, thinking, preparing. Unlike the Horde, whom she had studied long enough to know that all their Gates led to the same underground Halls, this place was one of four distinct and separate strongholds ranging along Edinburgh's Old Town skyline, which comprised the Titan domain. Pella, the birthplace of Alexander; Thebes, Ephesus, Persepolis. Geography and architecture defied any hope of joining these strongholds into one, but the Titans had long ago mastered the walkways, parapets, balconies and climbs that allowed them to move rapidly between each. Only road junctions broke their intricate aerial tapestry and forced them to ground, but they were practised in the art of crossing these obstacles unseen.

She sank below the surface again and swam an unhurried length underwater. Of course, just as the Titans knew the locations of the Valhalla Gates, so the Vikings knew the buildings that gave access to Alexander's strongholds. The doorway in the alley and A&K Finance would have long been marked by Valhalla scouts. But Pantheon rules forbade any attack through these public routes. If the Horde wanted to raid into Titan territory, they must come from the roofs.

Every night the Titans split themselves differently between the strongholds and the system used for allocating units to each place was a closely guarded secret, managed and constantly reviewed by Simmius, Adjutant and Quartermaster of the Palatinate. No one ever knew where Alexander would locate himself and each night the Companions and Band would prepare themselves in different surroundings. Tonight, for her, it was Persepolis.

At last, after many lengths, her solitude was disturbed by another woman entering, so she eased herself from the water at the far end, nodded to the new arrival, and walked through to a further room. She took a cold shower, while a young Schola girl waited with a towel.

'Thank you, little one. Are you going to make me look magnificent tonight?'

'Yes, ma'am.' The girl beamed shyly and then, over the next half hour, helped to oil the woman, comb her hair, and dress her. As it neared eleven thirty, other serving girls materialised and new women arrived, wet from the pool.

'You have made me invincible,' she said to the girl when she was finally ready and bestowed a kiss on the top of the little one's head. 'My foe will bow before me.'

She made her way into the final area, lit by moonlight coming through a large window at the far end. A man waited there, dressed in a simple tunic. He knew she would be the first and already held her sword, shield and helmet.

'Ninety minutes to kick-off, ma'am.'

'Indeed.' She smiled, strapping on the sword. 'I will take the air.'

'Yes, ma'am.'

The man strode to the window and pulled it open. Placing her helmet over her newly cleaned hair and fixing her shield, she stepped lithely past him, hunched and sprang over the parapet. She landed softly on a flat roof below and straightened to take in the view of the city. Chimneys, spires, domes shone in the moonlight and the sound of a few vehicles travelled up from the Mile far below. The bulk of the Pentland Hills was black against the stars to the west and in the other direction shone the lights of Leith. A faint wind caught her at this height and lifted the corner of her cloak. Blue.

Let the Season begin. I am ready. On her breast were the newly fixed Bloodmarks. One gold, two red. Seventeen kills.

I am Agape.

IX

In Valhalla too, they came early. Leiv – Hersir of Kill Squad Four in Wolf Company – had insisted upon it. The seven members of his litter arrived in the still-quiet hours of the early evening and took themselves through their rituals.

During the rigours of the Raiding Season, Punnr's role as White Warrior had limited his chances to get to know his Wolf team, but in the nights since Halvar had distributed the Bloodmarks, he had obeyed the Housecarl's instructions and trained hard in the Practice Rooms, first with his fellow new recruits and then alongside his Wolf litter colleagues.

Now Punnr changed slowly and observed his companions. His body ached from the previous nights of lunging and battering with wooden swords, but there was no doubt his skill had improved and, with it, some of the confidence that had been so undermined by the introduction of the Bloodmark concept. He pulled on his undertunic, cinching it with a thick belt, then stepped into knee-length boots. The room was scented with herbs and steamed from the hot showers. Leiv was already changed and he nodded crisply to Punnr and made his way through to the Halls.

The others took longer over their showers and prepared

themselves quietly. Hagen was stretched across the floor, arching his back. Fat Olsen waxed his beard, then slapped his cheeks and emitted deep huffs. Stigr sat in a corner with his eyes closed, his sinewy, muscled torso covered in tattoo swirls barely visible against his black skin. Knut emerged from the shower, short, with little stump legs, his beard greying, yet his chest still a barrel of strength. He paraded around naked and took no notice as Unn came through from the female area and sat her bulk down near to Punnr. That left only Ake next door, the one Punnr found most difficult to gauge. A skin-headed rage of a woman, as unapproachable on the daytime streets of the city as she was beneath her armour. Plain, beautiful and wild all at the same time. Punnr treated her with respect and wariness in equal measure.

'Word is we're being held,' said Unn to the room in general.

Olsen swore and slapped himself again.

'Keep your wolves chained,' said Knut, still happily naked. 'That's always the way to win a fight.'

Hagen sat up from his stretching and crossed his long legs. 'Makes sense. Let the Ravens find the scent first, then Sveinn will want us there quickly enough.'

'It's because of the Vestal,' Stigr said, without opening his eyes, and the others shot grim glances at Punnr.

'We all started as Vestals once,' Unn protested. 'All the more reason to get ourselves out there and let Punnr have his kill.'

'But we weren't in Wolf Company then,' retorted Stigr, sitting forward and giving Punnr a hard look. 'We had to earn our places.'

Olsen rumbled his agreement and spat loudly onto the tiled floor. 'And there's never been a season like this one. Nineteen killed in the Raids and now the bastards want twenty-five in the Cull!'

'They're fucking crazy,' growled Knut.

'Aye and they're fucking well going to destroy this Palatinate if most of that number comes from our ranks. This is my ninth year. One more and I'm telling you, I'm out of here. It's all getting too hot for me.'

'It's Knut's twelfth,' said Hagen, rising from his stretches. 'So he's free to leave at the end of any season. Are the rewards of retirement and Elysium sounding more attractive, old man?'

'Damn right they are. I haven't got this far to go out with Titan iron in my belly.'

'If that fate awaits any of us,' added Olsen, 'it should be during the Battle, in the press of the shieldwalls. Not because of some bastard cull.' He swore again and shook his head so his jowls wobbled like blancmange beneath his beard. 'Twenty-five. It's bloody ridiculous. We need to harvest Titan lives at every god-given chance or we're going to be in the shit.'

'Agreed,' said Stigr and his eyes were on Punnr. 'But perhaps our tactics need to be even better honed than that, my fat friend. Perhaps events will require us to make this a game of give and take.'

'What do you mean by that?' demanded Punnr testily.

Stigr pursed his lips. 'They are just words, Thegn Punnr. Make of them what you will.'

The room lapsed into strained silence and Punnr watched them. He knew all too well they resented his presence.

Firstly, he was a Thegn – more than that, an Electi, one who had been pulled from the outside world, rather than come up through the Schola system. They saw him as privileged and no one ever liked that. To complicate matters, they grudgingly respected what he had achieved as the White Warrior. They liked his trick of falling to Titan arrows and, for a time, he had been the hero of the hour. But that had passed. Now the presence of a bloodless, untested Vestalis in their elite unit left them ill at ease. He was a liability and no one wanted a liability on their team.

Brante, on Squad Three, was a different matter. He might be a Thegn too, but everyone liked him. He already had a Bloodmark to his name and was sure with his weapons. He had fought bravely against the Sacred Band at Old College and had borne the pain of his injury with grace. Most of all, he was easy company. He drank and laughed and argued with them all, and they had embraced him as a Wolf.

Ake came to the door, rubbing her hand over her bristly scalp. 'Leiv wants us in the Throne Room.'

The men finished dressing and followed her out. Unn held back and walked with Punnr. 'Don't worry about them. It's very simple really. Just make yourself a kill. Then they'll value you.'

'Can we take them?'

Agape had split the sixteen members of her Sacred Band into three groups and they spread wide that night, searching for the foe. Now she lay with five of them atop the flat roof of Edinburgh's Travelodge on the corner of

St Mary's Street and they had spotted Vikings kneeling in the darkness of an alley called Boyd's Entry. It was normally a bustling part of town and the alley led to a close with little eateries, but the time was now three in the morning and all was still.

She inched forward to where Kyriacos had spoken. He was placed in the angle between the parapet and the door giving access onto the roof, his helmet removed to ensure his plume wouldn't be silhouetted against the night sky. She eased next to him and followed his line of sight.

'How many?'

'At least seven – could be more in the alley.'

If it had been the Raiding Season, they might have loosed a few arrows and sent them scattering. But this Season was all about swordcraft. 'Then we wait and watch.'

The Vikings were in no hurry and it seemed an age before they began to file quietly onto the street, heading up towards the Mile and keeping close to the shadows of the buildings. Nine emerged and Agape studied their profiles and strained to see the insignia on their shields. At last one caught in the moonlight and she spied the wing of a bird.

'Ravens.' If it had been Wolves, she would have given them a wide berth, but Ravens – shorn of their bows – were a different matter. 'Can you make out any Bloodmarks?'

Kyriacos shook his head. 'Too far.'

She slunk away and raised herself to a crouch, strapped her shield to her back like the others and began to scamper across the rooftop, her Band following without a sound. The hotel was big and comprised all the southern half of St Mary's, giving the Titans easy flat roofing to navigate. When they eventually reached the older buildings with their angled tiles, the going was still good enough for their experienced bodies. They dropped to the far side of the sloping roofs and moved nimbly between each chimney stack, only rising again to peer over when they were gathered at the far end.

Of the Titans, only the Band and the Companions were abroad that night. Alexander and his officers had spent the previous days locked in tactical discussions and come to the conclusion that they would conserve their Hoplite Heavy Infantry, as well as Parmenion's peltasts and archers. Their reasoning was twofold. The Palatinate was too few in number to risk casualties before the Grand Battle, so the core of the troops would be wrapped in cotton wool and left in the strongholds. Secondly, unlike the Horde, which spread its new entrants across all its regiments, the Titans focused them in the Heavy Brigade. So keeping the Heavies locked away also meant shielding their least experienced troops from the ravages of Viking attentions. Alexander was in no hurry to expose his Vestals.

This first night, he had released the sixteen members of his Sacred Band to go hunting. Small, light and deadly. Their orders: find the Viking Blood Virgins and those with only a single Bloodmark on their breasts, and cull them. Seek to redress the Horde's numerical advantage before the meeting of the armies in a few weeks.

Kyriacos had his head above the skyline again. He waved down to Agape and she shimmied next to him. The Ravens were on the corner of the Mile. Despite the hour, a few pedestrians still roamed the main thoroughfare and Agape could tell the foe didn't like the streetlights. Instinctively she knew they would venture no further.

She patted Kyriacos. 'They're going to double back. Come on, fortune favours the bold.'

The Band scurried to the hotel once more. Between the old and new build, there was a narrow dizzying drop, six floors to street level. It was one of the Sky-Gods' many chosen descents and there was already a rope coiled and fastened. A trooper eased it over the edge and unwound it. At a signal, Agape took hold and leapt. She grappled downwards and could feel the movements of her Band following her example. She was on the pavement in moments and slunk into the dark between the buildings. Boyd's Entry was just across from her and she knew the Ravens would file into it and disappear. One by one, four of her troop landed. The final one would stay on the rooftop ready to help if a retreat was necessary.

Five against nine. They would need to proceed with caution. But her troops were Alexander's elite, while the Ravens probably had at least a couple of greener Drengrs in their midst – perhaps even a Vestal. If the Band could get across the road unseen and into the alley, they would fall on the backs of the foe. She drew her sword and the troops tensed. They could feel the violence about to unleash. *Ten seconds*, Agape calculated. *In ten they'll be half in the alley and half out. At their most exposed.* She tightened her shield grip. *Five. Here we go.*

Into her focus, a clicking insinuated itself. She lost her count and tried to zero in on the new sound. It was getting louder. The Ravens had heard it too and had frozen into the wall over the road. Heels. More than one pair. The night was broken by a woman's laugh and an answering titter. Into Agape's vision came two girls, short skirts and voices made loud by alcohol, leaning their shoulders together to peer at a phone screen.

They lurched to within touching distance of the crouching Titan and she thought they were going to pass, but then one looked up and stared wide-eyed at her. Her friend wobbled and turned too. A heartbeat of utter silence and then they screamed. The sound tore through the street. The phone dropped as they backed away, stumbling and competing to make the most noise. Kyriacos stepped livid towards them and Agape grabbed him, but she could already see the Ravens flying down the alley, for they knew what that scream meant. She hauled Kyriacos back, but the girls were just standing, yelling, so she jumped forward herself, raised her sword and hissed ferociously, 'Get out of here!'

They took one look at her and ran shrieking. Lights were coming on in the upstairs windows across the road and they could hear one of the hotel windows opening. Her troops were already climbing the rope. Get above street level. That was always the first rule in situations like these. She waited until last, then pulled herself up, boots against the wall of the hotel. It was a huge physical feat up six storeys, but they had trained over years to perform such tasks and in minutes the Band were on the roof again, panting and examining their sore palms.

Kyriacos watched her, waiting for her orders, and she waved tamely to him. 'Abort. The Ravens are long gone.'

'Where to now?'

She sighed and looked again across the moonlit rooftop landscape of the city. 'Return to Persepolis. The foe will know we're in this sector now.'

'A bloodless start,' he said.
'Indeed.'

X

Calder sipped her cocoa, slumped in an easy chair in the hospital's communal area. She was wrapped in a white dressing gown, but her drain and saline drip had been removed and she no longer required the rolling IV stand. Her wound was heavily bandaged, but it was healing and in recent days she had felt the first stirrings of strength. She longed for natural light and for air without the scent of antiseptic.

She was permitted into the communal area for four hours daily, always with the same group. She had protested about being locked up – sworn that it was less a hospital and more a prison – but soon she had realised her anger was useless and anyway the communal hours were just as boring as those spent in her room.

She caught movement and turned to the glazed partition onto the corridor. Two Vigiles had appeared and were speaking with one of the doctors. She had seen this man twice before and each time, he disquieted her. There was something about his eyes. They were not the eyes of a man who healed. Like the other doctors who did their daily rounds, he wore a white coat over a shirt and tie, but he paid no attention to the patients, never entered their rooms. To him, they were irrelevant.

She watched him talking to the Vigiles. He was angry about something and, even though the guards loomed over him, they were deferential in their body language. He glanced through the window and caught her watching. She looked away and swore as she dripped cocoa onto her gown, and when she looked again, he was leading the Vigiles to the lift. He placed a finger on the scanner, the doors opened and the group disappeared.

Calder was forced to remain for another hour in the communal area until the usual time for a changeover, but on this occasion she was champing at the bit to return to her room. Nurse Monique appeared and sat on the arm of a chair across from her.

'That's me almost done for the day, girl. Home soon to a bath, wine and Netflix!'

'You're very lucky.'

'Oh I don't know. One day soon you'll be out of here and your nights are going to be so very much more exciting.' She laughed, but Calder knew her point was serious. 'Alcohol, films and my own company – that's all I have to look forward to.'

'May I go back to my room?'

'It's a bit early, but sure.' She peered at Calder. 'You got a good colour, girl. I'd say we're not going to be seeing too much more of you soon.'

Calder followed her back to the patient rooms and waited as she unlocked her door. 'Who was that man?'

'Which one?'

'The doctor. The one who turns up sometimes and goes out back.'

'He's not important. Don't you go worrying your little head about him.'

'Those Vigiles seemed to think he was important. Does he work here?'

'No, he just comes and checks things sometimes. I think he's a specialist in something or other, but he's nothing to do with this wing.'

'He doesn't have the eyes of a healer,' Calder said simply as she pulled herself into bed.

The nurse busied herself with tidying the room and didn't respond. 'Well, you get some rest. Dinner will be round at seven. I've a couple of days' leave and then I'm on nights for the following three weeks. Eleven pm starts, which I detest. So I'll look in on you while you're sleeping. Okay, girl?' She smoothed down Calder's sheets and pulled the wheeled table to within easy reach.

Once she was gone, Calder lay motionless and listened to the changeover of the groups beyond the door. When at last it had quietened, she slipped from her bed and pulled the table over to the back wall. Then she pushed the chair across as well, mounted it and tried to step onto the table, but it was too wobbly on its wheels. She cursed, climbed down and looked around. The monitor still stood by the bed, but it too was on wheels. She eased it over and pushed it as firmly against the table as she could, then stood on the chair again. This time, when she placed a bare foot on the table, it shifted but held. Gingerly, she let it take her weight and by stretching herself against the wall, she was just able to bring her chin to the small window.

The day was waning. She was high, perhaps on the fourth

or fifth floor, and in the distance a field stretched away to a tree-lined hill dotted with sheep who were little more than lighter shades against the darkening grass. If she was still in Edinburgh, it must be on the extreme outskirts. In front of the field was a high-walled area, which was impossible to see inside even from her vantage point. She pulled up with her fingers and craned her neck to look down, and was just able to see the roof of a building below with skylights running along the top. She guessed the lift must access this.

The table was trembling and she thought how badly she could fall if the wheels took off. She was about to lower herself, when a man appeared below one of the skylights and she recognised him immediately. The doctor with the cold eyes, his balding head prominent from this angle. He was talking to someone and pointing. A Vigilis stepped into view, jerked an arm at unseen companions and strode out of her line of sight. Then she caught her breath. Children appeared. Three of them. Young ones. They were following the Vigilis and as they passed the doctor, he slapped the last one on the back of the head. In a moment, they were gone and the doctor turned in the direction of the lift. Just as he was about to disappear, she saw him glance up and, with a lurch, she knew how visible she must be set against her brightly lit room. Panicked, she pushed away from the window, the table trundled sideways and she slammed down onto the chair. Somehow she caught herself and stumbled back to the bed.

Long minutes elapsed and then she heard the lift doors opening. Footsteps approached. They came to her door and she could feel him just beyond. She thought the lock would click, but nothing happened. Just silence. He was listening.

Her breath caught in her throat and she scrunched the sheets up to her chin. He moved a fraction, paused once more, and then finally relented and retreated.

Air came to her in a great juddering wave and she gasped. All she could think about were the three little figures. There was something so strange about them, something serious, servile, unchildlike. Then she remembered the young voices she had heard before and gradually it knitted together. There could have been dozens of reasons why the children were there. But already her mind was dismissing these. No Vigilis would parade around a building that wasn't run by the Pantheon. No ordinary doctor would slap young patients.

Could it be possible?

Could she have found one of the Pantheon's Scholae?

To say the atmosphere in the Muir household was cool was a gross understatement. Oliver had said nothing about his father's fictitious conference, but he had made his manner plain enough for him to realise he was rumbled. Perhaps his mother sensed something too, for she was distant, formal, awkward around her husband. There had been no fighting over the last week, which was worrying. Instead, they had lapsed into stilted cordiality.

His father mostly ignored him, but sometimes Oliver caught him studying his son, pondering how much he knew and whether he could be trusted. For the first time, Oliver wondered if his father was going to leave them. Perhaps this girlfriend was important. A queasiness settled in his stomach at the thought, but he refused to let it affect him.

He settled into his room while his parents watched

television and he switched on his computer. The lights of the hard drives danced on the shelf above as the machine warmed up. He keyed in his password, checked through his various social media accounts, then pulled up a search engine and sat back to think. *Might as well start with the most obvious first.*

He typed *Morgan Maitland* into the engine and scrolled through the returns, mostly Facebook, LinkedIn, Twitter, all the usual suspects. If he hadn't known what Morgan looked like it would have taken far longer, but it was easy to see from the images that she wasn't present amongst the results. He switched to other less well-known engines, which searched the so-called "dark" web and this time he thought he found her, but it was a single old reference, years out of date, and without an image so he couldn't be certain. The lack of finds perplexed him. Almost too clean.

Okay, he would have to extemporise. He knew from experience that the banks' security systems were too good for him, as too were the passport agency's. So this time he would start more basic – her college. *Where had it been? Leith College of Art – that was it.*

Forty minutes later and he was in. Stripping databases was illegal, but he was only looking. It took him a while because he couldn't recall her course or date of graduation, so he had to trawl through the entire alumni base, but eventually he found the answer he had been expecting. Morgan Maitland wasn't there. Either she had not attended the college – or someone was assiduously erasing all trace of her.

It was getting late. He wandered out into the living room, ignored his parents and made a peanut butter sandwich in the kitchen. Then he returned to his room and prepared to take the search to a new level. He remembered one small reference by Tyler about his sister once driving him into the city. It took him five hours to force his way into the database of the Driver and Vehicle Licensing Agency. When his mother knocked on the door, he had to pretend to get ready for bed, clean his teeth and wish them goodnight. Then he kept his light off until he heard them retire themselves. It was gone midnight, when he could finally trawl through the Morgan Maitlands on the database, each with the photo used in their licence application, and it confirmed what he had already assumed. Tyler's sister wasn't there. She was gone. Ghosted.

He sat in the glow of his screen and tried to think. He was stuck. Her name was all he had to go on and if that had been properly erased, then the trail disappeared. Damn. He needed a different approach. What else did he know about Tyler's sister? What else?

XI

Punnr and his Wolves were released from North Gate at two forty-six on a calm, mild night. It had happened in a blur. One moment he'd been holding a training sword and sparring with Knut, and the next they were being ushered urgently to the Armouries.

It was the Second Blood Night and after the tumult of the Raiding Season and all the harbingers of doom, the Cull was proving distinctly underwhelming. Only the Ravens and Storm roamed each night, tracking softly through the city, listening and watching. The trouble was the Titans were keeping such a low profile that Halvar had sent only two of his four Litters out to hunt on the First Blood Night. A sighting by Storm had led to the release of Kill Squads One and Two. A chase, a fight. One dead Titan, too slow to avoid the Wolves, but caution seemed to be the watchword.

After all the pensive waiting, Punnr felt oddly elated to be running. Gone were his white vestments. Now he wore the same mail as his companions and carried a crimson shield with a black wolf's head. Only Odin's silver arm-ring set him apart, which he had required to be hammered in the Armouries to make it small enough to fit. The other

Wolves had mocked him about it, but he saw their glances and knew they were wondering about such recognition on the arm of a Thegn so new.

They went west along Market Street, under the bulk of North Bridge and on towards Waverley. They were Litters Three and Four, sixteen in total, led by Leiv. Halvar had sent his other two Litters from the North-West Gate via the castle, in what he hoped would be a classic pincer movement. Knut was beside Punnr, his legs working like pistons. Olsen was there too, puffing hard through his beard, but keeping pace despite his bulk. He could hear Unn's heavy footsteps behind and knew that Hagen and Stigr acted as rearguard. Ahead, mixing in with Squad Three, Ake ran in silence with her blade already drawn.

Behind the group came a Vigilis with the usual camera attached to his helmet. He was smaller and slimmer than those Punnr had seen before and it struck him that the man's bulkier colleagues were all very useful in the Raiding Season when there were known fixed points for the action, but the capricious, dynamic nature of the Blood Season called for Keepers of the Rules, who could keep pace with the combatants.

They wheeled onto Waverley Bridge and headed out of the Old Town. Tourist buses were parked for the night and a few figures dozed around the entrance to the station. Ahead lay the bright lights of Princes Street shops, a part of the city that was never entirely deserted. Pedestrians jumped out of their path and hoots and catcalls came from the rough sleepers. It felt odd to be racing amongst them. The claustrophobic maze of the Old Town lent itself to the pursuits of the Pantheon, but the wide boulevards to the north – with their Apple, Vodafone and Foot Locker windows – seemed alien territory.

Leiv took them over the bus lanes and tramlines of Princes Street and up towards St Andrew Square. They ran past Jenners and Punnr had a vision of sitting in there sipping tea with Lana. Another time. Another world.

A Raven awaited them at the corner of the Square and the Wolves slowed to a huddle. Brante was just a few yards from Punnr and they caught each other's eyes behind their helms. The scout was gesturing diagonally and Leiv pumped his shoulder and led them on.

They loped across the Square, past Harvey Nichols and then – suddenly and wonderfully – the city dropped away down the steep slope of Dublin Street and they could see the Forth beyond. As gravity lent them speed and their cloaks flew out behind, they felt kings of the world, but soon a Raven stepped from the shadows and signalled to apply the brakes. She pointed west along Abercromby Place. 'They're in the Gardens.'

'How many?' whispered Leiv.

'We think a dozen.'

'Unit?'

'Companions.'

'Shit. We've a fight on our hands.'

'Aye. Looks that way. And take note...' The Raven pointed to the corner of Albany Street. 'The boundary. Anything beyond there and you're out of the field of play.'

'What the hell are the bastards doing out here?'

The Raven ignored his question. 'Where are the rest of you?'

'Litters One and Two coming from the west.'

'Then go. No time to waste.'

Leiv led them towards the black mass of Queen Street Gardens. They jogged to the iron fence and began to climb. It was easy enough, but such a mass of troops and armour couldn't fail to make a noise. As Punnr jumped down the other side and Olsen landed with a thump next to him, the element of surprise must surely have been lost. They crouched and listened. Leiv raised three fingers and pointed left, then four fingers and pointed right. He was splitting the Litters.

Punnr saw Brante depart and followed his own squad. They formed a single line and wound between the shrubs. Lights from the road gave just enough vision to avoid banging into trees, but even so it seemed to Punnr's ears that they made a din. They filed deeper and the line began to stretch out so that he could only just see the figure of Ake in front.

A branch caught him under the chin and he was just mouthing an expletive when an enormous force smashed into his side, sending him sprawling. His head hit the grass and knocked his helmet aslant. A second blow bludgeoned his shield, which instinct had made him angle over his head. His ears rang and blood oozed beneath his tongue. Everywhere the night was broken with iron on iron. His opponent was wrenching his blade free from the shield and it gave Punnr precious moments to push the assailant away, bang his helmet in place and scrabble backwards.

A Companion faced him and Punnr shaped himself into the attack posture they had drilled in the training rooms. The man caught sight of his arm-ring and grinned savagely. 'The Wolf Vestal.'

The Titan came for him, smashing with his hoplon and

driving his shortsword over the top. *Dear god, this is it. The blood fight.* He parried and staggered as the Titan's hoplon punched once more and took him backwards into the fencing. He was at the very edge of the Gardens, as far as he could go, and as the hopelessness of his position hit him, survival instinct kicked in. To live, he must attack.

He launched himself off the railings and chopped at the man. It was wild, but it surprised the foe, who had to haul his hoplon up and gave Punnr the chance to shove his own iron-bossed shield into the figure. Now it was the Titan's turn to stumble. Punnr swung again, cracking his blade against the hoplon. And again. Smack, smack. The Titan leapt apart, gave himself a moment of respite, then grinned. 'Little Virgin's going to play hard to get? That's fine by me. I like them rough.'

Their swords came together and the impact hammered up Punnr's arm. The Companion crafted a new attack and the sword point flickered around Punnr's guard just an inch from his hip. Punnr backed off, took a few ragged breaths and remembered a move he had seen Calder perform. He let the hoplite come at him, then used the butt of his sword to strike against the bottom of his foe's shield to tilt the top forward. In one sweeping movement, he drove the point through this gap and clouted the Titan's helmet. The man's neck was thrown back and he gasped in pain.

An experienced killer would have followed through, but Punnr held back, almost more surprised than his opponent. The Titan adjusted his shield, but there was no grin now. 'Fucking prick,' he snarled and then shouted, 'Vestalis! Vestalis ho!'

In seconds another hoplite tore from the darkness and

charged into Punnr. His legs gave way and his world imploded in a rain of blows. There wasn't even time to comprehend his death.

Then a new sound. A wild screeching, like a cat. The blows paused and fresh violence erupted above him. A Titan boot stood on his shoulder, so he grabbed it, tugged and brought the man down. He staggered to his feet and saw the fight was now all around him. Ake was screaming and flailing her blade into bronze hoplons and Stigr was next to her.

Punnr saw the man he had tripped. It was his original adversary, on his backside and reaching for the shortsword he had dropped. *It has to be now. I must blood myself right here.* The Titan retrieved his sword, but he was still down and he grimaced as he saw Punnr coming for him, but then there were new orders in the confusion and Punnr's focus wavered. The Titan grappling with Ake thrust her away just as two more ran past. Punnr's opponent scrabbled to his feet and backed off as well. He extended his sword point at Punnr. 'You're marked, Vestal.'

Then he turned and followed the other Companions. Ake leapt after them, planted her feet apart and howled to the moon.

Relief surged through Punnr and suddenly his weapon was cumbersome and his body so heavy. Stigr was crouched by a dead Titan, wiping his blade.

'A kill,' croaked Punnr.

Stigr sized him up. 'But not yours, Vestal.'

There was movement and Punnr realised a Vigilis had been filming everything. Somewhere far away bastards with brandies had been watching his death fight.

The battle still raged further into the Gardens, but it was obvious the Companions were fleeing and neither Ake nor Stigr showed any inclination to give chase. The woman turned back to them, took in the fallen foe and scowled. 'Should have been more. We had them.'

'For a moment there, I thought they had me,' said Punnr. 'Thank you.'

'Your head's worth four credits to those bastards. We weren't about to let them have it. Rest assured, it was nothing personal.'

'Nonetheless, thank you.'

Gradually the night quietened and the Vigilis left them. Ake and Stigr cleaned their weapons, but nothing could compel Punnr to move.

At last more Wolves came from the centre of the Gardens. Brante was there. He strode to Punnr and shook his shoulder. 'You okay?' Punnr nodded and Brante looked down at the fallen Titan. 'Yours?'

'No.'

'Too bad.' There was blood on Brante's blade. 'Proper flippin' fight!'

Halvar strode into view. He had come from the west with Litters One and Two. 'How many Wolves down?' he demanded.

Leiv appeared. 'Five we think, sir. Two permanently.'

'Get the others tended to.' He pointed his sword at the Titan corpse and glanced at Punnr.

'Mine,' said Stigr.

Halvar nodded and swept his gaze away from Punnr. 'Okay, now we keep our heads. The foe are on Hanover Street and being tailed by Ravens, but the whole Titan

Palatinate will know the Wolves are here, so we want no nasty surprises. Litters One and Two will follow me. We'll track the Companions' retreat. Litters Three and Four wait here until the night's quiet and the Ravens give the all clear, then proceed at speed to Valhalla.'

He spun away and figures followed him, while Leiv took charge of the remainder. 'Spread out. Watch the fence line and the gates.'

Brante and Punnr felt their way back through the shrubs to the railings. Lights were on in some of the upper windows of the elegant properties curving around the Gardens and a small part of Punnr's weary brain supposed it was hard to sleep when there was a Viking battle waging outside your house. Adrenaline drained from them and the battle shock receded. They became conscious of birds calling in alarm in the trees and a rubbish lorry working its way up Dublin Street. Brante tried to clean his sword, then gave up and leaned against the railings, looking out at the houses. He let out a long ragged sigh. 'Wow.'

'Welcome to the Cull.' Punnr spat blood from his mouth and checked his teeth. He looked at his friend's blade. 'Number two?'

Brante nodded, stone-grim. 'Poor bastard's somewhere in there. What about you? Did you fight?'

'Yes.'

'That's all that can be asked of you.' He forced his sword back into its sheath.

'I wouldn't do that if I was you. It'll stick fast. Going to take some poor Schola kid hours to clean.'

Brante grunted and pulled it out again, leaning it carefully against the railings. They continued to watch for activity beyond, but gradually all sounds disappeared and the Gardens fell quiet.

'Screw this,' said Brante and slumped down to lean his back against the railings.

Punnr checked along the line at the other Wolves, but they were mere shadows, so he eased himself down too. 'I tell you, I bloody love wearing armour that's not white!'

Brante chuckled thinly. 'Look at us. Three thirty in the morning and we're sitting in Queen Street Gardens, dressed like Thor and Loki. What a pair.'

'We could be at home, sleeping in our beds like everyone else.'

They were quiet for a long while, bodies shaky and cooling. Punnr rubbed his jaw beneath his helm. His face felt battered and his mouth was still filled with the tang of blood.

'That Companion seemed to know Wolf Company has a Vestal,' he mused.

'He must have seen your mail has no Bloodmarks.'

'Maybe, but my shield was up and he worded it strangely, like he already knew.'

'Well, you got away with it.'

'And I'm still a useless Vestal.'

Brante shifted towards him. 'Perhaps you shouldn't wish that status away too quickly.'

'What do you mean by that?'

Brante stewed over his thoughts. 'You remember Freyja's speech in the vaults right back in our first weeks? What she said about people dying in the Pantheon? When I get back to my bed, there's no pretending I'm not a murderer.' Punnr said nothing and Brante brushed at some dirt on his shield.

'Tonight, he was a Titan and a foe. He engaged me and he would have killed me if I hadn't struck first. But I wonder what he would have been when the sun rises? Would he have woken in a house in Morningside or Portobello or somewhere in New Town? Did he have plans? Perhaps he would have been meeting someone for lunch or taking in a gallery? Or maybe he was simply going to crash on his sofa and watch sport. Did he have any idea that his life would be cut short tonight? I tell you, Punnr, killing is hard.'

They lapsed into silence. The birds had relaxed back into their nocturnal slumber and the city breathed easily again.

Then Punnr spoke. 'They say the Raids were particularly violent this year, but somehow they still felt like a game. The riddles and the secret locations and gaining the Assets. But this Blood Season is so different. Death is the only objective. And it's not even kill or be killed. That implies fighting to stay alive. This is more calculated. We're required to seek out victims to earn our Bloodmarks. We must spill lifeblood for credits, so riches will keep changing hands amongst the Curiate.'

'When you put it like that, it sounds pretty disgusting. Thank god the Pantheon doesn't allow families. I don't think I could deal with the thought that there's a wife and kids somewhere out there this morning, waiting for that Titan to come home.'

'Are you scared, Brante?' Punnr asked.

'Of course. I wouldn't be human if I wasn't. Are you?'

'I was when we first entered the Gardens, but during the fight itself there was no time to feel anything.' Punnr paused and pondered his next words. 'But I also feel worried when I'm with the rest of my Litter. Not raw fear or anything like that, just an unease. They see me as a burden during this Cull and I can't tell what they're thinking. It's like I have no one I can properly trust.'

'No one except me.'

Punnr nodded. 'No one except you.'

There was movement down the railings. Unn approached with Knut behind her.

'Get up, you wasters,' Knut hissed.

The pair rose and retrieved their swords.

'The Ravens have signalled all clear,' said Unn. 'Leiv's sending us to the gate.'

Knut pushed past and knocked his shoulder hard against Punnr.

'What's wrong with that prick?' Brante demanded as they began to follow.

Unn didn't answer, but pulled close to Punnr. 'Hagen's gone. This is a bad night.'

XII

Punnr remained in Valhalla long into the morning. Above, the city would be bustling, but the numbers in the Halls had thinned to a smattering as warriors returned their weapons to the Armouries, washed and changed, and gradually dispersed back to their daytime lives. He nursed his face. His lip was split and tongue badly bitten, but to his surprise the rest of the pain had receded.

The squad had said very little to each other. Hagen was dead and it was a bad omen. He had been a good warrior and a Wolf for three Seasons. Leiv enquired flatly if Punnr was all right and Unn had told him to get some rest, but otherwise they left him alone.

He sat in the Throne Room with a coffee, dressed in a fresh tunic and the fire drying his hair after using the showers. His stomach groaned for some breakfast, but he didn't want the flatbreads and fruit on offer in the Halls and wasn't yet ready to make his way topside for a bacon butty. He was disturbed from his thoughts by the sight of Sveinn crossing the Throne Room. The King glanced at him, paused and then beckoned him. 'Come with me, Thegn.'

Punnr followed him up the steps to the council chamber. The room was warm from a fire, which had been left unattended and burned down to a glowing ember. There was a teapot on a table beside the hearth and Sveinn poured himself a cup, added milk and settled into a chair. He indicated for Punnr to sit opposite him and he regarded him thoughtfully over the cup, his lined warrior's face jarring with the delicate porcelain.

'I wanted to tell you privately that you did well in the Raids.'

'Thank you, lord.'

'Radspakr seemed uncommonly keen to ensure you were chosen to be the White Warrior. He must have great faith in you.'

'I don't think those are his sentiments, lord. I'm not sure the Thane has my best interests at heart.'

The King pursed his lips. 'Your presence disturbs him and you disturb a viper at your peril.'

'He hopes for my swift end, I'm sure of it.'

Sveinn inclined his head. 'I have wondered that myself. You'll learn, Punnr, that in the Pantheon, friend and foe are an ever-changing and potent mix – and you'll have as many enemies behind your back as face you from the opposing lines. As King, I maintain a distance from the plotting, but I didn't reach this position without my fair share of infidelity. I've mastered all the tricks. I've played them all in my time.'

'And what should I do about this particular enemy, lord?'

'Abide by the Rules. But watch your back and don't be afraid to play dirty when you must.'

Punnr did not respond. He watched the embers and felt Sveinn's eyes playing over him.

'You remind me of my son,' the King said unexpectedly.

'I didn't know Pantheon warriors were allowed families, my lord.'

'That's the rule, but it doesn't always work like that in reality. I was in at the start when the Rules hadn't expanded into the complex absurdities that now give Atilius so many orgasms.'

'Is your son in Edinburgh?'

Sveinn stared blankly at the dying fire. 'San Francisco. He's been there for six years. Placed himself as far away from me as the earth would allow.'

'Does he know what you do?'

'Enough to despise me. He's a neuroscientist at the University of California, studying the development of multiple sclerosis. He's dedicated his career to saving lives – while I've dedicated mine to taking them.'

'That's a harsh analysis, lord.'

'I google him to see how his work's developing. I read his papers when they come online, though the gods know they're impossible for a poor soul like me to understand. I keep tabs on the conferences he speaks at. He's making his mark and I'm proud, but he'll never know it. He has nothing to do with me. To him, his father died a long time ago.'

The King rose and placed another log on the embers, prodding them with an iron poker until a flame flickered cautiously. When he returned, his mind was back in the Chamber. 'I was once a new blood like you, right back when it all began nineteen Seasons ago. That first year the Rules were few, tactics limited, regiments and specialisms non-existent. Each Palatinate started with the same number of troops – fifty – so it was an even playing field.' He chuckled.

'We thought fifty was a huge number and were convinced the police would close us down in days. But the Pantheon authorities were more powerful than we ever imagined and as we bludgeoned each other during the Blood Season nights, no one ever intervened.' His eyes were animated once more. 'Did you know that in the first six Seasons, Edinburgh was home only to the Horde. The Titans were headquartered in Athens. But then something happened and their whole Palatinate upped sticks and settled on the rooftops above our heads. Rumour has it there was a huge crisis amongst the powers that be and to this day, no one's the wiser about why the move was made. As a result the two rival Caelestes loathe one another and there's certainly an intensity between the Horde and the hoplites which is unparalleled. Yet, somehow, the move actually worked. The intimacy of our rivalry has made for enthralling contests over the years.

'The even playing field didn't last long amongst the other Palatinates. Money has a way of attaching itself to power. Shrewd gambles were played and there were winners and losers amongst the Caelestia. The Legion soon ruled supreme at the top of the pile with five times the blades that we can put into the field. Thank the gods we're never required to face them.'

'Have we only ever faced the Titans?'

'They have been our one foe. The Pantheon's Rules have locked us together throughout its history and that will only change if someone puts a sword in my belly... or in Alexander's. *Kill the King*. The joining of the Palatinates. Only then will we be permitted to look beyond this city and step up the rankings.'

'If I may say, my lord, there would therefore seem little objective to what we do.'

Sveinn shrugged. 'It wasn't always like that. In the early days it was such a new adventure. Every Blood Night was raw excitement – like nothing else in this world. We felt like gods. But now everything's become so weighed down by rules and ceremonies and the desperate accumulation of credits. Today's Pantheon is designed for the pleasures of its investors, not for the likes of us. And like gamblers everywhere, those investors welcome risk but not anarchy. The money flows most smoothly when the changes are subtle – a few troops dead here and there – a Palatinate a little stronger or weaker than the previous Season. Not for the Curiate anything as uncontrollable as the death of a King and the collapse of a Palatinate. There's an order to things in the Pantheon and that's the way they like it. You could say the whole thing about *Kill the King* is the Pantheon's nuclear button – never to be pressed.'

Sveinn pondered the fire silently, then drew a breath and pulled back from his reflections. 'Anyway, we digress. As I said, you did well in the Raids, but now you need a kill. Collecting Assets won't make you a Wolf. Only a Bloodmark can do that.'

Punnr rose. 'Thank you for your time, lord.'

'Good day, Thegn.' He waved gruffly. 'Get that kill.'

Christ knew what had propelled him, but during the gloom of the Christmas period eight weeks earlier – bored, indolent, alone, waiting for the Pantheon to find him again – Tyler had signed up to a dating site. It had been a game really, a touch of frisson during the long evenings. He had combed his shoulder-length hair, trimmed his D'Artagnan beard, hidden his silver Odin amulet beneath a smart shirt and snapped himself from various angles under the lights of the bathroom.

Then he'd played with his online profile, giving himself the name Zach, which he thought made him sound raffish. He began somewhere near the truth – an employee of Edinburgh University, but probably a lecturer in Ancient Norse culture. As each slug of whisky hit his belly, he grew more creative and became an oilman, working the rigs in the black storms of the North Sea and spending his leave on dry land training search dogs to sniff out climbers from the death grips of the Munros. Then, impetuously, he hated everything he'd concocted, and resurrected himself as a semi-professional musician, a fiddler for hire, who played bagpipes at weddings and toured the seedier hotels of Scotland with wild ceilidh bands. He liked that.

Most important, he lent himself a limitless passion, which had been torn apart by a spiteful lover and left him broken and desperate for the arms of someone who cared. Bingo. He grinned as he read it back, lit a cigarette and hit the submit button. To start with the replies had dribbled in, but then become an avalanche. They wanted to nurture him, share with him their own stories of shattered hearts and bring him back from the brink. He deleted most, laughed at some, checked out a few profiles and even sent the occasional short reply with enough left unsaid to hook them further.

Then the Pantheon came calling from its Christmas break. The *Agonium Martiale* and the first of the Raids. Suddenly he was the White Warrior of the Horde of Valhalla, and some part-time bagpipe player with a tender heart could go to hell. So he gave up checking his account and deleted most of the messages.

And at the end of the Raids came something else. The sight of Calder lying bloodied on the cobbles of the Upper Batteries and a dread that burned his soul. It was a fire that had kindled in him ever since and burned afresh whenever he thought of her.

Yet here he was, walking along George Street towards The Dome to meet his date, while Calder still lay somewhere in the bowels of a Pantheon hospital. Guilt flickered through his gut, but he told himself to stop being an idiot. Calder was a colleague; that was all. A fellow in a game that might kill either of them anytime. Feelings were for fools.

If truth be told, he had no idea how this date had become a reality. Sure, he had been attracted to her profile. A redhead, wide blue eyes and very pale Highland skin. Maybe she'd been more persistent than the others, her messages just testing and aloof enough to make him reply. Mostly, he thought, it was the Blood Season itself. That last fight in the Gardens and the blows of the Titans as they singled him out; then leaning against the railings with Brante and wondering why he wasn't dead. Something had made him go home and ask if she wanted to meet.

He climbed the steps to the grandiose entrance of The Dome and walked between its faux Corinthian columns into a hall dripping with gilt, velvet and Swarovski crystal chandeliers. He wore a jacket over a black shirt, faded jeans, smart boots and his usual hat, placed at a rakish angle. As he stepped into the immense space of the main bar, he was surprised by the crowd. Most of the tables dotted around between the marble columns were taken. On one side was a coachload of Chinese tourists photographing themselves from every angle as they sank wine. The bar itself, a temple to the finer art of cocktail creation, sat at the centre of the great circular building.

Tyler weighed up where best to pitch camp. He had been meaning to play it cool by taking his time on the journey, but in fact he was surprisingly early, so he needed somewhere he could witness her entrance. Beyond the bar, doors opened to a club room, from which even more noise emanated. He wandered over. The room was filled with an all-male throng dressed in bow ties and dinner suits. Champagne was flowing and the voices were alcohol-fuelled and coarse.

'Sorry, sir,' said a staff member behind him. 'Private party.'

Tyler nodded and glanced at a sign by the door. *Fettes College Reunion.* Edinburgh's leading boarding school. *Fifty grand a year at least*, he thought, *and you can ensure your son grows into a boorish Hooray Henry with the social skills of a braying mule.*

He doubled back and found a small table beside one of the columns where he could lean casually against the marble and appear hip and bohemian, like an itinerant musician.

'What can I get you, sir?' A bartender appeared at his shoulder, placed a bowl of pistachios in front of him and lit a candle that flickered impotently under the glare of the chandeliers.

'Just a beer.' He removed his hat, thought how much he wanted to smoke, and waited.

She arrived fashionably late and he was already most of the way through his drink. He waved her over and then thought awkwardly that he should have stood and greeted her. She ordered an eye-wateringly expensive cocktail and he had to remind himself the Pantheon paid him well.

And so they talked. Stuttering to begin with, but the alcohol soon warmed their blood and laced their words. She told him about her flat beyond The Meadows where she lived with her dogs. She worked for an animal charity and kept herself fit by jogging on Arthur's Seat and cycling to her office. She played guitar and wanted to know everything about his ceilidh bands. He'd forgotten the lies on his profile and her enthusiastic questions threw him. He survived by appearing enigmatic and non-committal, as he supposed a cool fiddler would.

She had a small tattoo of a dolphin in the "V" between her thumb and first finger, which he liked. Her hands were long and delicate. She was blonde now and he realised the redhead had come from a bottle. She was wearing war paint scarlet lipstick and had great teeth. Yet, even as she talked, he found himself losing focus. Afterwards, he would recall very little of anything she told him. The whole thing was, he had to admit, flat. How could it not be after the Blood Nights? After Freyja and Ake and Agape. How could any woman be interesting since someone like Calder had come into his life?

He felt obliged to order another round and then found himself wondering if it was possible for someone to drink a cocktail any slower. He realised his choice of table was unfortunate. It was directly in the path of the pricks from Fettes who were floundering backwards and forwards to the bar, stopping to honk and cackle near them. Tyler grew angry and couldn't hide it. Her original sparkle began to dull and she sat more reserved, still talking, but now watching him with hard eyes.

When she finally drained her drink, they both waited for the next move.

'So do you want to try somewhere else?' she asked.

Tyler shrugged apologetically. 'I'm really tired actually.'

'It's eight thirty.'

'I know, I know. I'm sorry. I've had a heavy week.'

'All that bagpipe playing.' She regarded him coolly.

'Yeah, something like that.' Tyler made a show of stirring. 'Well, it's been really nice meeting you.'

She watched him picking up the bill and seeking a staff member. 'So that's it. I get back from work, make myself up, cycle over here in the cold and now you're tired.'

'I'm sorry. Shall I call you a taxi?'

'I just said I cycled.' She stood. Her skirt had ridden up and Tyler had to admit she had beautiful legs. 'I know a twat when I see one.'

When she had gone, he sagged back against the column and stared grimly at the Chinese tourists. He really was feeling angry, though he was uncertain why and suspected it was aimed at himself for going on a damn date in the first place.

'Do you want the bill, sir?'

He was about to nod, then thought better. 'No. Get me a whisky. Large one. Something smoky from the islands.'

He toyed with his dram when it came and thought of Valhalla. He wondered if there were warriors in the Tunnels tonight, practising their swordcraft beneath the Mile. The Fettes lot were still milling past and he glared as one knocked his table. Two others had emerged from the room and were guffawing. He raised his tumbler moodily, flicked a dirty look at them, and froze, the glass on his lips, the whisky on his tongue.

The two men were standing close to one another, chests almost touching. They were both dressed in immaculate evening suits with brightly coloured waistcoats and cufflinks. They were laughing and giving each other a hug. The man closest to Tyler had his back to him, but he would have recognised that ramrod-straight posture, broad shoulders and bald head anywhere. It was Brante. The other man had an arm around his neck and was patting him goodnight on the back. Then he leaned in closer and kissed him tenderly on the lips. Brante reciprocated and they waved goodnight.

Tyler watched, the glass still by his chin as if it would hide him. The other man departed and Brante walked to the bar and ordered more champagne. There was an inevitability about what would happen next. The bartender went to find the champagne and Brante glanced left and right along the bar, then turned, leaned against it and looked straight into Tyler's eyes. His face went slack. The barman clinked a glass of bubbly down beside him and Brante nodded towards the club room to indicate the bill was covered, thought for a moment, then stepped over to Tyler's table.

'Well, I suppose it had to happen one day.'

'I guess.'

He checked around the room, still sober enough to think about eavesdroppers and cameras. 'May I join you?'

Tyler pushed the vacant seat out with his foot. 'Of course.'

Brante sat, pulled his vivid waistcoat down and self-consciously adjusted his cufflinks. 'What are you doing here, Punnr?'

'I got dumped by my date.'

'Deservedly?'

'She was lovely and I was an idiot.'

'Not your type?'

Tyler swirled his whisky. 'I'm not sure anyone outside Valhalla is my type these days. The Pantheon's insinuated itself into everything I think and do, while the whole damn real world's become a foreign land.'

'Aye. How can anyone or anything in this world ever compete with the Pantheon?'

Tyler looked at the other man and found his distemper vanishing. A mischievous smile played on his lips. 'You seemed fascinated enough by your friend.'

Brante dropped his eyes to the flute of bubbles in front of him. 'Well, seeing how you're obviously desperate to know, that was my ex.'

Tyler held his tongue. A strained silence developed. 'You're testing me.'

'I am?'

'Seeing if I have a problem.'

'And do you?'

'Jeez, Brante, that question doesn't even deserve an answer.'

Brante absorbed this, then gave a barely palpable nod. 'I guess not.'

'You just said nothing competes with the bonds we've forged in Valhalla. Out here, I don't care if you're the king of Abyssinia, because I know what you mean to me in the Pantheon.'

Tyler held up his drink and they clinked glasses.

'Me too, my friend,' Brante said warmly.

'I'm just sorry for all those ladies in the Horde who have the hots for you.'

They laughed and drank, then Brante scanned the room again. 'We should be careful.'

'Screw them. We met by chance. Anyway... what the hell are you doing with that lot in the club room?'

'It's a reunion of a few year groups from Fettes. It happens annually.'

'You went to Fettes?'

'From the age of eight. Like my father and his father before him.'

'Bloody hell.'

'Does it surprise you?'

Tyler pursed his lip. 'Soon after we first met – when I knew you only as *Thrall XII* – you told me the story of a Titan you saw on the rooftop when you were just a kid at boarding school, but I never realised it was Fettes.'

'I was a full boarder because the family home's in faraway Portmahomack.'

'Where's that?'

'A forgotten peninsula of east coast pastures caught between the Moray and Dornoch Firths.'

Tyler shrugged. The description meant nothing to him and Brante eyed him ruefully. 'So what do I call you, Punnr the Weakling?'

'What do you mean?'

'Out here in the real world.'

'Well... Tyler, I suppose.'

'Good evening, Tyler. I'm Forbes.'

'Forbes! What the hell kind of name is that?'

'One that goes back generations in my family.'

'It's your first name?'

'I'm sorry if it disturbs you.'

'It doesn't. It's just that... well... *Forbes*! Are you a lord or something?'

Forbes looked irritated and stirred in his chair, glancing back at the reunion room. 'Do you have trouble with my class background?'

'No, no. It's just that every last Drengr in the Horde loves you, treats you like one of their own. Whereas me? I come from the estates. Rough as you like. But they think I'm weird. The one they can't relate to. The bloody Vestal!'

Forbes said nothing and Tyler bit back his words. 'I'm sorry, I guess tonight's my night for being an idiot. I've been feeling shitty about being out on the town while Calder's still lying in a hospital bed. If truth be told, I've no clue why I even got myself on a date.'

'You probably needed a bit of downtime. Something – or someone – to take your mind off the Blood Nights. We all need that occasionally.'

'Downtime?' Tyler considered this. 'It's not downtime I wanted, more like some kind of meaning. Because real life feels like the thing we do in the breathing spaces between the Pantheon. In the intervals.'

'Perhaps the Pantheon's weregild has already purchased any meaning we used to own.'

Tyler quietened, uncertain if he liked that.

'You think I was enjoying myself back there with that Fettes mob?' Forbes continued. 'These annual reunions have only ever been made bearable by gallons of champagne, but tonight no amount of stimulants could make that crowd interesting – not even my ex. Like you and your date, I was just going through the motions.' He leaned forward with his glass in his hand. 'But, you know what? I think I *have* discovered something meaningful tonight.'

'What's that?'

'You, Tyler. I've discovered you. The real man behind the warrior. I'm not sure why, but I think this meeting feels significant. Like it was meant to be.'

Tyler considered this and then his lips arched slowly into a smile. 'I think so too.'

Later, as he walked back to Learmonth, Tyler had forgotten the girl with the fabulous legs and the dolphin tattoo. Instead, his mind was on the man he had just spent the last hour with. Brante of Wolf Regiment. His comrade-in-arms.

Forbes of Fettes. His new friend.

XIII

The Wolves were leashed. It was two-twenty in the morning, almost ninety minutes into the Third Blood Night, and rumours were flying. This time the Practice Rooms were forgotten and every last member of the Kill Squads was crammed into the Throne Room. Those of Hammer Regiment who weren't on duty at the Gates were present too, surly and sulking because they hadn't yet been permitted a single excursion. All wore their armour in readiness, and the warmth of the fire sucked beads of sweat from their bodies even though the pavements above sparkled with frost and the soil in the Gardens was iron-hard.

Brante peered over the heads around him and could make out Punnr across the Hall. Their surprise meeting two nights before had, if anything, bonded them still more firmly. He was shocked how quickly he had spoken of his ex, how easily it had come. Only afterwards did he think of the hurt if Punnr – Tyler – had reacted badly, if there had been a drawing back, a distance. The man had become too special to him. They had been in this together, up to their necks, right from the start and it would have killed him to feel the friendship slip.

Punnr wasn't wearing his helmet and Brante watched

him. It was strange that this man with the arm-ring, so meagre physically, so unsteady emotionally, still to make his first kill, still to earn the respect of his companions, nevertheless drew a sense of loyalty from Brante. He found himself looking to Punnr for shape and direction. Perhaps it was because his friend was committed to a personal emotional journey, a drive to seek out his sister. Perhaps his quiet certainty brought steadiness to others. Brante was unsure. He simply understood that if, one day, Punnr chose to lead, he would be there right behind him.

The clamour grew. They were saying Storm had been caught in a trap somewhere down on Cowgate. Asmund had sent four of his five Litters out, thirty-two of the forty-four in his ranks. Trained as archers and peltasts, they were a weak link in this season of swordcraft, but they were light, nimble troops who could filter through the streets as quietly as the Ravens. They were supposed to be seekers on these nights. Find the foe, alert Valhalla and bring the Wolves racing.

But tonight two of the Litters had been ambushed and long before they could send word back for reinforcements, there had been a bitter sword fight and, if tales were true, four Vestals were down. How could this be? Sixteen Blood Credits to the Titans. Surely these were lies. The Hall reverberated to howls of consternation. The Jarls and Housecarls had ascended the stairs to the council chamber without a word and slammed the door.

The Wolves bayed to give chase, knowing they could be on Cowgate in minutes. The Hammers yelled back. Someone pushed someone else and a scuffle broke out. Thankfully weapons were banned from the Halls even on these nights, otherwise iron would have been drawn. The shoving spread like contagion and became a wider brawl. Brante found himself jostled by the crowd as Hersirs waded in to regain control.

What fuelled the anger most were the claims that it was the Band. The filthy pissing Sacred Band, led by that whore Agape. Most of those present in the Throne Room had gleaned an inkling of the council's game plan this Season. Over the last few weeks, as Sveinn's officers debated strategies behind closed doors, the ranks naturally did the same, chewing over every piece of information and spitting out their own solutions. They knew Sveinn had gambled on Alexander not risking his scant elite troops on the Blood Nights and instead swaddling them deep in their rooftop strongholds to preserve them for the Grand Battle to come.

But now every trooper knew King Sveinn was wrong. The Band was abroad and death roamed with them.

As Valhalla feuded, Lana left hospital in style at two thirty-five in the morning. She had been woken after midnight by the duty nurse and informed of her imminent departure. She padded down the corridor for a shower and when she returned she discovered a black knee-length dress, jewellery, hosiery and smart shoes waiting for her. She worked at her hair in a hand mirror and even discovered a little make-up and perfume in a toiletry bag left on her side table. The scent jarred with the incessant tang of antiseptic permeating the ward and her heels sounded incongruous on the vinyl flooring, but she had grown to accept the ways of the

Pantheon. Treat you like beasts one moment, then lavish you with extravagance the next.

She perched on her bed, wondering if she would hear children's voices again, but it was late and the world was silent. Beneath her dress, her ribs still ached from the wound, but the bandages were gone and the scar, she suspected, might be the first of many. During these last weeks, she had been given too much time to lie in bed and mull over her life and she had come to the inescapable conclusion that the Pantheon was now her destiny; and, even though she would strive with every fibre of her being to avoid returning to the hospital, it wouldn't stop her seeking the fulfilment of adventure with her friends in the Horde. In a world without meaning, without a path, without her daughter, she had come to realise that the Pantheon was her home. She would embrace it, come what may.

At last the nurse returned and signalled it was time. She carried a smart wool coat on one arm and handed this to Lana, patting one of the pockets to indicate there was money inside. Lana followed her through the dark and empty communal area. As the nurse unlocked the exit door and led her onto a stairway, she felt a surge of freedom. At last she was being released. They descended four flights and came to a door. The nurse used a fingerprint scanner and the red light changed to green, accompanied by an audible click. Lana nodded her thanks and wished she could have said a more personal goodbye to Monique.

She had expected to step out into night air, but instead she found herself in an enclosed parking area and a limousine with blacked-out windows waiting for her. She opened the door and slipped onto the back seat. The interior was dark and she realised the windows were blackened on the inside too. The driver gave a small wave in his rear-view mirror, but she could make out little of him and as the car eased forward, he pressed a switch to bring up a partition screen.

Alone, illuminated only by the glow of under-seat lighting and blind to the passing world, she was taken from that place and it felt good. She was out. She was fit. Valhalla called. Punnr and Brante. She allowed herself a little smile, which broadened as she looked again at her clothes. Trust the Pantheon to escort her home dressed for a night on the town.

Her mind shifted to her flat and she thought of the food that would have gone off in her fridge, her cold and unmade bed and even the very air that would have grown stale from its sojourn. With a shudder she realised the last time she had been there was when she was attacked. She had risen from her bed, sensing something amiss, and come across the figure waiting for her in the living room. She replayed the fight on the sofa, his rancid breath in her face, his howl of pain as she butted her head into him and then kicked him to the ground. She had burst from the front door still clad in her nightwear, convinced he would chase her and bring her down.

Somehow she had found her way to the Tunnels and waited until Freyja and the Ravens came for the final Raid Night. Now she knew with a certainty she didn't want to go back to that flat yet. She yanked her thoughts away, felt for the money inside her coat and leaned forward to the partition.

'Where can I get a drink at this time of night?'

The partition slid down, so she could make out streetlights

and houses through the windscreen and knew they were deep within the city once more.

'Dropkick Murphys or OX184 are always lively,' said the driver, but then he glanced back and took in her dress. 'Although perhaps the Caley Bar in the Waldorf would be more suitable.'

'Take me there.'

At last they were underway. Halvar had bounded down the steps from the council chamber and consulted with his Hersirs, then they had been hustled to the Armouries. A tense gathering in South Tunnel and finally out through South Gate onto Blair Street and racing down to Cowgate. Litters One, Three and Four, twenty-one souls now, Halvar in front and followed by his Hersirs. Brante allowed his long legs to take him and drew level with the leaders. Blades were already drawn and his shield bounced on his forearm. The air was so cold, it burned his lungs and plumed from his mouth. Underfoot, the paving crunched with frost and as they reached the junction with Cowgate, he looked back and saw Punnr's helmeted figure following with Litter Four. Brante had to stop himself from laughing out loud. He was filled with the high that came before battle, a cocktail of fear and adrenaline and the sense of balancing at the sharp edge of life.

'Three and Four east,' whispered Halvar. 'One west with me.'

They broke apart and Leiv led Litters Three and Four down Cowgate. Vigiles had dropped in behind them on Blair Street, their cameras capturing everything. Figures materialised ahead. They were the remnants of Storm, with the lightning bolts clear on their shields. There was a pause in the pace, hurried discussion with Leiv, much pointing and then they were off again. Some of Storm joined their ranks, but others looked broken and continued their retreat to Valhalla.

Cowgate merged into Holyrood Road and the claustrophobic press of the old buildings eased and widened. They were into a university quarter and the blocks were more modern with coffee outlets and seating areas, but this change felt wrong. Their orders had been to destroy the Band on Cowgate. But there was no Band. They had lost the scent and their momentum began to wane.

They pulled up outside a darkened Pizza Express and gathered around Leiv in the moonlight. He was studying the rooftops, hoping for some lead and all too aware that cornering the Band was no easier than capturing the breath that steamed above his troops. Instinct whispered to him that the Band was already gone. Ghost in, make the kill, disappear: that was their favoured style. He swore, then regained his composure.

'Back west. We find Litter One. Go, go.'

The Wolves jogged once more into the tight blackness of Cowgate, under South Bridge and on towards George IV Bridge. Groups of homeless stirred from their layers and yelled at them. There were glows from a couple of phones trying to capture their movements. When there was no sign of Halvar or Litter One, Leiv slowed again and Brante could see the Hersir was uncertain what orders to give. A return to South Gate with their blades still clean would be a bitter blow, especially with a scoffing Hammer Regiment awaiting them, but the depths of Cowgate was no place to be milling around.

What none of them knew was that it was already too late. From the roofs beside South Bridge, Menes, Captain of Companion Bodyguard, counted their number and signalled to his couriers.

Leiv's eyes focused on a skip outside Tailors Hall Hotel in which old curtains and mattresses had been thrown, evidence that the hotel was using the gloom of February to get its refurbishments completed. At both ends of the building, scaffolding ran up to the gutters and the sight settled his questions.

'The scaffolding,' he hissed, pointing with his sword. 'We split up. Litter Three the eastern end. Litter Four the western. Get onto the rooftops, reconnoitre, and shout like hell for the other litter if you come across any of the bastards.'

Brante followed his squad. They sheathed their blades, shifted their shields onto their backs and ascended. The climbing was easy up a series of ladders and platforms, but they knocked against the steel poles and cursed as fear grew. They were heading away from the dark pavements they ruled and up towards a canopy of chimneys and rooftiles, dizzying drops and dangerous gradients, wide open spaces and a cathedral of stars. Brante thought of the Titans, remembered their speed and agility, and as he sweated under his armour and hauled himself over the lip of the gutter, he wondered what hell might await them.

Lana walked into the Caley Bar of the Waldorf Astoria. It

was smaller than she expected. A thin space of mahogany, with dark oak flooring and a long black marble bar. There were tables where she had entered, but otherwise the seating comprised a row of high leather chairs running down the length of the bar. A staff member was cleaning glasses, but otherwise the place was deserted except for three men hunched together at the far end. She seated herself at the nearest table and removed her coat. The bartender stopped his cleaning, retrieved a cocktail menu and came over.

'Just something with gin,' she said without needing the menu. 'Surprise me.'

He smiled and retreated. She wondered what had been happening these past weeks. She had got used to life without her phone, but still it felt strange not to be able to check the weather or the news. Her mind took her back to the night of the attack in her flat once more and she thought her phone must still be where she had left it near her bedside, but then she began wondering if the man had searched her things after she had fled. What had he found? What had he taken? Why had he been there?

'It's called Aviation,' said the bartender, placing a delicate glass in front of her with a cherry in the bottom and salt around the rim. 'Gin, maraschino, crème de violette and lemon juice.'

She sipped. It was good. Bitter, but refreshing, with the weight of the gin and the aftertaste of the salt. 'Perfect, thank you.'

She drank it faster than she intended and forced her mind away from that terrible night in her flat. She thought of Tyler and wondered what he was doing. Perhaps he was in Valhalla, but then again he was probably asleep on Learmonth. *Tyler, my god*. She found herself tensing. *I thought I'd lost you. I thought you'd gone forever*. She remembered her emptiness, her sense of aimlessness and the new purpose that had come to her to find Morgan. Then that night high in the castle, Erland's tongue on her face and Ulf with death in his eyes. For a moment she was tempted to take a taxi to Tyler's flat. Wake him from his bed and hold him. Press her cheek into his chest as she had done on that long descent from the castle.

She abandoned the idea and drained her glass. Damn, she'd needed that. She looked for the bartender to order another, but he had disappeared. Irritated, she rose and walked to the bar, but he was nowhere in sight. *Come on. I've been stuck in a hospital bed for god knows how long and I need a bloody drink*. She glanced at the three men. They were pressed against the bar, one seated on a high leather chair, the other two standing either side of him, bent over a tablet screen, with whiskies to hand. Businessmen, she guessed. In town for conferences and playing out on company expenses. She tapped the bar with her nails and flirted with attempting to make the cocktail herself.

'What the hell are they doing?' one of the men said staring at the screen. 'There's only twenty-three minutes until the end of play.'

Lana checked the clock behind the bar. Twenty-three minutes to four in the morning. Prickles danced across the back of her neck.

She looked again at the men. They were middle-aged, sagging at the edges, with receding hair and jowls from drink, but they wore nice shirts, designer jeans, expensive shoes and the Waldorf was a hell of an expensive joint for most businessmen to lay their heads. She reassessed. Could it be possible?

Slowly she eased her way down the bar. The man furthest away lifted his head over his seated companion and looked at her. She gave him her most inviting smile.

'Piss off girl.'

The other two turned her way and she was about to retreat when she felt the eyes of the seated man slide down her neck, over her dress and onto her legs. 'No, no,' he said in a gentle reprimand to the first man. 'It's late for a beauty like you. Are you staying here?'

'Just came for a drink.'

He gave her a knowing look. 'Of course you did. So what are you drinking?'

'It's called Aviation.'

'Give her another,' the man said over her shoulder and there was the bartender, nodding his acknowledgement as though he had been there all along.

The first speaker still stared at her with hostility, but there was no mistaking the look in the eyes of the other two. They smelled of expensive aftershave, but too much, as if they had showered in it, and there were serious rings on their fingers. *Okay*, she thought, *I'll play your game.*

'Want to have a look?' said the seated man when she had received her drink. She nodded coyly and advanced behind him so that she could peer over his shoulder. The other two pressed in a little too closely and a hand snaked round the small of her back.

On the screen was a jolting video taken by someone on the move. The footage was dark and blurry, and she could just see figures jogging ahead of the cameraman, but she would have known nothing more had it not been for the fact that down the side of the screen ran a list of information. Location, compass bearing, speed. There was a constantly changing series of numbers with pound, dollar, euro and yen symbols in front of them, but what really took her breath away were the words at the top: *Sacred Band*.

'Do you know what this is?' asked the man with his hand now on her bottom.

'I'm not sure,' she replied hesitantly and tried to look prettily perplexed.

'Whoa!' interrupted the central man. 'Contact alert!'

Warning signals were flashing down the side of the screen. He swiped right and a map replaced the footage. It was showing the Old Town and there were two dots blinking, one red and one blue. He zoomed in. The Mile. South Bridge. Cowgate. He touched the blue light and new data ran down the edge of the screen.

'Companions,' he said. 'Menes in charge. Eighteen of them, heading west. They've just made the crossing of South Bridge and up onto La Belle Angele.'

'They'll have to drop to Guthrie Street next,' said the third man.

'Yeah, but look what's beyond that!' He touched the red dot, which was blinking just west of Guthrie and read aloud the new data. 'Wolves. Litter Four led by Leiv. Only seven of them.'

Litter Four. A stone sank in Lana's gut.

'That's right,' replied the other man, removing his hand from her bottom in the excitement. 'They lost one in the Gardens.'

'Is this live?' Lana blurted.

'It damn well better be, girl.'

Their phones beeped. 'Odds are in.' They each consulted separately. '12–7, a Titan win.'

'It's obviously going to be a Titan win. I've got 4–1 for a Blood Count of three Wolves.'

'Forget that.' The seated man grinned. 'Look, Litter 4 has a Vestal! It's 3–1 he's a goner.'

Lana had never heard the term *Vestal*, but she knew well enough it was Punnr's litter. They were fiddling with their phones and leaving her to stare at the red dot. Then the seated man turned to her. 'I just bet three grand.'

He expected it to impress her and she tried to give him a smile of wonder. He returned to the screen, swiped it again and real-time footage appeared once more. 'Camera 27. He's right in there with the Wolves.'

She could see them now. Their Viking helms and shields bright in the moonlight as they worked their way across a slanting roof. They needed their hands for balance on the frosty tiles, so their blades were sheathed. She wanted to yell to them.

'Closer,' said the seated man, watching distance data on the right of the screen. 'Closer… yes! We have contact.'

Litter Four had just reached the apex of the roof and were dropping thankfully down onto a flatter area, when figures appeared on the building beyond.

'Shields!' yelled Leiv.

The seven of them sprung together in a line and locked with a clatter. Punnr found himself wedged between Olsen, who was still panting from the exertion of the climb, and the hard muscle of Knut. He placed his sword point on the rim of his shield and hunkered down, legs bent, shoulders rammed against his companions.

The Titans jumped onto the flat area a dozen yards from the shieldwall. Punnr counted ten and saw with relief that their cloaks and horsehair plumes were scarlet. *Thank the gods. Not the Band.*

'Hold,' ordered Leiv to his troop.

Ake let out a screeched challenge from the end of the line and the Titans hunched into attack posture.

'You better not give way, Vestal,' warned Knut next to him. 'Or I'll gut you myself.'

Punnr stared over his shield. The lead Titan was looking directly at him and as their eyes met, the man eased upright and lowered his hoplon fractionally. Punnr saw one silver and three red Bloodmarks and the moonlight illuminated a livid scar running across his lips. When the attack began, Punnr knew this man would come for him.

Another figure dropped from the parapet and stood to one side. 'Know that I am Menes, Captain of Companion Bodyguard, and you goat shits are outnumbered. Give us the Vestalis and we'll take the four Blood Credits and let you live.'

The entire Viking shieldwall bridled at this. 'We are the Wolves of Valhalla, Sky-Rat,' responded Leiv. 'And you'll taste our iron in your bellies.'

'Your funerals.'

Without another word or any sign from Menes, the Companions sprang towards them, covering the yards in a second and then leaping into the air. Their boots struck the shieldwall and their sword points thrust down seeking

Viking hearts. Punnr felt the full force through his shield arm, but the line held and experience lent the Wolves speed. The shields swung up and caught the descent of the Titan blades, iron smashing into wood. Somehow, Punnr's shield had been forced up with the others and he felt the point of the scarred man's sword smack across his shield rim and glance away.

Knut was shouting like a madman and Ake's shrieks of fury filled the air. Olsen let out a grunt on impact, then shoved back with the strength of an ox. His attacker slipped on the frost and Olsen yelled in excitement. Beyond him, Leiv struck over the shields and when he pulled back, there was blood slick on his blade. Punnr lashed wildly between the shields.

'Watch it, you bastard,' shouted Knut as a gap emerged in the interlocking shields. 'Get back into position.'

Punnr locked back in, but now his attacker had a grip on the edge of his shield and was grappling at it. Punnr tried to slice his fingers, but the aim was off and the man released his grip with an oath, then cracked his hoplon against Punnr's defence.

'Wolves!' yelled Leiv. 'Shieldwall advance!'

With a unified shout, the litter stepped forward as one, Punnr taken on the flow. They planted their front feet squarely, heaved their shields out and struck their sword points over the top. The momentum of the Titans was gone and the Wolves smelled blood.

'Come on, you bastards,' shouted Knut exultantly, but a warning cry came from Stigr on the far end of the line.

Menes had waved in more Sky-Rats. At least another eight dropped from the roof and broke around the undefended flanks of the Viking line.

'Circle!' bawled Leiv, and Ake and Stigr at each end began to bend round to cope with the fresh attackers. 'Where the hell's Litter Three?' demanded Leiv under his breath.

It was no good. The Companions had them and they knew it. Ake was already backing into Knut, and Stigr and Unn were fighting valiantly at the other end, but their flanks were moments from being undefended.

'Fuck!' yelled Knut and stared wildly for direction from Leiv even as he hacked at a Titan blade.

'We have to do something,' snarled Olsen.

Leiv parried a blow and looked down the line.

'Leave him. Leave the Vestal, for Odin's sake!' shouted Knut at his Hersir and Leiv's eyes fell on Punnr.

'I'm sorry,' he said.

Punnr was staggering from the blows to his shield, his arm already numb and his brain trying to comprehend. He started to say something back to Leiv, but already the line was breaking around him. He felt the reassuring bulks of Knut and Olsen pull away and suddenly there was just air beside him.

'It's you they want, boy,' said Olsen. 'Nothing personal.'

The Wolves fought such a rapid retreat back over the apex of the roof and down to the scaffolding, that Punnr found himself in a sea of Titans. Ake and Stigr were still defending the flanks, but Unn, Knut and Olsen were already using the frost to slide to the gutter and drop after Leiv. Punnr tried to follow, but knew that the moment he shifted his shield, the scarred man would hack him down where he stood.

He glanced behind as Ake swung at two attackers, screamed her defiance, took one long look at him and jumped for the scaffolding. The Companions were reluctant to give chase down to street level and they eased back. Two or three were nursing wounds and one had slumped to her knees. The others lowered their swords and turned towards Punnr. The blows on his shield stopped and in the sudden quiet, he could hear his heartbeat in his throat. He peered over the rim at the scarred man waiting for him and then around at the semicircle of foe.

He was alone.

XIV

'What's happening?' cried Lana in consternation.

'Don't trouble your little head with it,' said the man next to her and attempted to place his hand back on her rear, but she pushed him away.

'It's the Vestal,' said the seated man, absorbed in the images on the screen. 'He's a goner.'

'But he can't be. Why have they deserted him?'

'None of them are going to risk themselves ahead of the Battle if there's a Vestalis to be sacrificed. Too bad for him.'

The third man checked his phone. 'The odds are locked down. No more bets.'

'That's fine by me,' replied the seated man. 'It was 3–1. That's a cool nine grand coming my way when the kid's dead.'

Lana wasn't listening. Everything had faded except the image on the screen. The Vigilis was zooming in towards the action and she could see the Viking more clearly. His wolf's head shield held limply before him and his blade raised in defence. There was an arm-ring on his sword arm and, for a second, it gave her hope because she had never seen Punnr wear anything like that.

But then the camera focused closer and she could see the

long hair beneath his helmet and the little goatee beard. And there were his eyes in the moonlight behind the iron, searching his attackers. Bright with fear.

'I've been looking for you, Wolf Virgin,' the Companion with the scarred lips said and lowered his hoplon nonchalantly. 'I know someone who's going to be delighted we met you tonight.'

Punnr eyed him from behind his shield. He knew he must fight, but his mind was sluggish with shock. His breathing came in short pants, pluming up into the winter sky. The man gripped his shortsword with the point lowered as he played with Punnr. 'So what's a Vestal doing in a Wolf litter? No wonder they deserted you.'

Punnr took a cautious step towards him to bring himself in range of a strike, but he understood that any attack he launched would be parried and followed by the death blow. He sensed the rest of the foe watching him and knew somewhere on the roof above a Vigilis would be filming his last movements. He wondered if he should be spending these seconds considering his life; remembering his mother, his sister, trying desperately to grab on to something warm and wonderful from his past. But it was hopeless. All he could see was that horrible scar on the lips of the man in front of him and all he could think was that destiny had decreed its leer would be the final thing his eyes ever perceived.

'Need to do it,' Menes said from the sidelines and began waving his other Companions back to the roofs above.

The Companion grinned. 'You heard the boss, Vestal. Your last chance to take me.' He held his shield and weapon out from his sides, opening up his torso to tempt Punnr.

'I mean it, Proteus!' shouted Menes impatiently. 'Stop pissing about. There's only ninety seconds 'til Conflict Hours are over!'

At this Proteus glanced up towards the Vigilis who was circling a finger, confirming that time was almost up.

That was it. That was the moment. The gods had granted Punnr one final chance.

'Hey!' exclaimed the man next to Lana. 'What the hell's happening?'

The seated man took an age answering, his eyes glued to the screen. 'The Vestal's just killed him, that's what!'

It was true. Lana's jaw hung open and her hand sought the speaker's shoulder to steady herself. The Companion had taken a momentary look into the camera and was only just focusing again, his arms still held open and his torso exposed, when the Viking broke from his cower, stepped forward on his left leg and thrust with his sword – much longer than the weapon carried by the Titans. The blade found the softer defence beneath his opponent's bronze breastplate and burrowed through tunic, skin, flesh and gut.

'Down he goes,' stated the third man as the footage showed the Hoplite sinking to one knee and the Viking wrenching his weapon free.

On the edge of the screen the monetary amounts were going crazy, just as all hell was breaking loose on the rooftop.

'Well that's nine grand up in smoke,' said the seated man.

*

Now the Companions came for Punnr, even as Proteus was collapsing in front of him with blood breaking from his hideous lips. Fifteen of them, swords unsheathing again, boots flying across the frozen roof. Menes was yelling, but Punnr heard none of it.

His mind had come alive, as though the sword strike had pierced his own brain and shattered the barrier damming up his thoughts. He knew the foe had been returning towards the higher roof, so he knew equally clearly that the route behind lay open. He spun on the spot, dropped his shield and bounded up the rooftiles. The Titans were right behind him and he could feel their blades reaching for him. He teetered on the apex and saw the tiles slanting down to the scaffolding and then the drop to the street.

Just as the first sword tore at his cloak, he leapt. He hit the slanting roof, bounced and rolled, his blade flying from his grip. The scaffolding poles reared up, but he was already travelling too fast to grab them. He flipped onto his front and scrabbled desperately at the tiles, but they were slick with frost and with a sickening lurch he shot over the drop. For a heartbeat he looked up at the starlit sky, just long enough to tell himself it was an idiotic way to die, then he plummeted into the void.

'Well, some you win, some you lose,' said the seated man and switched the tablet off. He slugged his whisky and turned to appraise Lana. 'So what did you think?'

'I don't know.' She was desperate to see the outcome of Punnr's fall. 'It was all so confusing.'

'That's just as well. It's probably best you let it stay confusing.' He took her by the arm and walked down the bar out of earshot of the others. 'So, how much for your company until breakfast?'

'I'm sorry?'

'Name your price. I've a suite upstairs.' He smiled. His tanned face and silver hair lent him gravitas, but his eyes burned with craving. 'A pleasant enough place to spend what's left of a cold night.'

She faced up to him. 'Who the hell do you think you are?'

His smile evaporated and the ardour in his eyes chilled to something more glacial. He took a few moments to choose his words and when he spoke his voice was low with threat. 'You didn't see anything tonight. You forget it all. You understand?'

She was desperate to discover Punnr's fate and she could feel her arms shaking with frustration. If she had a blade at that moment, she would happily skewer this predator.

'Have you paid for your drinks?'

The question took her by surprise. 'Not yet.'

'Consider them on me. Now get the hell out of my sight.'

His eyes flicked open. He could still see stars winking at

him from beyond the dark masses of the buildings, but silhouetted against them were a dozen Titan plumes.

He was alive. The breath had been blown from him and his left leg hurt like hell, but he seemed intact. He tested his limbs, sensed his organs. How could this be? With a groan he shifted his head and found his nose pressed into cold, damp fabric. He was surrounded by curtains and old mattresses. The skip. The damn skip in front of the hotel! He pushed up and grimaced as he realised his left leg had caught the iron edge of the skip, but he tested it and knew the pain was only muscular.

He looked up at the Titans and wondered why they weren't coming for him. Then understanding flooded through him. It was over. The Blood Night. The Conflict Hours. It must be gone four. He rolled to the edge of the skip and lowered himself cautiously to the pavement, where he spied his sword. Retrieving it, he saw the black stain of lifeblood coating its point. He looked once more to the foe and waved the weapon at them and a cry of bitter victory broke from his lips. They watched him silently, then one by one disappeared.

Pain returned and with it exhaustion and cold and memories of the Wolves abandoning him. He began to limp down Cowgate, which was quiet now that the Horde was back in the Tunnels. The rough sleepers were still under South Bridge and they goaded him, but he waved his blade angrily and they kept their distance. He trudged slowly with his mind on Leiv and Litter Four. They had sacrificed him, left him to die because he was valueless to them and even now they would be arguing in the changing areas, caring more about the gift of four Blood Credits to the foe than the loss of one of their number.

He held his sword before him and was careful not to disturb the blood drying on it. He limped up Blair Street, dropped down a discreet set of steps and came to the small steel door, plastered in graffiti, which served as South Gate. He hammered on it with the butt of his weapon and hammered again when there was no answer. There was a camera above his head and he glared at it until he heard movement. The door creaked open and two Hammer sentries gaped at him.

'Conflict Hours are over. What the hell are you still doing out here?'

'Let me in.' Punnr shoved past them and walked painfully up South Tunnel towards the noise of the Throne Room.

'Hey,' a voice called behind him. 'Get that sword in the Armouries.'

But he ignored the instruction.

'You!' the voice shouted again. 'No weapons in the Halls!'

He kept going, arriving at the great south doors, from beyond which came a hubbub. He wrenched them open and stepped through. A sea of warriors raged, arguing about the losses of the night. Sveinn was seated on his oak throne under the ship's prows and Radspakr lurked behind.

'What the hell?' said a female Hammer near Punnr when she saw his sword, but the look in his eye quietened her. He shouldered through the turmoil and searched for the faces he needed to find. Warriors turned to spit curses at him as he pushed past, then spied the blade and swallowed their remonstrations. Gradually the throng opened to reveal Leiv and Olsen gesticulating in each other's faces, but Punnr's eyes locked instead onto the man who had first put voice to the flight.

He barged into Knut and grabbed a handful of his grey beard. '*Leave him?*' he shrieked, spittle flying. '*Leave the Vestal?*'

Knut grabbed at the fingers in his beard and made to use his short bulk to hurl the Wolfling from him, but he stopped when he felt the edge of Punnr's blade sharp against his cheek. The turmoil died and faces turned to the sight of a weapon carried in anger in Valhalla.

Knut's eyes were beads of hot anger and his breath ale-sour, but he held his tongue.

'Now then, lad,' warned Leiv.

'Don't you *lad* me. It was you who gave the order. You who left me there to die.' Punnr's voice had dropped to a quaver of fury. His words were for Leiv, but his stare was still locked on Knut. 'You left me there to face the foe and ran to save your precious hides. Call yourselves Wolves?'

'I made a tough battlefield decision,' answered the Hersir, his voice level. 'We were outnumbered. They were about to round our flanks. Another minute and I would have lost far more than one Wolf.'

'So I was the most expendable.'

'No. You were the most valuable. And every Titan knew it.'

Punnr's sword arm trembled with rage and a thin rivulet of blood sprouted from Knut's cheek and dribbled into his beard.

Knut glared at him. 'Get that blade off my face, Vestal, or I swear I'll kill you right here in this Hall.'

Punnr scrunched up his nose and took long, deep breaths. He was so close to splitting the bastard's ugly face in half. But, instead, he mustered his remaining strength and butted his forehead against Knut's, so that their eyes were as close as lovers, and said through gritted teeth, loud enough for the whole throng to hear, 'I am no Vestal.'

With that, he removed the blade, released his grip on the man's beard and stepped back. 'Look,' he shouted, raising the sword high, so that the flames from the fire played on its steel. 'Look at it, all of you. The lifeblood of a Companion.'

'A kill!' said a female voice close to hand. It was Ake and she raised her fist and let out a long wild howl that echoed through the Tunnels.

More fists were raised and her words spread amongst the Horde. 'A kill. A kill.'

The chants became a battle cry. Fists pumped. Boots stamped. 'A kill. A kill.'

Leiv stepped closer. 'Then you are now bloodied and a true Wolf.'

Punnr peered around him at the chanting mass, but his gaze returned to Knut. The warrior was still glowering at him, his eyes black below his brows and his lips pulled back in a snarl to reveal yellowed teeth.

Punnr lowered his sword and mouthed quietly to him, 'I am no Vestal.'

Then he swung on his heels, winced at the pain in his leg and limped back to the Armouries.

Part Two

The Field

XV

Tyler was dozing in his bed when there was a knock on the front door. He stirred groggily and reached for his phone. Three fifteen in the afternoon. Subdued grey light filtered through the curtains. *God, Oliver, not now.*

He sank back onto his pillow and lay staring at the ceiling. He had been in and out of sleep for hours, his dreams and his conscious thoughts merging into a mess of recurring moments. Knut's eyes, heavy with fury. Leiv's words: *Then you are now bloodied and a true Wolf.* Ake's look before she jumped from the building. Sveinn's gravel tones: *Get that kill.* Calder's body in his arms, featherlight and punctured. The hysteria in his mother's voice as she shouted at Morgan on that fateful day long ago: *Someone has to do something to save you!*

And the jolt up his arm as his sword broke through cloth and flesh and sunk into a thick mass of intestines. The pig-squeal choke of the Titan as he collapsed before him.

Tyler rolled onto his side. So it had come to this. There was his life before that blade strike and there was his life now and they would forever be separated by what had occurred. Because he had killed. The Pantheon could dress it up with all its Rules and ceremonies and flag-waving and declare it part of the game, but nothing could hide the fact that Tyler had taken a life last night. Brante's words tiptoed into his mind: *When I get back to my bed, there's no denying I'm a murderer.*

Tyler remembered striding into Sveinn's Throne Room, hurling figures aside and grabbing at Knut. He had no idea why he had focused specifically on the man. He had just been so angry. So utterly boiling with pain and rage. And Knut had become his target. There were moments while his blade dug into Knut's flesh, when he could have let loose and carved him, then swung and swung at the mass of warriors. Cutting and tearing and shredding everything in his path.

Now, lying in his underpants under a thin duvet, shocked, cold and utterly lonely, he could barely comprehend his madness. He could only assume it was the rage of a killer. The guilt of someone who had taken a life and could never give it back.

He shivered and forced himself up, pulled on a jumper and padded to look between the curtains. The scene took him by surprise. Early March, but Learmonth Gardens was covered in a blanket of white and the flakes were still falling. Already a snowman had materialised, surrounded by a flurry of little footprints. He lit a cigarette and watched the blackbirds squabbling, then walked through to the kitchen for a drink of water, wincing at his painful leg.

The Pantheon was now on pause. It was the break between the two sets of Blood Nights and perhaps it was apt that the city should have surrendered to the silent weight of snow. Apart from the calls of the blackbirds, he could hear nothing beyond the windows. No voices, no cars. It was strange how snow always brought hush.

The water made his stomach cramp. He realised his body was craving food, but it was the thought of whisky that made his eyes scan the room. How he needed its peated sting in his throat. How he wished to lose this silent day to it.

But, instead, his eyes found something else by the door. A folded scrap of paper. *What's the boy want now? Isn't he at school?* But it wasn't from Oliver.

I hoped to see you. L

He flung open the door and peered down the communal stairs, still dressed only in underpants and jumper. Cramming his heavy emotions to the back of his skull, he hurried into his bedroom, yanked on jeans, socks and boots, grabbed his hat, phone and thickest coat, and hobbled as fast as he could down to the street. There were several sets of footprints in the snow, but one of them looked smaller and more feminine, and he convinced himself they were hers. He followed them past Dean Bowling Club and out onto Comely Bank Avenue, then along the main road, where he lost them amongst all the others, but he guessed she was heading up towards the shops of Stockbridge and he strode in that direction as fast as his leg would bear.

People were milling through the charity shops and he peered into the cafés, wondering if he would see that blonde hair and those eyes over a cappuccino. He was through most of the town and chiding himself for ignoring her knock, when he spotted her. She was crossing the road and turning north up St Bernard's Row towards Inverleith Park. He chuckled with relief and quickened his pace. *You don't change*, he thought. *I'd recognise you anywhere.* The slim curve of her figure even beneath the long winter coat;

delicate, low-heel ankle boots under smart black jeans; the blonde hair pulled back in a ponytail and curling at the ends; a cashmere scarf; a Cossack hat; and those pearl earrings.

He dropped in beside her and waited for her to look.

'Oh my gosh,' she exclaimed and held her chest. 'You found me.'

'Hello, stranger.'

She beamed radiantly and threw her arms around his neck. They hugged tight and it struck Tyler that this was the first time they had ever held each other properly. She pulled back to study his eyes, her expression wistful now. Then she gripped him close again and kissed him lightly on the lips. 'That's for the castle.'

He thought to make a joke of it, but words failed him.

She pushed him away and punched him hard on the shoulder, making a couple of passers-by stare at them. 'And that's for making me think you were dead.'

He grinned ruefully and pointed in the direction of his flat. 'Come back. I can make us coffee.'

'No, come to mine. It's quicker.'

'Really?'

She indicated up St Bernard's. 'Just up there. But turn your phone off first because you never know who's tracking our locations. I always turn mine off when I come to yours.'

He complied and then walked with her, listening to the crunch of their feet in the snow as they drew away from the main street.

She noticed his limp. 'Are you okay?'

'Courtesy of the Pantheon.'

She wanted to tell him she had seen everything on a screen held by a member of the Curiate. She wanted to describe how desperate she had been when she had witnessed his fall from the building and how the man had switched off the feed before she could ascertain his fate. And, most of all, she wanted him to know of the relief that had flooded through her when she had marched to Valhalla in the early light and been brusquely informed by the Gate Keepers that judging from the scenes in the Throne Room, the Wolf Vestal was indubitably alive and kicking – and no longer a Vestal.

'Carried his blade into Sveinn's Hall,' growled one of them. 'If he'd tried that stunt on my watch, I'd have wrapped it round his bloody neck.'

'Well I never,' Tyler exclaimed as he followed her to the cottages on Reid Terrace and saw the Leith flowing beyond. 'To think you were only ever ten minutes away from me.'

She let him in, hung the coats, placed their shoes on a rack and bid him make himself comfortable on the sofa while she lit candles. The room was warm and smelt of flowers and herbs, conjuring up summer amidst the snow.

'Coffee?'

'Tea.'

He peered around curiously at her things, trying to piece together her life. On the walls hung paintings of ancient cities bathed in Mediterranean light. On her shelves were blue and white china cups and hardback books about history. He could make out the words: *Jerusalem, the Biography*; *A History of the Arabs*; and *Aristotle*. Through an open door to one of the bedrooms he spotted an exercise bike and on the other bedroom door hung a reproduction Byzantine cross. On the mantelpiece above the hearth were several more candles and a single photo in a gilt frame of a young child holding a teddy.

She brought in the drinks.

'Are you mended now?' he asked.

She rolled her shoulder. 'I ache some, but it's nothing compared to what it would have been if you'd not interrupted my dalliance with Ulf and Erland.'

'Those bastards.'

'They got what they deserved.'

'Not Ulf. If he hadn't fled like a schoolgirl, I swear I'd have sliced him into fillets.'

She toasted them teacakes and they lathered them with butter and jam, and munched companionably. She curled into the seat opposite and said, 'Tell me everything.' So he talked about the plan Halvar had hatched and the culmination of the struggle at the castle and the strange dancers at the Blood Gathering of Scotland. She was rigid as he described the execution of the woman beneath the *denarii* and his meeting with the Valhalla Caelestis. He explained the rules of the Blood Nights and imparted what he knew of the action to date.

'Vestales,' she murmured in understanding and thought of the boy she had pierced in the forest with a feeble arrow shot. 'They'll give me a Bloodmark because of Einar.'

'And you should be grateful.'

'What sort of heartless comment is that?'

'Because your first kill is done and dusted and no one will ever brand you a Vestalis. There is no love lost for those who have not taken life.'

She could see anger scrawled across his face, but she was riled by the flippancy of his comments.

'Einar was nothing more than a boy,' she retorted. 'He had barely embarked on his life and most likely only ever known the Schola. The Pantheon had its claws in him from such a tender age. The world gave him no chance to make different choices, to deviate from the path to that forest, where he died slowly and in dreadful pain. And you think I should be grateful? I will never ever forgive myself.'

He scrunched his face irritably, but stoppered his tongue and she roused herself from the sofa and took the plates to the sink.

'Forgive me,' he said quietly when she returned. 'It's a terrible thing, this game we play.'

The light was growing dim beyond the windows and she switched on lamps and settled back on the sofa to look at him. He sat cross-legged on the floor beside the fire, picking absently at some stain on the carpet.

'I need to thank you,' he said eventually.

'For what?'

'For taking on the search for my sister even when you thought I was gone. Oliver told me.'

'I'm afraid I got nowhere. But that reminds me…' She hopped up again and disappeared into the spare bedroom, returning with the sports bag she had taken from his flat. 'Your clothes. And this.' She held out his ivory Odin amulet.

'Thank you,' he said and placed it on the coffee table between them.

'And then there's the photo.'

He took it gently and peered at the smiling faces at his sister's graduation. 'Did you notice the man in the crowd?'

She nodded. 'Halvar. The mystery just gets deeper and deeper.'

'Morgan was never a member of the Horde.'

'But I thought she was why you joined Valhalla?'

'I did. But my assumptions were all wrong. She was never a Viking.'

Comprehension spread across Lana's face. 'A Titan?'

'Olena. Captain of Alexander's Companion Bodyguard.'

'My god. That explains the little Star of Macedon on the back of your amulet.'

Tyler looked at the amulet on the coffee table. It had been the one his sister had cherished in the years before his disappearance, though she kept it safely in a drawer and rarely wore it around her neck. Smaller than most. Wrought in ivory. A Triple Horn of Odin like those carried by the rest of the Horde, but containing on the reverse a tiny engraving of the Titan symbol. He had never thought to ask her about the embellishment and when he had discovered it wrapped in tissue paper beside a freshly cooked lasagne on the day she disappeared, he tied it around his own neck and cherished it too.

It staggered him now that he had accepted the design without deeper consideration. He picked it up and toyed with it, rolling the two sides in his palm. Perhaps, he realised, it was this very amulet that had twisted his thinking. He had always assumed Morgan possessed it because she was a member of the Horde and the Star was just an artistic addition. How wrong he had been.

'The Horn and the Star,' he said aloud. 'This amulet represented Morgan's union with Halvar. Their love and their dream that they could kill Alexander and bring the two warring sides together as one. Why the hell did I never see that?'

'You didn't know about Halvar,' Lana reminded him. 'So how could you have guessed?'

If he heard her, he made no acknowledgement and remained bent over the amulet, still turning it in his palm. 'Where are you Morgan? Where are you? If you're alive, why haven't you contacted me? Do the Titans know where you are? Are they hiding you? Are you their prisoner or have you fled their retribution?'

Lana watched him and gave him time for his questions to bubble to the surface, then asked quietly, 'So where do we look now?'

He placed the amulet back on the table and brooded over the question. 'Where do we look? Under stones, I suppose. Under every damn stone I find.'

'Be careful, Tyler. There are those who don't wish those stones overturned.' She shivered as she thought of Radspakr's attack dog in this very house. She glanced around the room, remembering the fight, the moments of sheer terror as a man forced himself brutally on her for the second time in her life. 'I need to get rid of this place,' she said, speaking her thoughts aloud.

They jolted Tyler from his own retrospection. 'Really? It's lovely.'

'Not to me, it isn't. It makes me feel... vulnerable. I need to rent somewhere else and start afresh. Somewhere without memories.'

Tyler didn't understand her meaning and they were quiet for a few moments until she spoke again. 'When I was thirteen my dad dumped my mum and ran off with a much younger model and it killed me. My whole teens were a disaster. God knows I was terrible to my mum, but it was him I really hated. Somehow I got a place in Edinburgh for university and it broke me out of the cycle of recriminations. I began building some success for myself and maybe I was even happy for a while. Not fathomlessly, like those later precious years with Amelia, but hopeful; aspirational.' Tears pricked at the corners of her eyes. 'And then... and then, it was all taken from me by another man.'

He made to get up from his spot on the carpet, but she waved him down.

'In the hospital, I saw more men abusing their power. Three little children bullied by adults. It made me so angry. And late last night, I met others in a bar. Men who think they can do what they want; who think they own you.'

'Not all of us are bastards.'

She pulled a tissue from a box on the table beside her and dabbed her eyes. 'Yeah, I know. I'm sorry. I don't know where all that came from.'

'Has Radspakr been threatening you?' he asked carefully. 'Or anyone else? Is that why you feel vulnerable?'

'No,' she lied. 'Just me being stupid. I shouldn't have said anything.'

He didn't believe her, but she rose to make more tea and so he excused himself for a cigarette outside, stamping around in the cold and watching the snow fall over the Leith.

'Will you stay for dinner?' she asked on his return, because she needed the company in this place of frightening memories.

'Sure.'

'There's one condition.'

'Spill it.'

'You come food shopping with me.'

And so he did. And the black mood that had engulfed him since the Blood Night began to lift. They trudged through the roads, kicking snow at each other and lobbing snowballs into the trees. They wandered the aisles of a little supermarket on Stockbridge main street and picked out items and laughed at little things like newlyweds. Then he sat in her kitchen and drank Merlot while she prepared a chicken tagine with Moroccan spices and minted couscous.

They ate opposite one another over the breakfast bar and Tyler thought he'd not tasted such good food since his mother died. They talked now of frivolous things, forcing away the deeper stuff, and sometimes when they laughed her fingers touched his.

'Can I have your number?' he asked when they had cleaned the dishes and sat again in the lounge.

'I don't think that's advisable. You know it's forbidden to communicate outside the Pantheon and they can check our call logs.'

'Well just give it to me on a piece of paper, only for emergencies. I worry about you and I need to know we can call if we have to.'

She acquiesced, reached for a discarded envelope on the coffee table and scribbled a number on the edge, tearing it off and handing it to him.

'What's your surname?' he asked, taking the pencil as well.

'Cameron.'

'Lana Cameron,' he mused.

'But don't put that,' she said hurriedly. 'You might leave

it lying around and you never know what the Pantheon spies can get hold of.'

'Okay… I'll call you Elsie.' He wrote the name above her number.

'Elsie? Why?'

'Say it slowly.'

'El… sie.' She grinned. 'Oh, very clever.'

He tore another strip from the envelope, pencilled his own number and gave it to her.

'And what shall I call you?'

'You'll have to come up with something.'

'WW,' she said and wrote the two letters beside the number. 'White Warrior.' She placed the slip of paper in a pot on the coffee table. 'Emergencies only.'

'Just for emergencies.'

She picked up her wine glass again and leaned back, observing him as she sipped. 'I've missed you, Punnr.'

'*Punnr*? You've never called me that before outside the Pantheon.'

She smacked a hand over her mouth. 'Oh my god, it was a slip. I'm sorry.'

'I don't mind.'

'But, you know, that's the whole point. You're both to me – Tyler and Punnr. The man I know is both those people.'

He pondered this and knew she was correct. To him, she wasn't only the poised, smart, intelligent woman before him, she was also the athlete, the competitor, the warrior he had witnessed so often in the vaults and Tunnels of Valhalla.

'Do you think,' she asked, 'we would have been friends if the Pantheon hadn't brought us together?'

'Not a chance. You're way too good for me. You'd have some lawyer boyfriend or something.'

He said it without thinking and they looked away, embarrassed.

'Will you stay the night?' she asked eventually.

He searched her eyes. 'Of course.'

'I'm glad I met you, Tyler Maitland. Whatever else the Pantheon has in store for me, it brought you into my life and I'm grateful.'

They opened another bottle and chatted the night away into the small hours, and when they could barely keep their eyes open, she tossed him a blanket and he rolled into it on the sofa.

'Goodnight, *Punnr*,' she said from her bedroom door.

'Sweet dreams, *Calder*.'

XVI

'I'll wager our King's rattled,' said Freyja, walking through from the female changing area in Valhalla to find a bare-chested Halvar securing his breeches.

'Aye. The Season's not going our way.'

She eyed the scars across his torso and the Valknut tattoo on his bicep. She was dressed in a simple tunic over leggings and her braided hair was damp from a rapid shower next door, having been pulled unexpectedly from her Saturday morning bed in Cramond by the driver at her door. 'Are the others here?'

'Bjarke's gone through. Asmund's in the Practice Rooms. He's taking it personally.'

'I don't doubt. His Storm Litters were routed.'

'*Four* Vestals,' Halvar seethed. 'A damn cock-up.'

He pulled on his own tunic, secured it with a thick belt and the two of them walked down to the Throne Room.

'Your Vestal did well though.'

'Aye. A Vestal no more. But his predicament was my fault. I was too quick to split the pack. Should've waited to catch a scent first.'

They found Asmund striking pells in the Practice Rooms

and stood by the door until he had completed a sequence. 'It's time,' said Freyja.

He placed the wooden sword back in the stands and followed them. Bjarke was in the Throne Room holding an espresso.

'Morning,' he grunted, almost politely, as though the early hour wouldn't yet permit them to discard their daytime, street-level civility.

They climbed the steps to the Council Room and found Sveinn consulting a laptop in the corner. He waved to coffee and tea on a side table and then they gathered around the map. At the last moment, Radspakr slipped into the room and joined them.

'My apologies for the unexpected call-up,' said Sveinn. 'I have news from Atilius. The Time Asset has been triggered. The Grand Battle will be precisely two weeks from today.'

There was a stir amongst the council members. They'd not expected this start to the meeting and the thought of the fight to come energised them. The Battle was the centrepiece of the whole Pantheon year, what every trooper waited for.

'Let me remind you about the four Assets,' continued the King. 'After a successful Raiding Season, the Horde is in possession of all four. The first – Time – gives this Palatinate two weeks' notice of the Battle and allows us – if we so wish – to transfer some or all our troops to an area within the vicinity of the actual battlefield at any point during this period. Alexander does *not* hold this Asset. His Palatinate will know nothing about the date of the Battle unless we are foolish enough to give it to them. He will be informed by Atilius only twenty-four hours in advance.'

There were glances around the table. Each could imagine

the turmoil and tensions of getting an entire Palatinate to the field of battle with only a day's notice. The Titans would suffer. It was good.

'The second Asset is Supplies. This too is held only by Valhalla and it lends us options. Choose to deliver troops to the relevant area during these two weeks and they'll be well provided for. When the Titans depart the city in the final twenty-four hours, however, they'll have access to no food or water until the Battle's over.'

'A hungry man is an angry man,' warned Halvar.

'A hungry man is also a vulnerable one,' countered the King and his Wolf Housecarl acquiesced. 'The third Asset is Distance. *Both* Palatinates hold this, which – I suspect – makes it null and void. If we had failed to gain it, we would have found our preparation area located at least fifty miles from the battlefield, a distance we would have needed to cover in a forced march during the twelve hours before combat. This Season, however, both sides will find themselves placed close to the conflict zone.

'And so to the final Asset – Field. This too is possessed by both Palatinates. It ensures we will receive detailed information about the battlefield twenty-four hours in advance; maps, topology, ranges, vegetation, hydrology, ground underfoot. Enough to let us make our final strategic judgements on the order of battle.'

The King fell silent and let his council digest the information.

It was Freyja who spoke eventually. 'From what you've said, lord, I draw two suppositions. First, it's a perfect storm for our foe. Kept blind until the last possible moment, they'll be hit by everything in the final twenty-four hours – the upheaval and confusion of transporting a Palatinate at short notice, just when data about the Field itself starts to pour into their ears and starvation rations kick in.'

Bjarke rumbled his pleasure. 'They'll be clueless schoolgirls on the ends of our spears.'

'What you say is true, Freyja,' concurred Sveinn. 'But Alexander will know it too and he'll not be unprepared. He'll ensure everything is ready to go at a moment's notice. Every trooper briefed. Have no doubt the Titans will arrive in respectable order and fighting spirit. And what is your second point?'

'If our possession of Distance ensures we aren't required to march fifty miles, it's likely the actual battlefield is located close to where we'll be dropped. We might be able to identify it well before both Palatinates are given that information formally in the final twenty-four hours.'

'Yes,' interjected Asmund. 'We can use the two weeks to get teams on the ground to make a full reconnoitre.'

Halvar was nodding his approval. 'Draw up battle plans based on the actual terrain days in advance. It would be a superb opportunity.'

Sveinn stroked his beard pensively. 'There's no guarantee we could identify the precise Field.'

'But given these two weeks,' said Freyja, 'we can map out considerable areas on the ground, determine conditions and make a damn good guess about the likely challenges awaiting on any field of combat.'

'So we go early,' mused Sveinn.

'Aye,' said Halvar. 'Use every available minute.'

The King gazed down at the city map between them as

though he could elicit some clue from it. 'Thane?' he said eventually, looking over to Radspakr.

'Lord, the arguments are logical, although you must maintain your strongest units here to complete the final three Blood Nights.'

A frown flitted across Sveinn's features, but he bit back a retort. 'Perhaps then, Thane, you should update the council about the Blood Nights to date.'

Once again, Radspakr retrieved his spectacles and consulted his iPad. 'Official figures at the halfway point of the Blood Nights from the *libitinarii* – removers of the slain – and confirmed by Atilius' teams. The slain of the Horde as follows: two Drengr; three elite troops, Wolf Company; one elite trooper, Raven Company. All at one Blood Credit each. And four Storm Regiment Vestales at four credits each. Total slain, ten warriors of Valhalla.'

'At a cost of twenty-two Blood Credits to the foe,' confirmed Sveinn and the room was silent.

Radspakr continued. 'Atilius, of course, hasn't provided us with the figures for the Titans. We believe, however, we may count four Companions killed during our encounters.'

'A poor show,' said Bjarke, eyeing his colleagues. 'And my Hammers kept under wraps in Valhalla on every night.'

'Wounded?' demanded Halvar.

'Numerous cuts and sprains. Eight are hospitalised, three of these in a serious condition. The latter unlikely to make it for the Battle. A further five are still recovering from wounds inflicted during the Raiding Season.'

No one spoke. Fourteen of the necessary twenty-five already culled and ten of them from Valhalla. Each of Sveinn's inner circle knew the King had misjudged his strategy. Worse, the loss of the Vestals was tantamount to throwing credits to Alexander. He might not be permitted to use them before the Battle, but if such figures still stood afterwards, he could spend well during the Interregnum, replacing his lost warriors before the start of the Twentieth Season, chewing up the thirty-eight-troop advantage Valhalla had held at the beginning of January. A year wasted and they all recognised it.

Sveinn cut through the silence. 'I'm removing the Wolves.' Heads jerked up. 'Housecarl Halvar, who is your most experienced Hersir?'

'That would be Turid. She commands Litter Two.'

'Turid and Litter Two will continue in the Blood Nights. The remainder I am removing.'

'With respect, lord, how in Odin's name are we supposed to catch-up the Blood Count if my Kill Squads have been gelded?'

'Alexander has made fools of us. He's resisted the urge to protect his best units – though they are dangerously few in number – and his Sacred Band and Companions have roamed freely.'

'Aye, lord, and we should resist the urge too.'

'I won't risk my Wolves any further in advance of the Battle. I need them on the Field in good order. Raven and Hammer will take over duties for the remaining Nights.'

Bjarke growled his support, but the King pounced. 'Enough of that, Jarl. Your Hammers will also be cut. Those Litters with new recruits – especially Vestales – will be removed. We don't need the weight of your numbers on the streets during these nights and the Vestals will be put to better use preparing themselves for shieldwall combat.'

Bjarke searched for a retort, but bit his tongue.

'What of Storm?' asked Asmund quietly, conscious of the negative impact his losses had already made.

'Storm will accompany the remainder of Wolf and Hammer out of the city to wherever our Pantheon masters have determined the Battle zone will be.'

'Do you know anything at all about its location?'

'Nothing. Atilius is as tight-lipped as the dead. But the less we know, the less we can give away to the Titans, and that's the key.'

'If I was Alexander,' said Freyja, 'I'd have people watching our Gates day and night. I'd have others at Waverley station and the airport. Anywhere to catch a hint of us departing. He knows we have the Time Asset and if his spies observe us leaving, he can make an educated guess when the Battle will be.'

'Aye,' agreed Halvar. 'And he'll know we're thinning our lines. So he'll send his troops in even greater force on the remaining Blood Nights.'

'Perhaps,' said Radspakr, looking at the Housecarl. 'He would even consider a Raid into our Tunnels like last year.'

Halvar glared back at the Thane.

'I'll speak of this with Atilius immediately,' said Sveinn. 'Ensure he has methods for transporting us that won't attract unwanted eyes. Halvar, you said earlier that we should use every available minute.'

'Aye, lord.'

'So we begin the transfer on Monday. I'll make the request of Atilius and he will ensure the logistics are ready. He'll send codes to each of your troops selected to leave, so they know to be prepared and remain at home to await the drivers.'

'Monday, lord?' queried Radspakr, unable to hold his tongue and his mind racing. Every time he believed he had arranged that Maitland brat's early death, the gods toyed with his plans. After his secret meeting in the Botanics, he had trusted that Cleitus' most loyal swords would despatch this particular thorn over the six Blood Nights. Yet now, not only was the Valhalla King removing Maitland's litter from the frontlines, he was sending them somewhere far away from Radspakr's grasping tentacles. The Thane would have no influence out there in the remote wilds of the Battle zone. 'Surely that's too soon to be practicable. The troops may not all receive the message. Atilius may not be able to confirm the travel arrangements.'

'He knows well enough that once the Time Asset is triggered by the Caelestia, we're entitled to make such a request of him and he will have his plans in place.'

Radspakr swallowed. 'Yes, lord.' He could feel the meeting slipping from him and tried one final tack. 'Housecarl Halvar, if I am not mistaken, Leiv is your best Hersir.'

Halvar fixed him with a hard gaze. 'Indeed, I consider Leiv to be my best Hersir, but Turid is my most experienced. And that's what my King asked me. Perhaps you've a better understanding of my Kill Squads, Thane?'

'Enough!' said Sveinn angrily. 'You've heard my decision. Freyja, your Ravens will lead on each of the remaining Blood Nights, tasked as always with finding Alexander's forces. Halvar, you'll inform Turid that Litter Two will be ready in Valhalla to give chase when the Ravens send word. Bjarke, you also will remain in Valhalla to command one half of

Hammer. I will release them when viable on the last three Blood Nights to give the Titans the impression of numbers and avoid any suspicion that the Horde is departing. Who is your trusted second, Jarl?'

'Ingvar, lord. Commander of the berserkers.'

'Then Ingvar will lead the Hammer Litters you send early to the Battle zone before your personal arrival at the end of the Blood Nights.'

Bjarke nodded his understanding.

'Jarl Asmund and Housecarl Halvar, you will both be in overall command of the troops that travel early. Use the time wisely. Learn everything about the terrain and evolve the battle plans. Train your troops hard. When the Titans at last make it to the Field, you'll reap devastation upon them.'

The council murmured assent.

'We are done. I'll make the necessary arrangements with Atilius. Good morning to you all.'

As they descended the stairs, Freyja was about to speak in Halvar's ear, when the King's voice came again. 'Housecarl Halvar, a word please.'

The Wolf commander returned to find Sveinn seated by his fire, but the King didn't beckon him to join. 'What is this thing between you and the Thane?'

'Lord?'

'There's bad blood between you – that much is obvious.'

'I simply don't expect the Thane to tell me how to run my Kill Squads.'

The King examined him. 'I haven't spent nineteen years in the Pantheon and risen to lead my own Palatinate without knowing when I'm being lied to, Housecarl. I suspect your differences are much more than you admit, but I also suspect they're not for the ears of a king.'

'If you say so, lord.'

Sveinn sighed. 'Be careful, Halvar. I wouldn't wish to count the Thane amongst my enemies. He plays this game better than most of us. And he also plays dirty.'

'I'm confident we can bury our differences, lord.'

'The Thane made a pointed remark about your Hersir Leiv. Tell me again, which litter does Leiv lead?'

'Four, sir.'

'Give me their names.'

'Olsen, Unn, Knut, Stigr, Ake and Punnr.'

Sveinn nodded thoughtfully. 'As I suspected. They will depart tonight.'

'*Tonight?*'

'I think it would be prudent. I will check that Atilius can sort the arrangements.'

'Yes, lord.'

'And you too, Halvar.'

'Lord?'

'You go tonight as well.'

XVII

In Stockbridge they slept late and it was nearing midday when Tyler was finally awoken by Lana emerging from her bedroom. She drew back the curtains and made drinks, while he pulled on his jeans and went outside for a cigarette. The snow had frozen and it was brittle beneath his feet. They dined on melted cheese on toast and coffees, him in his clothes from the previous night and she in pyjamas with tiny hot-air balloons and a cream dressing gown. He liked the "just woken" Lana. She was slower, less decisive, her hair rumpled and her face fresh and natural, like a youngster's.

They took a walk along the river and wound their way to Leith. They met a schnauzer like the one who lived below Tyler, and Lana made a fuss of it and asked him if he would ever like to own a dog. He shook his hands and said *no way*, then found himself thinking perhaps it would be nice; him and Lana and a schnauzer – in another life. They passed winter joggers and watched a group working out in the snow. They smirked as they thought of the Valhalla training vaults and the hell Freyja and Halvar had put them through. In Leith they ate a very late lunch of mussels, sea bass and drank a Marlborough white, then retraced their steps.

When they finally reached her cottage, she lit a fire in the grate and they collapsed on the sofa, red-cheeked and exuberant. As they watched the flames, it seemed natural to put his arm around her and she nestled into him. They talked quietly, but mostly they just listened to the snap of the burning wood and enjoyed the proximity of their bodies.

'You're different,' she mused after a long silence.

'How so?'

'There's an anger in you. A steel.'

'We're killers now. Things like that change people. Do you think less of me?'

She sat up to gaze at him. 'No. If I'm honest, I find it attractive.' Her hand came up to his neck. 'But you need to promise me something.'

'What?'

'Don't let it be the death of you. This game's dangerous enough without letting your anger make the decisions. I don't ever want you to leave me again like you did. When you fell at Old College, I really thought you were gone.'

He brought his own hand up to touch her fingers. 'Well, that goes for you too. I've spent weeks worrying about you. I've had the memory of you lying wounded in the castle locked in my head for an age. When I carried you down the steps, I didn't know if you were dying on me and I never want to feel that way again.'

'We started this together and we'll finish it together,' she said, her eyes on his lips. 'Promise me that.'

'I promise.' He leaned forward and kissed her, then drew back.

She could see the desire plastered across his face and she felt it reciprocated in the warmth of her belly. The years of preservation since her rape slipped away and for the first time she knew she wanted this man. This flawed and complicated man. She brought him back to her and gasped as they kissed again. She felt his arms wrap around her and instead of fighting his grip, she surrendered to it, rejoiced in the press of his body. She ran her fingers through the back of his long hair and worked her jaw to explore even deeper into his mouth. Her tongue danced with his. She tasted his saliva, felt the life in his breath and knew she didn't want this to end.

At last he broke the kiss, his cheek still pressed against hers. 'Oh Lana,' he whispered. 'I've barely been able to stop thinking about you. You're always there in my waking moments. I think – maybe – I'm falling for you.'

She pulled back at this and he thought he'd lost her, but there was a new light in her eyes and her mouth was parted in a tender smile. He kissed her hotly again and she let him, but then she pushed his face away once more and placed a finger on his lips.

'Not so fast.'

'Why?'

She put her head on one side and bit her lip coyly. 'Because what you just said, Tyler Maitland, makes this very special.'

'Okay,' he said, far from certain.

She rose unsteadily and kissed him on the top of the head. 'I'll open some wine.'

She went to the kitchen and he adjusted the tightness in his jeans, taking a long look over his shoulder at her bedroom. She returned with two glasses and another bottle of white. She cuddled into him again and they sipped while she played with his hair and ran her fingers over his neck and cheeks and mouth. He drank more deeply, took the glasses and placed them on the table and drew her back into him. Their lips worked together again, their arms around each other like clamps. Emotions cascaded from Tyler. Every black thought, every stress and tension, every fear left him, as though she were sucking them from his mouth. All he could think was how much this woman meant to him and how much he needed her.

He felt her shuddering against him and there was moisture coating their noses as well as their lips. He realised she was crying and the emotions ignited him still more. She dropped her face to let him caress her forehead and he ran kisses over her scalp and swept his fingers through her hair. But a new awareness was stealing beneath his passion and he grasped that her change had not been an invitation, so much as a disengagement. Gently, he tried to raise her head, but she was crying softly into his shirt and would not be moved.

'I'm sorry,' she croaked.

'What is it?'

She pulled back and her eyes were red-rimmed and moon-wide. 'I can't do this. Not now.'

He squeezed her hand and swept strands from her face, his ardour leaking out of him. 'That's okay. I understand.'

She retrieved a tissue from the sleeve of her shirt and held it to her nose. 'No you don't. It's not that I don't want to. I *do* want you. For the first time in years and years, I really want to. But not now. Not in the middle of these Blood Nights, with a Grand Battle looming on the horizon.'

'We can wait.'

She stared at him in earnest and gripped his hand hard.

'We *have* to wait. I can't risk giving in to my emotions and then losing you. I can't release my feelings when there may soon be Titan blades at our throats. I just can't do it. To have you and hold you tonight – and then see you fall in the Battle – well… it's too much. I've lost so much love in my life and I won't go through it again.'

Tyler knew she was remembering her daughter, Amelia, and the thought sobered him. 'I understand. I really do.'

He edged upright, but she clung to his hand. 'Live through the Battle,' she said earnestly. 'And then we have the months of the Interregnum to get to know each other properly. A peaceful, beautiful summer. No Pantheon. No blades and no death. Just us and a world to explore.'

He smiled. 'That sounds good.'

'Three weeks, a month. That's all.'

He reached out and wiped the damp from her cheeks. 'Maybe I should go.'

She looked disappointed, but she nodded in agreement. 'Maybe you should.'

He rose and tucked in his shirt, then fumbled with his shoes. She grabbed the holdall with his clothes and tucked the photo and amulet into it. 'Don't forget these.'

He pulled on his coat, slung the bag over his shoulder and stepped to her. He placed a tentative hand on her hip and she wrapped her arms around him in a tight hug. 'What you said about falling for me, Tyler Maitland – I want you to know it meant such a lot.'

She raised her face and they kissed gently.

'We get through these weeks unscathed and then you come back to me in the Interregnum and say those words again.'

He smiled into her eyes and nodded. 'That's a plan.'

That's a plan?

Tyler crunched his way through the old snow with beating heart. His left leg complained, but his mind was lost in the permutations of what had just occurred. Could he have chosen a more trite response as his parting words before hobbling off into the night? Halfway along Stock-bridge, he stopped abruptly and retrieved from his pocket the fragment of envelope with her number. He would call, come up with memorable, weighty words to which they could both cling through the whirling torrents to come.

He pulled out his phone and only then realised it had been switched off since the previous afternoon. He powered it up and was about to tap in her number when he saw a new WhatsApp message flashing. Weirdly it was from a number withheld – which he didn't think was even possible on WhatsApp – and the message read simply, '*Embarkation Sat 21.00.*'

He checked his watch and saw it was already 20.10. With a growing feeling of unease, he strode rapidly back to Learmonth Place. As he rounded the corner to his block, he saw the headlights of a car waiting outside and knew instinctively that the occupant was about to send his life spinning onto an entirely new trajectory.

Three hours earlier a local taxi firm had taken a booking from a number the telephone company was unaware it even hosted, from an account in the name of Trajan Holdings. The driver had been waiting outside ever since and had climbed up to Tyler's front door on two occasions. She didn't care. Trajan Holdings was more than generously paying for her time and sitting in the overheated vehicle scanning Facebook and eating chocolate was a damn sight better than taking clients around the city in this weather.

She lowered her window as he approached. 'Number six?'

'Yes,' he said cautiously.

'You're late. I'm here to take you.'

He stepped to her window. 'Take me where?'

'Airport.'

He blinked at her. 'Now?'

She checked her watch. 'Supposed to get you there before nine, so you've got ten minutes to be back down here.'

'Okay…' He hovered uncertainly, then came to a decision. 'Okay, I'll be back.'

Inside the main door, he kicked the snow from his boots, heard the schnauzer bark, and trudged the flights to his floor.

'Oliver!' The lad was sitting on the steps outside his apartment, iPad on his lap.

'Where've you been?' he asked flatly. 'I've been looking for you for days.'

'I'm sorry, mate.' Tyler sat down next to him and put the bag on the step below. The boy seemed subdued and didn't make eye contact as he flicked through Instagram. 'You okay?'

'Yeah – just haven't seen you for ages.'

'I've been here sometimes, but I've been busy as well. We must have been missing each other.'

'Pantheon business?'

Tyler shrugged. 'Sometimes.'

'You're lucky.' Oliver continued moving through the photos without really looking at them. 'You haven't even asked me how I've been getting on searching for your sister.'

Tyler admonished himself. 'God, I'm sorry. Have you had any success?'

'Not really. I've kept running into dead ends. I checked her college database, her driving records, all gone. I even went in to get her national insurance number, but that's been deleted as well.'

'Bloody hell, that's doesn't sound good. Is that... is that what they do when someone dies?'

'Dies? Why? Do you think she might be dead?' Oliver looked at him now.

'I'm not actually sure sometimes.'

The boy shook his head. 'No, I don't think they do. They'd deactivate it, sure, but the system would get messed up if they deleted numbers completely. There'd be no history of a record. That's what makes it strange. Someone's been doing a brilliant job of ensuring your sister never officially existed.'

Tyler lowered his head. 'So we've no way forward.'

'Maybe not, I'm sorry. But I'll keep trying.'

Tyler held the boy's eyes. 'Thank you, Oliver – I really mean it. What you're doing is so important to me. I wouldn't ask you otherwise.' He patted the boy's leg, then remembered his father and quickly withdrew his hand. 'But be careful.'

'Why'd you say that.'

'Just be careful. There are people in the Valhalla Horde who would react very badly if they knew you were looking for my sister.' He glanced up the stairs. 'Your parents at home?'

'Mum is.' He lapsed into silence and began to swipe through photos again, then stopped and clicked the tablet off. 'Mum's kicked Dad out. It's my doing – I ratted on him.'

'Oh Jeez, Oliver, I'm so sorry.'

'It's fine.'

'Where is he now?'

'Don't know, don't care. Probably shacked up somewhere with his girlfriend or on his boat.'

'He's got a boat?'

'Just a little Sunray moored at Cramond, but there's room to sleep in an emergency.'

'Is your mum okay?'

'She's been looking for an excuse to dump him. Can't you hear the music?' Lively club tunes were playing from beyond the wall. 'At least *you're* back, Tyler.'

Tyler gazed down the stairs, thinking of the woman waiting on the street. 'To be honest, I'm not. I'm going away.'

'How long?'

'I don't know. Might be just a night, might be longer.'

The boy started to rise. 'Well that's just bloody marvellous.'

Tyler caught his hand. 'Hey, I'm sorry. I have to go. You know… Pantheon stuff.'

'Where are you going?'

'Don't know that either.'

'You just won't tell me.' He pulled his hand away and turned towards his flat.

'No, I *really* don't know. But… but I think it could be the Grand Battle.'

Oliver paused at this. 'Seriously? The Horde and the Sky-Gods?'

Tyler nodded.

'Wow. The *big* time. I hope it gets online so I can see it.'

'I suspect they'll be trying to avoid that.'

'Well, maybe it's you who needs to be careful,' Oliver said tentatively.

'I will, I promise. And when I'm back we'll spend time together finding my sister and you can show me everything you've done.'

'Okay, deal.'

An idea struck Tyler and he picked up the bag and beckoned Oliver to follow while he unlocked his apartment door and went through to the bedroom. 'Here, have this.' He handed the boy his laptop. 'There may be useful things on it. I used to send Morgan emails ages ago before she disappeared, things like that.'

Oliver took the item. 'Password protected?'

'Niflheim99.'

'You're weird.'

Impulsively, Tyler leaned down and gave Oliver a hug, and he felt the boy's free arm come round him and squeeze. 'You take care of yourself, young man. You need to be strong.'

'I wish I was coming with you.'

Tyler waited until Oliver had disappeared, then stood indecisively in his lounge. Could this really be the Grand Battle? Apprehension rippled through his gut. Barely two nights ago he had killed a person for the first time and almost attacked his own litter with a naked blade in Valhalla. If the plane waiting for him at Edinburgh really was taking him to the Grand Battle, he would be travelling as a man with few friends.

He emptied his sports bag and then added new warm items. He suspected that wherever he was going, it was unlikely to be hot. He scanned around the room and rattled his brain for anything he might have forgotten. He already wore his thickest winter coat. His Odin amulet was safely round his neck. He tapped his pockets. Wallet. Cigarettes. Lighter. Phone.

He pulled out his mobile and wondered about contacting Lana. Maybe a text to explain he was being called away, but he thought better of it. She had agreed to exchange numbers on the condition they were used only in emergencies and if it was the Battle, she could well have a driver arriving at her place too. Wherever this journey was taking him, he hoped she would be at the other end.

He closed the front door behind him, debated whether to leave the key in the discarded wellies, then pocketed it and headed down the stairs.

Yeah, yeah, schnauzer, you know it's me. He stepped out into the cold air. *Okay, Pantheon. Let's do this.*

'Where are we going?' he asked from the back seat as she drove around the flank of the terminal and past rows of planes.

'Private charter.'

They arrived at a low-slung building sitting alone at the edge of the airfield, with the name *Signature Support* over the door.

'Have a good one.'

'Hello, sir,' said another lady as he pushed inside, this one in a smart purple uniform. 'Welcome.'

He stopped in his tracks in consternation as it struck him that he had no passport, no documentation at all, but she read his thoughts. 'You don't need anything, sir. All taken care of. Enjoy your trip.'

She waved him through a second door into a lounge area, decorated with purple lamps, pot plants, and prints of the Forth Bridge. Squeezed into two chairs were Unn and Olsen, each holding a plate of sandwiches and a cup of espresso, which looked so tiny in their paws. A table on one wall held more sandwiches and standing around it – like attendees at a humdrum business conference – were Leiv, Stigr and Ake.

The last occasion he had seen his litter had been in the tumult of Sveinn's Throne Room when he had been brandishing his bloodied sword and cursing their very existence. Now he faced them again and it was so alien to see them in civvies. These warriors of Valhalla who had left him to die above Canongate were extraordinary in their mundanity. Stigr's hard body was covered by a fitted Ralph Lauren jumper. Leiv wore a Scotland rugby top over chinos. Olsen sported a Rab down jacket and Unn a purple jumper. No, Punnr corrected himself, Ake would draw an eye. Her skinhead and pale complexion still exaggerated the granite of her eyes, and her rock chick outfit of skinny black jeans, grey T-shirt and leather jacket somehow complemented her screams of defiance when the Titans had advanced.

'Well, I'll be,' wheezed Olsen from where he was wedged into his chair. 'The damned prodigal son's decided to make an appearance. We were going to leave without you.'

Punnr edged to the chairs on the other side of the room,

dropped his bag and removed his coat. 'You seem to make a habit of that.'

Ake laughed hollowly and Olsen snorted and returned to his sandwiches.

'I'm guessing you didn't read your message,' said Leiv.

'Am I late?'

'Halvar's with the pilot. We've just been waiting for you.'

Punnr's lunch with Lana in Portobello seemed a long time ago and his stomach craved the sandwiches, but he refused to approach the table and affiliate with the group.

'Is it just us?'

'It would seem so. We're the vanguard. We will be joined by greater numbers in forty-eight hours.'

The tension in the room was palpable. Stigr studied him silently over a vol-au-vent. Unn kept her eyes on the carpet. Olsen stuffed his sandwiches and farted.

Through the wall came the sound of a hand dryer and then a door opened and Knut entered, zipping up his jeans. He was wearing a plaid lumberjack shirt and his long silver hair was tied back in a ponytail. He stopped and swore beneath his breath when he saw Punnr, his eyes diamond-hard. Then he continued to the table, grabbed a bottle of beer, wrenched off the top and took a long swig.

'Looks like I owe you, Stigr,' he said, wiping his beard on his shirtsleeve.

'It seems so.'

Knut jabbed a finger at Punnr. 'I had a hundred riding on you being a "no-show". My friend here reckoned you're made of sterner stuff. Says you've got guts.'

'Twelve Seasons under your belt, Knut,' Stigr said. 'But the lad here walks into Valhalla and puts a blade to your face. Cuts you in front of the whole Palatinate. I don't think I've ever questioned his guts.'

Punnr forced himself to shrug. 'So what? Am I supposed to be flattered?'

Knut scowled, but left a riposte bottled in his throat.

'Well that's in the past,' said Leiv. 'He's a Wolf now.'

'I thought I became a Wolf at the Oath-Taking.'

'It might say that on the packet,' continued Stigr. 'But you have to earn a position in a Wolf litter.'

'So you could say we did you a favour the other night,' added Olsen. 'Left you to kill that Titan and earn your place.'

'Thanks,' Punnr snorted, the word dripping with sarcasm.

'And not just any Titan,' Unn added. 'You took down a Companion, one of their elite.'

Punnr glanced at Ake, but she kept her lips sealed.

'Well,' he said brusquely and marched to the table to grab a handful of sandwiches. 'I'm here now. And if you don't like it, you can go fuck yourselves.'

'About bloody time,' came a booming voice from across the room and Halvar stomped in from the cold. 'Where the hell have you been?'

'There wasn't much notice.'

'Right you lot, time to go. Phones off.'

Punnr pulled his phone out and thought of Lana. He still had the scrap of paper with her number in his pocket, but he powered down the phone, then gathered his coat and bag.

'What've you got in there?' Olsen laughed. 'A nice little blow-up girlie to keep you warm at night?'

Punnr realised no one else carried anything. He

shouldered his bag irritably and they headed out across the slushy tarmac towards the lights of a Hawker Beechcraft 900.

Halvar drew close and looked at him quizzically. 'You okay?'

'Oh I'm fizzing with bonhomie.'

'They were debating whether you'd turn up.'

'And what did you think? Maybe you were wondering if all the Maitlands do runners.'

Halvar's brows came together. 'That's uncalled for.'

They clambered into a cabin the likes of which Punnr had never experienced and sank into huge cream seats, each with its own window. In minutes, they were underway and the plane taxied past larger jets. Once they were airborne, the others reclined their seats and sipped wine served by an attendant, but Punnr stared out the window and watched the lights of the airport recede. He guessed they ran east down the Forth, because he could see the city's golden glow to their right and then the bridges below. They flew over the little coastal villages of Fife, but then the plane climbed and cloud enwrapped them.

Hot food was served not long afterwards and Punnr bit hungrily into the sausages, mash and thick Dijon gravy.

'Don't get used to this,' warned Halvar from the seat behind.

After he'd eaten, Punnr made his way down to the small bar at the back. Knut was already asleep in his chair, Unn too. Ake was reading a music magazine. Stigr and Leiv were leaning on the bar, drinking shorts.

'You want a drink?' Leiv asked.

'Whisky.'

Stigr was silent while Leiv poured a generous measure from an Edinburgh Whisky Society bottle.

'Are we heading to the Field?' Punnr asked. The whisky was good, warming his throat.

'Aye.'

'Any idea of our destination?'

'Of course not, no one knows. But it looks like north or north-west to me.'

'How can you tell?'

'The turn we made soon after we lost visibility. It's nearly always north or north-west, because that's where the wild country is.'

'And the cold,' said Stigr without looking up from his drink. 'The Pantheon usually makes us freeze.'

It was less than an hour and two whiskies later, when the instruction came to buckle up and they felt the aircraft begin its descent. Punnr leaned into the window again but there was nothing to be seen. They heard the wheels come down and still he kept searching for lights, for anything, but the night was impenetrable.

'What the hell? There's nothing out there.'

'Must be still in the cloud,' said Knut from the seat opposite and no sooner had his words spilled out than there was a thud of impact. It was fair to say a few of the Wolves blurted their surprise, believing they had been several hundred feet up. The aircraft was sliding and crunching over a terrain that felt nothing like a runway and yet the night beyond remained utterly black.

'Where the fuck are we?' said Olsen from the back.

The plane slowed, began a turn and at last Punnr saw a sparsely lit building with vehicle headlights in front of it.

They came to a halt, the door was opened and the steps extended. He retrieved his bag and walked out into a night utterly different from the one they had left. A strong wind was blowing and the air that greeted them was sharp, clear, electrifying and deeply scented with the smells of the coast. They descended and trod onto soft, sinking ground.

'It's a bloody beach,' exclaimed Knut. 'We landed on sand!'

Ake knelt, powered up her phone and switched on its light as she took a handful in her palm. She pulled the fragments apart and Punnr bent to watch.

'Not sand. Billions of tiny, granular pieces of white cockleshell, pulverised over millennia by the ocean.' She looked at Punnr. 'I know where we are.'

XVIII

The killer stole so expertly into the block that even the dog didn't hear him. He hadn't, however, accounted for the lad sitting at the darkened upper floor window, who had watched him all the way down the empty street to the locked front door. The man noiselessly climbed the stairs wearing night-vision goggles, identified number six with the wellington boots outside and listened intently, ear to the door. He slipped a card into the crack, eased the latch and entered.

In his rucksack, he carried several items wrapped to muffle any sound. A stainless steel spoon and lighter, both dirty, smeared and ready for the victim's fingerprints to be transferred to them; a leather belt for a tourniquet, which would also be liberally peppered with his fingerprints and teeth marks; a capped needle; and two small syringes, one containing an undetectable, but lethal, cocktail, and the other a potent mix of heroin and eight milligrams of fentanyl. In his jacket pocket he also carried a face mask and third syringe, this one containing highly concentrated liquid sevoflurane. The victim would fall into a sleep from which he never awoke and the world wouldn't mourn the passing of another addict.

The killer stood in the lounge, took in every detail through his goggles and listened for any sound. He peered cautiously through the first bedroom door and saw a small room with sacks and exercise bags. He stepped to the next door, which was pulled closed. Listening again, he reached for the face mask in his pocket and screwed the syringe of sevoflurane onto it. Readied, he eased the door open and stepped towards the bed.

His night vision told him instantly there was no occupant. The duvet was thrown back and various items of clothing had been thrown on it. He checked the pillow for warmth, opened the cupboard doors, then stole around the rest of the flat until he was certain he was alone. Someone had cocked up.

He was just unscrewing the syringe and returning it with the face mask to his pocket, when there was a thud from beyond the front door and a small oath. Fast as a cat, he bounded across the room and sprang through the doorway. The welly boots had been knocked flat and a slim figure was stepping hurriedly back into number five opposite. For a heartbeat, the figure turned and streetlight from the window on the stairs caught naked fear on the features. A lad – a young teenager. Then the door closed and the lock clicked.

The killer considered his options. He was unmasked and there was every reason to suspect the lad could have seen his face. The cleanest solution would be to deal with the issue there and then. The lock of number five would likely surrender as easily as six and the lad would be a simple enough victim. But the killer was carrying only items for a very specialised death and bore no other tools of his trade.

What's more, there was no telling what company the lad kept in the flat. Most importantly, the money for this job didn't extend to collateral killings.

He pulled the door closed behind him, rearranged the boots, and departed.

Radspakr read the message on his phone and then deleted it. He was standing in his kitchen and the noise of the waves coming off the Forth penetrated through the windows and roared down the chimney, making the flames in his wood burner dance a jig. It was late and he'd been waiting expectantly for news.

In truth, this whole business with contract killers left a bad taste in his mouth. He was a proud Viking – an even prouder Thane – and he had spent twenty years believing problems were best solved on the edge of a blade during Conflict Hours. He had hated himself for sanctioning the attack on the woman called Calder in her Stockbridge home and he had perhaps felt a trickle of relief when its failure meant he must send Ulf and Erland to kill her more honourably at the castle.

But Tyler Maitland was becoming an altogether more resistant and unsolvable problem. Radspakr had clung to his belief that the answer lay with the Pantheon's blades and he might also give the lad an honourable death. He had ensured Punnr became Valhalla's White Warrior and thought it would be enough to watch him fall. When that failed, he had used his channels to Fat Cleitus to equip the Titans with everything they needed to kill a four-credit Blood Virgin.

But, no, Tyler Maitland simply would not die. And every week he lived increased the risk that Odin might learn of this man's presence in his Palatinate and of his Thane's incompetence. It was a danger too great for Radspakr. He was not about to lose everything he had built for his Horde.

He walked through to the sitting room and stared out of the bay window, where the white foam of the rollers could be seen beyond the cliff. But now this devastating news. Radspakr had once more resigned himself to the necessity of a contract killing and it had once more failed. Maitland had departed for the Battle.

Well that was it then, nothing more he could do. *Christ, what a mess!* Sveinn had said the Palatinate would begin transferring on Monday, so why the hell would Atilius start moving them that very night? He had thought he still had time.

Now what? Maitland was gone and Radspakr had no more knowledge of the location of the Grand Battle than anyone else in the Horde. Atilius and his Pantheon authorities were zealous about their secrets and merciless in their mischief-making. Even once the location was officially revealed, the Thane wouldn't travel to the Battle, so his hold over Maitland was gone.

And what of this boy on the stairs? Who the hell was he and why had he been snooping about at that hour? Like a wildfire on the Langholm grouse moors, every time he thought he'd stamped out the last flame, another flickered into life.

XIX

They were driven through the darkness in three Land Rovers, Punnr sharing the second with Ake and Olsen. The road twisted and turned and he had a sense of the sea always close to hand forcing them back against the safety of the landmass. Olsen seemed disinterested and soon dropped his chin onto his chest and dozed in the front seat, but Ake sat straight and stared into the night.

The Hebrides, she had told them on the beach. The Outer ones. Only on that chain of islands could you find the white shell beaches that shone like snow on sunny days. Knut had never even heard of them and most of the others greeted her news with indifference, although Leiv pondered the strategic significance of being on an island. Once in the vehicles, Punnr surreptitiously extracted his phone, turned it back on and tried to pull up a map, but the internet refused to play, as though modernity had never beaten a path to this godforsaken place. Vaguely he had a mental picture of a group of islands far out from the north-west of Scotland, the final bastions of Britain, clinging to each other against the might and fury of the north Atlantic.

With a sigh, he powered it back down and looked out at the impenetrable night. A loneliness began to paw at

223

him again and Lana suddenly seemed very far away. The warmth and light of her house felt like a different planet. The softness of her touch and the scent of her skin.

His sister, too, seemed more adrift from him than ever. How the hell had he managed to join the wrong Palatinate and then get himself stuck on an island in the middle of nowhere? He might as well have stayed in his old flat on the estate, wasting himself on drink and drugs. At least there was a chance Morgan might have returned there one day. But out here? One thing was certain. His search for his sister was colder than ever.

The cars wound around a corner and drove through a small one-road town with a church, tiny supermarket, petrol station, pub, a few pebble-dashed houses and a harbour with a jumble of fishing boats. There were lights in the pub, but nothing stirred and they were through in moments and the night reclaimed them.

'So it's inhabited,' Punnr said.

'I kind of expected that. What with the road and airport.'

'I wonder what they think of hosting the Valhalla and Titan Palatinates while we kick the crap out of each other.'

'They'll be delighted. Whatever our Pantheon paymasters have deposited into the islanders' accounts, it'll be Christmas come early for most of them.'

They lapsed into silence again. Ake had kept her head turned to the window throughout the short exchange and Punnr wondered if she was always this cold. He recalled her expression just before she descended from the roof. There was no doubting she had thought she was taking a last look at a dead man. Little would she have believed she would soon be sharing a car ride with that same man across a wild island to the Field of Battle. He glanced at her sourly and was tempted to force the subject, get the words out while she did not have the others for support. But, instead, he swallowed his bitterness and let the beast of loneliness get back to scratching his gut.

The vehicles slowed and turned onto an even narrower road. They ascended steadily and Punnr guessed they were heading away from the sea, pulling up and over the spine of the island. They reached the top and momentarily the clouds broke and a shaft of moonlight revealed the road dropping away again, snaking into the distance to a broken coastline and an endless ocean beyond. Then the light snapped off and the driver cranked into a lower gear and leaned into the first corner.

The descent lulled Punnr and his eyes were growing heavy, when there was an almighty clatter under the tyres. Olsen sat up with an oath.

'Cattle grid,' said Ake and no sooner were they over than the lead car was pulling up and they knew the journey was complete.

They stepped out into the wind. The vehicle lights shone on heather, rock and a stony track leading away down the hill. The dark bulk of a truck was parked on the final section of tarmac and Halvar came alongside Punnr and pointed at it.

'Your supplies.'

'What do you mean *mine*?'

'You found the Supplies Asset. If you hadn't, there wouldn't be any damn truck there.' He peered around. 'Which is lucky, because I've a hunch there's not a bloody thing to eat on this whole island unless you fancy commandeering a fishing boat.'

The Land Rovers reversed over the cattle grid. Only then did Punnr notice two other figures, wrapped up against the elements. They closed a gate across the grid and padlocked it, then hurried back to the warmth of the truck and slammed the doors.

'Our Vigiles friends,' said Stigr. 'It doesn't matter where we go, we can never get away from those bastards.'

'You'll be thankful of them soon enough,' remarked Leiv.

'Okay you pups,' said Halvar heading towards the path. 'I guess it's this way.'

They felt their way down, stumbling against stones and tussocks. Olsen switched on his phone's torch, but Halvar shouted at him. 'Turn that bloody thing off! We're Vikings now.'

Gradually Punnr noticed they could see the track more clearly and it was opening up around them. He dropped to his knees and felt the ground. Cockleshell fragments. The track was becoming a beach and, sure enough, over the wind they began to hear the beat of waves. There was a grunt just to their left and something huge shifted.

'Odin's bollocks! What was that?' exclaimed Knut.

'A cow, you moron,' said Stigr.

'Cows on a beach. Now I've seen it all.'

A labyrinth of dunes closed in around them and Halvar pulled them to a halt while he climbed one and scanned around. He pointed right and led them off on a new course with the sound of the ocean now to their left. A few minutes later, the dunes finally relented and they walked out onto firmer ground. Ahead they could make out the bulk of a building. There were other shapes clustered around and Punnr realised with sinking heart, they were tents.

'This is going to be comfortable,' he said grimly to Stigr.

'What did you expect? A motorhome?'

Halvar led them to the building, pushed open a heavy door and ducked his head to enter. Inside, they could see nothing and it actually felt colder. There was a reek of damp stone and history. Leiv sparked a match, held it close to the wall and spied candles in an alcove. They passed them around, lit them and the place revealed itself to be a rectangular building, larger than they had expected, with small arched windows and a flagstone floor. At one end was a fireplace, next to which stood a box of kindling and a neat pile of earthen bricks.

'What the hell are those?' asked Olsen.

'Peat,' said Unn, bending to pick at one of them. 'A gift from the Vigiles.'

'That's not the half of it,' added Ake, who was walking down the length of the interior, holding her candle high to inspect the ceiling. 'It's all brand-new beams and planking. I'll warrant this place was roofless until a few days ago.'

'Aye,' agreed Halvar. 'And the fireplace is new stone. Hasn't been there long.'

'Why wouldn't a hall have a fireplace?' asked Leiv. 'Surely the most important requirement on this godforsaken rock.'

'Because it's not a hall,' said Ake. She was at the far end examining runes and script carved into the wall. 'It's a house of god.'

'A church?' said Knut. 'The Pantheon's putting us godless heathens up in a church? Odin's balls.'

Ake wasn't listening. She had found an arch in the side

wall through to another area and when they heard her laugh, they followed and clustered around. It was an antechamber stacked with trestle tables. On the first were bowls, cups and knives, fashioned in the style of Viking utensils, along with flagons of water, ale and wine, but on the others were modern airtight plastic boxes filled with meats, breads and fruits. There were more boxes on the floor labelled with their names. In each they discovered thick leggings, walking boots, black tops, beanie hats and waterproof jackets, as always the correct size.

'Hi-de-hi, campers,' said Olsen.

Halvar took charge. 'Right, Unn and Knut, get that fire going. The rest of you, check out the tents. They'll be four-berth. Get changed and put all the gear you're wearing into the boxes, including phones, watches, wallets, ciggies and any other damn thing that a Wolf of Valhalla wouldn't carry. The journey's over and we're the Horde once more.'

Punnr collected his new clothing and followed the others outside to the tents, where he stood in the dark watching Stigr select one and disappear inside.

'You're with us, Wolfling,' said a voice in his ear and he turned to find fat Olsen. 'Well, what are you waiting for? Accommodation not soft enough for you?'

Punnr bit back a retort and crouched to enter. Stigr had lit a single lantern, which hung from a cross beam and sent shadows careering around the interior. The tents were fashioned from oak frames, with sail canvas lashed over them, pegged deep into the compacted sand. The floors were layered with birch bark and furs and there were more furs and linen rolled at the edges for bedding. Above each entrance was a beautifully crafted oak dragon's head.

'Are these the real things?' asked Punnr as he struggled to get into the new clothing before he froze.

'Near enough,' said Olsen. 'Though they were rarely used on land. These would've been raised in the longships on cold nights.'

When he stepped back into the night, Punnr was thankful the clothing was warm. He placed his valuables in a box, lingering with his phone and wondering if Lana was tucked up asleep in her flat. Earlier that very same evening, he had glimpsed her bed through the open doorway and had even thought he might end up sharing it with her. Now he had the dubious pleasure of spending the next few hours pressed up against Olsen and Stigr.

He deposited his box and sports bag beside the door of the church and went inside to discover the others had brought furs from the tents to lay near the fire. They feasted on roast chicken, flatbreads, apples and ale, and Punnr ate his fill, although he sat removed from the group with his back against the wall of the old building, where the warmth of the fire made little headway.

The food and flames relaxed the others and the ale greased their tongues. He listened as they talked more easily. The light played on their features and his eyes slid from one face to the next. There were smiles now and the affable glances of sword-kin who had shared violence and bonded on fields of blood. They teased each other and swore good-naturedly and raised their beakers of ale. And instead of hating them, Punnr found himself angry because he was not sharing their fire and they did not seem to care.

The peat gave off a deep, intoxicating scent, while the flames cast light dancing across the walls and revealed

Latin and Celtic inscriptions. Ake – unexpectedly – was the storyteller, even her hard shell softening. She described how the Viking invaders, long ago, had brought their longships to wreak havoc on these shores. How they had stayed and colonised, creating the Kingdom of the Isles, ranging from Islay to Shetland, and divided between the *Sudreyjar*, the Southern Isles, and the *Nordreyjar*, the Northern Isles. She spoke of the conflicts and the bloodshed as each island group was controlled by a separate warlord and how a king called Somerled finally combined the Norse tribes under a single Lord of the Isles.

Halvar grunted his approval. 'It's right, we should be amongst our ancestors when we face the Titan foe. No Greek hoplite has ever set foot on these lands.'

'And it's right,' said Ake, 'that we should be here in this church of god. Our Viking forebears were not always heathens. Cuthbert brought Christianity to these isles in the early centuries and converted the Norse kings. Dane and Celt. The old gods and the new.'

Knut spat into the peat at this, but they listened closely enough to her words. Punnr watched her as she spun tales and decided he should know more about the ways of the ancients. If he ever got off this bloody island – if the bastards didn't abandon him to the foe again – he would read and research and learn about the Viking forebears.

'What you doing over there in the dark, Wolfling?' Olsen demanded suddenly and eyes turned to Punnr.

'Our company's not good enough for him,' muttered Knut.

'I think,' said Stigr, 'our Wolfling is still smarting from our sudden withdrawal above Canongate.'

'Get over it, lad,' Olsen growled. 'Decisions are made in the heat of a fight, whether you like them or not. It's nothing personal.'

'That's what you said to me on the roof,' Punnr replied coldly.

'What?'

'*Nothing personal.* Those were your last words to me before you swung your fat arse to the rear and ran away like a schoolgirl.'

Olsen shot his bulk upright with startling speed. 'What?' he roared again. 'You dare insult me? Here? Tonight?'

'Sit down,' said Halvar sharply.

Olsen jerked a finger at Punnr. 'You're lucky we have no steel to hand in this house of god or I'd carve you for that, boy.'

'I said, *sit down.*'

Olsen stayed upright, glaring across the flagstones, his mouth opening and closing in outrage. But no more words escaped and Stigr pulled at his arm.

'Leave the lad be. He said what he said. It's enough.'

'Bastard,' muttered Knut.

Olsen shot a final glare at Punnr and then sank back on his rump.

There was silence. The warriors stared at the fire and Punnr watched them from his place at the cold perimeter, more ostracised than ever.

And then Ake said something none of them expected. 'Maybe he's right.'

'What?' Olsen glared at her.

'Maybe we did run too soon.'

Knut swore and threw a bone into the fire. 'Trust a bloody woman to feel sorry for him.'

Ake tensed and for a moment Punnr thought she was going to throw herself at the older warrior and tear his throat out. But she gathered herself and said calmly, 'There were only minutes left of the Conflict Hours. Maybe if we'd stayed, we would have seen Punnr gut that Companion and the odds would have seemed more even. We thought we were just six Wolves up there, but we weren't. We were seven. So maybe we should have remained with Punnr, kept our shieldline tight and taken out more than just the one of those Titans. It would have been a glorious fight.'

The litter was quiet as they digested her words. It was true. There had been only moments left on the clock. They had assumed Punnr would collapse and leave a gaping hole in their line, but in fact he had stood firm – all alone – killed a Titan, earned his Bloodmark and escaped to tell the tale. Perhaps their line would have held. Perhaps they left too soon.

The possibility did not sit well with them. Olsen harrumphed and Knut swore under his breath, while Stigr drank his ale solemnly and Unn drummed her fingers on the stone floor. Punnr realised he had been holding his breath through this exchange, his eyes locked on Ake. He would never have believed this wild, hardened Valkyrie could utter such words. Words that were almost contrition. Almost an apology.

It was Leiv who broke his thoughts. 'I gave the order and if I gave it too soon, then I am at fault. It is right that you live, Wolfling, and that you're here with us now. We are seven in this litter. Seven hunter-killers. Seven Wolves. And on this island, before the battle lines are drawn, we will forge ourselves afresh.'

'Well said,' murmured Halvar.

'So will you join our fire?' demanded Stigr. 'Or are you still smarting like a babe?'

Punnr searched their faces and looked long at Ake, though she had not raised her eyes to him.

'I'm comfortable enough where I am,' he replied.

'Obstinate bastard,' growled Olsen.

'He'll fit right in then,' said Unn and some laughed, although Knut's eyes in the dancing shadows were still black with anger.

'Here,' said Stigr. 'You better have one of these for your lovely little corner.'

He flung over a fur and there was more laughter, though the tension would not leak from the building. They returned to their ale and to new subjects and Punnr sipped his drink and pulled the fur around him. He wondered if he should have accepted the offer to join them, but a little speech by Leiv wasn't going to wash away everything that had happened.

He sat morosely against the cold wall and gradually the late hour quietened the others. None wished for the unwelcome interiors of the tents, so they wrapped themselves in furs and pulled close to the peat and slept.

Oh my goodness, yes! Why hadn't he thought of it before? Oliver was ensconced in his bedroom, the hard drives blinking out a silent waltz above his head as he bent over his laptop. Outside the Sunday walkers kicked through the remaining slush as they exercised their dogs in the Gardens and in the next bedroom his mum was awake and on the phone already, bitching to a friend about her soon-to-be ex-husband.

His search had been stuck for over a week. Everything he tried hit a roadblock. Morgan Maitland simply didn't exist. Then this morning, over a mix of muesli and cocoa pops, Tyler's words came back to him. *She was a Titan. They called her Olena*. He googled the name and quickly found it meant *torch of light*.

He scribbled a dozen variations of this onto a pad – *torchbearer, torchlight, flames of light, beam of light*. Then he began studiously working through social media networks, searching for any one of these. It took him several hours, stopping only for a snack of peanut butter on toast. He came across numerous credible options but they all fizzled out. Finally, he found a username on one networking site called TorchLight96. Trawling through the conversations, he noticed several references to the Pantheon and a number of occasions when TorchLight96 corrected others on their knowledge of the Palatinates. Obviously he or she considered themselves something of an expert. The posts had stopped three months earlier on fourth of December, but Oliver was able to break into the site's database and learn that TorchLight96 was the username for someone called Olena Macedon.

Macedon, the ancient kingdom of Alexander. It seemed too good to be true. And the 96 fitted too. Tyler had said his password was *Niflheim99* and Oliver guessed that if Tyler was in his early twenties, the nines probably related to his year of birth; 96, therefore, seemed like an appropriate year of birth for his elder sister.

Oliver stared at the name on the screen. Olena Macedon. *Hello, Morgan Maitland. I think I've got you.*

XX

The Wolves breakfasted on flatbreads, fruit and watered wine warmed over the embers of the fire. The church was chilly and they stayed wrapped in their furs as long as Halvar would allow. Gone was their spirit of the night before. Now the elemental sounds of the wild enervated them as a wind jostled down the chimney, carrying with it the cheerless cries of seabirds.

Eventually, Halvar rose and poured water into one of the earthen bowls, stripped to the waist and trudged outside. Leiv too emerged from his furs and kicked Punnr.

'Come on, Wolfling. These pots won't clean themselves.'

Punnr piled utensils into his arms and followed Leiv out into the grey morning. They walked through the dunes to a crescent of white sand. The sea was quieter than he had expected, with low waves lapping against the shore and wind-whipped white horses rising only further out. Another island squatted nearby, barren and colourless in the dull light, and the sea ran fast through the intervening channel.

The two warriors scrubbed at the bowls in the frigid saltwater, making their fingers redden and burn. A longer wave caught Punnr by surprise and snaked up over the top of his boots.

'Christ,' he swore, stepping back.

'Tide's on its way in.'

'How d'you know?'

Leiv stopped his washing and raised a hand to point behind. 'That line of seaweed's the high-water mark, and if the tide was going out there'd be more birds.'

'You're well informed.'

'East coast fishing stock born and bred. Dad and brother still go out.'

Punnr gathered up his utensils and walked over to join Leiv, who was looking out to sea. 'There's a shark in the channel.'

Punnr strained his eyes, but could see nothing. Then a black shape broke the surface. 'Jeez, that looks big.'

'Would make a great white look like a slip of a lad.'

'Bloody hell.'

Leiv laughed. 'Don't worry, Wolfling, it would spit you out fast enough. It's a harmless basking shark, all thirty foot of it, and only interested in plankton.' The fin bobbed up again, black and slick. 'Must be good feeding out there.'

The Wolf Hersir studied the changing currents in the channel and grew serious. 'I meant what I said last night. If I gave the order too soon, then I'm at fault and for that I'm sorry. But Olsen's right, you need to get over it. Make peace with him and Knut, and train hard with the others. When we meet the Titans, I need a unified Wolf litter. I need a solid shieldwall. I won't carry any passengers in this litter and nor will Halvar. You're either with us or you're out.'

When they returned to the church, the others were up and dressed in their gear, most already wearing the waterproof jackets and hats for extra warmth. Halvar, pink-faced from his wash, gathered them round.

'Today the work begins. We have an island to explore before the others get here. By tonight I want to know everything about this place. What size is it? What terrain? Where are the woodlands, the mosses? What's accessible; what's not? Which way do the storms come? Where are the heights? The best vantage points? Which folds can hide an army? Locate me the airport again; find where we landed. The Titans will come from there and, remember, they'll only get here hours before the Battle.

'Most of all, look for the Field. Sveinn won't be informed of its precise location until twenty-four hours before conflict, but that doesn't stop us finding the damn thing first. We're looking for somewhere flat, with enough space for a Hammer shieldwall and a Titan Phalanx. Some cover for archers and Wolf attacks – but not too much because our esteemed Curiate audience want to be able to see us!

'So get out there and look. Keep off roads. Don't trouble the locals. They know what we're about, but that's no reason to get up close and personal. Make a note of anywhere that has potential to be the Field and we can whittle down the options over the next few days.

'Right, we'll divide into pairs. Unn, you're with me. We'll take east. Olsen and Knut, inland and then northeast. Leiv and Ake, hug this western coast and go north. Stigr and Punnr, take the coast south.' He glanced at the clouds through the high windows. 'What light we have will be fading in six hours. Keep an eye on it and get yourselves back before dark, because I'm sure as hell not coming looking for you. Let's go.'

They bustled into their pairs. Punnr pulled up his hood and followed Stigr into the dunes. They travelled in silence, keeping the sea close on their right as they skirted the bay. Stigr was shorter than Punnr, but he strode with the relentless pace of an athlete. His black face was riven with creases and his short, wiry hair touched with silver, and Punnr guessed he must be early forties. He kept his hood thrown back and Punnr could make out intricate tattoos etched across the back of his neck.

As they reached the far end of the bay, the land rose and they climbed away from the sand and onto wetter, more squelchy conditions. Their boots sank and muddied and they swore. Stonechats rose around them, flitting across the tops of the tussocky grass with their chac-chac call.

Despite the wind, Punnr found himself sweating to keep pace with Stigr and eventually he pulled to a halt and looked back. The church and tents nestled amongst the dunes beside the white-tipped sea and behind the land rose steeply onto a heather-clad moor. Squinting, he could see Leiv and Ake climbing. His attention was drawn east to a ribbon of tarmac running around the outer edges of the grassland where a vehicle was pulled up and several figures were watching them. He called to Stigr and pointed.

'Vigiles?'

'They've been there ten minutes,' he said without looking over his shoulder.

'Filming us?'

'Doubt it. This place is top secret. Even the Caelestia and Curiate are kept in the dark, in case word finds its way back to the Titans and we lose the advantage of gaining that Time Asset.'

'An Asset,' Punnr called as he trooped after the other figure, 'which *I* collected.'

'That you did,' was the only response.

They must have squelched and slipped and sunk across the ground for another forty minutes. Always to their right the land rose before giving way to the power of the water beyond.

'If they make us fight on this, it'll be a circus,' moaned Punnr.

'They won't.'

They dropped into a shingle bay and picked their way across the stones. As they ascended again, the land changed. The ground became firm and the long grass was replaced by closely shorn blades, littered with dung droppings.

'Sheep,' said Stigr and slowed his pace to take in the surroundings. The turf was like a carpet, one side ending abruptly on the sea rocks and the other rising to meet the flanks of a hill.

'This looks more likely,' said Punnr.

Stigr took his time replying, but then agreed and they walked on. A squadron of oystercatchers ran in front of them, piping madly as they took to the air. The turf continued uniformly ahead, but then Stigr stiffened and stretched to look into the distance. Punnr followed his eyeline and spied a dip running across their path. As they approached, the dip widened and deepened into a ravine dropping to the freezing waters where the sea had mustered its forces over millennia and broken through the land's defences.

Stigr stared down into it, then began to walk inland to find a way around. It took them ten minutes to pass the obstacle and continue walking. They reached a low summit and paused to look back.

'I'm guessing that puts a downer on this being the Field?' asked Punnr.

'No chance of a shieldwall battle with that thing in the way. And the Curiate love their shieldwalls. Besides,' he continued, turning on the spot, 'there's no places for their cameras. Atilius wants a location where his Vigiles can film unobstructed and he wants different options to ensure the best angles and close-ups. He loves those death blows in 4k technicolour.'

They continued south for another two hours, but the land always sloped or dropped to rocky bays. They saw no sign of human habitation or anything manmade; even the sheep had long since deposited their droppings and departed. Only gulls, terns, oystercatchers and the constant song of the wind kept them company. Gradually the view began to open up and the sea stretched fingers from the west to creep across the horizon. They were nearing the southern extremes of the island and beyond was a vast panorama of white-foam waves.

They halted on the sea rocks and looked out. The wind had shifted direction and was thumping into their backs from the north. To their left, the southern coastline spread away in high cliffs and deep inlets. Impassable terrain. Punnr turned his face into the wind and swore. The grey clouds were yielding to a much darker mass and already the island's central hills were disappearing from view behind sheets of rain.

'Time to go?'

'I think so.' Stigr yanked his hood over his head and they

hurried back the way they had come. Minutes later, the rain stampeded into them with a physical blow.

'Shit!' yelled Punnr. Despite his coat, the wet infiltrated every nook and cranny of his body, snaking beneath his underlayers and pouring into his boots. The seabirds disappeared and the ravine, when they finally reached it, had been turned into a seething, deadly obstacle. Chilled to the core and half blinded, they reached the muddier grassland and stumbled into a quagmire. Afterwards, Punnr couldn't recall how many times he fell, how many times he cursed the gods or felt Stigr's firm hand yanking him up and shoving him on.

Finally, they dropped to the dunes and trudged disconsolately through the sticky sand to the church. Ake and Leiv were there and they'd started the fire again. The newcomers stripped, wrapped themselves in furs and laid their clothing around the hearth.

Ake passed a cup of warm wine to Punnr and he gulped gratefully.

A few minutes later, Unn and Halvar arrived. They were soaked, but not as muddy. Speech was too much effort and Halvar simply growled and grabbed the proffered wine.

Later, Punnr roused himself, picked up his clothing, as well as Stigr's, carried it outside and wrenched, beat and rinsed it of the mud as the rain hammered down. Hauling everything inside the doorway, he squeezed each item as dry as his strength allowed, then laid them again around the fire. Stigr nodded his thanks and Punnr could feel the eyes of the others on him.

Night crept in and they lit the candles. The Vigiles had visited in their absence and they found new boxes containing fillets of fish stuffed with capers and anchovies, which they grilled and ate with flatbreads warmed on stones by the flames. Afterwards, the three separate parties described what they had seen and they began to build a mental picture of the area. For the most part, though, they just listened to the relentless drill of the rain on the roof and retreated into their furs.

'Welcome to the Outer bloody Hebrides,' murmured Stigr.

'I wonder where Olsen and Knut can have got to?' Unn mused.

Halvar rumbled. 'If they've found themselves a nice warm inn, I'll flail them alive.'

Monday, mid-morning, and the man in the telecoms uniform stood on the front steps of the last block on Learmonth Place and rang the bell for flat number six twice, then tried number five three times. Satisfied, he pressed number one and an elderly man's voice answered. *Bingo*.

'Morning, sir, sorry to bother you. We had a call from the gent in number six to say his FTTH fibre-optic is down to ADSL speeds. I've checked the routing from exchange to street cabinet and all looks fine, as does the coaxial, so it may well be the receiver. The gent said he'd be at work. Would you mind letting me have access to his floor?'

'I'm afraid I don't have a key for his apartment.'

'That's no problem – I only need to get to the socket outside.'

'Well, I don't know. I'm not very good with all these

mod-con things. But I suppose I can let you up the stairs. Would you like a coffee?'

'That's very kind, sir, but I just had one.'

The buzzer went and he was in. He climbed to the top floor and rang the bell for number six. He gave it several long seconds, eyeing the lock as he waited. Good, a Yale tumbler. He retrieved a set of bump keys from his pocket, selected one and inserted it almost fully, then took out a small hammer, checked over the bannisters and hit the key hard once while simultaneously turning. *Bingo*.

Okay, part one of the job didn't require much. The client's orders were to photograph paperwork and take computer equipment. He pulled on latex gloves and roamed around the flat, opening drawers. He could find no computer, laptop, tablet or any other hardware, so he reverted to taking shots of papers with a compact camera. Mostly bills, statements, insurance, nothing out of the ordinary. There was a notepad with various thoughts and diagrams scribbled through it, so he snapped these as well. Then he tidied everything up, did one last circuit of the rooms, and went back outside.

Easy enough. Now for part two. He rang the bell of number five, waited, rang again and waited some more. No movement. He used his key again and slipped inside. This time the client had been much more specific. He padded around the property, touching nothing, looking into all the rooms before retracing his steps to the small bedroom at the front which, he deduced from a ceiling wallpapered with distant galaxies and a poster of some old sailing ship with shields along its sides, was the son's. He noted the hard drive stacks and the two laptops on the cluttered desk.

He placed his telecoms bag on the floor, pulled out the

camera again and photographed the desk from various angles so that he could replace everything exactly as he had found it. Then he began. First he checked the notepads and snapped anything the boy had written. Then he withdrew his own laptop from the bag, along with a very small screwdriver. Deftly he used the latter to remove the built-in hard drives from both laptops on the desk, inserting these one at a time into his own machine and thus bypassing any passwords and other security features that might have protected their contents. From there it was simple enough to break down any last defences and access the files.

Once downloaded, the man turned his attention to the stacks of portable hard drives above the desk. Retaining one of the copied laptop drives in his machine, he attached a cable to the first portable drive, but he couldn't get in. So he removed the alien drive from his machine, screwed it back into place in the first laptop, and inserted the drive from the second laptop. *Bingo*. The portable files came up and, one by one, he copied the lot.

Fifteen minutes after entering, he examined the photos he had taken of the desk and replaced everything in its original position, then walked back to the front door. A final scan around and he was gone.

XXI

Litter Four spent a desultory Monday continuing to explore their island home.

Olsen and Knut had finally returned the previous night when the others were bedding down. They admitted they'd become disorientated in the storm and walked for miles with no idea which direction they were heading. At last they'd reached a road and fastened on to this like a lifeline until they spied the lights of a vehicle. They had flagged it down and the driver – a local with a face as rugged as the coastline – took one look at them, thumbed them into the back and drove them to the gate by the cattle grid. Halvar was so disgusted he was incapable of swearing and simply rolled himself in his furs and left them to clatter about making a late meal over the embers.

By morning the wind had eased, but a sea mist had blown in, which refused to clear. The fine vapour droplets clung to everything, making the Vikings as chilled and sodden as the rain had done.

They had already determined that south held little of interest, nor north along the western coastline. Bogs, cliffs, bluffs and inlets broke the terrain and none of them could fathom Atilius selecting anything along its length to be the Field. So they hiked together back to the cattle grid, where the truck was now gone and Leiv wondered aloud if it was collecting more supplies, either from a plane or even a ferry that must surely ply the waters to the mainland. They fanned out in pairs and headed generally east over the central mass of the island.

It was mid-afternoon when they gathered once more at the church and compared notes. Stigr and Punnr had discovered the main town again, nestled around its harbour, beyond which sat the ruin of a castle on an outcrop in the middle of the bay. They'd explored closer and thought the surrounding livestock fields could be an effective battleground, being firm underfoot, well cropped and reasonably flat. Halvar, though, was sceptical and stated bluntly that the mist might have shrouded them that morning, but on a clear day every inhabitant in the town would have prime seating to watch the conflict without even leaving the warmth of their homes. Atilius, he suggested, was a man who valued privacy when it came to slaughter.

Leiv and Ake had found the airport again and taken note of the landing beach. A single plane was pulled up high to avoid the tide and the Land Rovers were parked nearby, but there had been no movement around the building. Unn and Halvar had come across a smaller community and taken themselves out onto swathes of machair grassland, which sloped down to the sea on the east coast. The mist stubbornly refused to reveal the full extent of the area, but both thought it the best potential site found to date.

Apart from a few wind-bent specimens cowering deep in folds, all agreed they had seen no trees. Whether it was the soil or the elements, these islands were obviously no home to woodland, which meant the Battle would be an open affair. No secrets, no ambushes, no initiatives seized from the depths of cover. As Wolves, this wasn't to their liking. In the presence of trees and shrubland, they could hunt with abandon; but a battle on the naked flanks of this island would become a brute struggle between the Hammers and the Heavies.

Halvar decided the mist would preclude any further exploration, so they returned to the church, where new boxes awaited them. Wrapped neatly in greased cloths to avoid any damage from salt or rain, they discovered their armour, shields and weapons. When Punnr pulled his chain mail *brynjar* into the open, he saw the single red Bloodmark freshly attached and thought of the man called Proteus, who was no more. Also wrapped in cloth was the arm-ring Odin had gifted him. He hefted it in his palm, then placed it to one side. This was not the time and place for such embellishments. They changed quietly and gathered again on the beach, wider now that the tide was retreating.

Punnr contemplated his companions. It was the first time he had seen them in the accoutrements of the Horde since the fateful Blood Night. Unn, Olsen and Knut – overweight in their walking clothes – now looked as strong as mules; Leiv, the east coast fisherman, had again the bearing of a Hersir; while Ake and Stigr – gaunt, lean, fast, shields slung with the insouciance of veterans – had a raw wildness about them, accentuated by the landscape around and the ocean behind.

No one commented on his Bloodmark, although he caught Knut squinting darkly at it and Olsen punched him on the shoulder, which he took to be some gesture of acceptance.

Halvar drilled them on the sand until the light failed. They closed together in a line, shoulders against each other and shields locked. Punnr recalled his lessons from the vaults during the early days of the Armatura. How to keep the shields tight. How to thrust underneath with a longsword, where the foe would be least protected. Cut them in the thighs; shatter their shinbones and stab up into their groins. He remembered how to focus not on the foe attacking him, but on the one attacking his neighbour to the right, because it was easier to drive his weapon at an angle between cracks in the shields and thrust into the exposed right flank of that warrior, while his own shield protected him from the nearest assailant and he had to pray that his comrade-in-arms on his left would look out for him.

There was an agreed pattern to their wall. Leiv took the centre spot, the place of honour. The bulks of Olsen and Unn wedged either side of him, while Stigr and Ake always took each flank. Leiv experimented with having Punnr slot in between Unn and Stigr on the right, but then swapped him with Knut, so that Punnr found himself hard up against Olsen's shoulder and the smaller, wiry frame of Ake. Locked in this line, they practised the advance, a steady repeated cycle of stepping forward, heaving their shields out, followed by a sword lunge. Each routine was accompanied by a howl and, as the afternoon evaporated,

Punnr found his own cry grow from a mere shout into something altogether more primordial.

In the last light, they practised a running advance and each time Punnr's shield unlocked from Olsen's, the big man swore at him. 'Get it right, you fool! I'm damned if I'm going to bleed because you can't keep your shield tight.'

'Useless turd,' growled Knut from along the line.

'Do it again,' ordered Leiv. 'No one's leaving this beach until I'm satisfied.'

Back and forth, they drilled. Then they switched into a diamond formation with Leiv as the point. Halvar stood on a dune and watched, letting Leiv command his litter as he saw fit. At last, blown from the exertions and barely able to see one another in the mist, they were dismissed and made their way back to the church.

They spent an age tending to their mail, blades and shields, wiping down, drying them, scrubbing at any spots, then greasing the metals and stowing them carefully back into their cloths. Only then were they allowed to stoke the fire, wash and change. Ake disappeared and returned glowing from a swim in the sea. Punnr stuck his head in a trough of rainwater and rinsed himself as best he could in the night air. Soon the smell of lamb cutlets roasting with garlic pulled them around the fire and Punnr was too cold to allow his pride to keep him away from the warmth. They ate in a tight circle, the cutlets blood-red, washed down with wine and ale.

Later still, as they relaxed and listened to Ake spin more tales of the ancient Norse Lords of the Isles, they were disturbed by commotion outside and the door was flung open. Into their somnolent circle trooped Litters One and Three, disorientated and slippery from the mist, but jubilant to find warmth and the smell of lamb. Brante was among them, beaming as he came to Punnr and grabbed him in a bear hug.

'There you are, you magnificent bastard!' He laughed.

The fire was stoked again and more cutlets and chicken thrown into pots. Halvar showed the newcomers the boxes of clothing that were once more piled in the antechamber, then ordered them to select their tents and change, and deposit their phones, wallets, watches and other sundry. By the time they returned, drier and warmer, the meat was cooked and they tore into it. Once the larger numbers of Hammer arrived, they would have to make use of the tents to sleep, but, for now, no one wanted to leave the welcome warmth of the fire and they would all bed down beneath the age-old Celtic inscriptions.

Halvar looked around as his troops chattered. *We are thin on number.* Trimmed from the thirty-two at the start of the year to just twenty-five, with seven of those remaining in Edinburgh to complete the Blood Nights under Turid's command and stop the Titans noticing the Horde was disappearing faster than the lamb cutlets. So the figures around the fire numbered only eighteen, a disturbingly sparse force. Nevertheless, these were his Wolves and when the slaughter began, they would be the troops on which the fate of Valhalla turned.

*

Several hundred miles away and on the other side of Scotland, Radspakr sat in his quarters below the Royal Mile and digested every word of a report, as nausea fingered its way up his spine. An hour earlier the specialist agency had completed its analysis of Tyler Maitland's and Oliver Muir's copied hard drives and sent the report as a heavily encrypted WhatsApp attachment to its client. The Thane had shut himself away and stared at the screen, scrolling back to key points and rereading.

Maitland's laptop had revealed few dramatic surprises. There were emails to and from his sister in the weeks before she disappeared, but nothing significant. The agency had searched on her email address and pulled up a few titbits, but Radspakr had found these himself long ago and they told him nothing new. Tyler's records showed he had conducted new searches for her since then, but with no success. He had also been searching on terms that were linked to solving the riddles in the Raiding Season, which was fair enough. Interestingly, Tyler had also attempted to find out more about Lana Cameron. So the man had a thing for the Raven Calder. He had suspected as much, but this was useful ammunition.

It was the young teenager's hard drives, however, that fascinated the Thane. Oliver Muir. A new name to him, but one that was suddenly becoming critical in this shambles. It was clear this lad – this neighbour – had become a close confidant of Maitland and party to far more information than any individual should if they wished to lead a long and peaceful life. For starters, he appeared to know everything about Maitland's position in the Pantheon, an outrage in itself, but one that paled compared to the subsequent revelations. It would seem that Muir had played a proactive part in finding the solutions to the Raiding Season riddles and then downloaded every fleeting video image of the corresponding Pantheon activities and posted them on fan sites. He was a focal point in the spread of online analysis and gossip about the Palatinates. Indeed, there were occasions when he even hinted he had insider connections into Valhalla.

Worse, though, far worse, Oliver Muir had spent the last few weeks searching extensively for Morgan Maitland. College databases, NHS records, DVLA, HMRC. This kid was good. Yet everything had drawn a blank and this fact gnawed into Radspakr's gut.

As Thane of the Valhalla Horde, Radspakr had privileged access to the personal details of every warrior in his Palatinate, as collated by Atilius' Pantheon logistics teams. He didn't, however, have any information about troopers from other Palatinates. Last year, when Halvar had admitted his relationship with a Titan, Radspakr had pressed and pressed for her name, but Halvar had refused to give up that information. The Thane could only accept and fan the flames of treachery, bringing Odin into the arrangement so that he could rig the Blood Season and gamble fortunes on the outcomes. For a few weeks the money flowed and the Titan body count exploded, culminating in their disastrous raid into Valhalla and the pruning of so many Companions, along with the head of Timanthes.

When the woman had disappeared, however, Halvar still refused to give up her name even under threat of crucifixion, and Caelestis and Thane had been forced to relent. Time passed. The Nineteenth Season kicked off and life returned to normal. Radspakr would have thought no more of it until Tyler Maitland appeared in his life and the man's indiscretions culminated in him revealing a photo to the Thane. From that moment, Radspakr knew the Titan traitor had been Tyler's sister and she was called Morgan.

Armed with this name, Radspakr had searched for her. He must locate her and stub out the threat. But even with the services of a professional, it had brought no joy.

Now there was this kid. This Oliver Muir, popped up out of the blue. And this lad could steal into data stores Radspakr had never even considered. Muir had broken down every last online hiding place for Morgan Maitland and come up empty-handed. Which meant, either Morgan was a world-class cyber fugitive, or some other hand – an unseen, supremely capable one – had hidden the trail for her.

He scrolled through to the end of the agency's report and stared at the final statements. Muir's last efforts had taken him to a small, low-profile chatroom and from there to new searches using the name Olena Macedon. That had to be a username for Morgan, it was too much of a coincidence. Christ, the boy was getting close.

Sweat glistened on his brow and his arms ached with age. This mess kept growing limbs and he was less and less certain how he could contain it. Halvar, Tyler, Calder and now Oliver Muir. All of them knew too much of how Odin had undermined the pillars of the Pantheon. Pillars of inalienable principle stating that no member of the seven-strong Caelestia – each an owner of their own Palatinate – could use illegally gained information to cheat the odds and make a cash killing. It was even more forbidden that such information could furnish an attempt to undermine, maim or destroy another Palatinate. There might be no love lost between Caelestes, but honour remained a requirement. Such illegitimate and prohibited activities, if discovered, could only lead to the ejection of the guilty Caelestis from the Pantheon, the stripping away of all privileges, the removal of Palatinate ownership, disgrace amongst Odin's wealthy Pantheon peers and, if truly unlucky, a single dark torturous journey to Erebus.

Radspakr was not about to join Odin in that downfall. He had devoted twenty years to the building of the Pantheon. He had been there right from the beginning when the Rules were forged by the Seven, when he and Sveinn were first given their fledgling Palatinate. Radspakr had dedicated himself to the Horde. He had led the construction of Valhalla beneath the Mile, extending the Tunnels, fortifying the Gates, designing the grandeur of the Halls. He had mastered Palatinate finances and prided himself on recruiting the best Drengr from the Schola. Valhalla had become his life and his love – and he would do whatever it took to hold on to it.

He pushed his chair away from the desk and leaned forward, elbows on knees and head between his legs. He felt faint. His breathing came in short gasps and his heart rattled. It was a panic attack. He had suffered from them in the early years when the Pantheon's demands were so stressful and he knew the tell-tale signs. He tried to slow his breathing, but it only made the dizziness worse. He scrunched up his eyes as waves of adrenaline coursed through him, cramping his muscles.

If truth be told, it wasn't the threat of Erebus that terrified him, it was the burgeoning conviction – heavy as lead in his stomach – of what he must do next.

XXII

Pop music blared from speakers nested into the ceiling tiles, but Lana didn't notice. She was too busy studying her figure in the mirror on the back of the changing room door. She had been perusing the clothing store for the last hour, holding items against her, smiling with the girls assisting and disappearing into the changing rooms to try on another piece. This particular top fitted beautifully and she liked the curve of her waist in it. She revolved on the spot and looked at her reflection over her shoulder. Decision made, she returned to the lights of the shop floor.

'I'll take this as well.'

'Perfect choice, madam. The colour really suits you.'

It was rare for her to go on a shopping spree, but Lana felt energised. Partly it was due to her escape from the grasps of the hospital and the strength flooding back into her core, but also she knew she owed her lightness to the man who had walked with her along the Leith and eaten her tagine so ravenously. The man who had slept on her sofa, then kissed her with more than just raw passion. Despite her head telling her she was a fool, her heart was flowing with emotions she had almost forgotten. Her scar no longer throbbed and her body felt ready for whatever challenges lay ahead. Ready for the Pantheon and ready, perhaps, even for Tyler Maitland.

She flashed a grin at the till assistant and took her bags out into the evening light of Princes Street. Buses and trams surged by and shoppers weaved around each other. Up on the Mile the ancient buildings were silhouetting against a pinking winter sky. She made her way along the street, stopped to study window displays, placed a few notes into a hat next to a man curled up inside a sleeping bag, and diverted to buy a takeaway coffee. Somewhere a busker was playing bagpipes and the melody floated above the traffic. There really was no city like Edinburgh and she was just beginning to love it again.

She crossed Princes Street and ascended The Mound, over the railway and past the galleries. Princes Gardens were dark now and she remembered hiding in the trees, arrow notched, watching while Punnr the White Warrior raced for the next clue. She turned up Cockburn Street and slowed her pace as she thrilled to the scents of the restaurants. She wandered a little way up to a vintage antique shop and stood sipping her coffee. When she was done, she pulled away and considered her options. The streets were still buzzing, so Victoria Terrace would be too crowded with diners and Blair Street full of drinkers. So North Gate it would be, on Warriston. She retraced her steps to the bottom of Cockburn, then began the long hard climb up Warriston's many steps. She revelled in her strength, taking the steps fast and easing past other pedestrians without breaking breath.

She came to a small metal door that resembled the rear entrance to a kitchen and loitered. Cameras above the door allowed the Hammer Guards to see her and to note when the steps were empty. She waited for the pedestrians to pant past her and for a man to skip down the other way, then she glanced at the camera and, sure enough, the door clicked open.

'Evening.' She beamed at the guard once she was through the secondary door and he grunted his response. She still carried her shopping bags, purse and coffee, and guessed he would share grins with his fellow Hammers, but she didn't care and strutted down North Tunnel to the changing areas.

Not long after, changed and her hair pinned up into a bun, she made her way to the Practice Rooms and began with gentle stretching exercises. Then she moved to boxing, strapping her hands and striking the practice dummies in bouts of increasing intensity. She built up a sweat, but her arms felt good and she pounded the leathers. Next she took herself to the mats and eased into the Muay Thai kicks, which had been her speciality these last few years. Again and again, she struck the hanging pells with the heel of each foot.

When she was ready, she took a wooden sword from the storage baskets, weighed it, extended it out before her, then returned to the largest pell and began a series of strokes. Faster, harder, beating the thing into submission.

'Looking good, *Cold Waters*,' said Freyja, standing in the doorway.

'I'm feeling good, ma'am. It's great to be back.'

'And I'm glad to have you. Are you fit and healed?'

'Absolutely.'

'Good. There's much riding on us. The Titans are ahead in this Blood Season and our Wolves are gone.'

'Gone?'

'Advance party to the Grand Battle, just Litter Two remaining.'

'Oh.'

Freyja saw the shadow of disappointment flit across the other woman's features. 'But don't worry, Raven, we'll join them in a few days. First though, there's the small matter of the remaining Blood Nights. I need you ready and primed. We'll be Valhalla's vanguard and we have ground to make up in the Cull. So keep with the swordplay. You'll have a real blade in hand soon enough.'

Odin studied her, entranced. The curve of her neck. The dark jewels of her eyes. Her skin, so much paler than he'd expected.

My god, you're beautiful.

Next to him, his companion was impatient and wanted to get on with it, but the man was a goddamn fool. It was moments like these that made it all worth the effort. He raised himself from his crouch and straightened to see her better.

Diceros bicornis. Black rhino. Critically endangered. Gone from Angola's Chobe Valley, Namibia and Botswana. Gone from the Transvaal, Chad, Cameroon, Nigeria, Ethiopia and South Sudan. Conservation status unclear in Liberia and Burkina Faso. Lost almost entirely to human eyes. A legend. A phantom.

Yet here she was. The last of her kind. The final south-central black rhino in a region that had once ranged from KwaZulu-Natal through Tanzania and tracts of Kenya, which had once comprised thousands of miles of pristine savannah grassland and thornbush, broken only by rocky kopjes and soda lakes. Officially she didn't exist. No one was supposed to know she still felt the African sun on her back or heard the *chrr-pop… pop… pop* call of the boubou as she maintained her lonely vigil amongst the acacia trees and baobabs.

But he knew. His dollars had sought out the right officials, the most corrupt national park authorities, the best guides, even found their way into the personal treasuries of the president. With enough dollars you could do anything. So Odin had flown from Manhattan to Burko Masailand in northern Tanzania and he had feasted in his luxury camp, distributed crates of vintage champagne amongst the grinning staff, looked down on two Serengeti dawns from the basket of a balloon, and then set out in a convoy of Land Cruisers on a long, crunching journey across the grasslands.

All so that he could see her now and be the last man to look into her eyes.

She knew he watched her, but when he stood upwind and refused to move, she found it hard to locate him. Yet she felt him close; this strange man who refused to leave her alone. This thing that reeked of danger. He had tracked her for six hours and she was tired now and had drunk nothing all day. At times she thought her speed and innate understanding of the scrubland had allowed her to lose him, but she heard them again soon enough. Coming closer. Always coming closer.

He smiled as he watched her snorting the air and pawing the ground from beyond the acacia trunk. He knew this spot marked the end of the journey. They could have halted her much earlier in the day, but he'd ordered the Land Cruisers to depart and continued on foot with his guides, following the signs of her progress under the withering glare of the sun, dropping into the defiles, pushing through the thorn thickets and climbing the rocky outcrops to obtain a better view. Although he would never admit it, the pursuit had been exhausting work for his sixty-four-year-old body, but it was these hours of hardship that he adored. Two point two million US dollars had been the cost to get him here, but that was nothing. He could make that in a day. Sometimes in a minute.

You've led us a merry dance, my damn beauty. I never thought you'd be so fast and elusive. I congratulate you.

He brought his .375 ivory-butted Magnum up against his right shoulder and aimed the bead between her shoulder blades. She dropped her wide elongated snout and turned to him. Did she see him? Did she know?

The bullet didn't take her between the shoulders. Instead it struck the top of her neck, shattered her vertebrae and sprayed blood, hide and bone in an arc across the stony ground. His guide clicked at the back of his throat in irritation.

The bastard thinks I've missed. I haven't missed, you fool. I'm enjoying the moment!

She was bleating. A high-pitched pitiful sound, more suited to a small duiker than this huge prehistoric beast. And she was dancing – springing lightly on her toes – but unsteadily, ungainly, like the girl at the hen party who's been drinking for hours. He watched incredulous as she threw her great head from side to side and stamped the ground and cried to the heavens. His heart pounded with unconstrained joy. To be able to see this. To be able to do this! Her little eyes burned brilliantly at him.

Then, at last, he relented and took her again. This time the bullet tore into her just beneath her left ear, exploding through bone and brain. She dropped instantly in a mass of armour and limbs. Just for a second she fought to rear her head, but then it was over, the mighty neck dropped, and all was still except for a cloud of dust swirling up into the darkening sky.

Diceros bicornis. Extinct now in south-central Africa.

His guides were racing forwards and fussing over the carcass. For most hunters, this was what it was all about – the photos beside the fallen behemoth, the detailed directions on how to skin the beast and mount her head. Christ, her horn alone was worth a hundred grand. But he no longer cared. His exultant heart had slowed and deadened. His adrenaline ebbed to nothing. She was just a carcass now. A heap of bone and sinew. Everything had been for that one moment – when he had her in his sights – when he knew unreservedly that he held a life in his hands.

The Land Cruisers were radioed in and soon he was back at camp. He washed, dined and then took a fine scotch out onto the veranda of his tent to listen to the cacophony of an African night. He was alone, save a Masai marksman posted somewhere nearby. Flames popped in the firepit and he watched sparks floating away into the night, an army of shimmering pinpricks.

He opened his laptop and logged into his stock accounts. There was a two-second delay as the signal made the forty-five-thousand-mile round trip from North America via the orbiting EchoStar XVIII and down to the lightless black smudge of the Serengeti. No matter where he was – no matter that he sat now in one of the last wildernesses on earth – he checked his funds every day. Geography was immaterial. Tomorrow his jet would whisk him from Arusha, but anywhere and everywhere was his home. Like most billionaires, he was effectively stateless, operating where taxes were lowest and opportunities highest. Technically he was a resident of Bermuda, but he was Philadelphian by birth and by nature. The son of a cab driver, he had broken the social bonds and gained a place at the Chicago School of Economics in 1971. A Rhodes Scholarship took him to Oxford for a year and it was there – shut away in his room at the top of a staircase on Garden Quad in Balliol while his fellow students partied in the college bar – that he began trading in convertible bonds.

He studied the lists of numbers scrolling up his laptop screen. The London Stock Exchange had closed four hours earlier and New York would follow suit in another sixty-three minutes. As of eleven twenty-seven that evening East Africa time, the net asset value of Raymond J Pearlman's Vanaheim Capital Management funds stood at $17.92 billion.

As prearranged, it was exactly eleven thirty when his mobile rang. He glanced around into the darkness, wondering where the Masai marksman lurked and if the man could understand English, then he tapped the screen and placed the phone to his ear.

'Are we secure?'

'Encrypted both ends, my lord,' came the voice of the Thane of Valhalla.

The phone Odin was using was untraceable, purchased

purely for these conversations, and its specially customised SatSleeve with Meganet encryption software meant he could speak with confidence from anywhere on the planet. No one would be listening.

'Go ahead, Radspakr. What needs my attention so urgently that you disturb my evening?'

'If you open your Google Play account, lord, you'll see I have sent the details.'

With a grunt, Odin launched the programme on his laptop and watched as six new tracks appeared, apparently purchased by him earlier that day. 'Mahler. Symphony Number 5. You know my tastes.'

'Track four, my lord. *Adagietto*. Twenty-one seconds in.'

He pressed play and listened as the strings began their theme. For a moment he was taken away by the beauty of the music, but he forced himself to watch the clock ticking away in the corner and after twenty-one seconds the music cut and carefully embedded files sprung open.

'So what are these?' he demanded, clicking through them. Zebra were honking in the distance and somewhere much closer a hyena cackled.

The voice at the other end sounded nervous. 'These, my lord, are a problem that I've been meaning to tell you about.'

XXIII

Halvar drilled them hard again the next day, though this time the extra numbers allowed them to oppose each other properly and the iron blades were replaced by wooden ones. As a fine Hebridean rain buffeted them, two shieldwalls smashed together on the beach beside the church. It was back-breaking, body-wrecking work and soon the air was salted further by the heavy smells of sweat and leather. Punnr rapidly learned that it had been one thing to keep his shield aligned with his companions when the beach had been theirs alone, and something entirely different when an equally determined opposing shieldwall came crashing into them.

On the first three occasions he was driven back several paces and lost all contact with Ake and Olsen as the opposing shieldwall attacked their flanks. When the lines were called apart, Olsen spat fury at him and dragged him back into place.

'Gods, what's wrong with you? Stand firm. Dig your boots into the sand and don't bloody give an inch! You break line like that when we're in it for real and Alexander will rip us to shreds.'

Wordlessly, Punnr locked his shield next to the fat Viking,

shoved his shoulder into the man's bulk and ground his feet into the sand. When the opposing shields came again, he took the hit and pushed back with every ounce of muscle, refusing to yield. He still slipped and gave ground, but this time only inches, and the shields of Litter Four held true and when it was done, Olsen's oaths were more temperate.

By the end of the morning, Punnr's arms shook, a calf muscle had pulled with the strain of finding purchase in the sand, and he had been hit twice on the helmet, once on the shoulder and several times on the thighs by the opposition's wooden swords. Had these been real blades, he needed no telling, he wouldn't be standing.

With the sun guarded by cloudbanks, they had no real sense of time, but when the flat metallic light seemed at its zenith, they noticed Vigiles bringing more boxes to the church.

'Company,' said Brante in a snatched breather across the shields.

Indeed, shortly afterwards, figures appeared on the dunes and the Wolves stopped drilling. More came out onto the beach near the church and one of these raised a hand. It was Asmund, and next to him the squat burly form of Ingvar. Storm and Hammer had come.

It turned out – once Halvar at last allowed his Wolves a break and the new arrivals had gone through the usual cycle of collecting their boxes, finding their tents and changing – that they hadn't flown from Edinburgh airport like the Wolves. Too many of them, Asmund said, over millet porridge. Such a crowd would have drawn the eyes of any Titan spies watching the main transport hubs. Instead, a fleet of taxis had called at addresses across the capital in the very early hours, then taken them out to the ring road, three warriors to each vehicle, and south through country lanes to a spot where coaches waited. The journey continued towards Border country, until eventually the coaches turned into a private airfield, which was deserted at that time in the morning. They boarded four aircraft and took off as the first smudge of daylight crept across the eastern sky.

Unlike the night flights of the Wolves, they had been able to see Scotland unfold below. One or two even knew their west coast geography well enough to pick out Oban and Mull, Ardnamurchan, then Coll and Tiree to the south. Well before they arrived, word had spread that their destination must be somewhere on the Outer Hebrides.

'Either that,' said Ingvar with porridge running down his beard, 'or we were flying Cessnas all the way to bloody Greenland.'

'Did you get much of a look at the island?' asked Halvar.

Asmund shrugged. 'A little. We're at the southern end of a chain. North there were larger islands and some of my guys thought these were Lewis, Harris and Uist. Looking the other way, further south, just a few small outcrops. The one we're on appeared broadly circular, with hills in the centre.'

'Main town's back to the east,' added Ingvar throwing a thumb over his shoulder. 'Far enough away.'

'Yes,' said Halvar. 'We've found that. There's machair on that side too; looked a likely spot for the Field.'

'Have you tried the northern coast?' asked Asmund.

'Not got that far, but we assume it's much the same.'

'Not from what I could see.'

'How so?'

'Flat,' said Asmund quietly. 'Open grassland, big sandy bays, shallow water between a few outlying islands and minimal housing. On a sunny day in summer? You wouldn't need the Caribbean.'

Halvar nodded slowly. 'Good to know. We'll get a scouting party out there.'

The room was growing rowdy. The new arrivals had filled their stomachs and were relaxing on furs. Amongst them, Punnr noticed Ulf. The same small eyes, weak chin, little mouth, pimples and moustache that refused to grow, but there was something changed in his demeanour. Less of the usual sneer; a quieter brooding.

'What shall we do with them?' Asmund asked, a half-smile playing on his lips.

Halvar looked around in disgust. Fifty-six Hammers, half the regiment, along with Storm's thirty-eight spears and archers, had joined the eighteen Wolves, and now there was barely space for them all to spread out on the furs. 'Make the bastards run.'

And that's exactly what they did. The troops were cajoled back out into the rain, ordered to shoulder their shields, and formed up as a single column on the beach – twenty-four ranks of five – with Halvar, Asmund, Ingvar and their Hersirs alongside. A sergeant-major yell from Halvar and they began to jog along the sand, their shields bouncing in unison. There was no laughter now, only a black silence as each individual inclined their head against the elements and concentrated on their footing.

They thought they would be pulled up at the end of the bay and ordered back the other way, but no such order came. Instead they found themselves climbing over the rocks to the muddy grassland that Punnr and Stigr had encountered two days earlier. Into it they ran with quiet cursing. The column shivered as ranks stumbled and tripped, but the Hersirs kept them going. Halvar was barking. Something about fitness, not tactics or courage or weapon craft, which won battles; the ferocious stamina needed in a slaughter-line; the endurance to make the killing thrust when an opponent had nothing left. But no one was listening.

Only when they reached the next rocky bay did he turn them, but not directly. Instead they wheeled inland towards the road. The big Hammers were really suffering. They were built to stand and hold ground against the foe, not run until they puked. Many had already fallen more than once and were one wrongly placed quip from smashing skulls. All semblance of ranks had disintegrated and now the column had a long comet's tail of stragglers.

Brante pushed up next to Punnr and grinned. He had streaks of mud down his face and his breeches were soaked from where he had fallen. 'Remember the drum race, *Thrall VI*? You and me, the last one's still running? First time I met you properly.'

Punnr's mind shot back to the vaults last autumn during the first nights of the Armatura, the twelve Thralls and Halvar beating that damn drum with as much malicious delight as he was cajoling them now. He tried to recall the faces of those early Thralls. Now only three of them remained.

Brante was laughing at the memory. 'Race you to the road.'

He surged ahead, slipping and sliding like a lunatic ice-skater, and something about the whole ludicrous proposal cut into Punnr and sliced through his pain. Before he knew it, he was grinning too and cursing Brante and shouldering through the front ranks. Brante chortled as he realised Punnr was giving chase, but his efforts only made him lose coordination further. 'Bastard,' he snickered as Punnr came level and heaved every last sinew.

They were nearly there, but now there was another set of footsteps squishing through the mud behind and then rounding them.

'You two think this is a race?' breathed Ake. 'I'll show you a race.' She let out a piercing gull-like cry and accelerated past them to the tarmac, where she turned with her arms wide to scream triumph. They arrived close behind and fell, heaving and spitting, but laughing through their gasps.

They heard others joining them, but then the roars of Halvar came to their ears. 'Keep going! Down the road, now!'

Punnr sat up and watched the rest of the column wheel in chaotic fashion and stagger down the tarmac. Halvar arrived to stand over them. 'Just what are you buggers playing at? Did I say *why don't you have a little race?* Did I say *break ranks?* Did you hear the words *forget all about military discipline?* Get up, you bastards, and run! You'll be washing the kit tonight.'

Sure enough, when evening arrived at its usual early hour and the troops collapsed on the floor of the church, Punnr, Brante and Ake were placed on cleaning detail. Outside, in the bitter air, with only candlelight from the doorway, they formed a chain; Punnr rinsing piles of clothes and boots in a trough filled with rainwater; Brante twisting items dry; and Ake carrying them into the building to lay around the fire. They worked for hours until Punnr's hands were so cold they were virtually incapable of movement. Only then did Leiv come out and inform them they could stop.

'Don't worry,' he said as they trudged inside. 'The boss would have been twice as angry if you'd let Hammer or Storm beat you.'

They were the last to eat and the church was redolent with the smell of food. Cauldrons had been suspended over the fire containing leeks, carrots, radishes, stock and meats. There were sorrel and sage omelettes with goat's cheese and hunks of roasted venison. Unn had saved them portions and spooned them out with a smile as they collapsed on the furs. Punnr could hardly hold his plate and had to place it on his knees. He gulped at some warmed wine proffered by Unn and gazed angrily over at Halvar, who was sitting with Asmund near the head of the Hall. To his surprise, the Housecarl looked back at him and Punnr could have sworn he saw a smile.

The Gulfstream G650 banked north-west and set its nose away from the approaching dawn. Odin watched the beacon on the port wing dip and then flatten out again as the plane settled on its new course. He lay on his bed, propped up by several pillows, sipping a Bloody Mary.

The plane was his workhorse. It carried him throughout each billionaire calendar. St Bart's for New Year, Davos in January, Beverly Hills in February for the Milken Institute, then the Super Bowl, Cannes in May, followed by the Monaco Grand Prix, Royal Ascot in June, Art Basel a couple of weeks later, the Seychelles for a month over summer, and

Africa in autumn for his hunting. His latest trip to meet his rhino had been an unusual and spontaneous one based on sudden tracker information and a chance too good to be missed, but now he glowered with frustration because he had been in the African wilderness when Radspakr had revealed the whole goddamn circus going on in Scotland.

He lit a cigar and drew venomously until the tip glowed. *Jesus, that bloody Thane is a loser. How fucked up can you get?*

One Titan traitor, whereabouts unknown. One Viking new recruit, brother of said traitor, asking dangerous questions. One Valhalla Housecarl, holding more secrets than was healthy for any man. And one stupid boy, meddling where he shouldn't.

All of them breathing. All of them very much alive. All with enough ammunition to hurt him.

The Caelestis pondered his moves. He needed someone he could trust. Radspakr was a waste of space – as was his henchman, that Neanderthal. What was his name? Bjarke.

He let smoke drift from his lips and stared out at the radiant clarity of the sky at this altitude. His pilots always took him as high as possible, where the air was thinner and turbulence minimal, so they could shoot through the heavens and get him to his destinations ahead of schedule.

Sveinn was useless. Too moral and upright for his own good. Being King had gone to his goddamn head. He thought the rules were there to be obeyed. *Play by the rules; die by the rules*. Odin laughed thinly. Yeah, right. Playing by the rules hadn't made him seventeen billion bucks.

He needed someone else he could rely on. Someone he

could own. Someone who would do anything to repay his debt to this Caelestis.

'Sir?' A voice came through his cabin door.

'What?'

'We're ten minutes from landing.'

He swallowed the dregs of his drink. 'Right, I heard you.'

A limitless bank of grey cloud could be seen below, getting ready to fold the plane into its embrace.

The pilot's voice crackled again. 'It might be a bumpy descent, sir, so you'd better strap in. I'm afraid it's cold and wet down there.'

Odin swore and eased himself up from the bed. 'But of course. Welcome to goddamn Edinburgh.'

XXIV

North Atlantic gales hurled themselves at the roof of the church, but also – for the first time – shafts of sunlight streamed through the high windows and burnished the flagstone floor on which the island representatives of Valhalla now sat. Those who could leaned their backs against the walls or columns and let the sun play on their faces, while the rest hunched cross-legged on their furs and listened to Halvar.

This morning would be dedicated to instruction of mind instead of body decreed the Housecarl and he sat, cup of wine in hand, with his shoulder against the hearth and the peat smouldering beside him.

'Let us tell you about the foe. To know your foe is half the battle. Many of you've faced them in Seasons before, but there are some who've not.'

He signed to Asmund sitting nearer the entrance and Storm's Jarl stood and spoke. 'The Titan Palatinate is divided between the Heavy Brigade and the Light, but don't let that fool you. Every one of them is modelled on the Hoplite, Ancient Greece's infantryman and the most heavily armoured soldier in the world at that time. They're arrayed in bronze helmets with full cheek, neck and nose guards; solid bronze front-and-back cuirasses, which can stop a swinging blade; and shin guards. Every trooper carries a short cut-and-thrust sword, which in the press of a shieldwall can be manoeuvred much more easily than our own longswords. They'll not slash or swing, but when they stab with those blades, you'd better not be anywhere in the vicinity. In addition, every Hoplite carries a circular oak shield – a hoplon – three-foot wide, smaller than ours, and faced in bronze.

'So – the Lights first, commanded by Cleitus, Colonel of the Brigade. They're divided into three. Parmenion captains the peltasts, fast-moving troops armed with throwing javelins and bows. They wear leather fish-scale cuirasses, which are lighter than the solid bronze. They're superb marksmen, so treat them with respect. They'll deploy to the rear, but they can take you down long before you reach them.

'Next are the Companions, Alexander's Bodyguard, captained by Menes. Armed with eight-foot spears, but they won't throw these like the peltast's javelins. Instead they'll strike with them from behind their hoplons and stick you as full as a pincushion before you can lay a blow on their defences. Sneaky, hard bastards, they're Alexander's most fanatical troops and will always stay close to him in battle.

'Third, the Sacred Band, captained by Agape. The blue-cloaked Titan elite. They'll be armed only with their shortswords and will roam wherever they wish on a battlefield, feinting in and out of the action. They're the Titans' hunter-killers. Ignore them at your peril.'

Asmund paused and looked around at the circle of

faces. He had their attention. 'Now let me tell you about the Heavies. Nigh on a hundred of them, with Nicanor as their colonel. These are the soldiers of Alexander's Phalanx. Their shields are strapped to their chests and are scalloped in the top-right corner. Through this, held in both hands and supported by a sling at their side, point the huge eighteen-foot sarissa pikes. When these come at you – four, sometimes five, ranks deep – you'll never get anywhere near their shields. You'll be skewered yards from the slaughter-line. When the Phalanx gets going, no shieldwall will hold. It cannot be stopped.'

Asmund looked to Halvar and the Housecarl indicated that he should sit, then spoke himself from his place beside the hearth.

'What happens when a rock hits a pane of glass? The glass shatters, of course, because it's brittle. But what happens when a rock hits a square of linen? The linen folds around the rock. When we face the Phalanx, we must be the linen. Our shieldwalls must bend, bring Alexander's great horned beast in, then swing closed and attack it on the exposed flanks where we can feed.

'The Phalanx is all about mass. Almighty force at one decisive point. But no advantage in a battle is greater than speed. Speed is everything. And if there's one thing Nicanor's Heavies lack, it's this.

'Of course, Alexander has faced us in Grand Battle for eighteen Seasons now and he knows his Phalanx's weaknesses. So he'll protect them. He may wedge his Heavies, so while the lead unit extends and exposes its flanks, the wing units will still pickle you on the ends of their sarissas if you try to attack from the sides. Alternatively, his Companions may be tasked with falling on you. They'll come with shields locked and spears ready for the punch.'

Halvar drank his wine and let the silence extend.

'So, like I said at the start, to know your foe is half the battle. If you find yourself facing the head of the Phalanx, you must yield ground. No Viking can stand against those pikes and live. But if you're ever lucky enough to catch a scent of their exposed flanks, fall on them mercilessly.

'If it's the peltasts you see before you, beware their missiles. They'll rain death from the sky and your shield is your salvation. But if you still breathe when their volley's done, charge them with all the speed you can muster.

'It's when the Companions come for you that you know you'll be in a real shieldwall fight, the type to tell your grandkids about. Their spears will reach over your defences and you must learn to use this to your advantage. Grab the shafts – hell, grab the iron blade if you must – but use the moment. Pull them towards you, get in behind the deadly points and then you'll feel your foe just a breath away beyond his hoplon. You have the longer sword – use it. Pierce them in the face, in the legs, whatever it takes to bring them down before they can wrest back control of their spear or unsheath their stabbing blade.'

'And what if it's the Band?' came a voice from the audience.

'If it's the Band you face, fight like Hel herself – like Loki possessed – because you're a whisper from death.'

In the absence of any Raven scouts, Halvar decided to send his swiftest and best Wolves to reconnoitre the north coast.

The journey would involve several miles on difficult terrain over the central spine of hills as they bent towards the west, so the team would have to travel fast to be back before the failing light. He chose Ake and Stigr.

They packed frugally in the pre-dawn darkness, throwing cold chicken and goat's cheese wrapped in cloth into a rucksack, and by the time the first hint of daylight glowed silver on the sea, they were already climbing hard above the bay. The conditions were calm as they scampered up the steep incline, grabbing tussocks of bog-rush for leverage, but when they finally crested the broad dome summit, a wind punched them from the north. Ake bent her bare head and accelerated into a steady lupine trot and Stigr followed.

The day matured and the elements warred with each other, as if trying to distract the runners from their grind. White clouds raced above them, interspersed by vast black buttresses reaching to the heavens. Every few moments the wind rent tears in the clouds and blue broke through, sending shafts of sunlight zigzagging across the island and colouring everything they touched in a vivid palette. They were chased by showers. Columns of water arcing down over sea and land, as though the gods pissed on the world. Crows wheeled above the runners' heads, hung on the wind and cawed to one another, and a skein of geese honked their way across the panorama and descended noisily on the fields near the main town.

Ake led down into a mud-slick valley and the wind abated for a time. They found a small stream and followed it uphill until the steepening gradient meant it ran fast and clear, then they scooped handfuls of the freezing water into their mouths and drank their fill. Once done, they climbed hard to gain the peak of the primary range of hills on the island. Stigr was blown by the top and Ake relented, waiting for him in a crouch against the wind. She raised her eyebrows in a wordless question when he arrived, but he was damned if he would be the weak link and pushed straight by with a scowl.

They rounded huge cliffs where gulls and fulmars circled, and as they reached the far side of the summits the panorama to the north unfolded. Between the storms, they could see the other Hebridean islands reaching in a chain to the horizon. Larger landmasses. Uist and Harris, they remembered Asmund saying. There was a fishing boat in the watery distance and a red and black ferry plying between the islands. Below them too, the place was opening up. There was rain, but they could make out the flatter contours of grassland and they glanced at one another. Even at this distance, it looked the best location they had seen for a coming together of the Palatinates.

It took them a further ninety minutes of slippery descent and hard running through soggy, lumpy terrain, to break out onto the wider land. A beam of sunlight turned the turf a brilliant green and the pair pulled up. The grass ran flat east to west, with sheep scattered everywhere. Only on its northern edge did it incline upwards in a natural rim before the shoreline.

'It's perfect,' said Stigr and he was right. The ground was hard despite the rain. There were pockets of gorse for cover and a long dip to the east in which good hunters could play unseen to their heart's content. Even the wind was subdued by the lower altitude and the sheltering coastal rim.

Ake bent and fingered the grass, looking at the myriad

of short green flower stems, which had been cropped by the sheep. 'This place would be exquisite in summer. Have you seen those photos of endless flower meadows? This would be one of them.'

'Aye, and this year the flowers'll be fed by blood and bone, I reckon.'

They searched the contours and looked to the sky to see how the sun moved. A flock of twite took off just in front of them, flitting up and down across the expanse until landing again as one. Ake unwrapped chicken from her rucksack and threw Stigr some.

'So?' he asked between mouthfuls. 'Which end?'

Ake mulled his question. 'Assuming the Battle's timed as other years and takes place in the afternoon, then I'd want to be right here at the western end, with the Atlantic wind and the lowering sun to my back. Let the Titans come from the east and take the elements in their faces.'

'They'd have more of that gorse cover where the birds went, but, aye, you're right.' He began to stride east down the centre of the turf, but Ake was drawn towards the raised coastal rim. She pulled herself up and stood looking out.

'What you're on would provide good vantage points for the Vigiles and their cameras,' shouted Stigr behind her. 'But I'm not so sure about that dip in the grass at the eastern end – it would give the foe a lot of cover.'

Ake didn't answer. She was still looking out to sea and eventually Stigr wandered back towards her.

'Remind me,' she said. 'How many Seasons have you done?'

'Seven.'

'And in all that time, have we ever been taken to an island before?'

'No.'

'So why are we here now?'

Stigr shrugged. 'Something different, I guess.'

Ake swivelled and looked at the grassland. 'Is that really so different? Basically it's just a large flat field and we've fought on those many times before in all the quieter corners of the Highlands. So why go to all the trouble of flying us to an island?'

She looked at Stigr, but when he had no answer, she turned again to face out to sea and he came up to join her.

'Fuck,' he said under his breath.

They were standing at the centre of a great crescent. On either side the grassland ran away from them and curved round at both ends. Caught in the crescent's embrace was a bay, but the tide was out and what confronted the pair, for as far as the eye could see, was a vast expanse of glittering white sand. In the distance stood another mound of grass, an island in the sand, and beyond this, on the very horizon, they could just make out a flat blue line where the sea began.

They jumped down and walked out onto the expanse, testing the solidity underfoot and searching for hidden dangers. The fine white shells crunched beneath their boots. There was a channel of seawater running down the centre, but it was shallow; an inconvenience, rather than a hazard. Oystercatchers and redshank bobbed along its edges and a flock of dunlin landed in formation.

The two of them kept walking. The wind blew harder once again, as though sensing these humans caught in the open. Sunlight broke through the clouds and dazzled them as it hit the sand. They followed the channel towards the grass island in the distance, turning sometimes to look back and study the perimeter. They knew instinctively that the turf around the rim would provide an ideal platform for observation and filming. There were no houses or roads. The main town was several miles back along the east coast and the only land behind the bay comprised the wild hills they had already tackled.

'There's not a shred of cover out here,' said Stigr. 'There'd be no secrets. We'd see everything the foe did – and they'd see every move we made. It would be a blood-fest.'

'Atilius doesn't care about that. Think how good it would look on his video. Everything played out on a featureless white backdrop. Get a few drones up and some choppers, and he'll have a blockbuster in the making. Hell, even the sand and water will turn an obliging shade of pink when people start dying.'

As they neared the island, the channel split in two, cutting off their approach, and each arm ran away either side and at last found the sea. These channels were shallow too, but they didn't bother to cross. Stigr simply stuck a boot in and prodded the bottom. 'Solid enough. Three strides and a trooper would be across, even with the weight of *brynjar* and weapons.'

'The island's a handy piece of ground.'

'Aye. Put King Sveinn on it and our backs against it, and the foe could hit us all afternoon and they still wouldn't get to him.'

Ake folded her arms and looked at her companion. 'So why would the Pantheon bring us to an island?'

'To watch us slaughter each other on this fine, white sand.'

They were silent, both turning on the spot and looking at the scene.

'People will die here,' Ake said at last. 'You can count on it. Friends as well as foe. By the time we're done, this place will stink of death.'

Stigr prodded a boot into the fine sand. 'Blood, flesh, shit and bone, all stamped into this beautiful beach. It doesn't matter where the Pantheon raises its banners, the devastation is always the same. This game we play is a terrible thing.'

'So are we in agreement?'

'Aye. This is the Field.'

XXV

The prisoner knew something had changed when his Vigiles guards opened the door to his cell and threw him new garments. He had worn the same soiled rags for two years, never taking them off except for the rare occasions they gave him a bucket of brackish water with his only meal. Long after their footsteps had receded, he remained crouched in the corner staring at the clothes in the dark as though expecting them to come to life.

He was used to the silence. To begin with, when they had thrown him in the first cell deep in the bowels of the earth, he had raged against it, hammering the door, hitting the walls and screaming his lungs hoarse, but time sapped everything and gradually he grew to tolerate the quiet. Occasionally he would hear the muted cry of another inmate and shoot upright and strain every sinew to listen, but the voice always ebbed away and left him alone again. If he was honest, he actually welcomed the arrival of the rats after his meals because their scurrying brought life and movement, and he would grin at every squeak.

To disorientate him further, the guards never brought his meal or took away his slops at a regular hour. They wanted to deprive him, not only of light and sound and freedom, but of the very concept of time. And it had worked. For an age piled upon an age, he had no idea how long he languished in their pit, how many seasons passed.

But then, without explanation, they moved him to a new cell and although still windowless, his senses came back to life. He noticed how the air alternated between extreme cold and stifling heat, and this told him he was now above ground. Nights brought the chill and sun the warmth. So he had started to count the days and scratch them into the walls with the handle of his spoon. His count in this new cell had reached two hundred and twenty-three. The alternating temperature told him something else too. The days never got cold. Wherever he was, it was a land where winter did not exist.

But the most wondrous, captivating thing about this second cell was the sliver of light beneath the door. Just a trace of it, but enough to begin calculating the differing lengths it crept across the floor. Using his spoon again, he scratched new marks into the flagstones to show its progress. He worshipped that light and over time he could tell the hour by it. Now it was mid-afternoon and he cherished this knowledge. It was a small victory; a one-fingered salute to the Pantheon masters.

When the sliver faded and the first tendrils of cold came to sit with him again, he pushed himself up and felt his way unsteadily to the clothes. He touched them with reverence and brought them to his face to smell the new scents. They were soft and clean. Slowly, he let the rags drop from his body. He needed no light to know his muscles had wasted away and his flesh was as pale as the moon. His hair hung in great ringlets and his white beard brushed against his collarbone. Both, he knew from his constant scratching and picking, were infested with colonies of mites.

Amazingly, there were trousers. Proper, real trousers. He pulled them up his legs and tied the belt around his emaciated waist. A T-shirt too. Nothing that would keep back the cold of the night to come, but he didn't care. The clothes made him feel human.

He stood in the centre of his cell and waited. What was one more night after weeks and months and years?

Sometime in the small hours, the flap on his door was unlocked and his meal pushed through. Potato soup, much the same as always. He left a little for the rats and listened to them arrive and skitter over his bare feet. Eventually he returned to his corner and perhaps he slept because the next thing he knew was the approach of footsteps again and the chink of daylight beneath the door. This was it, he told himself. Whatever these clothes were for, this was it.

He heard the keys and bolts and the movements of men outside, then the door was thrown back and figures were silhouetted in the entrance. He blinked and scrunched up his eyes to cope with the new sights. The Vigiles entered and pulled him to his feet. One held his hands while they clamped them, then another ducked and attached leg irons to his ankles.

Shackled, he was led out for the first time in two hundred and twenty-four days. His dulled senses were just able to make out more stone walls and much higher, vaulted roofs. They took him along a passage, through locked gates and past other thick wooden doors. Behind one, something banged hard at their approach, but stopped when they had gone.

The light grew and he kept his eyes down, but even the floor dazzled him. The air too was changing to a deeper warmth. Finally, the little party rounded a corner and daylight pierced them. He staggered against it, trying to bring his manacled hands up to his face. The guards held him for a few seconds until he could look again, then pushed him forward.

He came out into a world with infinite sky. The flagstones were hot beneath his naked feet and the air filled with dust particles that made him cough. At the foot of a stairway waited a Jeep with three more Vigiles and beyond that stretched a harsh land of rock and sand. A guard bent and unlocked his leg irons, then pushed him towards the stairs with his hands still chained.

Cautiously, his knees grating with the effort, he descended. Just above the waiting Vigiles, he stopped, shuffled around on the spot and looked up. Behind loomed a great broken castle with towers collapsed and walls crumbling, but its battlements still clear enough. He studied it for long seconds, taking in its contours under the baking sun.

As he turned back, his mind grasped two clear conclusions. He was capable of any act to ensure he never saw that castle again; and whatever awaited him now, he owed a vast debt to somebody.

For no one ever left Erebus without paying the toll.

Three and a half thousand miles away and thirty hours later, the company Mitsubishi used by Oliver's father drove along Queensferry Road in the early hours. As it approached a speed camera, it accelerated just enough to ensure its plate was captured by the flash, then slowed again and turned left towards Comely Bank. But it wasn't Mr Muir behind the wheel. Weighed down by a rucksack full of rocks, he was already three miles northeast of Dirleton at the bottom of the Forth, his boat rocking its lonely path into the North Sea.

The driver knew where the CCTV cameras were located and ensured they got a clear view of the vehicle making its way through the backstreets of Comely Bank, but then he parked carefully in a black spot not far from Learmonth Place and waited.

At the same moment, another man slipped into the corner property by the Gardens. It had rained earlier and he made certain to press his wet boots into the carpet in the hall and up the stairs – boots that were the same make and size as those owned by Mr Muir in his watery grave. The man had been inside before, when he had been sent to kill the resident of flat number six and found it empty. This time he used Mr Muir's key to open flat five and pulled on night- vision goggles. An earlier raid on the Land Registry records and he had the layout imprinted on his mind. He walked across the lounge to the second of two doors, which would lead to the rooms overlooking Learmonth Gardens. The door was only pulled to and he was able to listen to the regular breathing from within. Once again, he retrieved a face mask and small syringe of sevoflurane from his pocket. Screwing the syringe in place, he entered the room and came over the bed.

Even in the eerie green glow of his goggles, he could see the sleeping woman was attractive. A blonde somewhere in her forties. Her mouth was open slightly, showing a hint of teeth. He waited for her to exhale, then brought the mask gently over her mouth and pressed the syringe halfway down as she drew in another breath. For a moment there was no reaction, then her body jolted and she half woke, and at the same instant he pushed the mask more firmly onto her, although careful not to mark or bruise. With his other hand he gripped her rising head. If she opened her eyes, it was only for a moment, then she went limp. He released her back onto the bed, folded the cloth and returned it to his pocket. Using a new, dry cloth, he wiped carefully around her lips and nose.

Then he removed his rucksack and pulled from it a sealed plastic bag containing a pillow, one taken from Muir's new rental property in Blackhall and sufficiently covered in his DNA. He placed this over her face, pushed down on either side and held his position for several minutes until he knew the woman beneath him had gone. Leaving the pillow in place, he leaned over and took the spare pillow beside her on the double bed and squeezed it into his rucksack.

Satisfied, he walked out to the lounge and approached the other door. This one was closed and he sank to his knees and listened for an age. Gently, he turned the handle and eased it open. The curtains were thrown back and streetlighting shone through the rain-spattered panes. Over the desk a stack of hard drives blinked and above his head the ceiling glowed with luminous galaxies. He frowned because the lad was sleeping on his front, which would make things harder. Fortuitously, though, he had kicked back the bedclothes.

The man positioned the face mask neatly in the palm of his glove and leaned over the boy. No easy way to do this. He thrust his free hand under the boy's neck and hauled him up so that the back of his head was squeezed against the man's chest. The boy sprang awake. A cry broke from him and his limbs started flailing wildly. His assailant clamped the mask over his face and jammed the syringe fully down, while holding him in a vice-like grip.

The last thing Oliver saw was the poster at the head of his bed showing the Viking longship with its rows of shields, then the image faded. He knew nothing of being released onto the floor while the man tidied his bedding and retrieved a set of his clothing and a pair of his shoes. Nothing of being carried down the stairs, nor of the cold night air and the vehicle that eased around the corner.

And nothing of the other hands that grabbed him and took him from the life he had known.

XXVI

For the next four days, Halvar kicked them from their tents at daybreak and mustered them on the sands beside the church. If the tide was up, the hours were devoted to fitness and training at litter level. After the swordplay of the Blood Nights, they practised with different tools and Punnr found himself hurling a throwing axe time and again into the side of a sand dune until he had perfected the hold and the release. Next, they gathered in close and saw how their shorter seax daggers could be lethal in the press of a real fight. Then they split into pairs and duelled with both longsword and seax in hand.

Whenever the sea receded and gave them space to spread, Halvar cajoled them into their armour and they worked on larger set pieces. For these they used training weapons to avoid injury and focused on the four main phases of conventional battle – deployment, missile exchange, closing to contact, and close-order combat. They trooped onto the beach as one column of hundred and twenty, then repeatedly deployed from order of march to line of attack until they could perform it as smoothly as if they were on a parade ground.

They split into opposing forces and defended themselves

from hails of Storm's arrow shafts and spears. They learned that the arrows could fall on them from anything up to a hundred yards, while the killing zone for thrown javelins was closer to thirty. They waited for the volleys, then charged when there was a pause, until Asmund had his troops maintaining a regular rain of projectiles thundering onto Wolf and Hammer shields, which brought the warriors to a standstill.

Then they practised bracing against eight-foot spear shafts in a shieldwall and grabbing at them as they were shoved over shield rims. There were knocks and curses, as well as some laughter, but it was plain to see the terrors these weapons could inflict in a real battle once they were tipped with razor-sharp iron. Punnr found he could clutch the shafts as they came through, but more often than not he was then yanked out of position, creating a dangerous break in the Wolves' defences or making him stumble at the feet of his opponents, where, in a genuine battle, he would be butchered.

Time and again, Halvar, Asmund and Ingvar marshalled them and had them march as a single giant shieldwall across the beach, so they understood the differing paces, as well as the challenges of keeping together on a gradient. Sometimes they loaded the Hammer ranks on one wing to create a point of real strength piled ten or twelve deep, to which a foe would have to respond. More often, they placed Hammer at the heart of the wall and divided the Wolves across both flanks. Punnr and his fellows drilled in the art of bending the flanks into horns, which could close in a giant pincer movement. Alternatively they lurked behind Hammer where an enemy would find it difficult to spy what they were doing before they came out at a sprint.

After this, Asmund's troops were brought to the fore to fire a few volleys up the beach, then kneel to let Hammers' ranks march right through them, and form up behind, ready to send another volley over the receding heads of the warriors. Performed well, it could keep the enemy's shields up and heads down for most of the time it took Hammer to close on them.

By the end of each day, the Horde was spent. Their hair was matted and salted, their faces wind-cracked and their bodies throbbing. Finally dismissed, they peeled off their garments and washed in the troughs, thinking only of filling their bellies and sleep.

Whenever security allowed, it was the Ephesus stronghold four floors above South Gray's Close, just off the Mile, which was Alexander's preferred residence. Located over an assortment of small business premises and a backpackers' hotel, Ephesus was accessed via a cramped and pink-carpeted spiral staircase that led to an oak door so worn and rusted that a casual explorer would assume only a forgotten attic space lay behind.

In fact, for permitted visitors, the door opened onto a brightly lit stone and marble reception, off which were offices, changing rooms, armouries, practice areas and an aromatic plunge pool, lovingly coated in mosaics. Above this warren was a fifth floor barely observable from street level. It ran the length of the premises on the eastern side of Gray's Close and was roofed entirely in glass. Here, in this warm sunlit atrium, a garden of glorious proportions had been created, and here – under olive and fig trees – the King of the Titans could customarily be found.

After a week's pause in Pantheon proceedings, it was the evening before the Fourth Blood Night and Agape had been summoned to Alexander's presence. Her Band were preparing further up the Mile in Pella, while the peltasts and Companions split themselves between Thebes and Persepolis. So it was the Heavies of the Phalanx who gathered at Ephesus that night and they nodded to her and gave her space as she used the plunge pool, dried and changed into a simple tunic and sandals.

At eleven thirty precisely, she trotted up the steps to the atrium. The garden had been the pride of Alexander's predecessor, the second King of the Titan Palatinate. A decade earlier, he had overseen its planting and proclaimed it a modern garden of Babylon and home to the gods. The troops had been more dismissive, quietly thinking such energies should be spent on warfare, not horticulture, but they liked it when he declared the garden a symbol of Titan ascendancy over the Viking Horde. The sunlight, he claimed, the scents, the greenery, the very sense of life pulsing through the plants, represented everything Valhalla could never have in its dark ale-stinking subterranean Tunnels.

This second Alexander had been a virile embodiment of the warrior king and led his hoplites fearlessly, but at the Grand Battle in Glen Affric during the Thirteenth Year, he had been taken in the throat by a Raven arrow. Slumped against his Bodyguard, he had nevertheless remained conscious and continued to coordinate his troops until the bugle call of Battle's end, when he was flown to the Pantheon hospital and never seen again. The official story was that he had survived, but in a state too weak to offer further leadership to the Palatinate and had been retired from the Pantheon.

So the third and current Alexander was appointed by Zeus from amongst the officer cadre. Many believed the crown should have been Agape's – strongest, most fearless of all the Titan elite – but Zeus chose Attalus, Colonel of the Heavy Brigade before Nicanor, and, to be fair, during his first Seasons, he was a good King.

Agape wound along the stone pathways. The sky was black and moonless beyond the glass roof and all that could be seen were the reflections of the plants, giving an impression of nature flowing irrepressibly to the heavens. The borders were filled with ferns, palms, lilies, philodendrons and succulents, and over a decade they had grown tall, leaning over the walkways and forming arches. From the walls and iron roofing beams hung jasmine, clematis, hydrangea and ivy, but pride of place around the central terrace was given over to a perimeter of fig and olive trees, a nod to the ancient Mediterranean homeland of Alexander's hoplites.

As was his custom, the King was seated at a large glass table, laptop and bottled water to hand. He too was dressed in tunic and sandals.

'Sveinn's thinning his ranks,' he said without preamble when Agape appeared.

She seated herself cross-legged on the other side of the table. 'How can you be certain, lord?'

'Over the last few hours I've had people placed near his Gates, some in restaurants or bars, some just walking by. Okay, not strictly within the Rules, but Sveinn's not the only one who can cheat. They're reporting far fewer arrivals, perhaps less than fifty per cent. Unless most of the Horde's waiting until the last moment to turn up for the Fourth Blood Night, Sveinn's been sneaking them out of the city.'

'Which means the Time Asset must have been activated.'

'Exactly. And that means the fourteen days are already counting down. The Battle could be any time after the final Blood Night. For a week now, Simmius has been organising watchers at Waverley, the bus station, the airport. No reports of any untoward activity, so the gods know how the bastard has been sneaking them out!'

Agape looked at her King. He was older than his predecessor, probably early fifties. He had height – easily six-four – and when he was booted and helmeted, he could play the regal part well enough, but now – bare-headed under the spotlights – he looked gaunt and unimposing. His hair was grey and thinning on top. His skin sallow and his angry little eyes circled by black blotches. It was well known amongst his officers that this Alexander enjoyed his wine laced with opium as the ancient Greeks had, but Agape recognised an addict when she saw one and she suspected a more illicit coke habit was at play as well. When the drugs kicked in, he could be magnificent, but in between he was becoming a twitchy, paranoid husk of the man he had once been.

'We're *blind*, Agape.' He looked at her sharply. 'Blind to everything until the final twenty-four hours. We don't know the date of the Battle, we don't know the Field. How am I supposed to prepare the Palatinate in twenty-four hours?'

'It's just how the Raiding Season unwound, lord. We've been in worse straits.'

'A Raiding Season won by duplicity and dishonesty. That Valhalla White Warrior cheated each and every one of us. He should be whipped and expelled.'

His hands were screwed tight and Agape almost pitied him. It hadn't always been so. In his first years as Alexander, he had been strong and the Titan Palatinate had continued the success it had enjoyed under his predecessor. But then came the Eighteenth Season. A year of continual losses for the Sky-Gods. Too many defeats in both the Raiding and Blood Seasons, too many troops falling, culminating in the disastrous offensive into Sveinn's Tunnels and the death of Timanthes. It was too much of a coincidence and, although he couldn't prove it, Alexander was convinced his foe had again been playing dirty. Something in this suspicion had undermined him and the drugs stole around his defences and took hold.

Then came last year's Grand Battle when he saw the Wolves closing on him. He had already sent his Companions elsewhere on the Field and was bereft of protection. In that moment he had no answer and waited for the blade in his belly, which would surely bring the fall of his Palatinate. Destinies changed and Agape's Band had saved him, but he never recovered from the shock.

'Lord, if what your spies say is true and Sveinn thins his ranks, then we must be bold tonight. Don't hold your forces back in their strongholds. Put them on the streets.'

Alexander rubbed his chin thoughtfully. It was rough and hadn't seen a razor for a day or two. 'Make our numbers count?'

'Yes, if it's true that half of Valhalla's absent. This is our chance to make up for a bad Raiding Season.'

'What do you suggest? Counsel me, Agape.'

She had grown used to him seeking her advice. In the last year he had distanced himself from the other officers. Nicanor, he seemed to view simply as a tool to wield the Phalanx; Parmenion, he saw as a man of action but not of strategy; Menes, he distrusted; and Cleitus – well, all knew Cleitus chafed to take his crown.

She considered the situation. 'In the very first moment of tonight's Conflict Hours, send Parmenion's scouts for their vantage points over Sveinn's Gates. Get them there as fast as they can fly so they may see the first Valhalla movements and we may know from which Gates they leave.'

The King nodded. 'Then?'

'Bait a trap, lord. Use the rest of Parmenion's peltasts – light troops, not sword specialists. Too good a prey to resist. Wait for the Horde to take the bait and see if it's Wolves they send, or weaker troops. Use the Companions as a screen to hinder escape from the rear. Then, at the right moment, I will bring the Band.'

Alexander peered up at the roof and considered her words. It was commonly assumed the Vikings knew about this place, indeed may have already squatted on the struts between the glass and peered down into the garden. But during Conflict Hours the lights were extinguished and Alexander would be moved below or to one of the other strongholds. The roof was guarded by Heavies during these periods and rules forbade an attempt by the Horde through the door at the head of the spiral staircase. So it was a knowledge that helped Valhalla little.

'There's something else you should know,' he said and focused on her again. 'A little bird tells me Sveinn's submitted a formal request to the Pantheon for a warrior exchange amongst his Valhalla Wolves.'

'Now? In the middle of the Blood Nights?'

'My thoughts exactly. It must be an exchange he cherishes dearly.'

'Do you have any more details?'

'Alas, none. But there's one other snippet of information that's wended its way to my ear. They say a prisoner has been released from Erebus.'

Agape stared at her King. 'And is this release linked to Sveinn's exchange request?'

Alexander shrugged. 'Perhaps, perhaps not. The two things may be totally unconnected, but I don't like the smell of it, especially when Odin's in the city.'

'Odin's in Edinburgh?'

'His plane was logged landing yesterday.'

'It's not unheard of for a Caelestis to get up close and personal before the Grand Battle.'

'Indeed, it's not. And it may be totally innocent. But all I know, Captain, is when Odin's involved, foul play is never far behind.'

XXVII

After a week of final recovery, Calder was preparing in the Western Armouries. She had showered and was already in her undergarments – a layer of soft linen against her skin, then a thicker layer of wool and finally more linen. It could be hot and cumbersome, but it provided some protection against a blade strike. The ancient Vikings held to a superstition that a man wearing a chain mail *brynjar* should be capable of putting it on unaided otherwise he was unworthy to wear such fine protection and amongst the Horde's male fraternity, it had become an unspoken tradition to struggle alone with the mail. The women, however, cared nothing for such absurdities and Calder held her arms up as Jorunn, one of her Raven colleagues, pulled the *brynjar* – adorned with a single Bloodmark – over her head. The weight always shocked her even though modern expertise had reduced it to seven kilograms from the twelve in ancient times, but her body soon adapted and the armour became a part of her.

She did the same for Jorunn and then they helped each other strap iron vambraces to their forearms and greaves to their calves. Finally, they fixed their woollen cloaks over their shoulders and stood back to admire each other. They would pass muster.

They walked down to the Throne Room and entered to see Turid, Hersir of Wolf Kill Squad Two, descending the stairs from Sveinn's Council Room with fury blazing in her eyes. She stood over six feet tall, made all the more striking by hair shorn short, and Calder knew of her reputation as one of Halvar's most skilled and trusted lieutenants. Some of Turid's litter were in the Hall and she strode to them and spoke in angry whispers. Fingers were pointed to the Council Room amid noises of consternation, which drew more warriors in a wider circle, and then Turid pushed her way through the throng and marched back up the Western Tunnel to the Armouries. Calder looked at Jorunn and mouthed a question. As Turid had passed, the fury on her face had surrendered to an expression of abject shock.

Her Wolves followed and Calder herself couldn't resist returning to the Armouries, where Turid was pulling off her vambraces and hurling them on the floor.

'What's going on?' Calder asked Runa, her fellow Raven, beside her.

'She's being let go. Sveinn's put her on indefinite leave until the end of the Season.'

Calder had never heard of "indefinite leave" and wondered how such a concept could exist within the Pantheon. 'But she's in charge of the remaining Wolves. How can she be let go just before we start the Blood Night?'

It was a question everyone was asking.

Freyja entered the Armouries and the clamour died. She signalled for Turid to follow and both stepped back into the Tunnel. Calder craned her neck and could just see them talking earnestly. As the words tumbled out, Freyja's expression hardened. She quizzed Turid, jabbing fingers at her, then waved her to the Changing Rooms and turned on her heel to march back to the Hall.

The warriors followed as a flock, unwilling to miss a moment of this drama. Everyone knew that something of deep importance was occurring and, pumped already in readiness for the dangers to come, the atmosphere now became heady and addictive. Calder watched Freyja bound up the stairs and knock hard on the door. Hammer, Raven and Wolf – now little more than sixty in total – milled in the Hall and talked in subdued tones, waiting for the next act. The seven remaining Wolves looked astounded, for Turid was that moment throwing on her street clothes and preparing to leave Valhalla.

Hearing the noise, Radspakr emerged from his den and stood at the eastern corner of the Hall. He already knew the reason for Turid's departure, but he hadn't foreseen how the Horde would respond. His eyes met Calder's. It struck him that he'd never mentioned her involvement in all this mess to the Caelestis and now that he was just beginning to grasp what terrors Odin could unleash, he was glad he had not. He felt no care for the woman, but the less Odin believed the contagion had spread, the safer for all.

Calder returned his look and thought how the man seemed to have aged within weeks. He had shrunk and lost that cold, remote presence. Like others in the Hall, he looked shocked, but there was another emotion in his eyes, one of genuine alarm. She hated the bastard, but she also knew if the Thane was afraid, then something was very wrong.

The Council Room door swung open and Freyja

descended more slowly, her face frozen. The room was utterly silent. She reached the bottom of the steps and forced herself to focus.

'Fifteen minutes to kick-off,' she said in the firmest tone she could muster. 'Raven and Hammer, gather your weapons.' For a second, no one moved, then she yelled at them and there was a rush for the Armouries.

Calder jostled beside Jorunn and Runa as they collected their swords, shields and helmets from the lockers.

'What do you make of it, Jorunn? Will the Wolves go out tonight?'

'Litter Two's an experienced enough team. They'll go if they're called. But to have a Hersir removed at this hour and while Halvar isn't present – well, it's nuts, if you ask me.'

Calder belted her scabbard and sheathed her sword. 'Doesn't this put us at a disadvantage? I thought our numbers are based entirely on Blood Funds, so how can we just lose an elite unit officer without it being an unfair advantage to the opposition?'

Jorunn tossed out her hair and pulled on her helmet, so that her eyes peeked through the iron mask. 'It's impossible to dismiss a warrior without recompense, but it's not impossible to *replace* one under the right circumstances. Sveinn – or more likely Odin – must have made a decision that Turid isn't the right person to lead Litter Two for the rest of this Season and they've put in a formal request to Atilius for a replacement.'

'Now? Without Halvar knowing, and minutes before we head out?'

Jorunn nodded. 'Exactly.'

Armed and helmeted, they returned to the Hall and one Raven litter was sent to South Gate, while Calder's was ushered to the North West. She observed her team as she followed them. They were quietening now – Jorunn, Runa, Thurmond and the other three – drawing themselves into their personal killing zones, but she sensed their nerves and knew they were rattled. These Blood Nights were challenging enough for Ravens because they had to leave their beloved bows behind, so the last thing they needed was to witness such turmoil in the Tunnels.

Watched by a couple of surly Hammer Guards, they queued by the Gate in silence. Eventually Freyja arrived. She was still unhelmeted and the look in her eye hadn't eased. Calder began to voice a question, but the Housecarl rounded on her.

'Shut your mouth, Thegn. You've only one job tonight and that's to follow me and do exactly what I say. Understood?'

Calder nodded and Freyja slammed on her helmet, drew her sword and glared at the Guards.

The Gate opened.

XXVIII

The pair of Titan scouts arrived at their vantage point near North-West Gate just in time to spot the backs of the Raven litter as they slipped across Lawnmarket and descended Johnston Terrace below the castle. The scouts split, one following the litter from above, the other racing back to Ephesus.

Alexander was still there, though now with Parmenion in the War Room below the garden, while his peltasts waited just up the Mile in Thebes. Once he had heard the scout's report, he consulted the table map and came to a conclusion.

'Send two of your units to Grassmarket,' he said to Parmenion. 'Make some noise, get spotted. Then head south, lead them away from the safety of their Gates. And you—' he pointed to the scout '—hightail it to Persepolis, brief Menes and tell him I want the Companions spread north of Grassmarket to screen any attempted retreat to Valhalla.'

'Yes, lord.'

'Then on to Pella and inform Agape she may give chase.'

Fifteen minutes later, Agape received her orders from the scout. She was already armoured and waiting below Pella's ceiling hatch, ready to climb onto the rooftops.

'Which Company?' she demanded.

'Ravens, Captain.'

'How many?'

'Seven.'

She already knew the plan. It was, after all, her plan. She had only been waiting to know which Gate and which Company. 'Very well.' She dismissed the scout and looked to her fifteen-strong Sacred Band. 'We'll go as one tonight and overwhelm them with our numbers. Make ready.'

She was about to climb for the hatch, then reconsidered. 'No shields and no cloaks,' she said and discarded her own. 'Tonight we go fast and light.'

'Cover,' hissed Freyja and pressed herself into the shadow of the building.

They were halfway down the long staircase of Castle Wynd South and it felt exposed with the bare flanks of the castle's hill running away from them and the lights of Grassmarket below. Calder dropped into a crouch and peered down the steps. Behind them squatted a single Vigilis, camera fixed to his chest.

Grassmarket was always a popular place, its perimeter studded with pubs and eateries, and even at one thirty on a spring morning, there was life. A group of lads, worse the wear for drink, were milling around the foot of Castle Wynd, shouting at each other. On benches in the centre of the square, another group smoked and played with their phones. Three taxis were parked up, their interior lights on and the drivers reading papers or dozing. But it was none of these that had alarmed Freyja.

Instead, it was the figures materialising from Cowgate at the eastern end of the square and striding confidently into the open. Even from that distance, their plumes and cloaks were obvious under the streetlights. There were a dozen of them and they walked to the benches, scattering the smokers, and hovered in the shadows of the trees, a single Vigilis following. The lads at the foot of the steps had seen them now and began a chorus of catcalling. Phones were produced and video buttons tapped. One of them stripped off his top and paced forward with his arms in the air, daring the Titans to come get him and chanting as if he was on a football terrace.

Calder stared at the hoplites. Unlike the Horde, the Titans all bore the Star of Macedon on their bronze shields, so it was harder to tell one unit from another. This group, however, didn't have the shield with the scalloped corners which the Heavy Brigade used to hold their giant Phalanx sarissas, nor the burnished bronze breastplates of the Companions. Instead, their torsos were protected by multiple bronze scales, sewn together like those of a fish.

'Peltasts,' whispered Thurmond next to her.

Freyja was watching them intently. If the Horde had still been at full strength, she would have sent word for Halvar to bring his Wolves hunting. But now there were only six Wolves remaining in Valhalla and tonight they were leaderless and confused. That only left the Hammers, who would be too slow and too noisy.

She was amazed at how brazenly the Titans loitered in the square, even though they were obviously getting irritated by the yobs and concerned about the phones recording their presence. Sure enough, their leader signalled and they began to peel away towards the steps in the south west corner opposite where the Ravens perched. In moments they would climb towards the grounds of George Heriot's School and disappear. If they'd been Companions – even if they'd been Heavies – Freyja would have left them well alone. But they weren't. They were lightly armoured peltasts, no more skilled in swordcraft than the Ravens, and Freyja knew she could not have asked the gods for a better target.

She waited for the last Titan to disappear up the steps, then signalled to her team and led them down the rest of the staircase, followed by the Vigilis. The yobs were still taunting the backs of the hoplites, so when they saw this new group arriving in the square and realised, despite their inebriation, that most of the figures were female, they went into ecstasies of insults, swaggering towards them and thrusting their crotches obscenely. Freyja wheeled towards them and drew her blade with such panache, that it sobered them and they scurried backwards.

The Ravens reached the other side and pressed against the walls at the foot of the steps. Freyja looked at her litter. Twelve against seven, but if they could play it right, the element of surprise would be with them. She bounded up the steps and they followed.

The Sacred Band ran lithely along the top of the high wall marking the eastern boundary of George Heriot's grounds. Parmenion had sent word that his peltasts would make for the school having tried to draw attention in Grassmarket, so the Band knew the plan. Agape led her team around to the rear, then jumped from the wall and crouched behind the few vehicles still in the car park. Confident they hadn't been seen, she jogged across the open space to the foot of the main school building. Four floors high, with turreted bastions at each corner and a central clocktower, this grand Scots Renaissance structure was a stunning piece of architecture. Agape had played on it many times and now, swords sheathed and without their shields, the Band were ready to show off their supreme climbing skills.

Despite the floors rising high above them, every window had been given a decorative stone circumference by the original architects, with prominent sills and ornate canopies. Reaching up, Agape took hold of the lowest sill, swung her feet onto the wall and pulled until she could get a knee onto the sill. From there, she straightened against the window pane and peered inside at the dark and deserted office. She knew the pupils slept in dormitory buildings on the other side of the car park and the main building was given over to classrooms and administration, so there should be no risk of disturbing anyone at this time of night, but she checked all the same.

Now came the hardest part. Pressing her back against the stone edge and placing her feet on the opposite side, she levered herself a few yards up the window with her shoulder against the glass panes. At the top, she was able to claw at the decorative canopy with one arm. Years earlier, the Titans had driven hidden iron pegs into the upper lip of the stone and she found one of these now and gripped it. Using this as purchase, she swung out on one arm, scrabbled with the other to find another peg, then used all her upper body strength to haul herself onto the canopy. Once she was steady, she rested and watched her team working their way up windows to either side.

Above her perch, the bare expanse of the wall was broken by two decorative stone rims that ran around the whole building, like prominent dado rails. Again, the Titans had fixed pegs years ago which provided handholds. She reached up, felt along the lower rail until she touched the pegs, clasped with both hands and swung her legs in an arc up the wall until her feet found purchase on the rail as well. In this horizontal position, she was able to stretch one arm to the upper rail, grab the peg and pull herself vertical. Once her toes had good purchase on the lower rail, she could reach ever higher and grab the sill of the window on the second floor.

So the process started all over again. First the sill, then the leverage up the window, then the grab for the ornate canopy, the haul onto this and then the stretch for the next rail. With steady, rhythmic movements, she climbed, and her Band came with her. In fifteen minutes, they were all crouched on the rooftop in the shadow of one of the turrets, breathing heavily and shaking their arms to rid themselves of the painful lactic acid. As in so many strategic places across Edinburgh's Old Town skyline, coils of rope were stowed next to the turret, kept dry in weatherproof sacks and checked periodically by Titan scouts.

Signalling to Kyriacos, Agape left the rest of the Band and the two of them bounded carefully up the sloping roof to the very top, where they could head to each corner and look out. To the north, they could hear voices on

Grassmarket, and in the opposite direction some traffic still used the main thoroughfare of Lauriston Place, but below them the school grounds and the adjacent Greyfriars cemetery were black and silent.

'Take the northern edge,' Agape said. 'I'll take the south. Signal me at the first sign of movement.'

She didn't have long to wait. Little more than five minutes passed before she saw Kyriacos raise his arm and point west. She followed the line of his arm and saw the peltast squad jogging through the school's front gardens. Behind them, coming over the wall from the steps, were other figures. She crouched and peered down. As one of the pursuers levered over the wall, the lights from the alley caught the design on the shield. The wings of a bird. Ravens.

Calder was the last to drop to the ground and hug into the wall. Her unit knelt in silence and let their eyes adjust to the dark gardens after the brightly lit alley. Beside them, the Vigilis squatted wordlessly, filming every move. Freyja had reached the top of the steps just in time to see the Titans disappear into the school grounds and, after a careful check herself from the top of the wall, she had waved the others over.

The gardens were mostly laid to lawn and formal borders, so there were few shrubs for cover and they could see the peltasts a couple of hundred yards ahead, jogging across the grass towards the southern gates. Freyja moved and Calder followed as they slunk low to the ground, swords drawn and shields held away from bodies to avoid any knocking. They rounded the main building and looked south across the lawns. The peltasts had reached the gates and were clustered together looking out at Lauriston Place and gauging the traffic.

Freyja knew this was the moment to gain on them, while their backs were turned and attention elsewhere. A row of manicured yews ran down the centre of the garden and she led the Ravens over to these and slipped down their line. Little by little, they approached the foe until they had closed the gap to thirty yards and then she brought her litter to a halt with a raised arm. Crouched behind the yews, they waited.

Calder watched the Titans. She was close enough to hear their whispers. They were taking an age deciding whether to climb the gates, and even though they outnumbered the Ravens, the thrill of imminent battle flowed through her. She knew her team had the advantage of total surprise and her many weeks on the road to recovery had brought her to this moment. She tingled with adrenaline and thirsted to be unshackled. At last, the Blood Season was calling her.

Freyja raised an arm. In seconds she would launch them into the attack.

Calder gripped her blade and tensed for the release.

Then suddenly there was a hiss from behind. Freyja turned. It was Runa. She was pointing to the main building from where there was movement on the high roof. Calder strained her eyes and could just see figures flinging themselves over the edge and swooping down ropes. They dropped so fast and hit the ground with such swift purpose that Freyja knew instantly what came for her team.

'Fly!' she shouted, stealth no longer needed, and panic flared through the Ravens.

Calder sprang forward, but instead of launching into an attack, she found herself following the others in a headlong sprint towards the eastern exit to Greyfriars graveyard. She could feel the dread coursing through her companions and, without looking back, every last fibre of her being cried *run*! They hit the gates, tore up them and somersaulted over, then rushed into the maze of gravestones. She passed the old yew, which had once been the place for the Thralls to deposit their amulets if they wanted to leave the Pantheon, but she didn't notice or care. Her team was spread around her and she felt the jaws of their pursuers snapping at their cloaks.

Her foot caught and she crashed onto her shield, but was on her feet again without breaking momentum. Then, as she looked ahead, a long line of hoplites emerged from the night, shields locked, blades ready, eyes on her. She saw the bronze breastplates, knew they were Companions and knew, too, that death now waited. She heard Freyja scream in defiance and felt a yell burst from her own throat. Instinctively, she knew that momentum was the only advantage she had and she shot towards the line of bronze. Beyond any logical thought, she saw a squat rectangular burial tomb ahead and she leapt onto this, ran the few steps across and hurled herself into the air on the other side.

Time seemed to slow. She arced down onto the Titan shieldwall and suddenly her brain knew exactly what she had to do. Her left leg straightened and kicked into the shield of one Companion, giving her the leverage to push up and over it. At the same instant, she struck with her sword at the man to her right and felt the blade sink into the soft flesh of his throat between helmet and cuirass. She wrenched it free and knew it was a death blow, but even as he was sinking, she crashed onto the grass beyond the shieldwall, lost the grip on her shield, and rolled and rolled.

She was winded and partially concussed, but adrenaline forced her up. The shieldline had been broken by her impact. A Companion's body was crumpled and two more were turning and running at her. Behind, she could see the Sacred Band deep in the fray and knew her Raven team battled for their lives. She screamed her defiance and wanted to launch herself back into the struggle, but she had lost her shield and the two Companions came for her. Instead, the lights of Grassmarket called.

With a cry, she turned and charged down the steps, across the road and into Grassmarket proper. She ran to the centre of the square, oblivious to the drunks, and then forced herself to stop and look back. No one pursued her. The night was alive with the clashes and cries of conflict from Greyfriars, but she could only stand panting and gripping her sword, with shock and fury coursing through her.

And then came Freyja and Jorunn together, bloodied and wild. They still carried their shields and Freyja yelled at Calder and they rammed either side of her and raised their shields in a primitive defensive wall. There the three of them waited and hoped, but no other Raven emerged.

Minutes passed and the sounds of struggle grew slower. The entrance to Greyfriars remained black and empty, and gradually silence slithered across the square. If the yobs were still present, they were cowering somewhere.

Then, at long last, a single warrior stepped down to the roadside. The figure glittered bronze in the streetlights and stood, legs apart, uncloaked, sword sheathed and carrying no shield. They could feel the quiet confidence that surrounded her and none of them needed telling that this was Agape.

The Band didn't follow through its attack. Perhaps the lights and the wide space of the square made them cautious. Perhaps they were content with the scalps of four of Valhalla's elite. Another eight Blood Credits. Perhaps their lust for violence had simply been satiated that night. Whatever the reason, Calder, Freyja and Jorunn were able to beat a tentative retreat up to Victoria Terrace and back through the South-West Gate. A Litter no more.

XXIX

The wind had gone and the Valhalla islanders emerged from their tents to a silence they had almost forgotten. Save for the occasional cough from beneath the canvas, nothing could be heard. Even the seabirds had ceased their cries and disappeared.

Punnr laced up his boots and stepped from the tent he shared with Olsen and Stigr. The cold early morning air embraced him and he zipped up his jacket, but it was good to be out of the heavy fug created by three sleeping men in close confinement. He looked around at the other tents, where heads were appearing and a few individuals were wandering to the troughs for a wash in the pre-dawn gloom. He was gagging for a cigarette and a decent coffee, so to take his mind from his cravings, he thrust his hands in his pockets and climbed a dune above the encampment.

The sky was cloudless and a pale moon still hung above the waters to the west, while behind the central hills, silver light approached. Every sound seemed amplified in the hush. He could hear splashing from the washing troughs and the crunch of feet on the shell sand. Someone was hacking up phlegm and under another tent came a rhythmic snoring. There were bangs and low voices from the interior of the church as a fire was lit and breakfast begun. Nature, however, was completely muted. Even the sea slept.

He watched Brante wander bare-chested to the troughs and thrust his naked scalp into the water with a grunt.

'Hey,' Punnr called as his friend made his way back.

Brante waved, retrieved a jacket from his tent and scrambled up to join him. 'What a difference. I'd forgotten a world without wind.'

'It's kind of beautiful.'

'*Kind of!* Let me tell you, this is god's country.'

Punnr laughed. 'Yeah, right. Says the man who's never been anywhere near these islands.'

'Hey, Englishman – you're talking to a proud Scot. And us Scots don't actually have to *go* to these places to know we love them. They're in our blood.'

'Next you'll be telling me your whole family has ancient Celt running through its veins.'

Brante shoved him good-naturedly on the shoulder. 'Better than being a southern Saxon bastard.'

They fell quiet with eyes out to sea.

'I'm glad you're here,' Punnr said eventually. 'You and Halvar are the only people I trust on this island.'

'You still not forgiven your litter?'

'It's not about forgiving. When the shit really hits the fan, I don't believe they've got my back.'

'In the eyes of the others, neither of us are properly bloodied yet. We may have the Bloodmarks to show our kills, but we've never stood in a shieldline for real and never experienced the tumult and chaos of a Grand Battle. It doesn't matter how often we train together on the sand, until we've stood shoulder to shoulder with them against each Titan attack and survived, they won't see us as deserving of our places in these Litters.'

Punnr knew the truth of these words, but he disliked them nonetheless. 'Then we'd better look out for each other.'

'Aye. We've been in this together since the very first induction night. We've shared the entire journey and no one can take that from us.'

'Blood brothers?'

Brante nodded. 'Aye. Sword brothers. Always and forever.'

Punnr smiled, then found his mind turning to another. 'Calder too. Always and forever. I really miss her.'

'You worried about her?'

'Of course. Sometime this week there's three more Blood Nights and we've thinned ourselves to a fraction of our usual strength. If the Titans ever caught scent of how many of us have departed, they'd come from the roofs in waves. A hundred and fifty of them against – what – fifty of us? So, yeah, I pray she's safe.'

'At least *that* bastard's with us.' Brante pointed down to the tents where Ulf was making his way to the church. 'He can't get up to mischief here.'

Punnr watched the man below. He walked alone, head down and didn't see them on the dune. 'He's different.'

'Aye, I noticed that. Not the cocky shit who led the Perpetuals in the *Sine Missione*.'

'He's scared. He was under Radspakr's orders when he tried to gut me at Old College and kill Calder in the castle.'

'But the bastard still relished the opportunities.'

'He did – but he also failed and that won't have gone down well with his superiors.'

'You think our little lad's been given a few choice words in his ear?'

'I think he's been a hair's breadth from a very grisly end and he knows it.'

'Watch him Punnr. Scared or not, he's still a snake.'

'I will. I won't be forgetting what he and Erland did to Calder.'

Brante suddenly tensed, raised his nose and snorted. 'You smell that?'

Punnr sniffed too and his face split into a grin. 'Bacon.'

They plunged down the dune.

While they breakfasted in the church, Halvar approached and prodded Punnr with his boot. 'You're with me today.'

'Yes, lord. What are we doing?'

'I thought a day at the seaside would be fun.'

Twenty minutes later, his jacket pockets stuffed with flatbreads and cheese wrapped in cloth, Punnr followed Halvar up the flank of the northern hill and left the rest of the Palatinate to another day of war games. Halvar had been given route instructions by Stigr and Ake, and the two of them made steady, but slower, progress. The sun rose and the morning matured. When they summited the main range, Halvar paused with his hands on his hips and looked around. 'Mighty fine.'

He was right. Below them, the streams and pools of a waterlogged landscape, sparkled in the sunshine and high to their right came the cry of a buzzard. The sea was a flat calm and had metamorphosed into the most perfect blue.

Stretching away into the distance, the islands appeared suspended, floating exquisitely between water and sky.

It took them over three hours to reach the northern coastline. Halvar scrutinised the sheep-studded grassland with the eye of a general, taking in the gorse bushes and the long dip at the eastern end, but he said nothing and strode up the embankment to look out to sea.

'Bugger.' Being landlubbers, neither of them had thought to take account of the tide and what lay before them was not the endless white sand of a potential killing ground as described by Stigr and Ake, but a bay of pristine blue water. Ripples tickled against just a few yards of sand and sanderlings skittered in the shallows, pecking at morsels.

'We're here about the same time as the others would have been.'

'Aye, but five days later.' He jumped down from the embankment, scattering the sanderlings, and ground his boots into the sand to test it. 'As a kid, I used to spend time out at Prestonpans, but I never could get my head around the bloody tides.' He put an arm over his eyes and squinted out across the water. 'That little island looks interesting. Ake said it's accessible when the sea's fully out and if so, blood will be spilt over its possession come Saturday.'

Punnr descended as well and followed him along the ribbon of sand. The sun glared off the white shells and he wished he had sunglasses. The thought made him smile. Vikings in Ray-Bans. Halvar would burst a blood vessel.

They walked all the way around the perimeter of the lagoon, stopping occasionally to study the terrain. The water was as clear as glass and the white sand beneath turned it turquoise. It could have been Barbados or Fiji, but minus the tourists, and Punnr wondered if he had ever seen anything more beautiful.

Halvar halted again and squinted across the water. 'How deep do you think it is, Weakling?'

'The incline's really gradual. I reckon you could wade a long way out before it even touched your thighs.'

'But look at the size of this bay. You'd be up to your neck long before you'd made it halfway.'

'What are you thinking?'

Halvar remained scowling into the distance and took a long time to answer. 'My gut says Stigr and Ake are right – this would make a perfect field of battle. But the water worries me, makes me wonder if they're wrong. Perhaps Atilius has selected the grassland after all. It's just as suitable.'

'But not as unique.'

They continued walking around the perimeter until they came, at last, to the final finger of land and looked out across the channel to the little island. The water here was deep and they could discern its currents even on such a calm day.

'Holding the island might be a prize asset,' growled Halvar, 'but I'd not want to be caught on the sand when that tide comes in.'

Two glistening round seal heads popped up to look at them.

'So what now?' Punnr asked.

Halvar turned and clawed his way back up the embankment to the grass beyond. 'We wait.'

As the sun eased over them and morning grew into afternoon, they sat amongst the grasses, listening to stonechats and greenfinches. Out in the bay tiny terns swooped and danced, filling the stillness with their high, rasping calls and somewhere further along the shore, a curlew backed them up with its deep lilting melody.

Halvar stirred and said he was going to look at the turf again. When he had gone, Punnr lay back and let the sun play on his face. The air still had the bite of March in the north, but it also contained warmth and he surrendered to the peace. He must have dozed because the next thing he knew was Halvar knocking him awake and dropping down next to him. 'Good to see the Thegn's earning his keep.'

Punnr sat up and rubbed his eyes. 'So what do you think about the grassland?'

'It would make a fine enough Field. Plenty of camera points, good cover, solid ground. Stigr's right, we'd want to hold the western end.' He threw out an arm towards the embankment. 'Tide's turned. A lot more sand now, so we'll hopefully see the bay properly in a couple of hours.'

'Why's the tide so important? If the bay *is* the Field, can't Atilius just time the Battle to avoid a high tide? There's enough daylight.'

'No he can't, and that's what's making me question the others' assumption that the bay's the Field. The Grand Battle always begins at two in the afternoon and finishes at three. It's been the same every year.'

'It's only an hour long? Why so short?'

Halvar shot him a glance. 'You really have a lot to learn, Thegn. The big battles of ancient times were fought between armies of tens of thousands, so there was plenty of meat for the grinder. But us? We've less than two hundred on each side. Believe me, in the press and panic of a shieldwall, two minutes is a long time. Ten's an eternity. Give quality warriors more than an hour to butcher each other and there'll be no one left. That's hardly a sustainable model, even for the Caelestia's limitless pockets.'

Punnr thought about this. 'Okay, an hour. I get it. But that makes it even easier to avoid tidal worries. So why's it got to be so rigidly scheduled at two?'

'Because, Weakling, you're forgetting this is a spectator sport. It revolves around our wonderful viewing public. An early afternoon start here, means perfect late-night entertainment in Hong Kong and Shanghai; prime time evening viewing in Moscow and Dubai. New York and Washington will just be getting up and glued to their screens over their damn pancakes and muffins. Only those poor multi-billionaires in Silicon Valley have to force themselves awake in the early hours to watch us gut ourselves.'

'Do they all watch it live?'

Halvar looked at him in amusement. 'If you'd got a cool ten mill on a horse, would you watch the race live?'

'Point taken.'

'You don't get it, do you Punnr. Come Saturday, this little island hosts the Super Bowl.'

Punnr peered across the grasses. Perhaps he didn't get it or perhaps he'd been too wrapped up in the training to give it any thought. 'How many will be watching?'

'That's harder to say. No one knows for sure outside the Pantheon authorities. The seven-strong Caelestia, obviously. Then there's the Curiate. Some think they number four hundred, but that's just hearsay. And then there's a larger outer circle of people permitted to access the feeds and gamble, but the gods know how many they are.'

'When I went to the Blood Gathering at the start of the Season, the Curiate were the ones with the eagle and sword on their robes?'

'Aye – although that was just the Blood Gathering of Scotland. There are similar assemblies where each of the other Palatinates are located.'

'And the rest of the guests? Were they from this outer circle?'

'Most. If it was like the occasions I've been to before, there'll have been some extras on the invite list as well, who would have been – shall we say – hired for the pleasures they bring to the evening?'

'Yeah, there were a few of them. So what's the difference between the Curiate and the others in the outer circle?'

Halvar sighed. 'I don't know, I don't bother myself with the intricacies of our paymasters. All I know is the Curiate are carefully selected and Oathsworn like us. In return they get access to the real insider information, the sort of stuff fortunes are won and lost on. As for the outer circle? They're all handpicked, wealthy bastards as well, but their membership only gets them login details to the data stations, online betting and ultra-secure live feeds from the Vigiles cameras. You know, like when you only get bronze level car insurance.'

'That seems a lot of people with access to some seriously confidential material. Doesn't it ever leak?'

Halvar shrugged. 'Probably. There's always some morons in a crowd, so that's when the bodies start turning up. The

Pantheon's one of those clubs that's pretty damn zealous about its rules.'

'If you had stacks of cash,' Punnr said thoughtfully, 'would you pay to watch people die?'

Halvar stood and peered at the outgoing tide. 'I don't ask myself those kind of questions. What's the point? We're the ones doing the killing, so how can we say what's wrong and right. The way I see it, none of us are angels.' He swiped a dismissive hand towards Punnr. 'Anyway, enough of this quizzing, I'm sick of it. Bugger me, my stomach's rumbling.'

Punnr remembered his full pockets and pulled out the cloth-wrapped breads and cheeses.

'You're not a total waste of space,' said the Housecarl with a huge grin.

They sat and ate, and the food warmed Halvar's spirits. 'Ah, not a bad spot on a sunny day. A glass of Chablis and I might even be a happy man.'

Punnr swallowed his cheese and looked at his officer. 'Were you a happy man with my sister?'

Halvar tore a strip of bread and munched silently, his brows furrowed in memory. 'Aye, I was.'

'What was she like when she was with you?'

The Housecarl took an age answering. 'Playful, impulsive, featherbrained, petulant, whimsical, funny. Everything she couldn't be in the Pantheon. She would dance around the house in her knickers. Morning and night, no matter the time, always dancing. She loved cakes and sweet treats and would send me out on errands for chocolate pastries, which we ate in bed. She was happy in the house, said it was our special place. She could spend hours watching cartoons and playing video games and singing along to tinny pop. She filled the place with candles and made me take bubbly, scented baths with her. She would tease me because I was older and too serious and if I got irritable, she would tickle me.'

Halvar chuckled at the memories and Punnr studied the softness in the eyes of this rugged Housecarl. 'During those times,' Punnr said, 'I guessed she had found someone. She would come back to our flat with a new passion and vitality. She was the best I had ever known her. You should know that. You made her the best person she could be.'

Halvar squinted at him and nodded his thanks.

'I suspect I was a kind of father figure, replacing the one you and she barely knew. She liked me to be decisive and take decisions and that seemed to allow her to be such an amazing, sparkly woman during our times together.' Halvar brushed the crumbs from his front and a frown returned as he mulled his next words. 'And maybe that's where it all went wrong.'

'How so?'

'When the Pantheon hours were close at hand, Morgan transformed into Olena, a warrior, a leader. Tough, calculated, disciplined. We would say goodbye and we would go to our separate Palatinates and we would be the people the Pantheon needed us to be. Olena lived with her head, not her heart. Olena would never have been stupid enough to believe love could conquer everything.

'But in those other times, in that house, when we were sharing bubble baths or eating ice cream in bed, those were the moments when Morgan locked out the real world and dreamed her dreams. When your mother died and she had to be a grown-up for both of you, I think her moments with me became even more fanciful and illusory. She grew desperate thinking we should be together in the Pantheon, that we could stand shoulder to shoulder in the battle lines and nothing would come between us. The idea lodged in her and she would talk about it incessantly and hold me and whisper her dreams to me.

'God knows, I threw up enough objections, but somehow she always got around them and I started believing the whole crazy scheme. In that house, in her arms, listening to her passion and fizz, anything seemed possible. Her plan seemed simple. She would bring me news of Titan movements and Valhalla would be waiting to tear into them. If we could weaken the Titan lines enough during the Blood Nights, she was convinced I could lead my Wolves through their defences at the Grand Battle and kill Alexander. She hated the man anyway – a malignant, insidious, coke-fuelled coward, uncaring of his troops and unworthy of the crown – and she was so exquisitely certain that it would work.'

'So when did it start going wrong?'

'When I told Radspakr. Christ, I was a fool, but I couldn't just keep ambushing Titans so easily without raising suspicions and I knew how proud he was of the Horde and how much he craved success against the old enemy. I thought he would love our plan.'

'And did he?'

'Too much. He wanted more and more information from Olena and then – somehow – Odin knew about us too and that's when the dream became a nightmare. Olena was told she must lead the cream of Alexander's troops into a trap beneath the Royal Mile. If she refused, she would be exposed. I think that was when she knew everything was unravelling. I lost my beautiful, vivacious Morgan and instead she became subdued and distant and terrified. But we had gone too far already. Titans were dead because of us. If the truth got out, we were both goners, so our only choice was to do as Odin decreed. She must lead the Companions into the trap.'

'And that was the last time you saw her?'

'The final time I saw Morgan was in the hours before that fateful night. It was surprisingly mild and sunny for March and she had taken herself for a walk in the parks. But as dusk fell, rain came hammering in again and when she returned we argued like crazy and she departed for Ephesus in silence and without a look in my direction.' Halvar's words stuttered to nothing and it took him several seconds before he could draw breath and continue. 'Odin forbade that I should take part in the trap. He did not trust me. I was held in a secret tunnel in Valhalla while Bjarke and Freyja led the troops. It was a bloodbath. Freyja killed Timanthes and a third of his Companions were lost. But Olena organised a fighting retreat and disappeared onto the rooftops above the Mile and I've never seen her since.'

The men sat in silence with their thoughts as a breeze rustled the grasses.

'And that's it?' pushed Punnr. 'That's the end?'

'Except for the letter I told you about. She wrote to me last summer and described how she had returned to your flat on the estate after the disastrous ambush and there someone came for her. It wasn't the Titans or Radspakr or the Vigiles, but she used a strange turn of phrase. She said *"the one who appeared was so crushingly unexpected that you'd never believe me even if I could tell you and live".'*

'What's that supposed to mean?'

'I don't bloody well know! Don't you think I've asked that question a thousand times? But I do know this – if a warrior tries to run from this game, they always get found. Once you're in, there's nowhere in the world to hide if you try to leave. The reality is only the Pantheon can stop the Pantheon finding you.'

'So Atilius has got her?'

'Perhaps, although she was specific in her letter that it wasn't his Vigiles that came for her.'

A horrible thought occurred to Punnr. 'Do you think she's in Erebus?'

'I've wondered that many times and I've no answer. But I believe there's maybe one who knows more.'

'Who?'

'Agape.'

'Agape!'

'She found your sister on the rooftops after the cellar fight and she let her go. She could've killed her there or, worse, returned her into the hands of Alexander. But she didn't, because Agape and Olena were close.'

'What's that supposed to mean? I thought you and Morgan were the lovebirds who got us into all this mess.'

'I'm just saying your sister loved others too.'

Punnr stared out at the endless sky and tried to piece together what his Housecarl was telling him. Then he snorted angrily and shook his head. 'Sod's bloody law – of all the people, it just *had* to be Agape. Only the Titan's slaughterer-in-chief. What am I supposed to do? Charge over to her in the middle of the Battle and ask if she's time for a chat?'

To his surprise he felt Halvar's hand on his shoulder.

'I'm sorry, Tyler. I wish I could bring Morgan back. I truly do. But I'm not the one who has the answers.'

Punnr looked at the Housecarl suspiciously and a realisation dawned on him. 'You know how to get to Agape, don't you? How to communicate with her outside the Pantheon?'

Halvar removed his hand and frowned. 'Don't go there, Wolf.'

But Punnr would not be deterred. 'You know who she is – I can feel it. Don't pretend otherwise. If Morgan and Agape were so close, then you must have come across her on the outside. There was a moment on Calton Hill when she was about to split my skull, but she stopped when you shouted. She recognised you and then she realised who I was.' Now it was Punnr's turn to grip the other's shoulder. 'Halvar, you've got to help me.'

'I said, don't go there.'

'When we get off this island...'

'*If* we get off this island.'

'Show me how I can contact her. I'm begging you.'

Halvar thrust his hand aside irritably. 'Don't you think I've already tried that, you fool? Don't you think I've pleaded with her to see me and tell me what she knows? But she refuses. She's the Captain of the Sacred Band and

I'm a Valhalla Housecarl and there was never any love lost between us. She will not give me anything.'

'But perhaps she will for me. I'm Morgan's brother. Her flesh and blood. Her only surviving kin. If Agape knows something about my sister, she must tell me. Surely she would understand that.'

Halvar glared sullenly out to sea.

'Please, Halvar. Promise me, if we get off this island, you'll help me contact her. She's my only hope of discovering Morgan's fate. I've nothing else. Just ask her if she'll speak with me.'

Still Halvar fumed. 'I only said I *believe* she may know more. She may have nothing to offer.'

'But at least I will have tried.'

Halvar twisted to look at him. 'All right. When the Season's over – if we're still living and breathing – I'll ask Agape if she will speak with you. But I'm promising nothing more.'

'It's enough. Thank you.'

The men stood and examined the ever-expanding beach. The sun was lowering in the western sky, casting a metallic sheen over the sea. Flocks of birds were dashing all over the sand, their chorus the song of these northern outposts.

'We're losing the light,' said Halvar. 'We should start back. I'll post a couple of Hammers out here for a day or two because I still want to know what those channels are like when the water's coming in.'

'Can't we get the precise times of the tides from somewhere?'

'I was thinking that too. A visit to the town might be

called for. Come on, Wolfling, time to go see what Asmund has been putting the others through.'

A movement from the far side of the bay caught Punnr's eye. 'There's people over there.'

They shielded their eyes and stared. Three figures were standing on a knoll. A vehicle was parked up and a fourth figure carried something from it and placed it at the centre of the group. He fiddled and it grew legs. He was extending a tripod. Another in the group crouched and opened a bag, and even at that distance, Halvar and Punnr could recognise the shape of a video camera being retrieved.

'Well, well. Conclusive proof, lad. We've caught them setting up. So, whatever the bloody tide's doing at two o'clock on Saturday, you and I and the Horde of Valhalla will be standing out there on that sand, waiting for Alexander.'

Earlier that same day, under the same blue sky and on waters just as calm, the little Sunray was spotted wallowing off the Isle of May by a passing fishing boat heading back into the Forth. Within the hour, the coastguard arrived from Anstruther and the boat's registration documents revealed the owner to be Trevor Muir with mooring rights at Cramond. By early afternoon, the police had visited a flat Mr Muir had recently started renting in Ravelston and when there was no answer, nor on his phone, they called his employers. This was when they learned he hadn't been into work that day or the previous Friday and hadn't provided an explanation.

The first alarm bells began to ring and their inquiries led

them to his marital home in Learmonth Place. Again there was no answer at the door. They checked his wife's records and called her GP clinic employers. No, they hadn't seen her even though she worked mornings and should have been in that day.

So the moment came when they forced entry into flat number five and found the stiff, cold body of Mrs Muir in the bedroom.

XXX

Lana slouched on her sofa in pyjamas, watching the Tuesday evening sun setting through curtains she couldn't be bothered to draw. She needed a pee and probably a gin, but her body refused to move. Despite cocooning herself in her flat for the last two days, Sunday's Blood Night had still left her spent physically and emotionally. Her ribs were bruised and one of her knees scraped, but incredibly she had come through that murderous trap without a serious wound.

Her mind wouldn't let go of the sight of the armoured bronze line waiting for her, nor of the absolute fear of what had chased her. It was her first taste of the Blood Season and it made the Raids feel like playground frolics. She knew the Pantheon embraced risk and death, and she accepted these perils wholeheartedly because they were what made it so addictive, but to lose so many of her Raven litter in one fight was too much to bear. Four of the warriors by her side when they exited North-West Gate, when they raced down Castle Wynd steps and when they vaulted the wall into George Heriot's grounds, were gone. Thurmond and Runa, whom she had shared a perch above the Parliament building during the Raiding Season, were both now corpses in the hands of the *libitinarii*. She thought of Freyja and wondered where she was. The Housecarl had been a bloodied, shaking, livid figure in the Tunnels afterwards. She had soaked the cuts in her thighs and arms in gritted silence, bandaged them with the help of two Ravens from the other litter, and departed without a glance to Jorunn or Calder.

Her thoughts wandered to Tyler. How much she needed him to hold her at that moment. How good his arms would feel around her, like they had when he carried her from the castle all those weeks ago. She remembered the tenderness in his eyes on their final night together and she wished he was here again, ministering to her wounds and making her feel safe within these unwelcome walls.

With a sigh, she reached for her phone and began scrolling through rental properties, but her enthusiasm for a move had been ebbing since she realised any change of residence would need to be approved and recorded by Pantheon authorities, and that was pretty much the same as knocking on Radspakr's door and handing him her new address details in person.

She gave up and switched to Facebook, then flicked to *The Scotsman*. She scanned the headlines and was about to drop her phone onto the carpet, when a face appeared that she knew so well, under the headline: *Boy feared drowned in Forth*.

Wide-eyed, lips open, the Blood Night suddenly forgotten, she discovered the unfolding investigation and stared at the image of the smart, bright, effervescent lad. It seemed impossible that he could be gone and she visited other news sites to read their take on the story, as well as googling Oliver Muir and bringing up everything she could find. She toyed with calling Tyler, but wherever he was, she doubted he would have his phone with him and she knew it would do him no good to learn about this tragedy.

At long last, she got herself to the toilet and then to her new Krups machine for a flat white. The media were blaming Oliver's father for the tragedy and anger replaced her shock, but as she sipped her coffee, new questions began to spark.

Perturbed, she dressed, bolted some soup and toast and headed out into the gloom. She strode down to Stockbridge high street and then through the backroads to Learmonth Place. She wanted to see the property for herself, breathe it in, perhaps go up the stairs to number six and check if Tyler had left a key in his wellies. But, of course, there was a police constable standing on the pavement outside and her resolve disintegrated. She walked by with a courteous nod and kept going around to the other side of the Gardens, where she slowed and peered back. Lights were on in the lower floors, but the windows of both Oliver's and Tyler's flats remained dark, and for some reason this simple evidence of their absences caught in her throat.

She forced her emotions aside and tried to think. She recalled a line in *The Scotsman*, something about it being impossible to confirm death without a body. A spokesperson from the RNLI had described the predominant currents in the Forth and suggested where bodies would most likely wash up, but so far there had been no sign. Father and son. Both bodies missing. Both *presumed* drowned.

She remembered Oliver's contagious excitement as he looked for solutions to the Raiding Season riddles and then his search for Tyler's sister. The very same search that had brought Ulf and Erland to kill her at the castle.

Ulf. One of the Perpetuals. *Lost Children.*

The image of Radspakr appeared in her mind. The fear on his face on Sunday night. What had she thought? *If the Thane's afraid, then something's very wrong.*

And then a new face came to her. One with cold eyes.

She began to walk again, this time away from the house and back towards the shops, where she waved down a taxi.

'Marchmont, please.'

It took twenty minutes to break through the evening commuter traffic on Lothian Road and to see Bruntsfield Links ahead.

'Whereabouts in Marchmont?'

'Livingstone Place, but just drop me at the end of it. Do you know where the nearest bus routes are?'

'The 24 on Marchmont Road and the 41 on Marchmont Crescent. But if you need taking somewhere, just tell me. More comfortable than the bus.'

'Thanks, no. I'm fine.'

He dropped her at the end of Livingstone Place and she peered along it. The air was cold after a clear sunny day and she was thankful for her scarf and Cossack hat. Wrapping herself tighter in them, she walked west until she came to Marchmont Road and identified the nearest bus stops on both sides of the road. There were a few shops and she saw a café with a good view of the street. Once in the warm and ensconced at a window table, she ordered a glass of wine, then settled in to wait.

Two and a half hours drifted. The traffic outside dissipated and she felt compelled to order a pizza to ease the stares of the staff. She was thankful both bus stops were under streetlights, but the passing time also brought with it increasing doubts. Was she being stupid? There were so many factors she hadn't stopped to consider, so many imponderables that meant it unlikely her vigil would prove successful.

She checked her watch. Almost ten. Three hours before the Fifth Blood Night. What the hell was she doing there? By choice, she would already be at Valhalla, giving herself precious time to get into the right headspace. And the gods knew, she needed that headspace tonight. It felt almost laughably insane that she should be back out on the streets that very night with her sword in hand and life on the brink.

She was losing herself again in the blood struggle, when a figure materialised across the road beside the southbound bus stop. Her pizza half mauled, Lana shot a handful of notes to the waitress and hurried out, crossed the road further up and hung in the shadows fifty paces from the bus stop. The figure wore a winter coat and carried a plastic box, which Lana knew would contain a banana.

After a few minutes, a Lothian number 24 double-decker pulled up and Nurse Monique boarded, flashing her season card at the driver. Lana rammed her hat down and ran to the stop just before the driver closed the doors. Holding her scarf to her mouth, she bought a standard return with no idea where she was going and walked down the bus with her chin tucked low. There were only a few passengers on the lower deck and no sign of Monique, who must have climbed upstairs. Lana continued to the back seat and squeezed into a corner where she had a good view of the comings and goings.

They travelled south along Comiston Road, passed the Royal Edinburgh Hospital, through Morningside, around the Braids golf courses and on, inexorably, towards the edges of the city. The bus began to empty. They left the last buildings behind and crossed the ring road, then drove into darkness near the foot of the Pentland Hills. A few minutes later the bus slowed and turned into a large car park, where it pulled up behind several other empty buses. The final passengers departed and Lana waited with her scarf pulled over her nose again, as three more came down from the upper deck. The last of these was Monique, but she didn't look around and as soon as she had stepped off, Lana walked swiftly to the exit.

The other people were scattering amongst the cars and, for a moment, she thought she'd lost the nurse, but then she saw her crossing behind the bus and heading back to the main road. She followed at a cautious distance as the nurse led her a hundred yards along the pavement and then turned up a lane sloping towards the Pentlands. Beyond the rise of the road, Lana could see lights glowing in the distance and when she reached the crest her view opened up. Monique was just ahead, walking down the slope towards a barrier about three hundred yards away, manned by security guards. Either side of this, a solid twelve-foot chain-link fence ran around the perimeter of a complex, which comprised a brightly lit parking area and a large concrete building several floors high, but with windows only at ground level. There was no signage of any kind, no names, no branding. The place was judicious about its anonymity. But there were cameras. Mounted on poles above the entrance, over the parking area and beside the doors to the building itself.

Lana froze with indecision. Her crazy plan had worked.

She had remembered Monique's reference to her apartment on Livingstone Place and her bus rides into work, and thanks to some amateurish tailing, she was now looking at the secretive Pantheon hospital and its Schola. But she needed only a cursory glance to know implicitly the hospital was also a fortress and she could go no further. What the hell was she supposed to do? In seconds the nurse would be closing on the security guards.

'Monique!'

My god, that was too loud. She was certain sirens would blare and searchlights begin quartering the fields to find her, but all that happened was the nurse swung round and stared at her.

'What are *you* doing here? Did you follow me?'

'I saw you in Marchmont, yes.'

Monique peered at the guards, then paced back and pulled Lana against the hedgerow bordering the lane. 'Sweet Jesus, girl, you can't be here. You have any idea how much trouble we'll be in if they find us? Get yourself gone. Now! You hear me?'

She made to continue her journey, but Lana gripped her arm. 'Please, Monique, I need your help.'

'What you talking about girl?' The whites of her eyes were up close to Lana's, her lunchbox pressed between their bodies.

Lana tried to gather her thoughts. 'Listen, I know what's down there's more than just the hospital. I saw the children.'

'What is and isn't down there's none of your business. You were mended and then you were returned, that's all that matters. You mustn't breathe a word to no one 'bout how you found this place.'

Lana pulled out her phone and as the screen glowed, Monique turned in terror to check the guards had not seen. She pushed herself even closer to shield the light. 'You're crazy.'

Lana had the photo of Oliver from *The Scotsman*. 'Look at this lad. Look! They say he's drowned, but I don't believe it. I think he's in there, in that Schola.'

'You're mistaken. There's no Schola.'

'Please, Monique, he's special to me. So special. I *need* to know if he's there.'

'Calder, I told you, there's no place called a Schola and even if there was, I can only access the fingerprint scanners on my wards.'

'I just need you to tell me if he's there.' Lana was looking at the photo and tears were pricking the corners of her eyes.

Monique took her chin and forced it up so that their eyes met, then said in a more placatory tone, 'There's no Schola, but there are sometimes youngsters in transit in one of the wings, just there temporarily for check-ups. But you have to understand what they'll do to me if they find out about this conversation? I'm just a nurse. And I'm an illegal, so they own me. They can replace me with a click of their fingers.'

'I know, but the boy...'

'Calder, you don't get it, girl. They'll kill me.'

This sobered Lana. She looked at the nurse and could tell by her expression that she spoke the truth. 'I'd no idea.'

'So you need to turn around and leave, right now. You understand?'

'Okay.' Lana wiped the tears from her cheeks and Monique made to go. 'But *please* promise me you'll try. I just need something to confirm he's in there.'

'I make no promises,' the nurse said over her shoulder.

Lana watched her approach the barrier and flash her ID at the guards, then make her way across the car park without looking back.

She stared at the complex; at the fences, the lights and the cameras. *I'm sorry, Oliver. I'm so sorry. I tried. If you're in there, stay strong. Get through whatever they throw at you. Survive.*

XXXI

'Where in Hel's name is she?' Freyja demanded, but her Ravens could only shrug.

It was twelve thirty-six, little over twenty minutes to Conflict Hours and her Company, now so shorn that it was just one enlarged litter, was missing yet another member. The Housecarl swore and stomped to the female changing area, where Calder's locker remained untouched. Freyja opened her own, pulled off her day tunic and – topless – retrieved the linen underlayers that would sit beneath her armour.

'Missing a little bird?' said a man behind her and she froze. It was a voice from her past, a voice she had forced herself to forget.

'It's none of your business,' she replied and covered herself with the first layer of linen.

'But it is my business, now that I'm Hersir of Wolf Litter Two.'

Freyja refused to turn and give him the satisfaction of seeing her expression. She pulled on her padded woollen tunic and tied her braids back. 'You shouldn't be here. You should still be rotting in Erebus and, if I had my way, they'd throw away the key.'

'Now, now, forgive and forget.'

She spun around at this, unable to help herself. 'Forgive and forget! After what you did, you bastard!' She couldn't hide a spasm of shock when she took in the state of him and she cursed herself for letting him see. He was still tall and his hair still blonde, though no longer short, and there was the arrogance in his eyes that never left, but now he was a skeleton, his skin white parchment yanked across bones. He was already mailed and he held his helmet under one arm. 'You've no place in this Palatinate,' she spat. 'Whatever powers brought you back, they mean nothing. You'll never be one of the Horde in the eyes of the warriors here.'

His expression hardened at her words and she could see the old anger still coursed through his veins. 'It's precisely those powers who need me so much. How many people do you think ever leave Erebus?'

She refused to answer and turned back to close her locker. She could feel his eyes roaming over her and it made her stomach churn. 'Get away from me.'

He laughed ferally and thrust his helmet on. 'I hate to tell you, but I'm here for good, so you'd better start being sweet.'

She was about to reply, when Calder burst into the changing room, red and flustered. 'I'm sorry, I'm sorry.' She dived for her locker without taking in the Wolf.

'Where've you been?' Freyja responded angrily. 'We're minutes from Conflict.'

'I lost track of the time; it won't happen again.'

Calder was stripping and the man smirked, then caught Freyja's eye and walked to the door. 'I'll leave you to your little disciplinary situation.'

Once he was gone, Freyja stepped over to her Raven. 'You realise if you'd been late, I'd have no option but to report you. It's something the Vigiles don't take lightly.'

'My mistake, I know. Never again.'

Freyja looked at her more softly. 'Sunday night was brutal. I've never lost so many from my Company in one fight. If you need to talk about it, we can.'

Calder pulled on her wool tunic. 'Thank you, I appreciate that, but I think I'm okay.'

'Then get yourself dressed and armoured. I doubt we'll be going out tonight, so you're lucky. Sveinn knows what we had to endure and will send the Hammers and Wolves instead, so we may just be kicking our heels in the Halls.'

She departed and made her way down towards the Throne Room. Wolf Litter Two were heading the other way to take up station at North Gate, ready to leave on the strike of one, and the man was there again.

He leaned into her as she passed. 'Who's the girl?'

Freyja jolted to a halt and her blood ran cold. She turned on him and stared into the eyes behind the iron. 'You touch her and I swear I'll kill you.'

'Well, will you look at that,' whispered Brante.

They were leaning on the rail overlooking the harbour in the main town. All that could be heard was the gentle knocking of boats and the splashing of two otters playing below them, indifferent to their presence. Punnr watched in awe as they surfaced and rolled and kicked at each other.

'I think that's one of the most beautiful things I've seen.' One of them shot from the water to perch on the embankment. It clawed at the pebbles, and they could see the shine of its pelt and the beady brown eyes that peeked up at them. 'Funny, isn't it, how nature just carries on doing its thing. Here's us, caught in a game of such complexity, with rules coming out our ears, and secrets and suspicions. Foe, seen and unseen. Dressing up and slaughtering each other so arseholes with money can win more money they don't need. And – well – nature doesn't care. It just keeps on living around us like it's always done. Sort of puts things in perspective.'

It was eight thirty in the morning. Halvar had sent the two of them from the camp just after daybreak and it had taken two hours to trudge to town. The wind had been still for most of the week, but the bright weather of a few days before had turned to a flat grey, dulling the island, removing its scintillating varnish. Dressed in their black hiking gear, they had wandered down to the harbour where the ferry offices were located and found a small stone building saying *Harbourmaster*, with a sign on the door giving eight thirty as the opening time.

The second otter leapt out and the two tumbled together, then both dived abruptly and were gone.

Brante clapped Punnr on the shoulder. 'Show's over. Back to our complexities.'

Two cars appeared and dropped off occupants to unlock the ferry offices. Shortly afterwards, three more vehicles arrived, pulled into a lane on one side and switched off their engines. The couple in the first of these sat eating sandwiches and watching them through the windscreen. A man in the third got out, released a Labrador and took it for a wander around the piers.

'So the bloody place does come to life,' said Punnr.

'Aye.' Brante was looking out to sea. 'And I think I know why.'

Easing between the outlying arms of the island, noiseless, dwarfing its surroundings, came a ferry. The two Vikings were amazed they hadn't noticed it earlier. One second the horizon had been empty and now this goliath was upon them, making the castle on its outcrop in the bay look like a child's toy.

There was more movement across the car park and an overweight man in a short-sleeved shirt, black tie and badly fitting trousers, got out of a van, followed by an equally fat terrier, and opened up the harbourmaster's office.

'That's us,' said Brante as the first deep rumbles from the ferry came to them.

The terrier barked shrilly when they entered, but stayed on its cushion by the radiator and went back to gnawing a chew as it watched them suspiciously through its furry fringe. The man came out from a small kitchen where they could hear a kettle boiling, took one long look at their black clothes and disappeared again. They waited while he made tea and then joined them holding a mug saying Stornoway Highland Games '93. He seated his bulk behind a desk and sipped his drink, examining them with the same solemn expression as his mutt.

'We need to know about tides,' said Punnr. 'Do you have anything showing tide times?'

The man pointed to a sheet of paper tacked on a noticeboard and watched them try to interpret it.

'Pantheon?' he said at last with the soft accent of the isles.

'Don't know what you mean, mate,' said Brante, while Punnr focused on the sheet. 'We're just over from Edinburgh.'

'I been to the capital once.'

'Oh yes? What did you think?'

The harbourmaster considered this while he extracted a packet of biscuits from a drawer in his desk. 'I think, if I had to live there, I'd be killing folk too.'

Brante ignored the comment. 'I see you've got a ferry coming in. Where's it from?'

'Oban, like them all.' He chomped on a biscuit and threw a corner to the terrier who caught it dexterously. 'Busy one, this. Lot of folk on board.'

Punnr was running his finger along the lines on the sheet. 'So, let me get this right. HW means High Water and LW means Low Water?'

The man dipped his head once.

'And the Saturday marked is this next one in a couple of days?'

'Aye.'

Punnr held his finger to a figure on the chart. 'I was worried you were going to say that.'

'Problem?' asked Brante.

'Probably. What else would you expect? Come on, let's go before chatterbox here traps us in an endless conversation.'

The ferry was pulling alongside and men had emerged to catch ropes and haul them tight. The arrival of the boat had brought the town to life. A taxi was waiting at the end of the pier and a coach came down the main road. The little village shop had opened and the smell of hot sausage rolls drifted to them.

'Goddammit!' swore Brante. 'The Pantheon puts more

money in my account each month than I know what to do with, but will it permit me to have a few pence in my pocket for a tasty breakfast? Will it, my arse. Let's clear off, it's making my mouth water.'

But Punnr wasn't listening. He was staring up at the ferry's deck where rows of passengers dressed in black were waiting to disembark. Brante saw them too and whistled. 'The cavalry's arrived.'

'Too many for the planes, I guess.' Punnr stared at the figures and tried to spot a flash of blonde. 'I wonder if Calder's on there.'

The ferry's front opened and a lorry and several cars emerged. Then the foot passengers disembarked and a steady stream of black-clad, baggage-less men and women trooped along the pier. The harbourmaster came out to stare too, still holding his tea.

But there was no Calder, no Freyja and no Ravens. Instead, it was Bjarke and forty of his Hammer Regiment who slouched up the pier.

'Wolf pricks!' he shouted when he saw them, to the laughter of those behind.

The harbourmaster drained his drink, cast a look at Brante and Punnr, and returned to his office, saying just loudly enough for them to hear, 'City pricks.'

The troops began to clamber onto the coach and Punnr strode towards Bjarke, who was counting them on board. 'Where are the others?'

'Since when's it your place, Vestal, to demand questions of a Jarl of Valhalla?'

'I'm no Vestal and I'll ask you again, where are Raven and the rest of Wolf?'

Bjarke eyed him. 'Still in Edinburgh. Though there's fuck-all left of them.' He swivelled and boarded the coach. 'Get going,' he said to the driver.

Punnr waved for Brante and stepped on board. Bjarke was sat in the front seat and he scowled at the new arrival. 'Hammer-only vehicle, this. Have a nice walk back to camp, *Vestal*.'

To the Jarl's shock, Punnr stood aside to let Brante head down the gangway, then dropped next to the big warrior as the coach began to pull away.

'You need to get your facts right. The Bloodmark on my mail will attest I'm the killer of a Titan elite Companion worth two Blood Credits. But, more importantly, what did you mean *there's fuck-all left of them*?'

'Get out this seat before I break your legs.'

'Not until you've answered my question.'

Bjarke glared at him for many moments, weighing him up. 'Sveinn's trying one last attempt in the final Blood Night to make the Titans think we're all still scratching our arses in Valhalla. He wants Hammer out here, rested and prepared, so he's just kept back a dozen of my troops to guard the Gates, along with Raven and Wolf Litter Two to play with Alexander. Trouble is, they've been falling like bloody mayflies. Four Ravens gone to the gods on Sunday and two Wolves on Tuesday. With Turid out as well, you can count the Wolves on one hand and Raven's just a single litter now. Fucking stupid tactics! My Hammers have been screaming to be unleashed, but we were only allowed out on Tuesday.'

'Who's gone to the gods? Which ones?'

'Who cares? No one important. But it looks like the

bloody Titans will be taking the honours at the end of the Cull.'

Punnr wanted to hit him, strangle the information out of the belligerent bastard, but he knew it was useless, so he fell into silence and Bjarke jerked a thumb towards the rear. 'Now clear off, unless you want me to kick you and baldie into the verge without asking the driver to slow.'

Punnr was so seething with frustration that instead of complying, he found himself saying, 'Listen, Jarl, I don't know what your problem is. I don't know what I've done to piss you off. But here's something to think about. Despite everything that's been thrown at me, I've come up winning. Thegn of Valhalla, White Warrior, collector of the Assets, killer of Companions. I'm still standing and I'm only getting stronger. Whereas your little friend Ulf has failed at every task you've set him. Perhaps you should be asking yourself, which team you want to be on? The winners or the losers?'

He stood before Bjarke could respond and only heard a surprised snort as he made his way through the stares of Hammers to Brante at the back, where he plonked himself down, shaking. 'I think I just made a dangerous beast a lot more angry.'

'Don't lower yourself to the moron. He's all noise.'

The coach began to struggle over the central hills, but Punnr's mind was far away in Valhalla, praying for a Raven.

XXXII

It was the Final Blood Night and the remaining little band gathered in the Throne Room. They were pitifully few in number. The sixteen Ravens who had started the Nineteenth Season had been carved to nine. Twelve Hammers were retained to guard the Gates, and of the Wolves, only five were now present, including the enigmatic new stranger, who kept himself removed from the rest, leaning against a wall in the far corner where the shadows were deepest.

Calder stood with Jorunn amongst the Ravens and waited for Sveinn to descend from his Council Room. Freyja was out in front of the group, staring fixedly into space without meeting anyone's eye. Her arms were still bandaged and Calder thought a heaviness had descended upon her during this last week. She spoke little to her troops except to give orders and her cinnamon eyes, though still regal, were now unapproachable.

On the dais, Radspakr stood beside Sveinn's throne. He too was grim and avoided the looks of the group. Calder peeked over at a figure in the shadows in the far corner of the Hall. Was *he* the reason? She had barely noted him in these last forty-eight hours, but the timing of his appearance in the Horde coincided with this cloud that had descended on the officers, and the other Ravens talked about him in muted terms. His name was Skarde, but everyone referred to him as the Prisoner, and amongst the older warriors there was a wariness whenever he was mentioned. Calder knew instinctively that this man brought fear to the Tunnels of Valhalla.

The Council Room door opened and Sveinn stepped out onto the stairs above them. He was dressed for magnificence, his gold-trimmed mail *brynjar* already worn over his black silk undershirt and a wolfskin held across his shoulders by the Triple Horn of Odin. His long hair with its silver comet-trails was loose and hanging over his mail as he strode down the steps to a hushed Hall. He spurned the throne and stood instead on the edge of the dais, letting his eyes roam across those before him.

'My few! My brave defenders of Valhalla. The end of the Cull is upon us and you have again brought pride and honour to this Palatinate. In just a few hours the Blood Nights will be over and we can prepare ourselves for the glory of the Grand Battle. Before then, however, there is still a job to do.

'This Season the Caelestia demanded a toll of twenty-five from the Blood Nights and we stand now at twenty-two. So our task tonight is to seek out three more Titans and relinquish them of their lives, so they may not face us across the shieldwalls of the Battle.'

He was putting on a good front. Everyone knew that of the twenty-two slain, sixteen were Vikings. The King had got his tactics completely wrong. In the first set of Nights, he had sent out his Raven and Storm Regiments to find the foe, but these were troops who specialised in spear and bow and stealth, and were unsuited for the sword skills of this Season. He had gambled that the Titans would worry about their fewer numbers and thus keep back their Companion and Band elites. But he had gambled wrongly and their best had come raiding for Raven and Storm, and ravaged them. Most damaging of all were the loss of four Storm Vestales with a price of sixteen Blood Credits, while the Titans had husbanded their Virgins amongst their Heavy Brigade in their strongholds and not permitted them so much as a whiff of Blood Night air.

Sveinn swept his hand over the group. 'I know you wonder where your fellows have gone and feel the weaker without them, but I assure you everything is proceeding well. Through our capture of the Time Asset at the castle, we have been able to send them to the site of the Grand Battle in advance and even now they prepare the ground for us. Our foe have no such luxury. They remain locked in Edinburgh, ignorant of where and when the two Palatinates will come together. And it is this ignorance that will be their undoing when they finally face us, for we will be readied and practised. We will know the terrain intimately, its pitfalls and its opportunities. We will be rested, well fed, strong of mind and spirit, and we will prevail.'

Calder found herself drawn to steal a glance at the stranger once more. He hadn't moved from the corner and the shadows still slanted across him. She could see he was tall and strong – like Halvar – although that strength was more an aura than something physical because he looked thin, almost undernourished. She could just make out his white beard and she wondered what things he had endured in Erebus and what had brought him back to these Halls. His eyes glinted in the gloom around him and she suddenly had the sensation that he was looking back at her. She returned to the King and tried to focus, but a tendril of unease licked its way up her spine.

'So your duty tonight,' the King was saying, 'is to keep the Titans guessing, to make them wonder if the Horde remains at full strength in the city and to shape their plans accordingly. Spread wide, move fast, give them the impression of more of us at large on the streets. But also proceed with caution. We are few in number and it would be foolhardy to take on odds when they are stacked against us. Watch, wait, isolate the foe if you can – and take the lives of three, so we may complete this Cull successfully and look towards the Battle with renewed anticipation.'

He ended with a flourish and looked to Radspakr to see if he wished to add anything. The Thane shook his head, so Sveinn signalled to Freyja. She dismissed the troops in a clipped voice and followed the King as he climbed back to his Council Room.

The Conflict Hours began in twenty minutes and the Ravens made their way to the eastern Armouries where their weapons and helms awaited. As the nine of them checked their swords, Jorunn closed the door quietly and waved them close.

'Okay, that was the official pep talk. Now listen to the reality. Three deaths are required to complete the Cull. Those of you who've lived through a few Seasons will understand what that means. The King wants us to reap that toll on the Titans tonight, but they too – in all their full strength of over a hundred and fifty – will be set on prosecuting those final fatalities within our ranks. Let's be under no illusions what that means. The Hammers will stay safely behind our Gates; the Wolves may or may not come hunting. So those three death blows will be aimed at the nine of us.'

'Does Freyja know you speak like this?' asked one of the Ravens.

Jorunn gave him a hard look. 'She does. She has no more wish than I to see yet more of our number fall, but she's a loyal Captain of Valhalla and won't speak openly of such things.' She returned her attention to the group as a whole. 'The Rules of the Blood Nights dictate that if the Cull total isn't achieved by the end of the Sixth Night, each Palatinate must select the outstanding number for execution.'

She let them think about this and another spoke up. 'And that selection's made from the *whole* Palatinate?'

'Exactly. All one hundred and eighty of us. Three out of a hundred and eighty, instead of three out of nine. Do the maths.'

There was a long silence.

'So we'll follow Freyja wherever she takes us tonight and – if fates allows – we'll slim the foe of three of their number. But, for once this night, there'll be no heroics. The Valhalla Ravens will watch and wait, but we'll fight only if our lives depend on it. Do I make myself clear?'

There were murmurs of agreement and they continued to gather their weapons. Calder belted her sword, pulled on her helmet and wedged her shield onto her left forearm as she followed her troop down East Tunnel towards the Gates in the vaults on Market Street. Freyja was already waiting impatiently, hands on hips. She shot Jorunn a knowing look and watched her nine Ravens line up with Calder at the rear.

'Stay close tonight. We'll go east, under the railway to Carlton cemetery. Then, if it's clear, head for the Balmoral and North Bridge. Keep tight.'

The Hammer guard at the Gate raised two fingers to indicate the minutes before Conflict Hours. Calder heard movement behind her and glanced back to see Wolf Litter Two queuing up as well. Down their line came the Prisoner, helmeted and mailed, his shield held casually. As Hersir, he slotted into their lead position and she sensed him looming just over her shoulder, smelt the oil on his *brynjar*, imagined she could feel the tickle of his breath on the back of her neck. Tense silence descended and something turned in her gut.

'You have nice hair,' he said quietly.

Startled, she leaned away. He chuckled in soft derision and then she felt him touch her ponytail. Just a featherlight finger, but enough to make her freeze. He eased it down the length of her hair.

'I like blondes.' He bent towards her and she sensed his mouth right by her ear. 'But, of course, you already know that.'

It took her a moment to grasp the meaning of his words and then she shot round.

'Now, surely you haven't forgotten me?' He straightened and grinned, and although she couldn't recognise the blonde beard or the sickly pale pallor of his skin, her mind had never relinquished the memory of those teeth. Her heart spasmed and a vast weight plummeted through her. The years rolled away and she remembered them as though it was yesterday. The one that was pointy and the one that stood slightly out of line. Teeth that had been gritted with lust as they loomed over her.

She wrenched her gaze from them and sought out his eyes behind the iron mask. They glittered back, glacier blue even in the half-light of the tunnel and a moan of primal despair broke from her at their horrifying beauty.

For she had looked many times on eyes so similar. Eyes she had loved. The eyes of her dear lost daughter.

Calder's – *Lana's* – world collapsed.

XXXIII

'Go, go, go!' The Gate was flung open and the Ravens ran. Calder felt him grab her roughly by the arm and propel her towards the exit.

'You heard the Maharaja queen, get going! Titans to kill.'

Her legs wouldn't work and her throat was too tight to scream, yet she found herself out in the cold air of Market Street and his bulk pushing her in the direction of her receding team. She stumbled and fell to one knee and he swore, released her and ordered his Wolves to follow him west to Waverley. Their steps disappeared and she heard the Gate slam behind. It was spotting with rain and she knelt on the damp pavement, leaned forward and threw up a mouthful of acid that burnt her throat and strung out from her lips when she tried to spit. She wiped a fist across her mouth to clear the phlegm and through her scrunched-up eyes, she saw another figure nearby and realised it was a Vigilis, letting his camera roll.

'What in Hel's name!' Freyja had run back and she stood over her, blade drawn. 'Get up, Thegn! That's an order.'

Calder struggled to her feet, coughing miserably and trying to wipe her eyes, but the Housecarl was having none of it. 'You move now! Alexander has his whole army out looking for us.'

She pushed her roughly in the back and herded her along Market Street with the Vigilis following. They dropped down to the tunnel under the railway, where the rest of the Ravens were waiting. They eyed the state of her coldly, but said nothing as Freyja resumed the lead and they jogged onto a deserted Carlton Road, deep at the foot of the long climb to Carlton Hill. Calder struggled at the back, her body still spasming and her mind unable to grasp much more than putting one foot in front of another. She knew the Vigilis was filming behind her, but she didn't care. Nor did she care about the Blood Night, or the Titans, or the whole stupid, pathetic Pantheon. They could all go to hell.

The rain came harder and the road began to ascend. Her legs refused to carry her and she staggered again. The road took a sharp bend right and the Ravens had stopped to confer. She drew up next to them and looked around. The road rose to join the busier Leith Street and Freyja was considering next moves before they went out into the lights. To their left, deep in the darkness between the hill and the back of Waverley Station was a small car park with a few vehicles left overnight. Calder stared at it and craved its shadows. The Vigilis had moved forward to overhear the conversation and when Freyja gave the order, they all headed off towards the main road. This was her moment.

She ran heavily into the car park, dodged around the cars and dropped into the tightest gap she could find between them. Her shield clattered against a wing mirror and she dropped it, then sprawled on the wet tarmac, with her face inches from a tyre. She had a wall behind her and a vehicle either side, and by peering under them she could see if anyone approached. She stared out at the rest of the car park and let the rain pitter patter onto her.

Perhaps Freyja ran back to find her, perhaps the Housecarl cursed and snarled. But, if she did, Calder didn't hear her and the night remained quiet. Memories of Amelia toyed with her, beautiful moments of fun and love, mixed with images of the hospital bed as her daughter's life dwindled. She removed her helmet and laid her head on her arms without noticing the cold ground gnawing into her. There she sprawled, quiet and watchful, her blade in her hand.

She must have slept, for the next thing she knew she was frozen to the core and almost incapable of movement. The rain had stopped and there was a pale light in the sky. Groaning, she sat herself up against a car and hauled her cloak tight around her while she shivered uncontrollably. Her mind was numb. If there were memories and emotions, they were now locked away in her subconscious. She pulled herself upright.

A taxi went by and she became aware of the day's first commuters walking across the footbridge above her on their way to the station. She sheathed her blade, yanked on her helmet, retrieved her shield and hobbled painfully back towards Valhalla. A car pulled past her and the occupant slowed to stare. Two men came around a corner and stopped talking, one getting his phone out and taking a photo. On Market Street there were more people and they pressed themselves against the railings to let her pass. A man was opening up his car workshop in one of the vaults and he froze, key in hand.

She made her way to the fifth vault entrance and stood

under the gaze of the camera. People were still watching and a car hooted as it went by. After a long delay, the single door opened and a bearded face gestured angrily for her to get inside, slamming it behind her.

Two Hammers, helmetless and dressed ready to go home, gawped at her. 'It's six thirty-five,' said one of them, as if that explained everything. 'Everyone's gone.'

They began asking her where she'd been and telling her how much trouble she was in, but she didn't hear. She pushed through them and walked up East Tunnel to the Armouries. Mechanically, she deposited her helmet and weapons for cleaning, and continued on towards the Throne Room. Freyja was sitting alone with a coffee and wearing a tracksuit. She stared stone-grim at Calder, rose without a word and grabbed her by the arm. Calder let out a gasp of protest, but Freyja's grip was too strong and she dragged her into one of the empty Practice Rooms.

'Where've you been? The Vigiles have been scouring the city for you. They're assuming you've been culled by the Titans, but they need a body to confirm it and none of the foe has claimed the kill.'

Calder stared disconsolately at the floor and Freyja shook her. 'Speak to me, girl! If you've run – if you've been hiding – there'll be no mercy. The Vigiles will make an example of you.'

Calder crumpled before her inquisition. She put her hands over her face and sobbed, while Freyja watched her in consternation. 'What's happened to you? I thought you were one of my strong ones. From the very first night you arrived in that vault blindfolded and listened to Radspakr make his speech, I thought you stood out. You were small and weak and girly, but I saw the strength in your eyes and I told Halvar you'd make it. And you did. One of the few left standing, so I said to Sveinn I wanted you in my Ravens. I was proud of you, thought you'd make something of yourself in the Palatinate. Maybe even saw something of the younger me in your efforts.' She stepped back and opened her arms in distaste. 'But now look at you. Since you got wounded at the castle, you've never been the same. There weren't any Titans, were there? You got scared and fled.'

Calder's sobs ran dry and she wiped her face, pushed back a lock of hair and let out a deep ragged sigh. 'You won't understand.'

'To Hel, I won't. I understand enough to know you don't deserve to stand amongst my Ravens. I understand enough to know a coward when I see one. And the worst thing of all, I realise I've lost the trust I had in you.' Freyja turned to the door. 'I'll inform Sveinn you're alive and have no sufficient explanation for your absence. He can draw his own conclusions and decide whether to brief the Vigiles. I'm sorry, Calder, I thought you had a future in the Pantheon.'

'It was the Prisoner.' Her words spilled out before she could stop them.

Freyja halted. 'What did you say?'

'The Pris... He...'

'Skarde? What about him?'

Calder took a stuttering breath, paused for a heartbeat and then whispered, 'He attacked me.'

The Housecarl came back to her and stared fixedly into her eyes. 'Skarde? Tonight?'

'No, earlier.'

'When?'

'Before this. Before the Pantheon. When I was young.'

Freyja's gaze bored into her. 'When you were young, the man called Skarde attacked you? You met him up there in the real world?' Her tone was soft now, drained of its anger.

There was an eternal emptiness in Calder's voice when she spoke again and said simply, 'He raped me.'

Freyja's jaw set and her expression became iron. She swung to the door and closed it, then walked back to the other woman and took her in her arms, folding her head into her breast and stroking her wet hair. Calder went rigid at the touch and spasmed again, although no tears would come. The Housecarl continued to stroke her head for long minutes and Calder could feel the muscles in the arm that held her with such protective strength. Gradually, her body relaxed and she nestled into the warmth of her breast.

Freyja felt her tension disperse and said quietly, 'I give you my solemn oath, Thegn, I will protect you. That bastard will never lay another finger on you. We're in this together, you and me. Come what may.'

XXXIV

'The girl's been found,' said Radspakr.

'Alive?'

'Yes, lord.'

'And with sufficient explanation?'

Radspakr shrugged. 'It would seem.'

'Excellent. Then it's not another kill to the Titans.' The King returned his attention to the large sheet of acetate on the table in front of him, on which was depicted a map. 'We have it, Radspakr!' His voice was energised. 'The Field.'

'Now? Atilius has given you the Field Asset this morning?'

'Just an hour ago. Alexander will have it too.'

'So that means the twenty-four-hour mark has been activated and the Battle will be tomorrow.'

'Precisely! We knew it would be soon because the Time Asset was activated two weeks ago, but it's literally upon us tomorrow. Destiny calls!'

Radspakr slipped around the table to look at the map next to his King. 'Where is it?'

'On the far northern end of the island at Eoligarry, several miles from the camp.' He placed his finger on a name on the map. 'Traigh Sgurabhal. It's a beach.'

'Sand?'

'And a damn lot of it, Thane. The foe will have nowhere to hide from our Wolves. We must get these coordinates to Halvar and Bjarke.'

'The timescale's ridiculous, lord. What can Atilius be thinking? We've only just completed the Blood Nights.'

Sveinn laughed and his eyes were alight. 'But that's just it. Imagine the panic of Alexander right now. Picture the pandemonium that's going on around his council table this very instant. They're only just learning about the island. They'll be pulling up maps, calculating distances, realising the Field is on a pinprick of land in the Atlantic, about as far north-west as Scotland gets! He's got the remainder of today to transport a hundred and fifty troops. Their equipment, their arms, but not – crucially – any rations, for they failed to gain the Supply Asset and will travel on empty stomachs. They'll arrive on Traigh Sgurabhal tomorrow exhausted from the Blood Nights, disorientated, sleepless, hungry and utterly unprepared for the environment.'

The King banged the map. 'This is our time, Radspakr. We were so close last year. Halvar's Wolves almost had Alexander on the ends of their swords, should have, had it not been for that Agape woman. And that was in a year when we had none of these advantages. Now look at us.'

'We've not been so successful in the Cull, lord.'

'Stop being obtuse – that's insignificant on the grander scale of things. Tomorrow Alexander's troops will walk onto that beach and find the Horde of Valhalla drawn up in battle order and waiting for them. Strong, rested, confident and utterly ready for the fight. The victory's ours for the taking.'

Radspakr had rarely seen Sveinn so animated in recent

times and he had to admit the King's argument was persuasive. Perhaps they really could take Alexander. Perhaps the eternal struggle between Titan and Horde could be resolved this year. Maybe he, Radspakr, would soon be Thane of a much larger Palatinate. The thought was not unattractive.

'There is, of course, the small matter of the Cull total, lord.'

The King's shoulders sagged and he tutted angrily as he studied the map. 'I know, an unwelcome disruption.'

'The Wolves took one Titan peltast last night, which brings the total for all the Blood Nights to twenty-three. Two short.'

'So burdens will be shared.'

'One from each, lord.'

'And Atilius will conduct the rites on the island?'

'Yes. Most likely this very night for us. And later, perhaps, for Alexander, depending on how quickly he can get his Palatinate onto the isle.'

Sveinn pondered this. 'The troops won't like it.'

'They never do.'

'It mustn't be allowed to affect their confidence. We've not planned this entire operation, just for them to go weak-kneed and demoralised hours before the foe appears. It must be performed fast and without compunction.'

'In my experience, Atilius knows no other way.'

The King agreed and went back to the map. 'I hope Halvar's used his time well and found this beach already – he's had long enough out there. I must get this Field information to him urgently. Check there's a plane on standby for me, Thane.' He squinted at a spot on the map. 'There's a small knoll of land in the middle of the sand. That's the strong point, the place to hold. I will make my stand there.'

'Lord, we must inform Freyja and get word to all the remaining troops to be ready for the taxis within hours.'

'Do it. I want every trooper of Valhalla on that island by nightfall.'

'Yes, lord.' The Thane walked to the door.

'Oh, and Radspakr.' The King looked up from his map. 'I'm sorry you won't be present. As always, I leave our stronghold in your safe hands and will bring you news of our great victory when we return.'

Radspakr bowed to him. 'Lord, I look forward to it.'

Radspakr spent the remainder of the day overseeing departure logistics for the last of the Horde. By late afternoon he received confirmation that the taxis had deposited them at the airport and the planes were taking off.

He powered down the screens in his office, then made himself a coffee in the Main Hall and carried it as he roamed the empty Tunnels, checking the rooms and enjoying the solitude. After the fear and tensions of the last two weeks, it felt good to have everyone packed off. Except for the Interregnum, this was the only time each year when both Palatinates deserted their strongholds and even the Gates could be left unguarded.

He sealed the Armouries and Practice Rooms, then made the trek to each Gate to test the locks, set the silent alarms and switch on the laser fields. Satisfied, he proceeded through the Western Hall to the reception area in West Tunnel and changed into his street clothes.

It was five o'clock when he emerged into a blustery city, which was restless with Friday evening anticipation. Pulling his coat around him, he strode down from the Old Town to catch his tram on Princes Street. There was a queue to board and he had to perch next to a fat man and listen to tinny beats coming from the headphones of a girl opposite, but it almost made him smile. Sometimes it felt good to be nobody. Just one of the crowd.

Once cocooned in his Range Rover and crossing the Forth Bridges, it was Mendelssohn's Number 3, suitably known as the Scottish Symphony, which carried his mind from the Pantheon. Forty-eight hours, that was all. By the end of the weekend, those who still lived would be back in the city – Odin and Sveinn, Skarde and Halvar – and he would need to be stronger and more cunning than ever, but for the next two precious days he would jog on his beaches, watch the March light play on the sea beyond his windows, sleep and rejuvenate.

He pulled through the gates of his property and walked to his garden wall to peer over the cliff at the water beyond. The wind was whipping up countless white horses in the fading light and he wondered what conditions would be like on the island. For some reason, his mind drifted to Simmius, his counterpart in the Titans, and he thought grimly of the chaos that must still be surrounding him in Pella and Persepolis as he tried to get Alexander's Palatinate ready and gone before tomorrow's Battle. Perhaps sometime deep into the early hours of the night, he too would finally patrol his strongholds alone, check them, seal them and disappear to a home to recover.

Radspakr let himself into his house, flicked on the light and tossed his keys on the antique table in the grand entrance hall. He would make a paella, but first he craved a fine Shiraz from the Barossa Valley. He opened a side door and stepped down into his wine cellar. *That's strange.* He could have sworn he had a Shiraz on the top row. He pulled out the other bottles one by one, but there was nothing from the Barossa. Oh well, he must have drunk it. He selected a Cabernet Sauvignon from Coonawarra instead and proceeded up to the kitchen.

What the hell? Now the corkscrew was nowhere to be found. He banged about in the drawers, growing increasingly angry, then strode through to the gloomy drawing room and stopped. The reading lamp over his seat in the bay window was switched on and it was illuminating his desk next to it, on which sat the bottle of Shiraz, the corkscrew and a single glass. Warnings prickled through his bloodstream. Was it possible he had left the items there when he was last at home, to enjoy on his return? He stepped cautiously towards the light and saw that the bottle had already been opened.

'A fine vintage,' a voice said from the dark behind him.

Radspakr spun round to find a man ensconced in one of his armchairs in the corner. The figure reached out to switch on another lamp and Radspakr's blood ran cold. It was Odin, reclining comfortably, legs crossed, a glass of wine in his hand.

'I helped myself. Thought you wouldn't mind.'

'Of course not, lord. What's mine is yours.'

'Though the goddamn Aussies never could compete with a sweet US-of-A Napa.' Odin waved him towards the bottle. 'Don't stand on ceremony, man, it's your damn house. Sit, pour yourself a glass.'

Radspakr complied, turning his back to mask his terror and pouring the wine shakily, then perching on the arm of his reading chair. Outside, night was closing in and the myriad white horses could no longer be seen.

'Should you not be on your way to the island, lord?'

'Soon enough, but I've been having to clear up your damn mess. First on my agenda was removing that kid.'

'I saw, lord.'

'Hmm, it complicated matters having to silence the parents, but they'd have kicked up too much fuss if their son simply disappeared and, in the end, framing the father proved nicely convenient. More damn media attention than I wanted and some busybody cops, but a quiet word with the authorities and the case will soon run dry. I've had the kid questioned, but he doesn't seem to know anything more than what your report revealed about his searches. Pity, I thought he might have led us more directly to our missing girl. At least he's found us a potential point of communication. What was it? *Torch* something.'

'*TorchLight96*, lord. Olena Macedon. But it's not an account that's been used for quite some time. I don't see how we can encourage her to communicate.'

'With the right bait, Thane. You have to choose the right bait for the right fish. And we've had the right bait under our arses for the last five months!'

'I don't think I'm understanding you, lord.'

'No, Thane, I don't think you are.' Odin took several

slugs of his wine, then pierced Radspakr with his gaze again. 'Tell me about Tyler bloody Maitland.'

'Of course, lord. What in particular?'

'Everything. I want to know how he was recruited, what he said about his sister and what he thinks he's doing in my Palatinate.'

So Radspakr talked. He spun the facts as best he could to condemn Tyler and to make his own actions seem blameless. He recounted the usual process for receiving the selected names from Atilius' teams at the start of each year, how he had accompanied the Venarii parties over several nights through an autumnal city to track down each new recruit. He described meeting Tyler Maitland for the first time on the steps of Fleshmarket Close, the man's arrogance, his limp, his apparent poor health. He tried to recall the occasions he had noticed him during the Armatura and then he spoke about the first proper conversation in Sveinn's Mead Hall at the feast after the Oath-Taking in the Highlands.

'He thought his sister was in the Horde, my lord – that's what confused me. I knew there was no other Maitland in our ranks and never had been. I assumed he was wrong. How was I to know she was a Titan? No one has access to the records of all the Palatinates except Atilius, not even you and the other Caelestia.'

'That was your mistake, Thane,' said Odin jabbing a finger at him. 'You *assumed*. Assumption is a dangerous luxury.'

'It was more than an assumption, lord. It was hard logic. Atilius is who he is because he *never* makes mistakes. The Pantheon doesn't permit the recruitment of anyone who's a sibling to a current member, regardless of which

Palatinate – just as it doesn't permit the recruitment of husbands, wives, lovers, fathers, mothers, sons, daughters – so that we never have to deal with the complexities of relationships. So, Maitland had to be mistaken about his sister. He'd lost her, I assumed, but not to the Pantheon.'

'There's that word again.' Odin sipped his wine and Radspakr lapsed into hesitant silence. 'So, remind me when – what do you Brits say? – when *the penny dropped*?'

Radspakr thought fast. He wasn't about to tell Odin he'd made the link between Tyler and Olena of Macedon almost two months ago when he saw the photo of Morgan, nor about all his subsequent failed attempts to dispose of Tyler. He needed to skip ahead, tell his story sparingly. 'Just ten days ago, when I finally saw what the young neighbour had been researching. It proved conclusively that Tyler's sister was the missing Titan traitor, Olena.'

'Our little lost Olena. A girl who knows far too much.' Odin pointed to Radspakr's iPad by the window. 'Are Tyler Maitland's records on there?'

'Yes, lord.'

'Good. I'll want access to them.' Odin drained his glass and then peered at Radspakr hard. 'I have one final question for you, Thane, and I advise you to consider your answer carefully.'

The room went cold. Nothing but the sound of the wind in the chimney.

'Lord?' said Radspakr tentatively.

'What first drew your attention to the kid next door?'

Radspakr's mind raced. Odin's tone told him this was the critical question, but the tension was frazzling his wits and he was finding it hard to recall the precise order of events.

'Well… when I had Maitland's laptop analysed, there were items on the disk that incriminated the boy.'

'The reports indicate that the kid's laptop and hard drives were raided on the same night as Maitland's. So I assume he had *already* roused your suspicions. I'll say to you again, Thane, respond with care.'

Radspakr had the distinct impression Odin already knew the answer to his own question and the bastard was just toying with him. He closed his eyes, focused and spoke. 'The boy first came to the attention of a man I had sent to Maitland's flat a few days earlier.'

'For what purpose?'

'To search his possessions, download his hard drive.'

'Not what my sources tell me.'

Radspakr swallowed. A sickness was bubbling up into his chest.

'What my sources tell me, Thane, is that the man you sent was supposed to silence Maitland. You hired a goddamn hit.'

'We needed him dead, lord,' Radspakr blustered. 'He was becoming too much of a risk for us.'

Odin sighed. 'So let me see if I'm understanding this correctly. First, for you to consider Maitland such a risk, I can only presume you *already* knew Maitland's sister was the Titan snitch, long before you saw the kid's data. Second, you withheld this from *me* and thought you'd act alone. And, third, by killing him you risked drawing all sorts of unwanted attention to our little problem.'

'It would have been done well, lord. Made to look like an overdose.'

'Not fucking good enough!' Odin exploded. 'A member

of the Horde dies in his own flat. The White Warrior of Valhalla is found with heroin overloading his veins! You don't think that would have aroused Atilius' suspicions? Brought all his eyes to bear on me? Risked unearthing everything?'

'Well, it didn't matter in the end, lord, because Maitland had already left for the island.'

'And that, Thane, is the only piece of news in this whole damn shambles that pleases me.'

Odin lapsed into silence, rumbling under his breath. He forced himself to calm and then tilted his glass towards the door. 'I don't believe you've had a chance to get properly reacquainted with the Hersir here.'

Radspakr shot up from his perch. Leaning in the doorway was the Prisoner.

'Hello, Thane. I've never thanked you for the two years in Erebus.'

Radspakr's knees wanted to give way, but he drew himself straight and looked the man in the eye. 'There was never any place in the Horde of Valhalla for a creature with your tastes.'

'So you gave me over to Atilius.'

'Pantheon justice.'

'Live by the Rules. Die by the Rules.' Skarde nodded grimly. 'Except, I'm not dead.'

Radspakr dragged his gaze back to the Caelestis and attempted to imbue his tones with righteous indignity. 'Why is this creature in my house, lord?'

Odin sighed deeply. 'When you've done the things I've done to make the money I make, you don't ever allow your past to come back to haunt you. And I worry, Thane, that your incompetence is shepherding that past right back to my door. Olena of Macedon is still absent without leave. Housecarl Halvar still leads my Wolves. And Tyler Maitland is busy playing detective in my Palatinate. All on your watch and all with enough information to damage me. So, I ask you, what am I supposed to do?'

Radspakr's eyes flickered over the bottle of wine and corkscrew on his desk.

'I have devoted my life to the honour of the Valhalla Palatinate, lord. I have served you unstintingly for nineteen Seasons.'

In the corner of his vision, he saw the Prisoner ease into the room. The man was wearing black leather gloves.

'It doesn't have to be this way, lord. I can sort this out.'

'You've had your chance. Skarde here is a blunt instrument, but I suspect more effective.'

'We can make this easy,' the Prisoner said softly and cracked a hyena smile. 'But I hope you make it hard.'

The time for reason had passed and Radspakr knew it. Everything was crowding into this one moment and life suddenly became so simple. It was kill or be killed. The very ethos of the Pantheon he loved. In an explosion of movement, he grabbed the corkscrew and threw himself at Skarde, intent on burying it in his throat until the bastard's blood poured thick and black across his carpet.

But Radspakr was a bookkeeper with a bookkeeper's speed. The Prisoner had been born to kill.

He swatted away the attack, flung an arm around the Thane's neck and kicked his knees from under him. Radspakr collapsed to the floor with his head locked in the crook of Skarde's elbow.

'Lord.' Radspakr tried to focus back on Odin, but the pressure on his neck was inexorable. 'Call him... off.'

His head was forced down onto the carpet. His own carpet. The woollen Berber twist he had specially selected only a year before. The one he lay on to do his yoga.

Skarde's leather fingers were around his throat now. He scrabbled at them, but his strength was abandoning him.

'This is... not... the... answer.'

There was no air. The room darkened, the noise of the sea down the chimney grew faint.

'Odin... you bastard. It's you... who must die.'

With a final effort, he gritted his teeth, summoned his last vestiges of pride and spluttered at the Caelestis.

'You... will... not... win.'

Odin watched the last twitches of the Thane until there was no movement. Eventually Skarde released his grip and straightened with a grin on his face.

'You enjoyed that, you sadistic bastard. Remind me to keep a close eye on you.'

'What shall I do with the body?'

'Leave it. With the kid we had to be careful, but I should be able to rid myself of an incompetent Thane without too many questions. I'll have the *libitinarii* sort it.' He rose and retrieved Radspakr's iPad, then paused briefly to look out at the shipping lights. 'Nice place this.' Then he wheeled towards the door. 'Come on, we've got a plane to catch.'

'Going to kill Tyler Maitland?'

Odin halted by the door and shook his head in exasperation. 'I'm surrounded by bloody morons. Why does every idiot want to kill my asset? He's known as Punnr in the Horde. A Wolf like you. Get to him *before* the Battle;

before some Titan shoves a blade up his arsehole! Keep him
alive. Bring him to me. This worm's the bait that catches me
my prize fish. And when I have them both, *then* I'll let you
loose on them.'

Part Three

The Battle

XXXV

The two planes carrying the last of the Horde landed on the beach just as the day was being blown over the horizon. A fleet of Land Rovers carried them across the island and brought them to the track above the dunes. As they trudged down, they could see light flickering beyond and when they stepped out onto the beach they were greeted by the sight of a curve of sand lit by rows of burning torches, which had been forced into the ground and braced upright against the wind.

There was a shout of greeting from the camp and figures spilled from the church and tents. The troops converged and there were hugs and backslaps, but little laughter, for most knew what the lines of torches meant. Freyja slipped between the different groups and searched for Halvar.

'Have you heard?' she asked when she finally saw him coming from the church.

'Aye, twenty-three. The Vigiles informed me before they started erecting the bloody torches. I *told* Sveinn the Cull number was too high.'

'I don't think Sveinn had much say in the matter.'

'Already the troops are sullen. Atilius needs to get this done quickly and then we focus their minds on tomorrow.'

Freyja took the big man's arm and guided him down the beach out of earshot. 'I wasn't actually meaning the Cull total when I asked *have you heard.*'

'What then? I know nothing else.'

'Skarde's returned.'

Halvar stared at her, his rough face scrunched up. 'Skarde! Don't be stupid – he's rotting in Erebus.'

'That's what we all thought, but he's back in the Horde.'

'This is a joke, woman. No one can just come back and join the Horde.'

'You can if Odin says so.'

Halvar squared up to her belligerently. 'So who's he replaced? He ain't waltzing in unless he's a replacement; our Blood Funds don't allow.'

'Turid.'

'What!'

'He's replaced Turid. She's out – gone. And now Skarde's Hersir of Wolf Litter Two.'

Halvar was speechless. His mouth hung open. She watched the first volcanic tremors rising through him and waited for the explosion. 'I'll brain him! I'll crack his skull! I'll thrash the marrow from the bastard's bones! No one walks into my Wolf Regiment without my say-so!'

Heads were turning and Freyja raised a warning hand. 'Quieter, Housecarl, the troops have enough to worry about tonight.'

'Where is he?'

'I don't know. He didn't arrive with us.'

Halvar fought with his anger, desperate to roar expletives to the moon, but knowing Freyja spoke sense. He clamped his jaw and looked angrily out to sea. 'When did all this happen?' he said more quietly.

'Turid was informed before the Fourth Blood Night. Skarde arrived in time for the Fifth.'

'In other words, just after I departed. I swear, king or no king, I'm going to kick Sveinn from here to Greenland.'

'He knew nothing about it. Don't you think I grilled him as soon as I heard? He's as shocked as the rest of us.'

'So, now Odin meddles without recourse to the King? Bad things are coming, I can feel it.'

Freyja agreed. 'I think they've already arrived.'

Further up the beach, Punnr twisted his way between the rows of torches and searched the faces of the new arrivals. He saw her standing alone with her arms folded across her chest and his heart skipped.

'Calder, my god, there you are.' He strode towards her, but when she responded, it wasn't with the mile-wide smile he had been hoping.

'Hello, Punnr.'

He had been intending to hug her, but her tone stopped him short and he hovered hesitantly. 'It's so good to see you. I was so worried about you.'

'Were you?' Even in the light from the flames, she could see he had a healthy outdoor glow, browned and hardened by the elements. His long hair was salted, sanded and had grown wild.

'Thank god the Blood Nights are over. When Sveinn kept depleting our forces in the city and leaving you and the

Ravens to face Alexander, I couldn't stop wondering how you were. Thank the gods you're here safely now.'

Punnr thought she looked so fragile with her arms clamped across her chest, as though she might shatter if he dared to touch her. There were shadows around her eyes, which he put down to the freight of travel. 'It's not so bad here,' he said, throwing a hand towards the church. 'I know it looks shit in the dark and it's bleak with this wind, but the church is warm and there's food and the tents are okay. You should see this island in the sun! It's beautiful. I wish I could show you the island in the sun.' He was blabbing, but he couldn't help himself. There was a wall between them. A bloody great invisible wall and he had no idea why.

He stepped in and touched her on the arm. 'Calder...'

'Don't!' She flinched away.

'I was only going to...'

'Just don't touch me, okay? Just don't.'

He put his hand down and peered at her. She was gazing out to sea, her arms still clasped protectively and her eyes glazed.

'Are you okay? Did something happen in the Blood Nights?'

'The Titans won the Cull. They could hardly do otherwise by the time you'd all headed off here and left so few of us.'

'You know I didn't have any choice about coming here, don't you?'

'Of course.'

'I mean, I'd have stayed and fought with you if I was allowed, but I got whisked away as soon as I'd left your house that night.'

'The Pantheon does what it wants with us.'

Still she would not look at him and a panic swelled in him. 'Calder, please. *Lana*. I've missed you. What we shared in your flat, what I said – I meant it.'

'And what I said, I also meant. I can't do this. I won't.'

'You mean, not while the Grand Battle looms.'

'Not now. Not ever.'

A weight sunk through Punnr from his throat, through his ribs, to settle deep in his gut. 'Calder,' he said weakly. 'What's happened?'

This made her look at him. 'What's happened?' she almost hissed. 'What's *happened*?' She searched his face, mouth open, then seemed to shudder and her shoulders dropped. 'That's just it, Punnr. You'll always be asking that question and you'll never understand.'

'Tell me, please! I will understand. Just explain it to me.'

But she was shaking her head and dropping her eyes. 'No. This is my fight and mine alone. No one else can help. Now, I'm tired and I'd like to be with my Ravens.'

'Lana.'

'Don't use that name here. We are Vikings. Forget what occurred between us and move on.'

He shook his head in consternation and she stepped around him. 'Punnr, I mean it. I'd be grateful if you leave me be.'

Atilius at least allowed the new arrivals time to eat before he marched down the track with his Vigiles. Wooden steps had been constructed to allow him to climb the back of one of the highest dunes and he stood surveying the beach, with his robes blowing in the wind and Sveinn beside him. They waited while the Jarls and Housecarls marshalled their troops and had them file out onto the sand in three long lines, lit by the blazing torches and facing the Praetor of the Pantheon. The tide was just beginning to recede and the back row had their boots in the water. Fear rippled through the ranks, for all knew what was to come and those with more than a Season of experience had already warned the new intake.

Atilius and the Vigiles were the only ones wearing helmets hiding their identities. He had ordered everyone else to change from their modern clothing into the tunics and undergarments worn in Valhalla, but he had not required them mailed or armed.

'Warriors of the Horde of Valhalla,' he shouted into the wind as two of his Vigiles filmed. 'The total number slain from both Palatinates during this Season's Blood Nights is twenty-three, officially confirmed and verified. Of the wounded in the Pantheon hospital, all are expected to recover. So we remain two short of the total twenty-five required by the Caelestia during this Nineteenth Blood Season.

'The Rules dictate that the deficit must be accounted for from each participating Palatinate and we are here tonight to carry out that requirement.'

He waved curtly to a Vigilis who stepped forward holding a heavy sack and carried it to the end of the first line of warriors. 'Take a single pebble from the sack and hold it in your palm.'

Sveinn was the only member of Valhalla excused from this exercise and the first man was Asmund, Jarl of Storm Regiment. Without taking his eyes from Atilius, he reached into the sack and felt around amongst the pebbles, finally retrieving one and holding it to his side. The Vigilis heaved the bag on to the next warrior and waited while she repeated the process. Little by little, he made his way down the line and turned at the end and began again along the second row. No one spoke. Atilius and Sveinn watched from the dune.

The Vigilis was breathing hard from exertion by the time he came to Punnr and held out the bag. Punnr reached in and pushed his hand around. The pebbles all seemed the same, small, round and smooth. Feeling destiny waiting on his shoulder, he closed his fingers over one, began to pull it out, then suddenly dropped it and grabbed another. The Vigilis moved on and Punnr straightened his arm against his side, turning the smooth nugget in his palm and wondering what fate it held for him.

The Vigilis reached the end of the row and continued along the back one. He came to Calder and she dipped her hand in and took the first pebble her fingers touched. The bag was much lighter now and at last the Vigilis completed his task and walked back to the front. Every warrior held a stone.

Atilius began again. 'Now…'

Before he could say more, he was interrupted by a loud voice from the back. 'Hold!'

It was Halvar.

Atilius was stunned into silence and it took him a few moments to recommence. 'You wish to say something, Housecarl?'

'I do, lord. We're not all present.'

There was a murmur amongst the ranks and people looked at each other.

'Who's missing?' demanded the Praetor.

'Skarde, lord.'

The voices grew and individuals began to step out of line to scan the rows themselves.

'Is he right?' Atilius hissed to Sveinn.

The King searched the beach. 'He is.'

'Then where the hell is this man?'

'I don't know.'

'Can he be found? Has anyone seen him on the island?'

'I don't think so.'

Atilius gasped in exasperation and looked around at his Vigiles. The selection could not be delayed. To do so would bring the troops to bursting point. He straightened and addressed himself to the crowd with every ounce of authority he could muster. 'We will continue.'

'But, lord,' Halvar yelled back. 'How can you expect us to give ourselves up to the risks of this selection, if even one of us is permitted to avoid it?'

'We *will* continue, Housecarl. You know this needs to be done and I expect you to set an example! The troops will hold out their hands with the pebble in their palm.'

There was a wave of noise from the warrior lines.

'This is unjust, lord,' shouted Halvar. 'You know it is.'

Atilius exploded with fury. 'By the gods, you'll delay this no longer or I will take ten of you, not one! Do you understand me, Housecarl? Another word and I will select ten!'

Halvar glared around him and his expression was ferocious in the firelight, but he knew better than to open his mouth again. With a huge effort, he held open his palm and locked his eyes rigidly ahead. Gradually, the hubbub died as the warriors saw him comply and other hands were brought forward. A strained silence took hold beneath the moaning of the wind.

Atilius signalled angrily and three Vigiles began to move along the front row. One held a flaming torch, one walked behind the backs of each warrior, and the leader checked diligently in each palm. They progressed wordlessly and none of the Horde knew what they were looking for. Punnr cast a furtive glance at his hand. The pebble he was holding was black. The group started along his row and he tensed as they came close. He could sense the one behind him as the first man looked at his pebble. There was a pause and then relief surged through him as the group moved on.

Stigr was next to him and they checked his palm and moved again. Knut was the next one and Punnr watched them from the corner of his eye, waiting for them to continue. But this time they took a moment longer. The lead Vigilis looked hard at Knut's palm.

'White, my lord.'

The second Vigilis checked. 'I confirm, my lord. White.'

Knut was looking around him in bewilderment. He huffed and a growl came to his throat. If this was his fate, he would take these Vigiles bastards with him.

The strike through the back of his neck was so clean, so brutal, that he was still fully intending to attack the men, even as his legs gave way beneath him. The blade had severed his spinal cord and he was dead before he hit the sand. The third Vigilis pulled his sword free and wiped it on his cloak. Confusion raced along the rows. Voices were raised again. People threw their pebbles on the beach.

'A Wolf!' Halvar was yelling. 'You take a Wolf of mine!'

'It is done!' Atilius shouted back.

Vikings were striding towards the group, so the other two Vigiles drew their swords as well.

'Control your ranks,' Atilius ordered Sveinn, turning angrily on the King.

'Horde of Valhalla!' Sveinn cried against the wind. 'You will desist!'

Atilius waved the rest of his Vigiles forward and they drew blades and approached the first row. Valhalla was unarmed and one by one they gave way, huddling back and holding their hands up. The shouting calmed. The first three Vigiles stood around Knut's corpse with their swords ready to strike.

'This is all being relayed live to the Curiate,' warned Atilius from his dune. 'If another one of you moves, I will have the evidence on film and you will be formally identified and executed.'

The danger subsided. The Praetor glared at the faces before him, all semblance of the rows gone. 'In due course, when they are all arrived, I will travel to the Titan encampment and take the twenty-fifth life in the same manner, and I sincerely believe they will display more bravery and fortitude than I have witnessed here tonight. I suggest the officers amongst you marshal your troops hard tonight and get them focused on the Grand Battle that awaits. Alexander's hoplites will be ready and they will give no quarter to a rabble like you.' He swung a disgusted look at Sveinn and whispered, 'You need to silence your Housecarl or I will.' Then he brandished an arm towards the Horde. 'You are dismissed! Get off this beach.'

Punnr stumbled towards the group of Vigiles and stared

down at Knut's body. Black blood, thick as treacle, coated his throat where the blade had broken out. It had seeped across his tunic and even pooled onto the sand beneath. His mouth was frozen in a snarl and his eyes wide and livid. Punnr had seen that look enough times since his quarrel with the old warrior in Valhalla and he had suspected that one day he might need to kill Knut himself or risk a dagger in his ribs. But now, looking down at the sad remains of the man, he was appalled by the sudden, unexpected, utterly random end of his life. Knut had been a man who held a grudge, a man who might have harmed Punnr if the opportunity came his way, but he had also been a good warrior, a strong warrior, a Viking of twelve long Seasons, and he didn't deserve to die like this.

'Get out of here,' warned one of the Vigiles, brandishing his sword.

How could these bastards treat life so cheaply? Knut should not have ended his days with a pebble in his hand instead of a sword. Shaken and disgusted, Punnr trudged from the beach.

XXXVI

B attle is terror. The wait is worse.

Everyone in Valhalla knew this, from the greenest recruit to the most Bloodmarked champion.

The Vigiles had brought crates of firewood, which they piled beside the church and soon bonfires were burning between the dunes. Tables from the storeroom were carried outside and placed in a long line, so that shifts of a dozen warriors at a time could inspect and prepare their armour. More food was prepared even though everyone had eaten already. Why save it? Calories would be needed tomorrow and, for some, this would be their last supper. Drink, too, was available, but each trooper made their own personal decision about this. Some gave it a wide berth, knowing they needed to be at their physical and clear-headed best the next day. Many imbibed just enough to speed the dread of the wait. A few drank to excess and would drink more the next morning, because to stand in the press of a shieldwall and stab and stab again, they had to be inebriated.

Punnr queued early for the benches and was one of the first to tend his armour. In truth, he needed the focus of manual work to keep his mind from what had occurred. Knut's murder and Calder's words – her fathomless distance when he had found her – had left him numbed and shocked. So he had queued for the benches and now he forced himself to concentrate on the tiny labours of love that a warrior must dedicate to his equipment before he goes to war.

He laid out his chain mail *brynjar* near a burning brazier and inspected it minutely, checking for the slightest fault, a single broken link. He ran his fingers over the mesh to feel for any snag, held it up to study each ring, then oiled it with such care he might have been massaging the shoulders of a lover. Lying it to one side, he next took his iron vambraces and greaves, each etched with Norse designs, and buffed them with a dry cloth until every smudge was removed, as though these imperfections could undermine his defences in battle. Such attention to detail was a shared obsession that night. Up and down the tables, warriors pored over their armour, angling pieces towards the firelight to catch the slightest defect.

Next came his helmet, which he placed on the bench and then turned it in a full circle. It had dents from the Blood Nights – one in particular he recalled receiving when a Companion had charged from the darkness in Queen's Gardens and smashed him so hard that he had been unable to see through his eye-holes. The dents were battle honours, but he examined them diligently to ensure none had weakened the iron, then polished them until the helm sparkled.

Finally, he turned to his sword and seax. These would be his weapons. As a Wolf, he wouldn't carry spear or bow, and he didn't have the strength to wield the great double-handed war-axes, nor the skill to master the smaller throwing axes. So he would stick with blades. He unsheathed both and dripped oil down the inside of the scabbards, careful not to blemish the beautiful velvet exteriors. Then he turned his attention to the weapons themselves. The leather grips were in good condition with none of the gold threading broken. He polished the bone on the pommel of his sword and ran an eye carefully along the edges of both weapons to check for nicks. Many warriors were already sitting around the fires sharpening their blades and Punnr would do this later, a mechanical action to pass the time. For now, he cleaned them lavishly and eased them back into their oiled sheaths.

Satisfied, he wrapped the weapons and armour into the folds of his cloak, then carried the bundle back to his tent, with his helmet on top. Stigr and Olsen were elsewhere and he sank to his knees and placed his bundle on his sleeping rugs. No sooner had he done so, than the flap of the tent was thrust open and Halvar stuck his head in. His face was as black as thunder clouds and he flung an envelope onto the rugs.

'Take this. It's your sister's letter. You should have it. God knows, I've memorised its contents for long enough anyway.' He gripped the edge of the tent flap, shadows from the oil lamp playing across his rough features. 'Read it tonight, for none of us know what tomorrow brings. Things are wrong in the Horde. There are forces at work. Tread carefully, Punnr. Be on your guard.'

With that, he swung on his heels and departed. Punnr picked up the envelope and crawled to the opening to look out. Halvar was gone and the camp continued with its pre-battle preparations. He closed the flap and hauled himself over to the lamp in the far corner, then folded his legs and studied the envelope. It was grubby and creased and marked only with a single "H" in Morgan's hand. He put it to his nose and sniffed, but if there was any smell it was probably the leathery interior of Halvar's jacket.

Reverently, he withdrew two sheets of folded paper covered in his sister's slanted scrawl. There were smudges like raindrops or even tears, but the contents were clear enough. Quietly, he read. And when he had done so, he lay back immersed in his memories. He could see her clearly. He recalled the day she had first drawn the Triple Horn symbol onto his hand, her pride, her fervour, and then the anger of their mother. That day had been the beginning of the end. The very next morning, his mother had left to speak to someone and been killed in a hit-and-run.

His mother had been gracious and beautiful even through the poverty that embraced them when they escaped to Edinburgh. She was so fiercely protective of her children and so tearfully proud when her daughter graduated from Leith School of Art, because she believed Morgan had the world ahead of her. Perhaps it was for the best that she hadn't lived to witness her daughter's disappearance because it would have destroyed her. Not knowing whether Morgan was alive or dead, in pain or captive, happy or hurt, would have eaten her up. Wordlessly, he pledged an oath – to his mother, to his sister, to himself. *I will not give up the search.*

He replaced the pages in the envelope, pulled his tunic up and tucked it into the waist of his breeks, then belted his tunic and crawled back to the entrance. As he emerged, three warriors approached. He couldn't make out their faces in the dark, but their body language was abrupt and aggressive.

'Thegn Punnr?' enquired the central figure in a low voice he didn't recognise.

'Who wants to know?'

'Come with us.'

'I said who wants to know?'

The man stepped close. His hair and beard were ice white and his eyes in the dim light were black holes. 'You don't ask questions, boy, you just obey me. Now you can make this easy or you can make this hard. Either way, you're coming with us.'

The other two men, neither of whom Punnr recognised, stationed themselves either side of him.

'Then maybe I'll make it hard.'

The man brought his face right into Punnr's and in the same instant Punnr felt the kiss of a knife through his thin tunic. 'I'd suggest you don't do that, boy, because I'd seriously enjoy cutting you from balls to throat.'

The point of the blade broke through the material and pressed hard into Punnr's naked stomach. He relented and raised his hands to indicate he wouldn't resist.

'Good boy. Follow me.' The man withdrew the knife and began to lead him between the tents, his two companions keeping step behind.

What the hell is happening? Punnr's brain was all over the place. Calder, Knut, Morgan. What had Halvar said? *Things are wrong in the Horde. Tread carefully.*

'Where are you taking me?'

'To see the boss.'

They left the tents behind, walked silently onto the beach and headed for a gap in the dunes.

'Skarde!' a new voice called from a few yards up the beach. 'So now you make an appearance. Where are you going with Thegn Punnr?'

It was Leiv, his sword on his hip.

'None of your business,' Skarde snarled dismissively and made to continue.

'Hey!' Leiv shouted much more loudly and heads turned from around the fires. 'Just who the hell do you think you are – speaking to your senior Hersir in that tone? No one's taking a Wolf from my Litter without my express permission, least of all the bastard who missed the final Cull.'

Skarde rounded on him. 'You want to make trouble?' he hissed.

Leiv stepped back and drew his full longsword with a flourish. That captured attention. Warriors stepped from their fires and approached the group. Skarde eyed them and looked at Leiv's blade. His knife was no match. Punnr was behind him and he considered spinning and gutting him in one satisfying sweep, but Odin's words rang in his head: *Keep him alive. Bring him to me.*

With a curse, he turned and stepped so close to Punnr that no one else could hear his words. 'You're mine, *Tyler Maitland*. I'll be back.'

Then he waved to the other two and they marched off into the dunes.

Leiv sheathed his sword. 'What was that about?'

Punnr shook his head. 'A minor disagreement. Just nerves before the Battle.'

Only it wasn't. Alarm prickled through his brain. He had never seen his assailant before, but the man had used his real name. How could that be? Only Radspakr, Halvar and Calder knew his true identity. *Seriously, what the hell is happening in this Palatinate?*

The other warriors had returned to their fires, the spectacle over. Leiv looked sceptical, but shrugged his acceptance of Punnr's explanation. 'I think you'd better come join the litter. There's going to be enough trouble tomorrow, without things kicking off tonight.'

Punnr followed the Hersir. As they passed one of the fires, he saw Calder. She was sitting tight next to Freyja, with her knees pulled up to her chin. He desperately wanted to go to her. More than anything he needed her to smile at him like she had done in Stockbridge. He thought, if he felt her arms encircle him, he would probably lose control of his emotions and cry and cry and cry. But she was lost looking at the flames and did not see him and the moment passed.

His own litter was further down the beach. They had brought rugs from their tents and Stigr sat on one of the firewood crates. Leiv dropped into a place in the circle, drew his sword again and began running it back and forth across a whetstone. Unn was stitching some of the thread on her own weapon's handle. Olsen drank from a beaker of beer, while Ake was using a small stone pendant on a leather thong to sharpen her seax. Punnr sat beside them, lay back and watched the flames, and then his eyes shifted to Ake's face. She was staring unseeing into the fire, while she ran her knife along the sharpening stone. Her skinhead and bone-white flesh made her look almost skeletal in the flickering light. A death mask for what was to come.

Olsen swallowed a mouthful of beer, then spat a second one into the flames. 'For my shieldman Knut. I swear those bastards will pay one day.'

He passed the beaker to Stigr, who did the same. Then Leiv and Unn. It came to Punnr and he drank and spat. 'For Knut.'

Ake took the beaker, imbibed and spat. 'To the Wolf Knut, who should have died facing the foe, with a blade in his hand. We will avenge him.'

They swore their agreement and Unn said, 'Something bad comes to this Palatinate.'

'Don't speak like that on the eve of battle,' Olsen rebuked.

'But it's true and you know it. The selection should never have been allowed to happen without the Prisoner present. He's returned to the Horde and he must abide by the Rules.'

'Why the fuck's he back anyway?' growled Olsen. 'Leiv. Do you know?'

The Hersir shook his head. 'It's well above our pay grades to wonder what schemes our leaders hatch. We're just here to fight.'

'We lost Turid for that bastard.'

'The Wolf officer with the most experience and a sword I would have trusted with my life. Her absence is a grave loss.'

'Like I said,' agreed Unn, 'something bad's happening.'

'And it won't stop tomorrow,' murmured Ake.

'What's that supposed to mean?' demanded Olsen.

'That battles never go to plan. Unexpected things happen.' She looked across the fire to Punnr. 'There will be twists.'

Unn rose and walked away to the tents, to return a few minutes later with a bowl. She knelt beside Ake, dipped her finger into the bowl and applied a line of blue paint across the other woman's nose and cheekbones. Then she ran a second from her scalp, down the bridge of her nose and over the centre of her lips to her chin. Ake took the bowl and did the same to Unn. Then the big woman moved around the circle, applying the war paint to each member of the litter. It felt cold and gritty to Punnr and it dried into a stickiness on his skin, but he could see it was important to the others and he bowed his head when she was done.

There was movement beyond them and figures converged on the fire as Halvar gathered all his Wolves. He squatted on the far side of the fire and his face was still rigid with anger, but he kept his voice even. 'So we come to this again, my Wolves. The eve of battle. And some of us won't see the next sunset. So, to all of you now, I say it's been my honour to stand alongside you.' Olsen passed him the beaker of ale and Halvar raised it. 'To the Wolves of Valhalla, the Kill Squads of the Horde. There are no better.'

He drained the drink and threw the beaker back to Olsen, wiping his sleeve across his chin. 'Don't let the King's confidence lull you tomorrow. He's convinced himself of our advantages; believes the foe will be in disarray. But he's wrong. Come what may, the Titans will be ready. Even as we speak, they land on the island. Their officers will spend the night studying the Field. Tomorrow the hoplite lines will march onto that sand as prepared as ever and we'll have a bloody death struggle on our hands.'

He peered around the larger circle of faces. 'On a

battlefield, it's impossible to see what's happening on the grander scale. So just stick with your litter, follow your Hersirs and remember what you are – hunter-killers. Probe the foe, find their weaknesses, and strike. And, if you get the chance...'

'Kill the King,' interrupted Punnr and all faces turned to him.

He thought Halvar would tear a strip from him, but the Housecarl paused and then nodded. 'I was going to say, take out the officers, but Thegn Punnr's correct. Perhaps one year it'll actually happen and – when it does – I want it to be a Wolf that puts the blade through Alexander's heart.'

There were muted cheers for this, but most faces were contemplative. Beneath the hiss and crack of the fire, a low sound began to insinuate itself. At first it was little more than a moan, but then it grew and blossomed and became song. Punnr looked to where Stigr was sitting on a crate. He was leaning on his knees, his eyes on the flames, and his voice came deep and melodious. Words floated into the night. Ancient words, at once alien and universal. They formed with rolled "r"s and clicks at the back of his throat, and Punnr knew he must be listening to a Viking song of war. He watched Stigr – a black man in a Viking army – and wondered what unseen trials he had endured on his journey to this place.

Stigr's voice was magnificent and the notes carried far amongst the dunes. More warriors were drawn from their fires. Others came from the church and the tents. Soon almost all the Horde was gathered to listen to his ethereal sound and to witness this song from a different millennium.

A Hammer shieldman edged through to Halvar and bent to speak in the Housecarl's ear. Halvar rose and followed the man out of the circle of light.

Punnr closed his eyes and lost himself in the voice. Each exquisite note pierced him like a seax in the heart. Half-thoughts washed over him. Questions, fears, cluttered memories, desperate promises. The man called Skarde: *You're mine, Tyler Maitland.* Morgan's final note to him: *I love you, little brother.* Lana in his arms, her eyes on his lips: *We started this together and we'll finish it together.* And Halvar, sitting with him on the dunes: *I'll ask Agape if she will speak with you.*

The helmeted champion of the Titans flickered into his head. Agape.

Gradually, other voices had joined with Stigr's and the sound swelled. A choir of fighters. When, at last, the final note hung in the air, Punnr opened his eyes to see that every face was tight with emotion.

There was silence, for nothing else needed to be said.

Beyond the dunes, Halvar began to walk along the beach.

The Titan Palatinate arrived on the island in plane after plane and stepped into wind and darkness. They trooped disconsolately across the sand to a fleet of waiting vehicles and were driven to a field near the northern end of the island, where lines of burning braziers awaited.

There were tents as well, but the hoplites just laughed mirthlessly at the sight. What good were tents when they had only hours before daybreak and their armour and weapons were still being unloaded from cargo planes? What they wanted most was food and they all knew there would be none of that. No Supply Asset meant nothing to eat, and for the first time, in that desolate, cold wind, Lenore – Titan White Warrior during the Raiding Season – felt them resent her failure to gain it and turn against her.

The Praetor of the Pantheon arrived soon after and the Titans were forced to march out to the braziers and go through the pebble ritual. A man from Nicanor's Heavy Brigade was executed and, although there was none of the belligerence displayed at the Valhalla selection, mutinous bewilderment seethed silently through the lines. Cold, hungry, disorientated and scared, they could have endured nothing worse than witnessing a Pantheon punishment.

Agape felt the anger as she stood in the front row and considered the randomness of Atilius' methods. What if it had been one of her Sacred Band who picked the white stone? The elite of the elite. Would she simply have accepted it? She eyed the armed Vigiles and wondered what she would have done in that moment if she had her blade at her hip.

Thankfully, the armour and weapons arrived soon after and this gave the troops something to concentrate on. Fires were lit and the cornel caps and oil-fleeced covers stripped from the huge sarissas, so the iron points could be inspected and cleaned. Hoplons and breastplates were buffed to perfection and horsehair plumes combed straight. Bows were oiled and strung, javelins laid in long rows and the standards of the Lion of Macedon unpacked and pressed. As the first glow of dawn peeped from the east, some of the troops finally collapsed in their tents exhausted. They might at least be permitted to close their eyes for a few hours.

Dressed still in her wind jacket and hiking trousers,

Agape strode across the campsite to where Alexander was speaking with Cleitus.

'I want to see the Field,' she said and the King nodded. Atilius granted them two Land Rovers and the Titan officers were driven the short distance to the northern shore. They climbed the embankment and looked out, but their timing was against them. The bay was a sheet of water that winked back at them in the dull dawn light, its surface rippled by the wind. Cleitus swore gruffly and smacked his arms against his sides in frustration.

'What bloody use is this?'

Menes and Parmenion jumped down onto the thin strip of beach and oystercatchers and redshank exploded from the shallows in alarm. They kicked the sand and tested it as best they could, and Menes pushed a boot into the water and stamped.

'Will it take my Phalanx?' asked Nicanor from above, but Menes could only turn back and shrug.

Agape walked along the ridge a little way and stared out. If the Land Rover's clock had been correct, it was six in the morning. Eight hours until the start of the Battle. 'Am I correct to think tides take six hours to go out?'

'There or thereabouts, maybe a little less,' said Parmenion.

So, low tide before midday. The next high after five that evening. Agape studied the bay and pondered.

Alexander came up behind her. 'There's the little island out there that we saw on the map yesterday. Are we still planning to claim it as soon as the Battle Hour begins?'

Agape felt the force of the wind against her back, blown from the great Atlantic to the west, and she peered at the sand dipping away from them. 'It looked good on paper, but here now, I'm less convinced, lord. The wind's strong and the beach slopes. I'd prefer to fight downhill and with the gale at my back.'

'It's imperative we get this decision correct, Captain.'

Alexander looked gaunt in the cold light, his thin hair blowing from his scalp. She wondered when his last hit of coke had been and could see the paranoia throbbing in his eyes as he thought about the Battle last year, when the Wolves had got so close.

'Do we know the agreed perimeter of the Field?' she asked.

'Atilius says it's the circumference of the bay.'

'So the ridge we're on is out of play?'

'Yes.'

'You're certain, lord?'

'The Battle must be waged on the beach.'

Agape turned back to the view. 'In that case, the Horde can't circle us unseen behind this ridge and that means our backs will be safe.'

'So I plant my standards just below us?'

'No. We plant your standards closer to the centre of the bay. If we can line ourselves across the sand, we can cut off this half of the beach and keep Valhalla pinned out by that island, where the elements will be at their worst and the sand will be the most treacherous.'

'She speaks well,' said Cleitus, coming up behind them.

Agape bit her tongue. As Colonel of Light Infantry, Cleitus was her line officer, but the man was a bumptious sod and she wished for the umpteenth time that Timanthes still lived. There had been an officer she would have followed into the gates of hell.

Alexander looked over his shoulder. 'Nicanor, we'll load the Phalanx as we discussed.'

'Aye, lord, that should do the trick. As long as that sand holds us. We still have the morning, so I'll return in a few hours and test it when the water's gone.'

'By the gods, I'm cold,' said Cleitus. 'Let's get back to the camp. I've seen enough bloody seawater for one morning.'

He began to stomp towards the vehicles and Alexander looked hard at Agape. 'You're sure?'

'Yes, lord.'

'We hold this end of the bay and let Valhalla have the island?'

'Trust me, lord.'

He examined her carefully. 'I do, Captain. Though I would sooner place my life in Sveinn's hands than trust some of those here this morning.'

He followed Cleitus to the vehicles, and Menes and Parmenion clambered back up from the shore.

'I'm staying,' said Agape. 'It's not far back to camp. I'll see you there soon.'

The cars departed and the Captain of the Sacred Band walked slowly around the edge of the bay, noting the sounds and the views. She listened to the birds, observed the dappled light on the water. She reached the far end and looked out to the little grass-studded island. The water between looked benign enough, but there were sure to be currents. Then she peered across to the shoreline on the far side of the bay and could see trunks and metal boxes piled at different points. Camera equipment. The grandstand for the Vigiles.

She turned in a circle and took in the island, the hills

behind, the vast palette of the oceanic skies. So this was the place Atilius had chosen. The place the Horde had known about for two weeks. They would be oozing with arrogance. Sitting around their fires, bellies filled with food, their troop numbers greater than Alexander could muster. They would have stamped all over this beach and spent hours laying their plans. They must think victory was theirs for the taking.

She placed her hands on her hips and felt her hair thrash wild in the wind.

Well, Vikings, be careful. I am Agape. Greatest of the Sky-Gods. Captain of the Sacred Band.

And I do not intend to lose.

XXXVII

Calder was already wide awake when she heard the engines approaching.

She had been lying in her furs for an age, staring up at the tent's canvas while Jorunn breathed softly next to her. She wanted to puke and guessed there would be plenty of other Vikings kept awake that night by churning stomachs and liquidising bowels, but her own nausea had nothing to do with the forthcoming Battle.

No, her mind was only on him. *Him*. The man who had first thrown her life spiralling out of control all that time ago. The one who had forced himself onto her – *into* her. The father of her dead child. The bastard she had spent so long making herself forget. He was out there now, somewhere amidst the low conversations and coughs, only metres from her, separated by just a few layers of canvas. With every pore of her body, she could feel his presence creeping over her, oozing through her orifices, filling up her lungs, squeezing her heart, forcing her down, as though he was once more physically on top of her.

God, what was she doing on this island, dressed like a fool, fighting for nothing, forced to kill when the only person she wanted dead was so very much alive and still – after all this time – laughing at her? She had thought the Pantheon offered her a new way forward. In fact, it had led her in a circle, right back to where she had started.

The engines grew louder and Jorunn stirred. 'What in Hel's name is that? It can't be time already, I've only been asleep a few moments.' She raised her head and stared at Calder in the dark. 'You awake?'

'Yes.'

The Raven reached out an exploratory hand and found Calder's shoulder. 'Don't worry, we'll be sharing a fire again tonight soon enough.'

There was movement outside and Freyja stuck her head through the entrance flap. 'Rise and shine sleepyheads. Move it.'

They threw their furs aside and shivered as they pulled on linen undertunics and leggings, then stumbled out into the dawn light. Land Rovers were bumping down the track, their headlights illuminating a startled and sullen army coming awake. Vigiles emerged from the vehicles and began to dump trunks on the sand.

'Ravens, commandeer four of those,' Freyja ordered. 'Pack your blades in one, your bows in another, and your mail in the rest, but keep your helmets. Then give your shields to these kind gentlemen. They'll be taking them ahead to the Field. And make sure they damn well mark the trunks so we can find them at the other end.'

Calder returned to the tent and retrieved her mail neatly wrapped in her cloak, along with her sword, seax, bow and quiver of arrows, then mechanically followed the others to the trunks. She had waxed her bow the previous night, strung it with the help of Jorunn and inspected every feather on every arrow shaft.

'Not your cloak,' said Freyja as she was about to place the bundle in one of the trunks. 'You'll be needing that soon enough on the tops.'

Calder followed the team behind the tents to where the Raven shields had been laid under a tarpaulin. They carried them to the vehicles, then trooped to the water troughs to wash and splash themselves awake.

Half an hour later, the Land Rovers lurched back up the track and it became standing room only in the church as Valhalla queued for breakfast. Bacon was frying, as well as chicken. Oat flatcakes and crumpets baked on a griddle over the hearth and there were sorrel omelettes and a steaming vat of honey-sweetened wheat grain porridge. Calder heaped her bowl with the porridge and stood in a tight group with her Ravens. She had no appetite, but she forced herself to spoon it down and felt it smother the nausea and warm her insides.

There was little talk amongst the warriors, just a movement of bodies and a low murmuring. They were waiting for leadership, for someone to speak up and give them direction. So far there had been no official confirmation of the tally from the Cull, but the troops had already quizzed the newcomers and done their calculations. Of the required twenty-five body count, seventeen had come from the ranks of the Horde, with a further four still hospitalised. So now – as morning filtered through the high windows – Valhalla numbered a hundred and sixty-eight and all knew the Cull had been a travesty of strategy. Perhaps it was little wonder that Sveinn was nowhere to be found.

Calder peered through the crowd and glimpsed Punnr. The Wolves were gulping down their food at the far end of the church, still streaked in their blue war paint. He saw her too and stared back, a moment in time, shared between them amongst the throng.

Olsen swore through his food and broke the spell. 'Here comes the bastard.'

Sure enough, shouldering towards them was Skarde. His vivid white curls and beard epitomised an ancient Norseman and his face exuded savage strength now that it was recovering from the ravages of prison. His gaze passed over them and he was about to wave Litter Two around him, when Leiv pulled him by the shoulder.

'This way, Prisoner.' He gathered the Hersirs out of earshot of the Company. 'Where the hell's Halvar? Has anyone seen him?'

'Not since last night,' replied the Hersir of Litter Three. 'He must be with the King.'

Leiv harrumphed. 'A damn fine time to be in conference. Valhalla needs its officers right now.'

He left them and pushed his way through to Freyja by the hearth.

'Anything?' she asked.

'No one's seen him or the King.'

She nodded. 'Okay, we can't wait any longer.' She signalled to one of the breakfast attendants. 'Is it ready?'

'Yes, ma'am, all set.'

Freyja heaved a table against the wall, cleared a space amongst the bowls and stepped onto it. 'Horde of Valhalla!' Faces turned to her and the murmuring dropped. 'Our King awaits us at the Field and soon we'll march out to join him. Then we'll unfurl our Wolf, Raven, Hammer and Lightning banners and face down our foe until they piss themselves with fear. But first I want to hear you, Vikings! I want to hear you roar!' A few voices shouted back at her. 'I said, I want to hear you roar!' This time most of the multitude howled. 'And again!' A wave of thunder hit her as every warrior filled their lungs and bellowed to the heavens.

'Horde of Valhalla, once more we're gathered for the glorious ending to the Blood Season. This is the day we've trained for. This is the day we're paid for. This is why we exist! The Grand Battle!' The Vikings clamoured their approval, pumped their fists and smacked each other. 'Some of us will fall. Some of us will not recover. But none of us will ever take a step back from our shieldwalls. For we are the Pantheon's greatest warriors and we will never break!' Whoops, chest thumps. 'Now, as is our custom, we will look to each other, make our solemn oaths and share Odin's mead!'

Freyja signalled to the hearth attendant to pass her the great drinking horn, which had last been used at the feast of the Oath-Taking. She raised it above her head to yells from the crowd. 'To Odin, High King Sveinn and the Horde of Valhalla! Together we stand. Together we shall prevail!' She drank and then willing hands reached up to grasp it for her, so that she could scoop more liquid into her palms and rinse them through her braids. Rubbing her face, she nodded and allowed the horn to begin its journey through the crowd as each warrior drank and wetted his or her scalp.

It came first to the Ravens, and Punnr peered through the bodies to see Calder sip with a dark intensity and then sprinkle her golden hair. Fifteen minutes later and the horn had reached the Wolves. Each of them drank and then Ake held it while the whole company dampened their scalps with the sweet liquid. Finally, when Unn had taken it for her to wet her own shaven head, she raised her face and let out a piercing wolf howl, which filled the church. The cry was taken up by others and the sound swept through Punnr, forcing a yell from his own lungs and making his body tingle. If the Titans were waiting outside, they would surely turn tail and flee.

In his hand he clasped the arm-ring gifted to him from Odin. Grimly, he tugged it into place on the bicep of his sword arm.

The Palatinate departed their encampment shortly after breakfast and began the three-hour hike to the Field. They marched in column, two abreast, and in Company order, with the Ravens at their head, followed by Storm, then the mass of Hammer and finally Wolf. They travelled light, dressed only in their linen tunics, breeches and boots, with their wool cloaks wrapped around them and their helmets tied to their belts. They climbed the first hill above the bay and the columns became more ragged as each trooper leaned into the work. The small group of Ravens in the vanguard soon built up a lead over Storm and, despite her thin layers of linen, Calder could feel sweat prickling her armpits. She was about to throw off her cloak when Freyja motioned to the sky, where the high cloud of morning was rolling away to the east at speed, revealing swathes of blue. 'You'll be thankful for that when we reach the top.'

Sure enough, they came over the lip and the wind hit them hard. It was the first time Calder had a proper sense of their location and she stared around at the blue, white-flecked sea and the island chain to the north. Freyja, too, stopped and peered westward over the vast Atlantic from where the wind hit her full on. Sveinn had shown her the map of the Field before they departed the city, so she knew the plan to take the islet in the bay. It made strategic sense, but now, squaring up to the elements, she also knew it meant the Horde would be battling this wind as much as the foe. She tore herself away from the view and signalled them on. No point in waiting for the other companies on this exposed spot.

It took a further two hours for the Palatinate to hike the intervening valleys and gather above the final descent to Eoligarry. There had been little conversation during the march as each warrior considered how their destiny might unravel that day. Amongst the Wolves in particular, there was a growing unease. Where was their Housecarl? Perhaps he had indeed been ordered to accompany the King to the Field ahead of the Horde, but it was so out of character for him to be missing when his troops most needed marshalling.

Punnr stood with Brante and studied the bay in the distance, where water glistened over its lower reaches.

'It's about halfway in,' said Brante.

'Halfway out, would be more accurate. So it should be fully out in another two hours.'

'And we reckon another four before kick-off?'

'Something like that.'

As the Palatinate paused on the summit, a new sound

came to them and they squinted up into the sky. Far above, two dots appeared from the east and flew towards them. As they approached they slowed and hovered high overhead. Helicopters.

'Helmets on,' shouted Freyja and the order was passed through the ranks. 'Get your faces hidden. Then smile for the cameras and wish our viewers a warm good morning from the Horde. Let's hope they're getting comfortable.'

Beneath the whine of the rotors and with faces concealed by iron masks, Raven, Storm, Hammer and Wolf dutifully waved one-fingered salutes at the helicopters and jeered.

Then began the long descent to battle.

It was midnight on a balmy Sunday morning in Sydney and beyond the black door and the huge man in the tux, the party at Level 6 of The Ivy had been in full swing for a couple of hours. The vigorously vetted guest list had already enjoyed cocktails on the veranda, dined on oysters and steak, and watched the "hostesses" perform pole-dancing routines. Now, laughing and jostling, they began to settle along the curved seating in the sunken lounge and consulted their phones for the latest odds while they waited for the live feed to kick in on the big screen.

Five thousand miles north, it was ten o'clock in Tokyo and a considerably more bracing four degrees. The night breeze bustled across the balcony of the Roppongi Hills Club on the 51st floor of the Mori Tower, forcing its guests to remain cosseted in the main dining room, where they had been enjoying diamond-studded sushi and Wagyu ribeye. Only a few stepped outside to smoke and peer over the endless lights of the metropolis known as Electric Town. The dress code was black tie and the conversation a civilised affair. Quietly, they discussed the changing values on their phones, considered their options and placed their bets through the ultra-secure portal.

On the shores of Dushu Lake in Suzhou, just beyond the western limits of Shanghai, a leading light in the Politburo of the Chinese Communist Party sat himself down in his dimly lit study. Despite the thirty-two bedrooms in his country residence, he had packed his family off to relatives because he loved to be alone on Battle Nights. In honour of the Scottish Palatinates he had opened a 220,000 Yuan bottle of Glenfiddich and he sipped it appreciatively as he stared out towards his floodlit gardens, modelled on the nearby UNESCO World Heritage classical gardens. His bets had been placed that afternoon, so now all he had to do was wait for the alert to tell him the live feed was ready and then he could flick on the giant screen and lie back.

Not many miles east, it was a far less relaxing atmosphere as the chairman of the country's second largest steel conglomerate yelled at his driver. The limousine was caught in traffic on Shanghai's Bund and he was damned if he was going to arrive at his colonial-era waterfront property after the action started. It was his own fault. He had cut it too fine leaving his headquarters in Century Park and timing it to hit the Saturday evening crowds drawn to the lights and entertainments along the famous street, but this didn't stop him throwing every obscenity he could think of at his driver. The poor man consulted his satnav, pumped his horn at the car in front and swerved onto a side road.

Seven time zones and five thousand miles west, the afternoon shadows were just lengthening around another property along the banks of a great river, this one the Bosphorus. The owner of the neo-baroque style mansion in Yenikoy had hired a DJ and every room in the 3,600 square-metre space reverberated to dance anthem beats as the beautiful, hip and rich denizens of Istanbul partied like there was no tomorrow. Only a few on the guest list were even aware of the Battle feed due in less than an hour and when the signal came, this privileged group would disappear to the basement cinema.

The Russian chapter of the Pantheon's Curiate gathered at a giant dacha in the Gardens of Meyendorff, seven miles from the Moscow ring road. It was minus two degrees and the thousand-hectare garden with its century-old pine trees of Far Eastern and South Sakhalin breeds, was swathed in a blanket of snow that sparkled in the late afternoon sun. The guests liked to observe the same traditional ceremony for each Pantheon Battle. Wearing their eagle and sword robes, they stood in a circle in the giant atrium and toasted the Pantheon with glasses of priceless Château Margaux while intoning together the Curiate Oath. As the final line – *may neither earth nor sea receive my body, nor bear fruit from it* – passed their lips, they gave three rousing cheers and then broke out the caviar and vodka. Shortly, they would proceed to the home theatre for the Battle performance, then move on to dinner in the great glass-walled dining room overlooking the winter wonderland and devote the evening to celebrating their winnings or drowning their losses.

On the shores of Lake Maggiore in the Italian-speaking

region of Ticino in southern Switzerland, the wealth manager of the Princely Portfolio hedge fund surveyed her guests. There were only eight of them around the dining table, but they were all dear friends, as well as banking associates and colleagues in the Curiate, and she always counted this occasion as the social highlight of her calendar. So she had ensured the lunch was not only spectacular, but also quirky and fun. They had begun with shark fin soup, containing abalone and sea cucumber. This had been followed by a series of miniature dishes, all extravagantly crass. First there had been sushi topped with Mikimoto pearls, then a lobster frittata. Next came a tiny pie containing matsutake and winter black truffles, and finally a delicate bowl of crab curry with quail eggs and beluga caviar.

They laughed delightedly at the composition and toasted her health. Now she smiled as she listened to them exclaiming over a humorous dessert of €600 cupcakes, sheathed in twenty-three-carat edible gold. Soon they would take their claret and champagne through to the library, draw the blinds to shield the afternoon light, and settle down around a temporary cinema screen she had erected in front of her leather-bound collections.

Above Manhattan it was one of those spring mornings when the sky was an achingly endless blue. In a duplex penthouse on West 57th Street, the CEO of Regency Associates breakfasted with his family by the pool overlooking Central Park. Far below they could see the many Saturday morning joggers already beating out their circuits around the lake. His wife was enjoying champagne, but he stuck to black coffee with his bacon and eggs. He was dressed in tennis whites and would be heading to the club as soon as the Battle Hour was complete. He checked his stocks on his iPad, then switched to the Pantheon odds and made his final betting choices. His kids were busy zapping dragons on their own iPads, but his wife would take them inside shortly. She knew how important Conflict Hours were to him and how much he tried to prioritise these live viewings within his hectic schedule. The least she could do was to give him a quiet hour in the sunshine with his coffee.

The tech billionaire's alarm burst into life with another rendition of Queen's 'Don't Stop Me Now' and he fell out of bed trying to grab the phone. Six in the morning in San Francisco and he'd been up until three playing the odds and shooting tequilas. Damn, his head hurt. He stumbled through to the bathroom, tripping over a foam guitar, which had somehow found its way into his bedroom. Then he took the elevator to the kitchen on the top floor of his residence on Broadway and threw some orange juice and paracetamol down his throat. He flicked on the coffee machine, filled a bowl with honey-nut Cheerios and wandered onto the veranda still dressed in his boxers and Golden State Warriors T-shirt.

The sun was just rising and it was cold, but the sweeping views from Pacific Heights over the Palace of Fine Arts and beyond to the Bay always took his breath away. With growing excitement, he gulped a mouthful of cereal and waved his spoon over his head. Yay! Welcome to the morning of Battle. The Titans and the Horde. Plumes, shields, javelins, war-axes. He loved those Scottish guys! Forget damn basketball, there was nothing to beat a bit of hardcore sword-on-sword action to start the weekend. And best of all? After the killing was done and the bodies were counted, there was still a fortune to be made.

Rock on.

XXXVIII

'Keep your snouts to the ground, Wolves.'

The four depleted Litters of Wolf Company House Troop crouched on the turf, heads down, shields grasped, waiting for the signal. In front of them, in a long line running the length of the grassland, stood the rest of the Palatinate, facing the bay, but hidden from it by the rising escarpment. They were arrayed with the full panoply of war: chain mail *brynjars*, shin and wrist armour, thick furs to soak up blows, helms, shields, battle-axes, longswords, knives, spears and bows. The sun glinted along this wall of iron and the wind unfurled their cloaks.

The seaward half of the line was taken up entirely by the hundred shieldmen of Hammer and at their very end were a dozen berserkers commanded by Ingvar. These were the only warriors not maintaining order and Punnr watched them as they paced in small circles, growling and spitting, rocking their shoulders and working themselves into a rage. They had fixed their shields to their backs, so that both arms were free to wield huge double-bladed axes and he wondered what substances they had thrown down their throats. He didn't mind admitting he feared them. Not so much because of their contrived anger, but because they seemed only a hair's breadth from anarchy. Even Ingvar was shaking in a way he had never seen before.

Punnr glanced at the grassland behind and noticed the wildlife had scarpered. No birds danced across the open space and even the sheep had headed to rougher ground on the hillside. He wondered if they sensed the violence to come, but guessed it was more likely due to the noise of the helicopters. At least four now hovered above the bay, along with as many drones, their deep-throated roar competing with the wind to create a wall of noise.

Sveinn stood several paces in front of the Palatinate line, flanked by Freyja, Bjarke and Asmund, as well as two bannermen ready to unfurl their flags at the signal. When the Horde had descended to the bay two hours earlier, they had found their King waiting. He had greeted them with a carefully scripted speech given from the bonnet of one of the Land Rovers, but he couldn't hide his nervy expression nor the one huge omission from his oratory – the whereabouts of Housecarl Halvar, the true leader of this Palatinate in war. After he had dismissed them and they milled in bemusement, he consulted with his officers and it was Leiv who represented the Wolves on his council and who returned to them eventually with the plan.

So now the Wolves hunched low, braced to spring.

Further down the line, Punnr could see Calder's back. She had untied her ponytail and let her hair hang free over her mail. As her cloak whipped out in the wind, he studied her slim figure and thought how meagre she looked compared to the berserker animals. He desperately wanted to call to her and say something – anything – before the hands of fate threw them onto the sands, but he dared not shout and could only burn a hole into her with his eyes.

Leiv swivelled on his knees at the head of the twenty-three Wolves. 'Here we go.'

Sure enough, beside a cluster of vehicles, one Vigilis stepped away from a group and waved an arm. Sveinn nodded and flicked a hand to his bannermen. Stooping, they grasped a flagpole each and raised them high. The wind snatched avariciously at the banners and threw them out in snapping ripples, so that the giant Triple Horn of Odin and the Valknut were visible to all. At the same instance, the flags of each regiment were raised along the line, all except Wolf. Freyja, Bjarke and Asmund dispersed to stand in front of their troops and the King took one sweeping look along the line and then turned and began to walk up the escarpment.

In that moment Punnr realised Calder was peering at him over her shoulder. He tried to mouth something, but even though her eyes were hidden behind her helmet, he could see the rigid set of her mouth. A sharp expressionless line.

Give me something, Calder. Anything. Just a sign, a tiny show of emotion before we are hurled at the Titans. If you care for me a jot, show me something now before it is too late.

Orders were thrown down the line and the Palatinate began to follow Sveinn up the incline. She held his gaze for one more heartbeat, then turned away without a flicker. Punnr watched her go, his mouth open, his breath held, and the weight in his stomach, which had been so constant since she arrived on the island, stirred, rolled and settled once more, heavier than ever.

Calder's line reached the crest and the expanse of sand opened up, hard white in the sunshine, and the wind punched into them all. Calder could see the channel running down the centre until it broke in two either side of the islet, but it looked shallow and harmless, perhaps even inviting in the bright light. Above her, the banners whipped so frantically that their rapping drowned out the din of the helicopters. She stared across to the opposite arm of the bay, where nothing stirred except a few groups of Vigiles filming beside their vehicles.

'Come on,' said Jorunn nervously.

And then they did.

First they heard a beat beneath the wind. Drums, deep and persistent, thumping at marching pace. These were joined by a new sound: a hundred and thirty voices raised in an ancient battle hymn. Then from beyond the long grasses came a forest of spikes and Calder knew she was looking at the sarissas of the mighty Phalanx. The voices crescendoed and with them advanced the Lion and Star of Macedon standards, rising steadily up the faraway slope. Then she saw the first plumes, the first helms and shields, their bronze glittering in an unbroken line, and she felt the glory of the foe reaching across the sands as they sang to them. The sarissas of the Phalanx were concentrated towards the landward end of their line, while the javelins of the peltasts and Companions extended towards the sea.

'Don't just bloody gawp,' yelled Bjarke. 'Show the warbling pansies your appreciation.'

Valhalla screamed its response, drawing their swords and thumping them against their shields. The noise rippled up and down their line and, when they were finally done, they realised the Titans had fallen silent.

Leiv called up from his crouch. 'Where's the Band?'

Freyja searched, then shouted back. 'I can't see them. They'll be readied out of sight.'

'Great,' said Leiv grimly and drew his blade. Behind him, the Wolves did likewise.

So the world waited. The flags pounded. The helicopters whirred. A skein of geese flew in from the sea and spiralled down onto the sand with a song of their own.

Then a klaxon blasted from a single Land Rover at the head of the beach and that was it. Two o'clock.

'Go!' Leiv cried.

The Wolves exploded from their squat and Punnr found himself charging up the slope towards the backs of the berserkers. At the last moment, Ingvar opened them up and the Wolves streamed through the gap. They reached the crest and flung themselves into the void. With a gasp of pain, Punnr landed on the sand and felt his knees take the full weight of his armour, but he had no time to think. Already the other Litters were racing towards the islet. He could see Brante's tall figure ahead and Ake was beside him, snarling as she sprinted. He ran as hard as his lungs would allow, his shield banging against his side and his boots sinking into the cockleshell sand. With a flurry of wings, the geese scattered in a cacophony of alarm and rose heavenwards.

The Wolves reached the central channel and followed it down towards the split. Behind them, he knew the berserkers would be following, then the rest of Hammer. He shot a glance over his shoulder to the other side and felt a surge of relief because the sand was empty. They reached the point where the channel broke in two and Leiv signalled Litters One and Two along the edge of the right-hand channel, while Three and Four splashed across the main channel and followed its left-hand tributary. The berserkers filled the gap between the two groups and only then, when they were arranged in a defensive line in front of the island, did Leiv slow the pace and allow them to turn and look up the beach.

Punnr panted through his visor and could see the Sacred Band arranging itself in similar fashion at the top of the beach. Thank the gods, the Titans had not wanted the island and had not sent their elite to carve into the Wolves as soon as the klaxon sounded. There was a female leading them and he guessed it must be Agape. Words from his sister's letter the previous night slipped into his mind: *It was Agape who found me in the first light.*

He let his pulse subside and watched as Bjarke steered Hammer into line at the centre. In their midst, studiously protected, Sveinn marched with his Bodyguard. Unlike the rest of his troops, this small group crossed the tributaries and walked up onto the islet, where the bannermen did their best to secure the flags of Valhalla. Storm and Raven arrived too and positioned themselves either side of Hammer.

Punnr looked back to the foe and could see that Alexander had placed himself behind the Band, with his own group of close Companion Bodyguard and the Macedon standards. The main body of Companions and peltasts were already providing a screening line that cut off the upper half of the beach, and the Heavy Phalanx was slowly descending from the perimeter, still carrying their sarissas upright in their slings. Out there on the empty expanse, the wind was stronger than ever and smacked into Punnr's face. Grimly, he squinted into the glare of the afternoon sun and guessed why the Titans had wanted that end of the Field.

There was a nervous lull. Everyone knew Plan A had worked. If the Band had wanted the island as well, they would already be neck-deep in a blood fight, but instead both sides now had a few moments to adjust and marshal themselves into position.

Punnr glanced behind him at the channel. It was shallow enough and easily crossable, but – he noted from the ripples – the water was coming in. Well, come what may, this would be their line. After all the practice, all the studying, all the planning, everything came down to this little stream of heartachingly clear water flowing over its bed of white cockleshells. Their orders were to defend it with their lives.

Sveinn braced himself against the wind and looked across the Field from his vantage point on the island. Encased in his ornate silver helm and holding his shield as protection against any stray arrow, he allowed himself a moment of satisfaction. Halvar had been correct about taking this island. Raised up above the action, the King felt secure. It would need a real hotshot to get a missile into him from down there and any swordsman amongst the foe would have to navigate the channels and attack uphill.

Halvar, by the gods. Sveinn cursed himself for his

weakness. When they came for his best Housecarl on the beach in the deep hours of night, Sveinn should have railed against it. He should have stood tall, harnessed every ounce of majesty and threatened blood and violence against those who sought to undermine his Palatinate. But he was too old these days. Too tired and jaded. He barely understood the whirl of events which had forced Halvar's removal mere hours before the Battle, but he had not survived as King for nineteen Seasons without knowing when to protest and when to turn his eyes away. Once upon a time, to be in the Pantheon meant simply to fight the foe and win the glory. But now, the real enemies were those closest to you. The ones who whispered sincerity, then plunged the knife – or more likely the bullet – into your back.

Sveinn summoned his reserves and shook himself into the present. Alexander's Phalanx was grinding its way towards the centre of the beach, its inner columns already splashing down the spinal channel.

Take the initiative. Follow the plan. This was the moment. Don't let Alexander decide the course of this fight. *Take the initiative.*

He signalled to one of his runners. 'Tell Jarl Bjarke to send the berserkers and then begin moving his troops.'

The man ran down the slope and splashed through the channel. Sveinn watched as he spoke hurriedly with the huge Jarl, then saw the order passed to Ingvar. The berserkers began to strut and preen, growling, rocking, pacing away from the channel, and while the Titans' eyes were on them, the back rows of Bjarke's Hammers trotted to the King's right, towards the northern edge of the bay.

Always be one step ahead of your foe; act – first and

foremost – to deceive him. Come on, Alexander you bastard. Fall for it.

*

The first Hammers ran past Punnr and formed themselves up as three ranks of twenty in front of the Wolf screen. The remaining forty still held a single line stretching across the centre ground, while Raven and Storm protected the southern side of the bay with the other two Wolf Litters.

Out in front, the dozen berserkers roared their challenges at the oncoming Phalanx. They swung their axes and made feinting charges towards the mass of Heavy hoplites who marched inexorably towards them in seven rows of twelve. Three hundred yards now between the fronts. With blade and butt spike, the sarissas weighed seventeen pounds and the Heavies still held them two-handed at the vertical in their carrying slings. When they hit a hundred yards, the first four rows would bring them down and present a bristling wall of murder.

The Titan command might have been transfixed by the berserker show, but they had also noted the shields strapped to their backs. From either side of the slow-moving Phalanx, fifteen of Parmenion's peltasts rushed into the gap, formed a line in front of the Heavies and loosed a volley of arrows. The shafts arched into the blue sky, caught on the wind and sailed over the berserkers. Ingvar's men roared their laughter and charged at the lightly armed foe, but the peltasts held their ground, gauged the wind better and loosed two more volleys. This time the missiles rained down on their targets. The quicker thinking of the berserkers managed to hunch and use the shields on their backs as protection, but others were not so fast. One bellowed as an arrow struck cleanly through his mail and into his shoulder. Another dropped helplessly as a feathered shaft thudded into his thigh, and a third was hit full in the chest by two arrows. He died as he crumpled.

It was enough to halt the berserkers' rush and they retreated, spitting fury at the peltasts who melted back behind the Phalanx.

'Come on, you Heavy bastards,' breathed Leiv next to Punnr. Once the two Wolf Litters on the northern side had become concealed by the new Hammer lines, he had called them together. 'They must be able to see what our Hammers are planning. Change course.'

It was the critical moment. Just as the full might of the Titan Heavy Brigade trudged down the middle of the beach, Valhalla had thinned its centre. Either the Sky-Gods would react to the new danger on their left flank, or they would throw caution to the winds and march right through the single Hammer line and up the islet's slopes to take Sveinn's head.

Now Asmund sent Storm scurrying forward and they fired volleys of arrows into the right-hand side of the Phalanx to encourage the Heavies to steer left. They were so tightly packed that Storm could barely miss and hoplites dropped.

As Punnr watched, he felt his feet growing cold and looked down. The incoming sea had already broken from the channel and was inching up his boots.

*

'Sveinn's loading his left flank,' said Alexander anxiously to his two Brigade colonels. 'We must respond.'

'It's a bluff, lord,' said Nicanor. 'He wants to divert my Heavies from the centre ground. Don't let him. Keep the Phalanx on course and we'll rip through his innards.'

'He has three ranks of shieldmen on the left, ready to skirt the Heavies and blow a hole through the Companion's line. Then they'll have open beach all the way to my standards.'

'Nicanor's right, lord,' growled Cleitus. 'Don't let Sveinn dictate the battle. Hold position. I can load Menes' twenty Companions with another twenty from Parmenion and we'll hold any Hammer flanking attack. By the time they've realised the way's barred, Nicanor's lot will be relieving themselves on Sveinn's flagpoles.'

'Lord, you must change direction!' It was Agape, running back from where the Band waited thirty yards down the beach.

'You keep out of this, Captain,' seethed Cleitus. 'We know what we're doing.'

'But look at the water.'

'I said zip it, Captain. I'm your commanding officer and we hold with the plan.'

She ignored him and addressed herself urgently to Alexander. 'We need to change, lord. It's a double bluff.'

This caught the King's attention. 'Explain.'

'Scenario one, the Phalanx keeps marching down the middle. In a hundred and fifty yards it'll hit the exact point where those channels come together. The water's risen fast in just the last ten minutes. They'll be calf-deep and with the weight of the sarissas, that'll spell trouble.'

'I've already advised the King,' spat Cleitus furiously, 'that my Companions and peltasts can hold any Hammer flank attack.'

'Hammer's got no intention of coming down the flank. As soon as the Heavies are caught in the water, they'll swing in on them from the side and carve them up.'

'I've heard enough!' commanded the King. 'Signal the Phalanx to change course left to the Hammer lines.'

His adjutant shouted to the drummers behind and they beat out a new rhythm. For long seconds there was no response down the beach and then they saw the front ranks of the Phalanx begin to angle out of the central channel and set their sights on the mass of Vikings to the left.

A hundred yards. Orders were flung along the lines of the Heavies and the first four ranks of sarissas swung down to the horizontal. Nothing could change the attack now.

'You said it was a *double* bluff,' said Alexander to Agape, without taking his eyes from the action.

'Yes, this is scenario two and we're doing exactly what Sveinn wants.'

'*What?* You'd better start talking fast, Captain.'

'Trust me, lord,' she said with a thin smile. 'It's time to turn the tables.'

'Brace!' bellowed Bjarke.

The front rank of Hammers locked shields and dug their boots into the sand, now covered by ankle-deep water. The second rank locked in too, pressing up against their comrades. The third rank sheathed their swords and stood more loosely as they had been drilled to do time and time again when facing the Titan Phalanx machine.

Ulf stood in the second rank. His shield was pushed into the back of the man in front and his sword rested on the upper rim. He peeked over the man's shoulder. *Christ, here they come.* Twenty yards. The sand itself seemed to be pulsating as they splashed towards them. Fifteen.

The front rank of Hammers let out a huge roar and just as the sarissa points came for them, they ducked. Ulf barely had a moment to react. A sarissa blade shot past his neck and a second crashed into his helmet. He fell backwards, but the warrior behind swore and pushed him back. Gasping with panic, he hunched like his fellows and the huge sarissas passed over him.

The training kicked in. It was ugly. It was unorthodox. But it was the only chance they had against Alexander's Phalanx. While the third rank grabbed at every sarissa point they could and heaved at it, the forward ranks shouldered upright. Now they were deep within the forest of sarissa poles and swung their swords wildly, trying to create as much mayhem as possible. Ulf found his head wedged between two of the poles. He twisted and cursed and hit at them with the upper rim of his shield. Then he saw the points of the Phalanx's fourth rank coming straight at him and screamed. With a final surge of animal strength, he managed to dislodge his head and get his shield up to catch the blade. It hit the iron rim and deflected upwards.

He fell to his knees in the water and found himself in a strange subterranean world. The front rank of Heavies were still ten feet away, but the overlapping sarissas of the first four ranks were all now above his head, filtering the light and creating a canopy of hardened Cornelian cherry dogwood. He watched one of the points take the Hammer next to him square in the mouth. The man was carried backwards, then shaken into the water in a fountain of blood.

A claustrophobic terror exploded through Ulf. Water below, death above. Shields behind and marching boots coming straight at him. He had to get out! More Vikings were dropping into the water now, crouching with their blades ready. One of them saw his immobility and whacked him in the shoulder. '*Move*, you bloody Thegn!'

He was shoved forward and began crawling through the water as snot and tears leaked behind his mask, but other Hammers were doing the same and suddenly the first rank of Heavies was right there within striking distance, their legs and groins exposed below the shields strapped to their torsos. In a split second Ulf would be trampled beneath the water. With a hysterical yell, he stabbed and stabbed again. Below the breastplate. Into their guts. Keep hitting them. An ecstasy of killing. He butchered the figure in front of him. Five times he must have stabbed him, until he could see the blue of the intestines through the blood streaming into his face. The man collapsed on top of him and Ulf squirmed like a fish to keep his head clear of the water and stabbed at the next figure stamping towards him. Strike. Strike. *Gods above, someone help me.*

To live was to kill.

*

'They've taken the bait,' yelled Leiv and spun to look up at Sveinn on the island. The King saw him, nodded and gave the signal. 'That's it, we go!'

In front of them it was mayhem as Hammer fought tooth and limb with the Heavy Brigade. The three Viking ranks had almost disappeared into the forest of sarissas and Bjarke had wheeled his remaining single line of forty into the Phalanx's flank. Leiv waved his shield towards Wolf Litters Three and Four who were still screening the southern approach to the island. Skarde saw him, but didn't respond.

'Get over here, you bastard!' Leiv yelled, although the tumult drowned everything out.

The Prisoner watched him behind his helmet, toyed for long moments with disregarding the order, then finally relented and waved the Litters to follow him, leaving Raven and Storm still guarding that flank of the beach. They splashed across to Leiv and Wolf Company was reunited. Leiv rallied his twenty-three troopers, checked the bloody struggle before them, then led them around the inside and charged up the centre of the bay.

Two hours earlier, it had seemed such a great plan. The officers had gathered around Sveinn on the turf, eyed the swathes of sand before them and agreed they should be bold. As they had done last year, they would go again for the jugular. Take the initiative immediately and load Hammer on the far northern side of the bay. Force Alexander to respond by diverting his Phalanx and sending his Companions to screen the outside of the Heavies to stop the expected flank attack. Then trick him and launch the entire Company of Wolves charging straight up the centre of the beach with nothing but empty sand between their blades and Alexander's throat.

But there had been no Halvar present during that discussion. No voice with his experience, nor anyone who had spent as much time observing the island and the bay. So no one took account of the tide.

It's too slow, thought Punnr as he ran with the pack. Already the main channel was thirty feet across and in its deeper parts the water came almost to his knees. His boots were sinking and slipping on the sand beneath and he could hear Brante beside him, heaving with exertion. The Wolves might be charging with all the lethal abandon they could muster, but even their superb agility couldn't cope with the elemental rules of the sea.

Atilius. Punnr found himself thinking about the Praetor. *This is exactly what the bloody man wanted.* He'd planned it down to the last detail. The place. The date. The time. All so that he could stage a Grand Battle at sea. As the Wolves rounded the terrible struggle between the two big regiments and Punnr glimpsed the floating bodies and the murky scarlet veil expanding into the clear purity of Western Isle waters, he also understood the beauty of the art involved in this moment. From the cameras in the helicopters and drones above, this blossoming cloud of blood would be colouring the canvas for the watching audience with a vivid new shade.

And yet Punnr had to admit they seemed to be making progress. They were passing the Phalanx and before them the head of the bay was opening up. Three, maybe four, hundred yards ahead they could see Alexander surrounded by his entourage and a thin screen of Companion Bodyguard. Perhaps this plan was going to work after all. He remembered something Halvar had said when they were training by the church. *It doesn't matter if you're losing in all the other areas of the battlefield, it only matters if you have numerical advantage where the action is decisive.* And they did. Hammer might be taking a beating from the Phalanx, but here in this moment, it was twenty-three Wolves charging at a dozen Companion guards. Kill the King. Combine the Palatinates.

Punnr yelled in exaltation and Ake spun and grinned wildly at him from a few strides ahead. Brante too could see their quarry and leaned forward into a clumsy run. Wolf! Wolf!

And then the Titans pulled the trap.

From the rear of the Phalanx on their right, Menes led his Companions in a dead sprint straight towards them. The Wolves had thought this foe was on the outside of the Heavies, protecting the northern flank, but in fact they had been lurking at the rear, their attention always focused on the central belt. They were still on dry ground above the channel and they closed the gap in seconds. A sixth sense made Punnr glance the other way and, sure enough, from behind the peltasts on the left flank, the Sacred Band also flew towards them.

'This is it, Punnr!' cried Brante who had seen the twin threats. 'Nothing else matters. Fight for your life!' He threw his shield into the water and, gripping his sword, he drew his seax in his other hand and bellowed at the oncoming foe.

The Wolves just had time to close into a defensive ring

and then the Titan elites were on them. At that instant, no training or tactics or strategy mattered. They were all now in the realm of pure chance. Iron rang against iron. Shields thudded. Soldiers slipped.

Punnr swung his blade at the first Companion spear and felt a jarring pain up his arm as he hit the shaft. He thrust the spear aside with his shield, followed through with a wild stab and saw his sword bury itself beneath the Companion's helm, splitting her mouth. He yanked it back and stood dumbfounded as blood burst from her lips. She placed a slim hand across her face, stared at him in astonishment and sank into the water. He started to reach for her, but then another spear punched into his shield and suddenly he too was underwater, clawing and squirming within his helmet, trying to work out where was up and where was down. Sand and blood surrounded him and he could see nothing. The sounds of the struggle were muted behind the hammering of his own heart. He grasped something and realised it was a corpse – the woman he'd killed, her hair swirling against him.

He flung himself away in panic and broke the surface. A hoplite was above him and a spear thrust down onto his helmet. Under he went again, dazed and half-drowned. Water flooded his lungs and he burst upwards, coughing and spewing. Somehow he still had his shield and he dragged it from the water just in time to counter another blow, but he was sinking under the weight of his mail. Then another figure loomed over him, took the Companion in the neck with a knife and hauled him up.

'On your feet, Wolfling.' It was Stigr.

Punnr dragged himself upright. The Wolves were bunched

tight and locking shields. He thrust himself next to Stigr and rammed his shield into the wall. Unn was on his other side and finally there was some semblance of organisation. The Companions held back for a heartbeat as the advantage of their charge waned and Punnr had a moment to glance down and see the fat corpse of Olsen floating face-up in the water, blood billowing from his groin. He could feel Brante's back pressed against his and knew his friend was facing an even greater threat on the other side as the Band launched itself against that wall.

The Companions came again with spear points aimed above the Viking shields and the Wolves ducked and stabbed over the rims. But they were in the deeper part of the channel and although their foe also had water up to their knees, they were able to use the advantage of being higher on the sloping sides to thrust down with their shafts. It was hopeless and Leiv knew it. He grabbed Brante and pulled him between the two shieldwalls.

'Plan B. We have to reset the line back by the island. Not just us, the whole damn Horde. Find Bjarke. Tell him the Hammers *have* to retreat. We'll suck the Sky-Gods into the deeper water and then hold our line. Go, damn you! Run!'

He pushed Brante towards the gap at the rear of the Wolf circle and the big man began to run, his back straight as always, his knees pounding up through the surf. He broke from the press of the conflict and raced towards the battle with the Phalanx. Dimly he was aware of the Ravens off to his right, deep in their own private fight against the javelins of the peltasts, but he had no time to take it in as he searched for Bjarke amongst the carnage.

'Disengage!' yelled Leiv behind Punnr. 'Step by step, Wolves. Let's show them how it's done!'

Without a single shield unlocking, what remained of Wolf Company retraced their steps. They braced as the hoplites attacked once more, threw them away, then trod rearwards again. Yard by yard in this orderly fashion, they retreated, never letting the foe find a gap.

'Hold!' bellowed Leiv.

Punnr was still locked between Stigr and Unn, and the strength in their frames gave him confidence. The rising water meant it was almost impossible for the enemy to strike underneath Valhalla's shields, so they could focus entirely on protecting their upper bodies and parrying any spear thrusts over the top. They inched back past the battling Phalanx and as the water got deeper still, the Titans eased their assault.

This was the breathing space Leiv had been waiting for. 'Now Wolves. Fly!'

As one, the whole formation spun around and threw itself towards the dry slopes of the island. Punnr was taken by surprise and lost his footing in the confusion. He fell and splashed again under the water, but his feet managed to scrabble in the sand and he shot back up. As he did, gasping and coughing, he had just one heartbeat of clarity amongst all the fleeing bodies and saw Leiv in front of him and the other Viking – the one with the ice-white beard – pushed against him. Punnr watched the seax blade slip out and pierce Leiv's lower back, so fast, like a wasp sting. It was done in a split second and the Prisoner barely broke his run towards the island, but it was enough to arrest Leiv's momentum. Punnr yelled in dismay, but it was too late.

His Hersir was feeling for the wound beside his spine and collapsing as he spun.

'No!' spluttered Punnr aghast and tried to reach a hand towards him.

Leiv looked briefly into his eyes, mouthed a silent question and sank below the water.

XXXIX

Brante swung his sword at an assailant and realised how stupid he had been to discard his shield. The rear ranks of the Phalanx were still ploughing ahead in some semblance of order, but those still living in the forward ranks had dumped their sarissas in the close-quarters struggle and were wielding their Titan shortswords. He parried a blow from a female Heavy and knocked her backwards into the water. A Hammer stepped in and stabbed her before she could recover and Brante grabbed him by the shoulder. It was Ulf.

'Where's the Jarl?'

Ulf pointed shakily to where a knot of Hammers were fighting in the hottest part of the action and Brante spotted the braided blonde beard and throat tattoo of the Hammer colonel, swinging a double-headed axe in great arcs. He thrust Ulf aside and splashed through the crimson water. Bjarke's eyes were glazed beneath his helm, his jaw clenched in a snarl and Brante could plainly see the battle fury that had hold of him. The axe came sweeping round in another huge arc and he had to stumble backwards to avoid it. Bjarke was carving at anything that was foolish enough to get within his reach.

Brante yelled, but the Jarl was beyond hearing. A sarissa point came lunging at the Wolf and he only just managed to strike it away. He could see the rest of his Company retreating fast and knew that if he couldn't get the Hammers to do likewise, they would become isolated and surrounded. He stumbled round behind Bjarke, chose his moment and launched himself to the man's side.

'Jarl! Jarl! You must signal the retreat.'

Bjarke leapt in surprise and brought his axe up to strike at this new threat.

'No, Jarl! Valhalla! Orders from Sveinn! We must retreat.' It was a lie, but it appeared to work. Sense sparked in Bjarke's eyes and he arrested the axe's swing.

'What?' the Jarl bellowed. 'Never!'

'Sir, we get the line back to the isle and hold the dry ground. We must!'

'Hammer doesn't run!'

Bjarke shoved him away and heaved again at the oncoming Heavies. Brante tried to step back in, but he could see the great weapon would no longer discriminate between friend and foe. What in Hel's name was he supposed to do?

A hand gripped him roughly by the shoulder. 'Why are you here, Wolf?'

It was Ingvar. The berserker madness had abandoned him and his eyes were lucid as he stared at the other man.

'The attack's been stalled. We're moving to Plan B. We can't fight in this water. We have to get everyone back to higher ground. Feign the retreat! Look! You can see the Wolves are almost there.'

Ingvar peered behind and, sure enough, the Wolf units had reached the original channels and were wading in thigh-high seawater across their deepest parts. Beyond, the beach sloped up to dry sand and Raven and Storm were already lining this at the water's edge.

The Hammer Hersir could instantly see the sense. He shoved Brante to the rear. 'Get everyone back. I'll deal with the Jarl.'

Ignoring the swinging axe, Ingvar waded to Bjarke, grabbed his cloak and yanked so hard that his colonel fell backwards into the water. Bjarke came up spluttering and swearing hell on earth, but his eyes had lost their craze and his roar at the Hersir was one of recognition.

'Sir, the waterline. High ground. Let's make these bastards swim!'

Bjarke understood. He swept his gaze behind and took in the battle, then grinned and crunched in next to Ingvar. Shoulder to shoulder, they arced their weapons to keep the Heavies at bay and trod backwards. Behind them, Brante rallied the other Hammers and they began to stumble back to the deeper channels.

'Hold!' cried Agape. 'Don't give chase.'

But it was in vain.

The Band were still under perfect military discipline and she simply had to raise her arm to bring them to a halt, but the same could not be said for the Companions, who only had eyes for the backs of the fleeing Wolves. They whooped and took the bait. Menes himself was at the front and lost to the moment. He flung his spear at the receding foe, drew his shortsword and sprang after them. His troops followed suit. They could taste victory, so nearly in their grasp, and it seemed so easy. Everyone knew when an enemy fled the real killing could begin. Chase the Vikings through the knee-deep water and tear into their backs. Cut them down, then run onto that goddamn island and butcher their King.

Either side of them, Alexander's other units scented the same outcome. On the left, the Heavy Brigade roared its victory song at the sight of the fleeing Hammers, and on the right the peltasts – still on higher ground and only in calf-deep water – could see Raven and Storm trying to organise themselves after their retreat. This was the moment to attack.

Far behind, on dry sand at the top of the beach, Cleitus laughed delightedly. 'The day's ours, lord.'

Alexander nodded cautiously. Beneath his grim demeanour, he was a sack of nerves and utterly convinced Valhalla would contrive some means to murder him before the klaxon finally signalled his reprieve. But even he had to admit events looked promising. The Wolf attack had been overcome and from this distance all he could see were the backs of warriors, friend and foe alike, running in the other direction.

But the Titans had never won the Time Asset. They'd not been given the opportunity to spend two weeks understanding the island's capricious nature, nor used the previous evening well enough to study the Field. Only Agape had wandered alone in the dwindling light and stared down at the twin channels running around the edge of the islet, where the water was deeper and the currents strong.

Now the Captain of the Sacred Band stood helplessly with her troops as the rest of the palatinate lost their heads. She scanned the shoreline of the isle on which Valhalla would make its stand and noted where their weaker spots would emerge. Mind made up, she signalled to Kyriacos and led her Band back into the fray.

'Cover them,' ordered Freyja.

Raven and Storm were lined along the sand beside the rising seawater. Below them, the Wolves were wading back across the channel, now waist-deep in places. Calder loosed another arrow and watched it arch into the peltast ranks on the other side. It seemed as though every Titan in Alexander's palatinate was splashing towards them at full pelt. The foe could see the Wolves and Hammers floundering in the deeper channel and were desperate to carve into their unprotected backs.

The peltasts were so keen to give chase with their javelins, they had abandoned their bows, so the Horde's archers could fire without needing to worry about protecting themselves. Calder strung another shaft, aimed it loosely at the converging mass and let it go. The string cut into her fingers and smacked along the iron vambrace on her forearm. Her shoulders and biceps were already shrieking from the effort needed to draw the weapon, but she forced the pain to the back of her mind and maintained a steady rhythm. Notch, draw, raise, loose. For a moment, she remembered the first arrow she had ever fired in the forest during the *Sine Missione*. How pathetically she had released the shaft with only sufficient power to cover a few feet. Yet, it had pierced Einar enough to give him a slow death. Einar. A boy she had barely known, who was now commemorated on her breast in the form of one of her two Bloodmarks.

Only the gods knew how many more she had killed now. Bloodmarks were impossible to count in this battle. Every arrow she loosed landed somewhere in the mass of the foe and could hardly miss.

The Wolves were pulling themselves out of the channel and the Ravens opened up to let them through. Calder searched the new arrivals for Punnr or Brante, but instead found the eyes of Skarde. He dragged himself from the water and came next to her. For the first time, his expression behind his helmet had none of its perpetual arrogance and he turned to stare uncertainly at the bodies in the water. Calder's insides squirmed and she held her bow rigidly drawn with an arrow still notched, her fingers refusing to release it.

After several heartbeats, Skarde grunted with satisfaction and shot her a glance. 'Well, well. Look at you. The little girl who let me fuck her is all grown up and magnificent. I'll wager you're loving the madness. It gets to you, doesn't it? The sheer bloody violence makes your spine tingle.' He grinned. 'Maybe one day we should have that second date. I'll let you carry a knife, even a damn sword if you want, and we'll make a real good fight of it.'

Furiously, she swung the bow towards him and released her arrow, but the range was nothing and his mail too strong. The missile chinked off his chest and fell to the sand. He looked at it, then laughed and hit her hard on the shoulder.

'Bottle that anger, girl. Save it for when we have some private time.'

Then he began striding away to rally the Wolves and before she could react, Freyja was beside her.

'Here comes trouble, Ravens. Draw swords!'

Calder looked back to the scene below and, sure enough, there was trouble indeed. Through the ranks of the peltasts, came hoplites in blue cloaks.

Punnr hauled himself out of the water, gasping and coughing. There had been seconds when he thought he'd never make it, such was the gradient of the sand and the weight of his armour. Behind him, Unn had fallen on her hands, literally incapable of climbing the last yard to the shore. Punnr stepped back in and grabbed her arm.

'Come on, damn you.' He dragged her up the slope flapping like a seal, then collapsed next to her, panting and spitting seawater.

'Leiv's gone,' he gasped. He wanted to tell her what he had seen, but it was as if his brain was closing down from the shock of everything. The noise, the violence, the sheer speed of events. He tried to find the words, but instead his lungs just spasmed.

A figure loomed over them. 'On your feet, Wolves. It's payback time.'

It was Skarde, cold-eyed and brandishing his sword.

Punnr staggered upright. 'You bastard,' he croaked. 'I saw... I saw what you did.'

The Prisoner's expression froze hard and he stared at the Thegn. Unn hadn't overheard and was busy securing her footing by the water's edge to repel the next attack. Skarde came close and pushed his helmet to within inches of Punnr's. 'What are you saying, Maitland?'

'You killed him,' Punnr snarled. 'You stabbed Leiv.'

Without breaking his glare, Skarde dropped his free hand and drew his seax again. 'You mean with this?' He looped his sword arm around Punnr and yanked him close, so that the point of the knife rested just below Punnr's mail, pressing through his breeches into his bladder. 'Did you see how quick it was? In and out like lightning. It looks nothing to a casual observer, but the art is knowing precisely where to insert it.'

The knife pressed harder and Punnr dared not move.

'Would you like another demonstration? It would barely hurt. Just the smallest prick, in and out. Then I would lower you to the sand and it would be over. No one would notice. Not a single soul.'

'Where's Halvar, you bastard?'

'Out there.' Skarde jutted his chin towards the horizon. 'Fish food.'

Punnr was stunned into silence.

'You listen to me, Tyler Maitland. You're Odin's now. He knows *all* your secrets. You and your bitch of a sister. Halvar's already paid the price. And when this is over, your pain will be so exquisite, you'll cry to the gods that I didn't kill you today. You understand? No one will help you. No one will care. You're Odin's and the game's over.'

Skarde jerked the knife once for impact, then pulled it away and turned to survey the line of Wolves and Hammer extending along the edge of the channel. The Titans were dragging themselves up the slope towards them, but they had failed to catch their foe in the depths and now the tables were turning.

'Pick your mark,' Skarde yelled to the troops. 'And send them to a watery grave.'

The Wolves snarled in reply. All except Punnr. Next to him were Unn, Ake and Stigr, who were the remnant of his litter. He could still see Leiv's body floating alone further up the bay. He thought of Odin and Radspakr, and then that single image of Calder peering at him from the line of attack, her face a rigid mask of disdain, so cold, so distant, a million miles between them.

He gripped his sword to stop it shaking and tried to hurl the memories from his mind.

But then another image broke to the surface. A picture of him and Halvar sitting in the dunes and talking of Morgan. Halvar, the true Housecarl. Halvar the Rock – the Horde's only link to his sister. Gone now forever.

There – as the battle turned in the final minutes before the end of the Conflict Hour – something slipped in his mind and Punnr the Weakling, Thegn of Valhalla, stepped out of the line.

'She's mine.'

Freyja's arm extended and pushed Calder back from the edge. Below them, sodden but climbing the underwater slope at incredible speed, was Agape. Freyja placed herself so the water just curled around her toes and raised her blade.

Calder knew she should herself be preparing to repel the other attackers, but she couldn't drag her eyes from the two women and she sensed even the rest of the Sacred Band was slowing. Because this was it. This was the duel.

Agape launched herself upward with the power of a croc ambushing a drinking wildebeest. Her sword reached for

Freyja's stomach and the Raven Housecarl had to dink to one side, the attack had been so fast. She righted herself and thumped her shield down onto the Titan, bludgeoning her to a standstill, then swept her own sword round in a graceful arc aimed at the woman's neckline. Agape ducked and the blade sliced through her plume. Then, as Freyja's effort overreached and she exposed her unprotected side, the Titan struck. On firmer ground, her shortsword point would have found the sweet spot above her opponent's hip and cut into her gut, but the cockleshell sand was anything but firm in the eye of the angry current. Agape's sword point caught the bottom of Freyja's *brynjar* and forced a couple of the iron rings into her flesh, but it was no death blow.

Freyja needed a moment to breathe and recover, but if she gave her opponent a second, the Titan would be out of the water. The Housecarl rated herself one of the deadliest warriors in the Horde, but she was under no illusions. On firm ground, advantages even, the Captain of the Sacred Band would have the taking of her. So, no matter what else occurred around them, her only task was to keep this Titan down in the cold Scottish sea.

Without a pause and only the briefest squeal of pain, Freyja returned her sword in a backhand and forced her opponent to fend the blow with her hoplon. The blade crunched into the bronze sheathing and made Agape stagger a step back. The water clawed at her thighs and the sand sucked at her. This time both swords came together with an almighty clang and they switched and impacted again. They fell into each other, shoving with their shields and their faces only inches apart. Freyja shifted her balance and kicked out. She caught Agape in the groin and almost succeeded in flinging her bodily back into the channel, but somehow the Titan stayed upright, flicked to the side and struck again as Freyja was off-balance. The blow would have skewered a lesser athlete, but Freyja's shield dropped just in time and the blade ricocheted off its rim.

Now it was Freyja's turn to attack. She rushed into the surf and swung her sword forearm, then back-arm. Agape had to fend for her life, catching each blow on her blade, then holding her opponent back with her shield. The women clung to each other again, their swords behind each other's heads as they wrestled. For moments, they seemed irretrievably locked, then they hurled each other away with such force that Freyja was sent back up the slope and Agape tumbled into the deeper water.

Freyja righted herself and hunched into battle stance again, but this time Agape did not attack. Either side of them, far along the shoreline, Vikings were carving into their struggling foe. Agape stared at Freyja, raised her sword in salute to a worthy adversary and bowed her head once.

Then she turned and retreated the way she had come.

Punnr strode north along the sandy rim of the islet, away from Raven and Storm, away from the Wolves and behind the lines of Hammer as they thrust the Titans back into the water. He passed the last man and kept walking around to the place where he could see the sea opening up to his right and the last finger of the bay's grassland perimeter stretching on the other side of the now full channel.

It was quiet here. Strangely forgotten. A group of Vigiles stood on the grass filming and they watched him, wondering what brought this lone figure to this flank of the bay. Punnr studied the channel. It was as he had remembered in his mind's eye from the afternoon with Halvar. A large rock perched in the centre, damp and glistening, but secure enough above the water level. Beyond, the water hadn't quite reached the very edge of the bay and there still remained a thin strip of sand running around the perimeter below the grassy headland. Birds scurried on it and pecked at morsels, as though oblivious of the carnage in the centre of the bay. Make it to that strip and someone could run entirely around the waterlogged Phalanx, which was the closest of the enemy units.

Punnr sheathed his sword and began to descend. The current whipped at him and he discarded his shield. Holding out both arms for balance, he waded towards the rock and felt the sea lick up to his thighs.

'What the bloody hell are you doing?' shouted a figure running along the sand from the Hammers. It was Brante.

Punnr reached the rock and pulled himself up to kneel on it. 'Go back. I have to do this alone.'

Brante halted at the edge of the water. 'You're crazy!'

'Yes, I think I probably am – but you're not going to stop me.'

Brante scanned around, gauging distances and deployments, then stared back at his friend. 'You're mad, Punnr. Totally stark-raving insane.'

He began wading into the water with his sword held above his head. Punnr swore and checked to see if they had been noticed. 'For god's sake, go back.'

Brante reached the rock and grabbed it, holding on below Punnr. 'Remember our evening in the Dome?'

'What? Why the hell are you talking about that now?'

'You'd just been dumped.'

'Yeah and I found out your name was Forbes. It was a bad night all round.'

'We also said we'd die for each other.'

'But not like this.'

'Blood brothers, remember?'

'Blood brothers, yeah but...'

'So are we just going to perch here until some Titan notices?'

'Oh for Christ's sake! Okay, follow me.'

Punnr pushed himself off the rock and dropped to his waist in fast water.

'What are we doing anyway?'

'Meeting someone.'

They struggled beyond the current's grasp and waded up the far slope until the water was down to their calves and rippling gently. There was another shout from behind. Skarde was charging along the sand, blades in both hands.

'Run!' Punnr grabbed Brante's arm to yank him onwards. 'Run for your life!'

They threw themselves out of the water. Above them, the Vigiles peered down, one of them filming every move they made. Another pointed to his watch and Punnr waved his understanding. With every last drop of their strength, the two Wolves began to sprint around the edge of the bay.

'Christ, here they come,' panted Brante.

Five Titan Heavies had detached themselves from the struggle and were wading through the water, sarissas dropped and swords in hand. Much more worryingly, Companions had seen them too. They assumed it was a suicidal attempt on their King and they rushed from the fight with the Hammers and hurtled towards the pair at an angle to cut off their approach.

'Come on!' Punnr yelled as he gasped for breath beneath his helmet. 'We've got to get around them or it's all over!'

Brante glanced behind. 'That bastard Skarde's still chasing us! What the hell's happening?'

They raced along the sand strip until their hearts were ready to give out. Three hundred yards further round, Alexander and his officers had spotted them and his close Companion Bodyguard stepped in to protect. But Punnr had no intention of making it that far. Instead he threw a glance over his shoulder and calculated they'd outstripped their pursuers, then changed direction and plunged back into the water.

'This way!'

Only a fool believes you can see on a battlefield. But perhaps some warriors – hardened by years of struggle, attuned to the nuances of conflict – can sense changes in the field of action, which lesser beings fail to recognise.

Certainly it was only instinct that made Agape raise her head. She had been wading back out of the channel and pulling her troops from the futility of the fight, when something made her look beyond the struggle to her right. She saw the group of Companions pulling away, the five Heavies wading fast with them, and she shifted her focus further, towards the far side of the bay. Two figures were hurtling through the shallower water, arcing round between the King's party and the main body of the Palatinate, curving towards her side of the bay.

Just two of them. So little threat. And yet. And yet...

With a noise in the back of her throat, she caught Kyriacos's attention and led her Band to intercept.

Bjarke had seen them too. Raised by the sloping bank, he could look over the heads of the Heavy Brigade and spot the two Wolves charging behind the fray. He bellowed with delight. *Those crazy bastards are going for it!*

Swinging his axe madly, he threw himself into the water and began carving a path through the Heavies.

From his rock on the summit of the islet, with the banners of Valhalla slapping above him, King Sveinn had an even better view. He had been watching the two warriors from Wolf Company since they had separated themselves from the other units and crossed the channel. Armoured and helmeted, it was difficult to tell their identities, but Sveinn had glimpsed an arm-ring on the first figure and recalled the smoke-wreathed room at the Blood Gathering when Odin had tossed such a trinket across his desk.

Then the King saw Skarde give chase. Skarde. A killer too sick even for the Horde. Thrown into Erebus and forgotten. Then resurrected by order of the Caelestis. Odin's man. Sworn to him. Eager to murder for him.

In that moment, Sveinn knew instinctively what the two Wolves were going to do.

Perhaps some small part of him had always known. He rubbed his beard and thought of his son in California.

Farewell, Punnr the Weakling. Sometimes family is more important than loyalty. God speed you in your search.

'Punnr! What the hell are you doing? That's the Band coming for us!'

This far up the bay the tide was only halfway in and the pair were moving fast through the ankle-deep water, but it also lent speed to the blue-cloaked Titans who were sweeping towards them.

'Keep going, don't stop now!' Punnr steered a course directly for the oncoming foe.

'You're insane! We're dead meat!'

The Band were almost on them. Fifty yards, no more.

'Agape!' yelled Punnr, as he unsheathed his sword and waved it towards her, then flung it hard into the water.

'What are you doing, you madman?'

'Throw your blade away!' Punnr spun on Brante mid-sprint. 'Lose it. Now!'

Brante cursed the gods and sent his weapon cartwheeling behind him.

'Agape,' Punnr shouted again. The two groups were only yards apart now. He crashed down onto his knees in the water and Brante collapsed behind. 'We yield to you!'

She came over him, legs apart, sword raised for the kill. A vision of terror.

'Olena of Macedon,' Punnr cried in desperation. 'I am the brother of Olena of Macedon and we yield to you, Agape!'

He raised his face to her glare and the eyes that bored into him from behind their mask were emerald green, hard, dangerous, but also now debating. He remembered the very same expression as she stood over him on Calton Hill. Then, like now, her blade had been poised to strike, but it was a strike that had never come.

'I yield to you,' he said more evenly.

A cry tore her attention away. The giant Hammer Jarl had broken through the lines of Heavy Brigade and was running towards them with his axe swinging. He'd seen the Wolves throw their weapons and now knew the cock-sucking pansies were surrendering. He'd kill them all.

Then she saw the other Viking. The man with the ice-white beard, still hurling himself across the beach with blades in both hands.

Agape made her decision. She waved her Band around the fallen pair.

At that moment the air was rent by the scream of the klaxon.

Three o'clock. The Grand Battle of the Nineteenth Season of the Pantheon was over.

Agape hunkered down in the path of the lone sprinting Wolf and for a heartbeat it seemed he would rush her. But then he pulled to a halt and swaggered just a few steps further, rolled his shoulders arrogantly at her and spun his blades.

But Bjarke's anger was beyond reason. He ignored the klaxon and kept coming, so the Sacred Band took one step forward and yelled their defiance back. The sound finally broke through to the Jarl's crazed mind and he slowed. Panting heavily and glowering at the two Wolves, he lowered his war-axe and accepted the reality of fifteen members of the Titan elite blocking his path. Taking a huge breath, he howled to the heavens, then flung his weapon angrily into the sea.

'Get up,' ordered Agape and grabbed Punnr by the scruff of the neck. 'You're now prisoners of the Titan Palatinate and Alexander will determine your fates.'

She began wrenching him away towards the King's flags and Kyriacos booted Brante upright, but Punnr tore himself from her grasp and spun back round. Skarde was standing twenty yards away, pointing his sword straight at him. Everywhere warriors were motionless, arms drooped, weapons lowered, the fatigue of conflict finally hitting them. He peered through the armies and up onto the raised beach. The white-sanded Hebridean islet was now surrounded by crimson water. A blood isle.

And there she was. Bow discarded, sword held loosely by her side, blonde hair billowing in the wind, staring right back at him across the water and across the void of two rival Palatinates.

'Forgive me,' he whispered. 'Please forgive me. We started this together, but I must finish it alone.'

Author's Note

Dear Reader

The Grand Battle is over and we are left on a beach littered with the detritus of war. I have chosen not to name the island, but those of you with even a passing knowledge of Scotland's glorious Hebridean landscapes will locate it easily enough. It is a place which I have visited on many occasions, spending days wandering the dunes and hills and dazzling sands, while revelling in the sense of being somewhere so remote and timeless. It seemed the perfect place to set the bloody culmination of the Pantheon's Nineteenth Year.

Back in the city, I had great fun traipsing up and down the Royal Mile, looking up at the rooflines to determine where my Titan strongholds should be located. I knew it would be impossible to house the whole Palatinate in one place, so I split it into four – Ephesus, Persepolis, Pella and Thebes – and divided the regiments into each. Alexander's glorious garden beneath its dome of glass is – alas – entirely a figment of imagination, but perhaps one day someone will create it up there amongst the spires and turrets.

Thank you for continuing on this journey with me! So where do Punnr and Calder go from here – a love which spluttered briefly, but is now irrevocably divided by rival shield lines? What will the Titans do with their new prisoners? How will Calder face the monster from her past? What terrible twists and turns have beset young Oliver? And where, oh where, is Morgan Maitland?

If you would like to connect, please visit:

cfbarrington.com
Facebook: @BarringtonCFAuthor
Twitter: @barrington_cf
Instagram: @cfbarrington_notwriting

Meanwhile, read on for a teaser from the opening of *The Hastening Storm*, Book Three of the Pantheon. I hope you stay with me – it's going to be a hell of a ride!

BOOK THREE
THE HASTENING STORM

I

Alexander of Macedon – High King of the Titans, Commander of Companions, Protector of Pella, Persepolis, Ephesus and Thebes, Lord of the *Sky-Gods*, One of the Seven – stubbed out his cigarette, knelt forward and snorted the blade-sharp line of coke his pageboy had prepared for him. He grunted and blinked as the floral-scented powder hit the back of his nostril and the diesel undertones slunk down his throat.

God, he needed that.

Only hours earlier he had been on that wind-blasted, gull-infested, blood beach and he was still greased in the sweat, salt and muck of the whole damn exploit. After the klaxon had sounded, cutting through the battle frenzy like a scythe through wheat, the rival Palatinates had prised themselves apart and waded to opposite sides of the great bay. Vehicles bumped down to the shoreline and disgorged Vigiles, medics, orderlies and *libitinarii* – removers of the slain. Field hospitals were erected, arms and banners collected, water distributed and cookhouses thrown up arbitrarily, their scents soon blossoming across the dunes and drawing all those warriors who could still walk.

Later, as night descended and the sea drew back once more

to reveal swathes of sand, Pantheon planes landed one by one, their wheels ploughing furrows across a battleground washed bare. The Titan regiments gave up their armour in return for jumpers, coats, loose trousers and boots, then hauled themselves onto the waiting planes and collapsed into the depths of unconsciousness even before the engines roared and took them from those blood isles for good.

'Enter,' Alexander barked in response to a timid knock.

It was his Royal Page carrying a flight case, which he placed on a glass and gilt table along one wall of the King's private chamber in the Ephesus stronghold, four floors above Gray's Close, just off Edinburgh's Royal Mile. The lad opened the case and gingerly removed the King's war helmet. It was a thing of beauty. Burnished bronze that gleamed in the downlights. Intricate grape vines etched lovingly into the cheek guards. A snarling snout above the eyepieces to symbolise the Lion of Macedon. And a rich horsehair plume that swept over the helm in an unbroken scarlet wave.

'And what about the rest?' Alexander snapped. It was lost on him that a sovereign's helmet should perhaps look less perfect in the aftermath of a mighty battle. There were no chinks in the bronze, no tousles in the plume. For Alexander was not a King who led from the front. He had spent the duration of that blood struggle behind his Bodyguard, beside his banners, peering at the carnage from a safe distance.

The boy's eyes bulged with fear. 'My armour,' Alexander barked. 'My cloak, my greaves, my sword, you blithering idiot.' He swept his hands down the front of the knee-length tunic he had changed into as soon as he arrived back in Ephesus. 'Do you expect me to do this dressed only in my undergarments and my helmet?'

The boy scampered from the room as Alexander grabbed a goblet of wine laced with opium and drank deeply. He dragged a bare arm across his lips and began to pace. Memories of the Battle flooded back to him and his gut knotted with exhilaration. He knew it was the coke beginning to work its magic, but he didn't care. He heard again the clamour of his Phalanx as it hit the Hammer's shieldwall, their mighty sarissas splintering limewood shields and breaking the line. He saw once more the speed of his Companions as they had launched their ambush against Sveinn's Wolves. *Yes!* Alexander clenched a fist and punched the air. They had cleaved into Valhalla's finest and cut them down. The formal Blood Tidings would be announced in a few days, but he needed no certified body count to know Wolf Regiment had been broken in this struggle across the sands.

He flung the goblet triumphantly against the far wall and grinned, but then his lips skewed into a snarl as his mind's eye jolted to the Band. His elite unit. His Sacred Band. The warriors that epitomised every quality in a Titan hoplite. And yet... and yet... What the *fuck* had Agape been thinking when she accepted the surrender of that pair of Viking deserters? What possible reason could she have not simply to slice their heads from their shoulders and be done with it?

The boy returned, this time too agitated to remember to knock. He carried the King's breastplate, greaves, cloak and sword, already unpacked from their flight cases and Alexander forced himself to settle while the boy began lacing his breastplate. A commotion from Ephesus' Armoury bled through the walls as those troopers not already released back to their homes busied themselves cleaning and storing weapons. There was laughter, for the exhaustion of the journey back to the capital had been replaced by the nervous release of emotions as each individual realised they had made it through the annual struggle and still lived. And no doubt there was alcohol now. Not strictly permitted in the Armouries of any of the four Titan strongholds, but no one was going to begrudge them their wine tonight.

The boy finished fixing the breastplate and picked up the sword, but Alexander slapped his hands away and belted the weapon himself. Then he waited impatiently while the lad attached the red woollen cloak to clasps on his armoured shoulders. Finally the King snapped his fingers for his helmet and pulled it over his head until his eyes were hidden in the recesses above the great cheek guards. He stalked to a mirror and admired himself. *You'll do.* Even the ancient Lord of Asia himself would approve.

It was unusual to carry a blade and wear a helm within the sanctity of the stronghold, but what was about to happen required concealed identity and he knew his officers next door would be similarly helmeted and armed.

He pointed to the discarded goblet. 'Get me a refill, boy, and bring it to me in the Bladecraft Rooms.'

Right, let's get this bloody thing over with.

Acknowledgements

Originally, much of the action in *The Blood Isles* was supposed to take place in Book 1 – *The Wolf Mile* – because it seemed appropriate for one entire Pantheon year to be contained in a single volume. But it quickly became apparent that I could never fit the eddies and permutations of the story into just one book and so I broke the Pantheon's Nineteenth Year at the climax of the Raiding Season and left the Blood Season and Grand Battle for the second instalment.

I wrote *The Blood Isles* long before I had a publishing contract for any of the books, taking a gamble that the series would one day see the light of day and determined to give my characters the adventures they deserved, even if no one else ever enjoyed them. Thankfully, the gamble paid off, because in 2020 Head of Zeus offered me a three-book contract and I was able to show them that I was already well into the planning for Book 3! Thank you to my editorial team at HoZ – Holly Domney and Lizz Burrell – as well as the wider team members, including Lottie Chase and Thorne Ryan. They brought wonderful insight to the first drafts of *The Blood Isles*, prompting me to look again at the interplay between the characters, encouraging me to ramp up the tensions, showing me the points in the story where the reader was desperate to feel even more of the simmering hatreds, rivalries and – yes – loves, which would transform these warriors into much more complex personalities.

Once again, I am indebted to Annabel Walker for her copywriting and proofreading, as well as to Dan Mogford for his absolutely awesome covers for both books! I totally love the tumultuous skies he has brought to each volume, which have become such a dramatic feature for the Pantheon going forward. Thank you too to my agent, Laura MacDougall, and fellow team member, Olivia Davies, at United Agents.

Huge gratitude must again be extended to my circle of early readers and friends who have given me their wisdom and support, coaxing me forward even when times have been difficult and I have suspected I may be the Pantheon's next victim. David Follett, Mark Clay, Mike Dougan, my brother Steve and my sister Shireen. Thank you too to fellow writer Helen Reynolds, who taught this luddite about social media and all things digital. To this group of supporters, I would also add Fifers Ronnie Mackie and Sandy Duncan for all their encouragement, as well as Steve & Lynne Thomas at Smash Digital for their help with promo films for *The Wolf Mile*.

Since the publication of *The Wolf Mile*, it has been wonderful to be build relationships with fellow authors and I would particularly like to thank three (bestselling) colleagues who have embraced the whole Pantheon concept with such enthusiasm: Matthew Harffy, Ruth Hogan and Giles Kristian. Thank you for all your wisdom and support.

Finally, so much love and thanks to my parents and siblings, to my step-daughter Sarah, and – of course – to my wonderful Jackie and the pooches Oscar (who we loved and lost during the first drafting of *The Blood Isles*) and Albert (who arrived as a bundle of relentless energy during the editing stages). I have only been able to disappear into my world of Vikings and Titans knowing I have you around me when I re-emerge.

About the Author

C. F. BARRINGTON spent twenty years intending to write a novel, but found life kept getting in the way. Instead, his career has been in major gift fundraising, leading teams in organisations as varied as the RSPB, Oxford University and the National Trust. In 2015, when his role as Head of Communications at Edinburgh Zoo meant a third year of fielding endless media enquires about the possible birth of a baby panda, he finally retreated to a quiet desk and got down to writing.

Raised in Hertfordshire and educated at Oxford, he now divides his time between Fife and the Lake District.

@barrington_cf
www.cfbarrington.com